MAD ROGUES AND ENGLISHWOMEN

ELIZABETH ESSEX

All rights reserved.

No part of this publication may be sold, copied, distributed, reproduced or transmitted in any form or by any means, mechanical or digital, including photocopying and recording or by any information storage and retrieval system without the prior written permission of both the publisher, Oliver Heber Books and the author, Elizabeth Essex, except in the case of brief quotations embodied in critical articles and reviews.

PUBLISHER'S NOTE: This is a work of fiction. Names, characters, places, and incidents either are the product of the author's imagination or are used fictitiously. Any resemblance to actual persons, living or dead, business establishments, events, or locales is entirely coincidental.

Copyright © 2023 by Elizabeth Essex

All rights reserved.

Published by Oliver-Heber Books

0 9 8 7 6 5 4 3 2 1

To Tameri Etherton, friend and fellow scribe, whose help was essential to the development of this story. For welcoming me to her adopted city of Edinburgh, conducting me on an unforgettable tour of the medieval closes, taking me to the highest of high teas and making my stay in Edinburgh both memorable and highly enjoyable.

And to Jenn LeBlanc, photographer, writer and kindred spirit, for the photographic inspiration, but more importantly, for the delightful introduction of contrapposto.

And to the Tortoise Conclave of my dear fellow writers Tracy Brogan and Sherry Thomas. I never could have plodded my way through this manuscript without your daily encouragement to keep crawling along at our turtle's pace. You two are simply the best of the slowest.

PROLOGUE

EDINBURGH, SCOTLAND, JANUARY, 1802

*I*t was the poor, miserable beggar girl huddled against the bitter Scottish wind on the corner of Queensferry Lane that caught Miss Margaret Conway's eye. The dark-eyed, raggedy lass with an even more raggedy, hollow-eyed child clutched to her hip.

She could picture her clearly—an urchin Madonna and Child.

The vision alit in Miss Conway's head like an errant angel and hovered, insistent and watchful, glowing with the sanctity of a Verrocchio, the holiness of a Raphaelo, the humanity of a DaVinci.

Our Lady of the Gutter.

She could make it so, if she dared.

And so, despite the difficulties that nearly always stopped her, she bid the chairmen put her down so she could make her lame, careful way crossing the icy pavement.

She crouched down low, despite the ache and strain, and

offered the girl the few coins in her pocket. "My name is Maisie. And I should very much like to paint you."

CHAPTER 1

$\mathcal{A}$rchie Carrington was the sort of fellow who was always delighted to find himself with an armful of lass—in fact, it was his favorite state of being. Dairymaids, housemaids and countesses alike—Archie opened his arms to them, one and all.

The present armful came out of nowhere—nowhere being the new Lord Advocate's mist-shrouded stableyard up Kirk Brae Head—falling into his arms with all the force of a banner headline.

"Whoa there, lass." He held fast to keep them both from falling to the icy cobbles—if not to also keep his sole pair of satin evening breeches from being ruined by the slick stable mud. He had taken pains with his appearance that evening, scrubbing himself diligently so as not to smell like printing ink, but he would certainly not be readmitted to Sir Richard Conway's elegant drawing room if he looked—let alone smelled—like he'd rolled in horse shite.

"You whoa there." The armful's voice was low and pleasing, despite being full of breathless objection. "You're the one who ran into me."

"So I did!" And he was not sorry—not with her supple form beneath his hands.

She pushed out of his arms, putting one hand to her chest and the other against the rough stable wall for balance, as if their brief contact had knocked the wind out of her. Or perhaps he just had that effect on women—his smile *had* been known to make barmaids weak at the knees.

Archie put that smile to work on this lass, who was also clearly a maid of some sort—serviceably dressed in a nondescript, dark, hooded cloak over an equally nondescript gown and splattered apron. But he was no snob. "My apology, lass. Quite right—my fault entirely."

With the exception of her ginger hair, keeking out from the edge of the hood, everything about her was nondescript. Which was perfect for Archie's needs—he had wandered out into the stableyard looking for one of the new Lord Advocate's servants to chat up. Or, if worse came to worse, bribe. A groom or a footman had been his original intention, but a maid from Sir Richard Conway's house might serve better—footmen and groomsmen were dressed in livery to catch the eye, but a maid-servant was dressed and trained to be invisible.

He had tried getting his questions about the new Lord Advocate's sudden assignment to Edinburgh answered in the more usual, straightforward way—but his straightforward questions had not been answered. Evasion seemed to be the name of the game. Well, two could play at that—Archie had made his reputation as a man who found out uncomfortable truths.

"I hope I didn't frighten ye, lass." Archie made his voice warm and his accent more broadly Scots in an effort to set her at ease.

"No," she said, contradicting herself by sidling further away and casting a wary glance toward the house and the kitchen stair. "I'm not afraid."

Not of him anyway.

But no, not *nay*—she wasn't Scots, then. Likely an English

servant brought north with Lord Conway's household when they had relocated to Edinburgh—from London, presumably, though no one seemed to know exactly. Which was better yet—a lass far from home, away from familiar friends and family would be easier to sweet-talk out of a little harmless information.

All he had to do was turn her up sweet.

"You're English then, lass?" He broadened his smile to show her he took no offense. "Welcome to Scotland."

"Thank you." Her voice was low and calm, but her wariness remained—she took another hesitant, almost lurching step nearer the stair. "I didn't realize there was a welcome committee."

"Oh, aye." Archie laughed at her wry humor. "Are ye all to rights then, lass? That was a devilish bit of a bump ye took." He put out his hand to aid her, but she drew back. "Lass, I mean ye no harm. I imagine it's got to be hard, aye, coming all the way up to Auld Reeky not knowing a soul. Devilish lonely I was, when I first went down to London." He cocked his head to one side, all inviting innocence, and gave her his sunniest, most maid-pleasing smile. "I'm Archie."

Her lips curved into the barest trace of a smile, as if against her will. Or her better judgment. "You would be."

Archie was amused, but also buffeted back a wee bit by the sharp nick of sarcasm in her tone. But now that he took a second look, she had a governess-y air about her he hadn't noticed at first—a probing, acute gaze, as if, in her spare glance at him, she had already seen through to his flaws.

He fell back upon his strength—charm. "Governess then, are ye? Just rid of the bumptious bairns for the evening and catching a wee moment to yourself?"

She raised her eyebrow, leveling that acute gaze at him. "What sort of a governess would I be if I felt my *bairns* were *bumptious?*"

Archie couldn't help but laugh. Oh, but how he liked the clever ones. "Don't worry, I won't tell."

Her smile grew enough to warm the corners of her hazel eyes. "Such favors."

Clever and wry. Delightful.

He took a casual step closer, to get an even better look at the lass, but a noise from the bottom of the kitchen stair—the door slamming open—diverted both their attentions.

A cultured voice floated up to them. "Maisie?"

Maisie—now that name was Scots, even if her accent wasn't. "I won't keep ye from yer mistress, lass," he whispered, letting his brogue fully loose on her, along with another sure-to-please smile. "But if ye e'er find yerself lonely, in need of a friend, I live over Cowgate way. Ask anyone there and they'll tell ye where Archie lives. Mayhap I could meet ye for a walk on yer halfday, or for an amble along the gardens of the old loch?"

"*Such* favor."

Her wryly self-possessed voice didn't give anything away, but Archie had softened harder hearts. "Or you could send a message to the Review—that's an important literary and political quarterly, by the way—by way of one of the crossing sweeps. No one need know."

"No one?"

"Well, just ye." He gave her a wink. "And me."

"Ah." Her smile was rife with irony. "Intrigue along with favor."

"Maisie?" The voice called again, astonished and insistent.

Archie peered through the raw mist to find the owner of the imperious summons was the Lord Advocate's daughter, Miss Flora Conway, a strikingly attractive, golden-haired young lady who was being newly acclaimed as Edinburgh's version of a diamond of the first water, even if her father was a politician of the second. As beautiful as she was gracious, Flora Conway was another lass Archie ought to try to turn up sweet.

But Miss Conway's gaze was all for her servant. "Maisie, I've been looking everywhere for you!" she scolded her charge. "What in heaven's hour are you doing out here in all this freezing damp?"

"I needed some quiet," the governess returned in that same low, calm tone, as if she were impervious to the disgruntled lady's summons.

"Out here? What you need is to attend the soirée. Do come. It's only just started." The beautiful daughter of the house glanced down. "Oh heavens, Maisie! Your hems are at least four inches deep in this awful slushy mud—I'll never get used to this coal soot! But—" She gasped in horror at the mud streaking up the side of her charge's skirts. "Whatever happened? Are you all to rights?

"I'm fine," this Maisie countered in a decidedly non-deferential, but still patient tone. "It's just an old smock. Pray don't take on."

"My fault, I'm afraid." Archie stepped into the small circle of lamplight and turned the full force of his charm on the mistress. "Miss Conway, pray forgive me for losing my way and discommoding your Maisie. She was only trying to direct me back inside."

"My Lord Carrington!"

Clearly, his reputation preceded him—though he had been at some pains to reform it. The pretty young Englishwoman's glance filled with fresh anxiety—and just enough outrage to be amusing—darting from him to her charge. "What on Earth are you doing out here with my sister?"

Surprise was like a well-aimed boot to his backside. "Your sister?"

He had no intelligence of more than one Conway sister, but perhaps he had partaken too freely of Lord Conway's copious liquor instead of listening carefully. He would change that. "Pray forgive me, Miss Flora."

But what was any sister, or daughter of the Lord Advocate,

doing in a stableyard in the gathering dusk, dressed like a tatty governess?

How curious. And how intriguing.

It only remained to discover if it might be useful.

He gifted his slyest smile yet to this enigmatic Maisie. "Delighted to make your acquaintance, Miss Conway." He sent her a surreptitious wink as he swept her a gallant bow. "Archie Carrington, at your service."

CHAPTER 2

$\mathcal{H}$e would be an Archie. So very Scots, the way he rolled the name off the clever tip of his tongue. And her sister Flora's outrage was as amusing as it was predictable—though younger than Maisie by some ten years, there was nothing like a rogue to set Flora's protective instincts on guard.

And this Archie Carrington, though a lord, was certainly a rogue. He could be nothing but, coming out of the mist to catch her, all swirling, madder black velvet coattails and unruly raven dark hair. Satan in a crimson waistcoat—he all but exhaled brimstone.

But what had the man been doing in the stableyard instead of hobnobbing with the good and great of Edinburgh within the drawing room, seeing and being seen, drinking her father's freely flowing liquor? Because clearly, Lord Carrington was a man who intended to be seen. The cut of his form-fitting coat alone was far too French to be the product of fusty old Edinburgh, though his strong grip, where it had braced up her arm, had been far more like a farrier than a fop.

She gave him another covert assessment. Now that he was

gazing in predictable stupefaction at her beautiful young sister, Maisie was at leisure to admire the form beneath the tails of that madder black coat and satin breeches. If the well-shaped calves beneath his stockings were any indication of the rest of his physique, he was truly a fine specimen of a man.

A vision of him, nude, stripped of his civilizing clothes and bare as God made him, standing in the flat northern sunlight of her attic studio, swept into her mind like a hot, exotic wind, blowing away the dust and cobwebs.

But before her face could color even the slightest tint of rose madder, Maisie dismissed the idea. It could never be. But what might she do if taking a life study were not forbidden to women, even accomplished portraitists like her. Especially lady portraitists.

And especially like *her.*

As a result of her collision with Lord Carrington, the ache in her hip was acute. She had to take the hand her sister offered in place of Carrington's—a loss, to be sure.

"Heavens, Maisie, you look done in." Flora reverted to her mother-hen mode, taking Maisie's arm to navigate the slippery, steep kitchen stair. "You're all tumbled up. You'll have to change and let Raines—Raines?" Her sister called down to the Scots maid who appeared at the bottom of the stair. "Help my sister into a fresh gown before you conduct her to the drawing room, if you please."

"Aye, miss," Cora Raines agreed stoically.

"And see if you can do something about her hair and—" Flora made an encompassing gesture. "—and everything else for that matter."

As if at nearly thirty years of age, Maisie would agree to any part of being mutton dressed and trotted out as lamb. And besides, any attempt to turn her into appropriately dressed mutton would take far too long at this hour.

She firmed her resolve. "Flora, you don't need me."

"Of course we do," Flora insisted. "This is Papa's first soirée in Edinburgh, and he requests your company."

Maisie only just refrained from making a decidedly rude noise. "Papa would never request such a thing." Sir Richard generally preferred that his lame eldest daughter assume a retired life that did not require making a display of said lameness in his drawing room.

"You can't always hide, Maisie—it's not right. Come," her younger sister coaxed. "It will be right as rain. I promise."

"And when was the Scottish rain ever right?" In Maisie's limited month of experience with Edinburgh's dismal weather, all the cold, raw rain ever guaranteed was a persistent ache in her leg.

But as she had no want to argue with her sister in front of either Raines or the keen green gaze of this Lord Carrington fellow—who was still eyeing her with entirely unfathomable intent—she settled on the non-confrontational. "I'll go up."

Anything to keep Flora from questioning why Maisie had been out in the first place—bribing beggars to sit for her.

And so, to go up, Maisie went down, though she was acutely conscious of her slow, inelegant movement down the kitchen stairway—the easiest, narrowest, least formal entrance in and out of the house, only a half story down, instead of the wide, icy, stone terrace stairs up. But she needn't have wasted her worry— the big, bonny devil of a Scotsman had already turned the bright lantern of his smile upon her sister, a perfect girl who lit up a room with her incandescent beauty, her lively conversation and her brilliant blue eyes.

Maisie was the dark horse, the lame spinster sister with nothing to recommend her but her talent for paints. And thank goodness for that talent—as her father had often said, a spinster must have a profession.

"Your pardon, Miss Flora." Carrington's dark baritone was low and soothing, and interestingly free of that Scots burr he had so recently wielded like a blunt weapon upon Maisie. "I hope I didn't discommode either you or your sister."

"Not at all," Flora answered in a reserved, but softened tone—clearly some of her starch was softening under the persistent press of Lord Carrington's charm. "It's only that it's such an important evening, you see."

"I do see," he agreed amiably. "That's why I've come, myself."

"I've heard of you," Flora informed him. "You're the newspaper man." Flora delivered this bit of news as if she had only just happened upon the information and not spent the past month—their first month of residence in Scotland—memorizing the names of Edinburgh's great and good and influential, while Maisie had been far more interested in the low and forgotten.

Young Lord Archie Carrington, Flora had learned, was the third, but most brilliant son of the Marquess of Aiken, a wealthy and influential landowner on the west coast of Scotland who occupied his seat in Lords for the seeming sole purpose of digging a thorn into the side of the previous Prime Minister, Mr. Pitt. Papa had made a sound of derision when Flora had mentioned both the son and his father, but he was clearly canny enough to add the son—who was not only a newspaper man, but the youngest-ever editor of the Edinburgh Review, which the young man had revived from obscurity to become a highly acclaimed quarterly publication full of politics, literature and satire—to the invitation list.

And Flora was more than canny enough to take advantage of the acquaintance. "You're very kind to help my sister, but we can't have either of you getting wet out in all this dirty weather. Let me show you back in," she was saying as she took the arm young Lord Carrington dutifully offered and began to lead him away, earning Maisie a much-needed reprieve—her sister would soon forget Maisie with such a distraction on her arm.

But Flora was not so docile. "Don't think I'm forgetting you,

Maisie," she called over her shoulder. "Twenty minutes, or I'll come looking."

"Witch," Maisie muttered.

"Termagant," Flora countered amiably before she returned her regard to the influential young lord. "But don't let us give you a bad impression of the Conways, my lord. It's just that my sister is shy of people, you see, and needs to be encouraged."

Shy, Flora called her. Uneasy would have been closer to the truth. Unwilling to do what was expected. Uninterested in making nice.

But young Lord Carrington hadn't seemed interested in making nice—his interests were clearly in making something altogether more mischievous.

"She's an artist you see," Flora was explaining. "She's achieved some renown as a ladies' portraitist."

Some renown was a bit of a stretch. Maisie had indeed had some success painting portraits of Flora's small circle of society friends in the neighborhood of Richmond, outside of London, where they had lived—she had even had the honor of painting the illustrious Duchess of Northumberland at her beautiful home just down the river at Syon Park. But before Maisie could truly take advantage of her growing reputation, their father had unexpectedly relocated the family from Richmond to Edinburgh, where Papa was to take up a post as the new Lord Advocate.

Renown would have to wait.

But Flora was clearly not so patient as Maisie. "Have you ever had your portrait made, Lord Carrington?"

"Ah, no," the young man said, sounding wary of the trap Flora was setting. "No time for such a thing, really. I'm a working man, not the heir, you see?"

"Tut," Flora said, and Maisie could imagine the gently rebuking tap of her fan against Lord Carrington's arm. "Your brother, Viscount Lanark, may have his virtues, but he is not the youngest-ever editor of the most influential political quarterly in Scotland, my lord."

"Miss Flora, you flatter me." The roll and sway of his brogue came rollicking back.

"Of course I do, my lord," Flora laughed. "For I want something of you."

"And would it surprise you, lass, that I want something from you, too?"

Maisie suppressed both her laugh and her sigh. Archie Carrington would certainly have his work cut out for him if he thought thick lashings of his Scot's charm would work their wiles on Flora. Although her young sister was exactly as she appeared to be—perfectly and completely lovely with her spun gold hair and delicate features—she had cut her teeth on London's bachelors. Viscounts and rogues alike had fallen to their metaphorical knees before Flora's radiant youth, beauty and cunning—the clever girl had not been born yesterday.

Nor had any of the Conways. They were, none of them, soft touches.

So Maisie, at nearly thirty years of age and firmly on the shelf, was happy to let Flora lead the man away. It gave her time to ponder out just what Lord Archibald Carrington, youngest-ever editor of the most influential political quarterly in Scotland, had been doing, skulking about the inky dark of her father's stableyard.

Perhaps she would get changed after all.

CHAPTER 3

$\mathcal{B}$y the time Maisie had been pinned into a suitable green silk round gown, had her unfashionably cinnabar red hair tamed into order and made her slow way to the divan in the second drawing room, where Sir Richard was holding court for his soirée, Flora had made a thorough job of it —Lord Archibald Carrington stood contemplating Maisie's quarter-sized, elegant portrait of Papa hanging just above the mantlepiece.

"Remarkable," he said.

"Ah, Maisie, there you are." Flora left her conversation with Carrington to quietly greet her older sister. "You certainly took your time." She held Maisie at arm's length. "But it was worth it—Raines has managed to make you almost civilized. Now," she said before Maisie could give her a tart piece of her mind, "I've got him all softened up, but he's asking technical questions—in Italian!—about your 'facility with rendering surface textures,' and I've nothing of usefulness to say except, 'Yes, hasn't she done the lace detail on that cuff beautifully.'"

"It's *impasto* technique, for future reference," Maisie supplied.

"But you need not tout me like a carnival barker." She had not thought to take up her trade as a portraitist in Edinburgh so soon —her mind was too entirely taken up by her waifs depicted as saints. But a spinster must have some profession. "It won't do, even in savage, slushy Scotland."

But Flora was a force of nature, sweeping Maisie's plan before her. "What do you take me for?" Her smile was sweetly arch. "I have no need for any savagery, when all I have to do is point to your exceptionally civilized work hanging on the walls and let people marvel for themselves. And do you see the woman in the lavender silk Lord Carrington is talking to? That's Lady Augusta Ivers, who is a very influential hostess—she regularly hosts literary and artistic salons and is a great patroness, especially of women artists. Her niece is a famous novel writer."

A young woman of society pursuing an artistic career—how interesting to hear. "Then oughtn't you be cultivating her, instead of the slippery young lord?"

"Do you think him so?" Flora frowned at the inconveniently handsome man before she recalled herself to her purpose. "But as to Lady Ivers, it's already done—she'll be your next commission. But she said, and I quote, 'You concentrate on getting Archie, here. I've got a good feeling about this and I am never wrong!' Isn't that delightful?"

"It is something," Maisie agreed with as much good humor as she could muster. People like Lady Ivers would always have good feelings when two young and attractive people were thrown together—especially two young people as attractive as Miss Flora Conway and young Lord Archie Carrington, she with her spun-gold fineness and he with his brooding dark.

Maisie refused to let it grate upon her that no one ever had good feelings like that about someone like her.

"Well, I completely agree with Lady Ivers," Flora was saying. "Lord Carrington is the more important commission to take, because if you take him on, your reputation will be set beyond your being a mere *lady portraitist*, which I must say is demeaning to a talent of your stature."

Maisie clasped Flora's hand in sisterly gratitude, even as she teased. "And you are so very sure of my talent, are you, with all your extensive learning and erudition? Did I miss your Grand Tour?"

"You know you did not, because we would have taken such a tour together if the world were not such a hidebound place. But this, my dear sister, is our chance—we are no longer inured in the country. Edinburgh shall be our new beginning, I promise you. If you take Lord Carrington's commission, followed by Lady Augusta Ivers', you will make your fortune and then we may take our Grand Tour together. Papa cannot object with you as my chaperone."

"But who will chaperone me?" Maisie teased. It was all a lovely dream, what Flora proposed. But the sad truth was that Maisie had stopped believing she was ever going to be able to walk through the galleries and salons of Europe some time ago— not without some hideous Bath chair wheeling her about. And that was not to be considered.

Far better to stay at home and be uncomfortable privately.

"Why not Lady Ivers for a chaperone?" Flora was far more enthusiastic. "We will cultivate her! They say she always wears lavender satin as a sign of love and respect for her dear, departed husband. Isn't that romantic? And you, with your talent for *surface textures* with your exquisite *impasto* technique, will do her silks to perfection. The future lies before us!"

Maisie squeezed the warmly reassuring hand in hers. "Your future does," she amended.

"And yours," Flora insisted. "Come then, let's secure him, shall we?" She all but towed Maisie across the room without waiting for anything approximating agreement from her sister. "You're in luck, Lord Carrington, I've almost convinced her to take you on."

"Have you?" Lord Archibald Carrington turned that considerable Scot's charm toward her beautiful sister and for a long, breathless moment, Maisie felt she would have done almost anything to paint such a man.

He had an impressive physique, but more interestingly, he fairly bristled with character, much the way a fox bristled with fur—despite the civilizing clothing, she sensed that underneath that pliable veneer of urbane charm there was something of the sly savage.

What hues would she pick to portray that alluring aura of sulfur and brimstone?

"Your sister, Miss Flora," the artful Adonis was saying, "tells me that it is her fondest wish that I engage you, Miss Conway."

Ah. Flora's wish.

"Oh, yes!" Her sister was unapologetic. "The thing that would make me most happy would be to make my sister happy, first."

"Flora, what are you saying?" Papa, whose interest had been aroused by the uncommon appearance of Maisie at an evening entertainment, queried. "I pray that our Flora is not up to one of her tricks, my Lord Carrington."

"A trick, Sir Richard?"

"In pushing her sister at you in this way." Papa's censorious gaze was, as usual, all for Maisie. "You've been too polite to stop her from speaking, my lord, so I will instead. Our dear Margaret is but a *ladies portraitist*, my Lord Carrington. I'm sure a man of your stature would want your portrait done by the famous Mr. Raeburn or one of his school."

Maisie was sure her face flamed at least five different shades of vermilion. But she said nothing, because what was there to say? She ought to be used to such offhand dismissals by now, but this time, her father's habitual denigration stung like a turpentine poultice.

Maisie might have been humiliated into silence, but Flora, bless her, did not hold back. "Maisie is far more talented than any student or studio assistant of Mr. Raeburn, who, for your information, is not resident in Edinburgh at this time—I made his acquaintance but recently in London."

Maisie could not tell if Flora was telling the truth or an advantageous lie—neither was beyond her abilities—but she sailed on regardless. "And I am sure had either Lord Carrington or Lady Ivers wanted Mr. Raeburn to make their likeness, they would have done so before now. And having seen both Mr. Raeburn's work and Maisie's, they will know that her work compares favorably." Flora turned with a flourish at the portrait of Papa. "Such delicate *impasto* technique. Stunning."

"Indeed," Lady Ivers acknowledged. "Though Raeburn may be the current favorite, I find he has an alarming tendency to paint all of us women as if we were indistinguishable, one from the other, amongst all the same lace and ruffles. While Miss Conway —do I detect this smaller canvas to be your portrait of your sister, Miss Flora, at a younger age?" The lady gestured elegantly to a small work hung over a side table.

"It is not a canvas but a pastel on paper, my lady," Maisie felt bound to correct.

"But I think it makes it all the more charming and intimate, don't you?" Flora put in as she drew Lady Ivers off to take a closer inspection of the pastel.

"Spontaneous," Augusta Ivers agreed as she was carried away. "And exceptionally charming."

Which left Lord Carrington to charm Papa and convince Maisie—or perhaps it was the other way around. "I notice you have been largely silent in this discussion, Miss Conway. You have not said if you are willing to take on such a commission."

Maisie felt all the novelty—and irony—of being consulted. "No," she agreed with her own wry smile. "But I should be a very great fool if I did not want such a commission."

"Margaret," Papa warned, insisting on her formal name,

instead of the far more Scots childhood nickname he himself had given her—it was as if he had become more inexplicably English in the return to his homeland.

But Lord Carrington smiled in acknowledgement of her wit. "And you do not strike me as a fool."

A curious feeling of pleasure worked its way under her skin—she was not as immune to his charm as she might have thought. "No, my lord."

"But Margaret," Papa began. "Your health—" Her father sighed away the rest of the implication, as if he could not bear to bring up what ought to remain politely unsaid. As if Maisie's affliction were somehow a burden to *him*.

"My apology—I had not realized." Lord Carrington looked from Papa to Maisie in polite consideration. "Is there some impediment to your taking on my commission, Miss Conway?"

He was looking at her. He was asking her.

Not Papa or Flora or anybody else. *Her.*

Perhaps that was the real power of his charm—this steady acknowledgement of people.

"No, my lord." Maisie hoped her voice was as firm as her resolve. "My health is—"

"Precarious, Margaret," Papa insisted, as if his daughter's health were in jeopardy now and not the result of an illness some sixteen years in the past.

Maisie felt the humiliation paint her with dark slashes of raw Sienna and burnt umber. But she would not let Papa have his way. The time had come—as Flora said, Edinburgh could be a new beginning. Opportunity had come knocking in the form of this recklessly charming man. She could snatch her chance up with two skilled, capable hands, if not steady legs.

All she needed was steady nerve. "Both my health and my talent are more than adequate to render an attractive likeness of a man of Lord Carrington's obvious youth and handsomeness."

The tartness of her reply was more than enough to rebuff

Papa. "Margaret! That will do." Papa put on an offended air. "I am only trying to protect you."

Protect or prevent—they were all the same to Maisie. Still, she ameliorated her words. "I pray you will remember I am old enough and experienced enough to make my own considered decisions about my art, Papa."

Her father ignored her and tried again to appeal to the gentleman himself, as if both Maisie's wishes and presence might easily be disregarded. "You must excuse my daughter, Lord Carrington, for she has not been much in society and her manners are somewhat blunt."

Burnt Sienna. Raw umber. Madder—maddest—deep.

"Her frankness is refreshing," Carrington rejoined, diplomatically.

Maisie felt the colorful heat and humiliation dissipate a little. His charm was certainly a powerful thing.

"You are kind to say so, my lord," her father agreed with another put-upon sigh. "But a young lady painting a young man, you see." Papa lowered his voice, as if he could barely bring himself to say the words. "So indelicate. My opinion is against it."

Papa's opinions were largely antithetical to Maisie—an obstacle she was becoming increasingly determined to overcome.

And she had help. "Not if done properly," Flora interjected, rejoining them. "With proper chaperones, at a proper time of the day. All entirely above board. And only a few sittings are actually required. Three, typically, isn't it, Maisie?"

"Four at most." But she could not bear to have a chaperone in the room while she worked—not even Flora. Especially Flora— the temptation to flirt with Lord Carrington, and he with her, would be impossible for her sister to resist. They would drive Maisie mad with their chatter.

"I don't know," Papa quavered. "It isn't done. Think of what Dr. Johnson said."

"Is Dr. Johnson Miss Conway's physician?" Lord Carrington asked considerately.

Maisie almost laughed out loud. "My father is referring to Dr. Johnson the philosopher and dictionarist, who held that the public practice of any art—the 'staring in men's faces'—is very indelicate in a female." She had long noted that Dr. Johnson and his adherents somehow had no opinion about what must be the reciprocal indelicacy of a male portraitist staring into his female sitters' faces.

"Dr. Johnson was an old windbag," Carrington contradicted with what was a nearly conspiratorial smile.

Oh, yes—powerful, absolutely delightful charm.

"Yes! Thank you, Lord Carrington," Flora added her own opinion. "Just because it's how it has been done in the past doesn't mean there isn't a new or better way to do it, Papa," she asserted. "Lord Carrington is an important man in Edinburgh. A commission from him will open up greater possibilities for our Maisie."

"I thank you for the distinction, Miss Flora, but the decision to take the commission must belong to Miss Conway," Carrington clarified. "Perhaps she prefers to paint Lady Ivers instead?"

Lady Augusta Ivers gracefully recused herself. "You are all kindness, my dear boy, but I unfortunately have not time to sit for Miss Conway at the present, though I should very much like to engage her for later in the spring."

"Certainly, my Lady Ivers," Maisie agreed. "I would be honored."

"Maisie?" Flora was saying. "Surely you must also want to take Lord Carrington's commission?"

"Must I?" Maisie murmured with a gently teasing smile for her sister, already knowing she *must*.

Madder black, of course, would be the background from

which his personality would blaze. And phthalocyanine green, mixed with a clay gray and something metallic—verdigris—for that glint in his green eyes. Of course, vermilion for the ruddy undertones in his glowing, dark skin. And carmine and cinnabar as well—every red pigment she could find, to convey that almost lusty, sly delight.

Maisie started from her pondering of pigments to find they were all looking at her in expectation. All but Carrington, whose gaze slid silently sideways until it landed on golden Flora. The way all men's gazes naturally did.

Normally, Maisie had become inured to playing the lame spinster sister, left behind or overlooked. But that evening, something within her—pride, she supposed—objected.

And so, while she held their attention, she asked him, "Why?"

"Why am I arranging for my portrait? Well, as your sister said, I've recently become the editor of the Edinburgh Review—"

"No. Why are you willing to commission me?" Maisie asked baldly, because frankly, he didn't seem the type of man who wanted to be immortalized or historified in a portrait. He might be a rogue, but he did not seem an egotist. He seemed less concerned with self-interest, than in self-amusement. And if he was offering solely to further his chances of falling in love with Flora, it were better she understand that now. Forewarned was forearmed.

But Carrington surprised her. "Because *you* think me handsome."

Maisie would have laughed and rolled her eyes, but under the circumstances—and under her father's disapproving eye—she settled for fixing young Lord Carrington with what she hoped was an acidly amused expression. "What I think is immaterial. You *know* you are handsome, my lord, which is more than enough confidence for both of us."

Archie Carrington threw back his head and laughed, as if

surprised to find himself given as good as he gave. "You have me to rights, Miss Conway. But while I am merely handsome, you are very talented, so I will offer you the going rate for Edinburgh portraitists like Raeburn—fifteen guineas," he declared, "to convince you to take me on."

Maisie was shocked by her own delight—but not so shocked that she did not again wonder *why* the young lord should make such an extraordinary offer.

But his lordship was all blithe, easy explanation. "These portraits"—he turned to the various paintings displayed in the salon—"are an exceptional calling card for your talent. And, as to your question, I will add that I have had my portrait made before, when I was quite a bit younger, in Paris, by a woman artist. And I must say that I found that experience to be quite…" A small smile grew upon his lips and his voice drew low and quiet. "…pleasurable."

He did not exaggerate the word, nor put any salacious intonation into his tone. And yet, an unanticipated shiver of delight tickled across Maisie's skin, giving her gooseflesh.

"So you see," he explained with that easy smile, "I am partial to women artists."

"Excellent." Flora was all but beaming her approval of the man, before gazing at Maisie intently, as if she could will her sister to accept him.

And why should she not? Even if he were not entirely sincere, it would be—dare she think it?—exciting to paint such a handsome specimen of a man.

Even with all his clothes on.

Why should she not wring some pleasure of her own from the experience? Despite her father's opposition. Despite the indelicacy of gazing at this man's face. Despite the fact he was probably up to no good.

"I accept your commission, Lord Carrington. Be here tomorrow morning. Early." When she could see him with the clarity of the early morning light instead of cloaked in inky charm.

His answering smile was all sly fox being invited into the hen house. "I look forward to it, Miss Conway. With a great deal of pleasure."

CHAPTER 4

$\mathcal{A}$rchie presented himself at the front door of the Conway's townhouse at the busy triangular intersection of Kirk Brae Head with Hope and Princes Streets at the unsociably unheard-of hour of precisely eight o'clock in the frosty morning.

The new Lord Advocate's house stood at the meeting of the old and the new—the tall, stone house itself was of an older era, weathered and deckled with moss and lichen in the manner of the modest gentry estates which had once stood at the verge of the countryside, had now been all but subsumed by the encroachment of Edinburgh's regimented, elegant New Town.

Archie's father, the formidable and canny Marquess of Aiken, had sold off some of his family's ancient holdings for the development of the area and now presided over his family fortune from a magnificent, modish townhouse overlooking the New Town's St. Andrew's Square. Archie avoided the place like the plague, preferring to keep his own set of private rooms over the Review's offices on Liberton's Wynd, just off the Cowgate, in the heart of the ancient city, where the pulse of Edinburgh beat to a decidedly more Scot's tune.

As did his own. Or maybe it was the anticipation of a new undertaking that had his blood pumping in his veins. However it was, he rapped the wrought iron knocker to find the oaken door opened by the pretty, gilded youngest Conway daughter herself.

"Miss Flora!" He doffed his hat with a smile. "How kind of you to greet me." If he were waiting for some sign, this was surely it.

"It is not so much a kindness as a necessity," she warned as she bobbed a graceful curtsey. "Maisie is notoriously prickly in the morning. I'm here to ease your way. I'm having coffee brought up —do you care for some?"

"I care for quite a lot, I thank you," he joked. "Although, if your sister is so prickly, why did she insist upon such an unfashionable hour?" Not that he wasn't an early riser, but he normally spent the dark of the morning ensconced in a snug coffee house off Stinking Court, listening to what others might dismiss as idle gossip, but which he knew was a good gauge of the mind and mood of the city, while guzzling down mugs of the magical brew before he loosed himself upon other human beings.

"She'll have her reasons," Flora explained away inexplicable behavior with a wave of her dainty hand and led the way to the back of the house—giving him a delightful view of her gracefully swaying hips as she preceded him through the green, hobnailed door separating the public part of the house from the servants. "Maisie's studio is in the attic—her preference, I will add, as my father was more than happy to give her a properly furnished, finished room for her *atelier*. But she chose the attic and again,"— Flora held up her that delicate hand as if to forestall his question —"I'm sure she has her reasons."

Flora led the way up the narrow, switchback flights of the servants' stairs at the back of the house and Archie was left wondering if he had ever seen behind the baize door in any other house besides his own? Or rather, his father's, as neither the Aiken townhouse nor the grand estate in Lanarkshire would ever belong to anyone but the heir—which Archie most assuredly was not.

Which is why he felt a bit disingenuous having his portrait made. It seemed an extraordinarily vain way to get what he wanted—information about Sir Richard Conway, his recent elevation to the rank of knight and his unexpected and sudden posting to the Lord Advocacy of Scotland. What had the man done to deserve such reward—the knighthood—followed so quickly by banishment to the political hinterland of Scotland?

Something was amiss. And this excellent access to all portions of the Conway abode was a very good start at finding out what.

"Here we are." Flora cast a warning smile over her shoulder. "Now, gird your loins," she joked before she pushed open the creaking attic door. "Good morning, Maisie. I've brought your Lord Carrington."

"He's not my lord anything." Maisie Conway hurriedly pulled a Holland cloth

cover over a small painting on her easel and turned to face them, her annoyance somehow writ large across her otherwise impassive face. "Next time I will be more precise. If you're going to while away the morning chatting your way up here to my aerie, I suggest you arrive earlier, Lord Carrington—at dawn, which moves earlier by three minutes per day at this time of year."

"Archie, please." He held out his hand in greeting. He would begin as he meant to go on, with an open, informal manner designed to charm and put her at ease. Flora Conway had made it clear last night that if Maisie was not happy, then neither was she.

And Maisie Conway was unhappy—she ignored his hand. "You've almost wasted the good light, Lord Carrington." She began to herd him, like an arthritic, irritable collie from one of his father's tenant farms, into the large dormer bay, where the flat gray light from the tall window slanted across the floor. "Sit there."

Granted, he was only the third son, but he was the third son of a marquess and even in his decidedly more rough-and-tumble working life as a political newspaperman, he had been used to being treated like something other than an inanimate lump of flesh. If this was any indication of how his mornings were going to be spent for the foreseeable future, he needed a different approach.

"Have you not had any coffee yet?" he tried. "I cannot reasonably expect you to flatter me without the elixir of the magical bean."

Miss Conway dashed him an arch look from the side of her eye. "You know very well you won't need flattery, Lord Carrington. Not even in those clothes."

"Call me, Archie." He was beginning to warm to the *staccato* rhythm of their banter. "May I call you Maisie?"

"No, thank you, Lord Carrington."

"Here you are, Maisie." Behind Miss Conway's unbending back, her more pliant—and more pleasing—sister was at the door, taking a tray from a servant. "Coffee, strong and dark, with a pot of sweet cream, just as you like it. And chocolate for myself."

"Oh, no. Take your chocolate pot and begone." Miss Conway began to shoo Flora out.

"But I convinced Papa that you would be chaperoned—"

"Absolutely not," Miss Conway insisted. "You may have promised, but I never agreed."

"But—"

"Call one of the footmen if you must—Robert is getting on in age and could use the rest. He can sit outside the door and doze there, without interfering with me."

Flora looked decidedly uneasy.

"Your portion of the proceedings is done, Flora, dearest," her older sister said, not unkindly. "I promise to return *your* Lord Carrington to you in an hour's time, which is all he looks capable of enduring. Why don't you come back then to collect him?"

"And his fee," Flora agreed. But she smiled at him as she said it, to make the parting with his money and his affection easier.

"My purse and I are at your disposal, Miss Flora," he said.

"Good luck, Lord Carrington," Flora called, before adding in a voice meant for her sister's ears only. "See if you can manage to take him down *only* a peg or two this first time, Maisie, dear, although he looks as if he might not only survive the fall, but will also enjoy it."

"I'll try," Miss Conway muttered before she shut the door on her sister.

But Archie had a journalist's ears and heard it all. If clever Miss Conway thought she was going to discommode him, it would be her morning for being taken down a peg.

"Alone at last," was his teasing opening gambit.

"Pray don't waste your charm on me, Lord Carrington," the irascible woman rejoined, "when you had much better save it for later."

Archie could feel himself rise to her bait—it was the curse of liking the clever ones. "Charm never goes to waste." He gifted her with his most interesting, enigmatic smile.

"I'm sure you could fill the potholes in the streets with it," she assured him in that amused, governess-y way she had. "At the moment, what is required is that you scoot back a bit—no, too much. Rotate your body more to the right. Now. Yes. Turn your chin toward the left. Stop!"

"Do you treat all your sitters so peremptorily, as if they were dogs to sit and heel?"

"Not if they come on time." That amused wisp of a smile grew another measure. "And wear proper clothes."

That was the second time she had dismissed his clothes. He looked down at the garments he had selected—a bottle green coat of superfine over butter-hued doeskin breeches and worn, but well-polished boots. Exceptional fabric, excellently tailored in London, in the Continental style of a refined sportsman. "What's wrong with my clothes? And your direction was only to be here 'early.' I was at your door—"

"At the break of dawn, then—no matter what time that is—here, in this studio, to make the most of the light. Not downstairs making eyes and trying to make love to my sister."

Was that jealousy he heard? "Do you object to my friendship with your sister?"

"Not at all!—if you do it on your time and not mine." She spoke without looking at him, busying herself strapping large sheets of paper onto a slatted board. "I shall only need three or four hours of your time—each in an hour's sitting. After that, she is yours to woo as you will."

"I rather think any time I'm paying for is my time," he murmured, just for the amusement of provoking her reaction. He did love a challenge—he would find a way to charm her, even against her will.

"You would be rather wrong—you are not my only client, my lord, and any time wasted waiting for you, is time not spent working on another painting or earning another commission."

Miss Conway's opinion was so close to his own, he had to laugh. "How refreshingly mercenary of you."

That brought her up short. "Are you mercenary for wanting to run your newspaper at a profit?"

"Oh, yes." He agreed just for the fun of it—because as much as he took her point, it was far too early to let her know she was right. "I've been called that—and worse—many times. How else would a man like me know such a ten-guinea word?"

"A man like you—educated by tutors before being sent to France and Italy for a Grand Tour in advance of a full university degree at St. Andrews? You should curse your tutors and dons if they hadn't taught you such a word."

"Why, Miss Conway, you flatter me after all. You seem to know a great deal about me."

While he knew next to nothing about her, other than the fact that she walked with a pronounced limp and was reportedly "shy of people." She didn't seem shy of people—in fact, she seemed perfectly capable of defending herself. As if she'd had practice.

God's teeth, how he was fascinated by the clever ones.

"Your Edinburgh is a gossipy place," she answered. "But it is my job to understand the background and nature of the people I paint so I can show them to best advantage."

"So you can flatter them."

She almost smiled and waited the space of a breath to collect herself before she answered with a question of her own. "Did you find my portrait of my father flattering or true to life?"

"True to life," he had to admit.

"There you have it. Now, as I've heard the nursemaids across in Charlotte Square say, kindly hush your whisht."

He did so, mostly for the novelty of being told to do so—not even his childhood nursemaids had needed to tell him to stop and listen. He was always listening.

And also looking.

So he looked at Maisie Conway. She was dressed in much the same sort of nondescript clothing as she had been wearing in the stableyard last night, but with the addition of a very old and very voluminous smock that he could now see was stained not with food or children's fingerprints, but with smears of paint.

And she thought his clothing less than presentable? "You never did say what was wrong with my clothes."

"Too ordinary."

Archie was nonplussed—he had chosen these clothes specifically because they were rather sporty and dashingly Corinthian, the sort of thing one could wear both in a corner in Stinking Court and while charming spinsters. "But I am an ordinary working man, Miss Conway—I put in a good few hours work before I came here this morning, and I will put in many more after."

"You misunderstand." She waved her charcoal in a short gesture of dismissal. "But for now, pray sit still, my Lord Carrington."

"Archie, if you please." He smiled to mitigate the request. "Since we're to be so intimate with you staring indelicately at my face."

"I am currently staring at your hands, which you are constantly moving, making it impossible for me to capture them adequately."

"Apologies." He folded his hands obediently in his lap. "I find it hard to be still, if I'm honest. Much prefer to be moving about. I can't think if I can't move." His best ideas came when he was walking, striding about the city talking to people, learning what they knew.

"Then don't think."

He tried to do as requested, but found his attention wandering, from the frankly cold, open windows of her attic to her newly lime-washed walls of his alcove—to better reflect the light, he reckoned. It seemed Maisie did have at least some of her reasons.

The rest of the long room stood untouched, with some bits where the darkened plaster had cracked off, exposing the lath and brick. Against one such wall were stacks of canvases, most facing away with their backs turned, so to speak, and others draped in Holland cloth. Nearer to the cold fireplace, an old, cast iron-railed day bed with a rolled-up mattress and linens was pushed against another wall.

"This is a very well-fitted room. I imagine it was an attic for storage prior to your arrival?" And perhaps other items from the Conway family's past were stored about the place as well.

"As you say," was her simple response.

He suffered a few more moments of silence before he tried

another conversational gambit. "And you've only been in the house a month?"

"As you say."

His eye wandered back to the canvases. "That is a great many commissions for only one month."

She followed his gaze without turning her head. "They are not all commissions. I have other work."

Clearly she was busy. In contrast to the hotchpotch nature of the furnishings, her work area was as neat and organized as a typesetter's letter box. Paint brushes were set out by size in separate glass jars. Wooden boxes of colored sticks were stacked along the length of her table and behind, on shelves, were an array of clearly labeled glass jars with more pigments and oils. Even the rag basket, set at the foot of the table, within easy reach of her stool, was filled with neatly folded scraps.

Everything efficient and utilitarian. Just like her.

And although her easel and stool were set in front of him, there was evidence—a sagging, once well-padded armchair was pulled up close to the window behind him, where cushions had been laid across the sill—that she might have sat there, drawing the city.

"Do you find the rooftops an intriguing subject for your study?" he ventured.

She glanced at him, as if she were startled, almost. "No."

"No?" But Archie was used to employing persistence on people he wanted to know more about. "But do you sit here to paint? Or perhaps just watch?"

That she was surprised by his acuity was evidenced by the loft of her brows. "Both," she finally answered. "I am a portraitist, Lord Carrington—I am far more interested in people than pediments. Fortunately, my vantage point over the busy corner gives me access to ample characters to satisfy my curiosity." She nodded at the chair. "If you tire, feel free to use it. But you'll have to move it around to it face me, instead of the street."

"And moving furniture is, I imagine, difficult for someone in your…condition."

She waited the length of a breath before she asked her own question. "Is that what you waste your imagination on?"

Her reply was so blandly tart he almost laughed. "Are you sure you're not Scots?"

"My hair may have the unfortunate tendency to tend to auburn, thanks to my father's Scots ancestors," she answered. "Yet, I remain thoroughly, stubbornly English. It is an unchangeable fault."

Her only fault, that he could see, was that in an unflattering light, Maisie Conway would be called plain—although that auburn hair could never be plain. It lit her somehow, like a banked flame.

But outside of her hair, her eyes were a hazel-ish, brownish color, her nose regularly shaped and her mouth adequate, if not pleasing. Altogether, she was a pleasant-enough looking lass, with nothing special about her.

When she moved, of course, she became much more noticeable, firstly for the pronounced limp, which showed itself in the way she seemed to drag one leg into line behind the other. But it was that fierceness, he decided, that insistence on hitching her leg along when it clearly didn't want to come, that gave her such a curious, determined aura of purpose.

A sense of purpose he understood and shared. "I should like to see your pictures of these characters you see from up here."

She peered at him then, with that acute, intense gaze, as if she could see his thoughts as easily as she could see his face. "Really?" She sounded unconvinced.

"Yes." Archie felt an unexpected heat begin to creep under his collar.

He was used to convincing. He was also used to being looked at—he was a braw lad in his prime, with his own black hair and strong white teeth. He was, by all accounts, a fine figure of a man.

But Maisie Conway remained either unconvinced, or uninterested in his believability. She seemed not just to look at him, but look through him—as if she saw all the small, unbecoming, petty parts of himself he had worked to eradicate or, failing that, hide from public view. All the doubts and uncertainties he hid behind his flattering smiles.

And here he had put himself in a position where he was to be scrutinized by someone sworn not to flatter him. What in hell had he been thinking?

He had been thinking that it would be an easy thing to charm or seduce someone in the house—it had not mattered who. And it might not matter, still—but he really did like the clever ones. They were so much harder to get.

Yet his curiosity was demanding answers. "Your chair here is padded," he asked, probing her limits the way one probed a sore tooth. "Why is your stool not also padded for your comfort?"

Her gaze flicked away. "Because I don't require it."

"You said you were limiting the sitting to an hour for my benefit, but if the task proves too much for you…"

She refixed him with that acute eye. "Too much what? Too much money? I assure you, my lord, I will give you very good value."

"Too much…" Under the unrelenting stare, his well-honed instinct for self-preservation urged him to prudence. "Too much exertion? Your father seemed concerned for your health."

"It is my reputation he worries for, my lord, not my health."

"Is your reputation that precarious, lass?" he teased.

"Not at all," she retorted. "But yours is. You are the subject of a great deal of chatter about the town, we find. As I said, your Edinburgh is certainly a gossiping city."

This time, he could not keep his face from going ruddy with heat. Clearly, a few barmaids, not to mention any number of countesses, had talked. "You shouldn't believe every piece of gossip you hear."

"Even if I believed only some of it..." Maisie Conway let the rest of her thought trail away, but, he noted, she also had two high spots of color on her pale cheeks, though she put down her charcoal and folded her hands composedly. "I walk with a limp, Lord Carrington. That is the extent of my infirmity. Yet, too often, people think that physical infirmity makes me infirm of mind or purpose. Which I assure you, I am not."

It had cost her something of her frost—which was really just self-possession, he now realized—to tell him that. "So noted," he said respectfully. Yes, he liked the clever ones. But he admired the honest ones more.

"Thank you." She nodded, though her color remained high. "That seems to be enough for our first day, my lord. I think it best if we take up again tomorrow."

"I regret I have a previous engagement tomorrow, Miss Conway, but I can make myself available to you the day after, if that could suit?"

Her brows rose briefly, as if she thought better of her idea. "Actually, that would suit. Then the day after, at—"

"The crack of dawn, in this room," he confirmed. "I look forward to it, Miss Conway."

"Thank you, Lord Carrington."

"Archie," he said, determined to get the last word. "I warn you, Miss Conway, I will wear you down. Nothing less will do."

CHAPTER 5

$\mathscr{M}$aisie called for a sedan chair as soon as dawn made the streets safer to traverse, but the early hour was the most reliable time of day she might escape the house undetected. Though the steep, slippery cobbles and stony stairs of the city made her leg and hip ache, she wanted the exercise without her father or sister—who were still abed—interfering.

Back in Richmond, it had been easier to escape notice. There, she had been able to wander the countryside without worrying about seeing a soul. Yet Edinburgh was so crowded her worries did not matter—no one noticed her in the throngs, much less commented on her limp. And when she became too tired, she could hire one of the old-fashioned, but convenient, sedan chairs she had first seen ferrying the curious up to the parapets of the lofty Castle.

Dirty and down at heels as the city appeared in the gray of the morning, she liked being about before the fashionable people—including her sister—had stirred from their beds. At this hour, only the last, lost and lonely of the city were abroad.

She found her Madonna in the same spot along the Grassmarket, but looking much the worse for wear this time. Lurid bruises covered one side of her otherwise perfectly proportioned face, giving her a ruined, penitent look that was sure to pluck the heartstrings of passers-by—far more Magdalene than Madonna. Yet, there was simply something special about this girl, something luminous and beautiful about her, despite the bruises and grime—or perhaps because of them.

"Are you hurt?" she asked.

The girl's gaze swiveled up. "It's ye again, is it?" she sighed. "Naw," she very obviously lied, even as she winced in answer to the second question. "Nae much."

Maisie forbade from asking the next series of questions—what happened and who did that to you—in favor of a more purposeful approach. So, first she proffered her pennies. "I have a new offer for you. Instead of letting me draw you here, for pennies, I would like to pay you to come and pose for me, where I have more time and comfort for us both, out of the raw weather." Her aerie was safe enough from the rest of the house, accessible only by the servants' stair and with nothing of value to steal —surely she could entertain this harmless waif without endangering them all. "I will pay you more, certainly, than you could make begging."

For all her wounded angel looks, the child proved clever. "How d'ye know how much I make beggin'?"

"Because you're going to tell me." Maisie nodded to the coins fisted up in the girls grip. "And I'm going to offer you more."

"Are ye?" The girl squinted up at her. "Is it manky pictures then? Though ye don't seem like a dirty sort of leddy."

Maisie was startled enough by the suggestion that she could only laugh. "I am not and it will most assuredly not be for dirty pictures like in the print shops, I promise. But you can come and decide for yourself, if you like. After you set me your price."

The girl, whom Maisie judged to be a young twelve or thirteen years old, looked down at the clutch of coins in her hand

and whispered. "I'm one o' the best, ye see. I takes in mor'n t'others."

Such misplaced pride, Maisie was moved by pity. "It looks to be quite a lot, so I will pay you a guinea a week." She named the outrageous sum. Her earnings over the years had not yet amounted to a fortune, but her savings were more than adequate to her needs—she only ever spent a few coins at a time on painting supplies, rather than on costly clothing like Flora.

"That's gold, then?" the girl queried with round, wary eyes. "Every week? Whatta ye want me ta do fer gold?"

"A few hours of posing—sitting quietly, much as you do here —in the evenings, in my studio at my home." That was also when Maisie could be assured of being left alone—when Flora and her father were off to their social engagements for the evening and the servants were playing least in sight. "All you have to do is sit, or stand, while I draw or paint a picture of you."

"Wit' me claes on?"

"With your clothes on," Maisie assured her, although she ought to see if she could find clean clothing for the child—as well as soap and water. She had no want to afflict the household with the possibility of lice.

"An' I can leave when I'm scunnered like?" the girl pressed.

"Yes, you can leave if you tire. You have my word," she pledged. And there was something desperate about the bruised, pinched face. "And food to go along with it, as part of the pay. Soup," she offered, wondering if the poor girl's teeth were still sound. "And warm, soft bread. All you can eat."

"S'truth? I won't have tae pay ye back outta the guinea fer the food?"

Maisie was both saddened and heartened by the girl's cynicism—what sort of life did she have where the offer of food was taken with suspicion? "The food and clothing are part of your pay, on top of the guinea. But you may try out the work first, to see if you like it."

"Haven't I heard tha' afore." But then she seemed to screw up her courage. "When do I hafta start?"

"You can come to me this evening," Maisie offered. "I live on the other side of the city, up on Kirk Brae Head, past the West Kirk."

"Aye, I know where tha' is," the girl said with narrowed eyes. "Happen I'll meet ye there, at the kirk?"

"Certainly," Maisie agreed, happy she might take her time, to make preparations in preparing a canvas for the girl's arrival. "Whenever you'd like."

The child nodded. "Ye go'way wit' yerself an' I'll meet ye there, end o' the day."

Maisie did as requested, because she did not want to badger the poor child any more than she clearly already had been. And when the appointed hour arrived, it proved easier than expected to slip away from the house for the short walk down the steep hill to the kirk. And whatever pains it cost seemed worthwhile to win the girl's trust.

Maisie's patience was rewarded when the girl duly appeared at the end of evensong, skinny, shoeless and shivering without the rough cloth that had seemed to swaddle her in the Grassmarket.

Lord help her, but she would find adequate clothing and shoes for the child as soon as they got home. Maisie paid her promptly and immediately wrapped her own cloak around the child. "Thank you for meeting me."

The girl accepted the warmth and the money gratefully. "Reckoned if ye were a bawd, ye wouldn't meet me at a kirk in front o' God an' all. An' I asked around about the hirplin, scribblin' leddy and folk sayed ye were right enough so."

"I am glad to hear that," Maisie answered, though she wasn't entirely sure if the girl's cant Scots expressions had been an unqualified compliment. "If you'll help me by lending me your arm," she said to the girl, "we'll go up Kirk Brae Head to my house, there." She pointed up the rise. "I'm Maisie," she offered again.

"Agnes."

"It is nice to meet you, Agnes." Maisie measured her words between the efforts of walking. "Thank you for helping me."

"I'm helping ye?" The girl scoffed.

"You are. Not least by giving me your arm up the road."

"Easy work then, missus. So how'd ye come hirplin?"

"I beg your pardon?"

"What happened tae yer leg?"

As the query seemed to be for simple information, Maisie gave the simplest explanation. "A childhood fever left me lame."

"Had one or two of those meself, but ne'er went lame." Then Agnes started and pulled away. "Ye don't still have it now, have ye?"

"No, you may rest easy. It was long ago, when I was about your age."

"Been years, then?" Agnes stepped closer again. "Yer well old now."

"I am." Maisie took the assessment without rancor. "I'm well over it. Except for the leg."

"What kind of soup, do you ken?"

Maisie had to stretch her brain—she never made note or kept track of such things, which were part of the household management meant for Flora, who would one day be a wife with a household to manage herself, unlike Maisie. Not that she wanted to be a wife with a household to manage—her aspirations were now only to paint in peace and relative comfort, a spinster plying her profession.

"Barley, perhaps," she suggested, thinking of the most commonly Scottish soups. "Or leek."

"Cockie Leekie?" The child breathed out a sigh of hope. "Haven't had that in a dog's age."

The girl looked as if she had had very little else to eat within that dog's age. "No matter what is in the pot," Maisie promised, "we'll get you a good hearty meal."

"Ye've a strange way wit' ye, missus. Ye're nae from Scotland, are ye?"

"No, I am English."

"Ye sound it, all class, like."

Maisie accepted the assessment as neither a compliment nor a complaint, but as simple fact. "But you're Scots," she said. "Have you lived in Edinburgh all your life?"

"Nay, missus. Come from up east. My village is Prestonpans. My family's fisherfolk there."

"Then, may I ask, why are you in Edinburgh and not at home where your family might take care of you?"

"My da's dead now—lost at sea—and there'r too many bairns fer my ma ta feed. Sent me an' Fergus—he's me brother—ta seek our fortunes in Edinburgh."

Some fortune—begging in a marketplace, exposed to all elements in all weathers.

"I don't mind telling ye," Agnes confided. "I was pure glad we were sent together. Didnae fancy comin' alone an' leaving Fergus behind."

"And where is Fergus now?"

"He'll have his corner to sweep at Cowgate Head. I can see him from me spot in Grassmarket. That's who I went to see—I didn't fancy taking this work without telling him, ye ken like?"

This was Agnes's way of telling Maisie that someone was looking out for her, should Maisie prove of malicious intent. Smart girl.

"I'm glad he knows. But Cowgate?" That was where Archie Carrington had said he lived. Perhaps she might ask him to look out for the lad. "Could you not find better work than begging and sweeping the crossing for pennies?"

"We did look fer work," Agnes swore. "Honest, missus, must have climbed a thousand steps and knocked on a hundred kitchen doors when we first come. But no one wanted ta take one an' t' other. Either or, they said, an' Fergus an' me didn't like ta be parted. But sweeping's nae so bad. Better'n begging, he thinks—he don't like the pity, ye ken?"

As Maisie had endured more than her fair share of pity, she did indeed understand.

"Me, I weren't so bothered," Agnes chattered on. "No need ta do anything but sit an' hold out my hand. They told me ta look scunnered—well, I were pure knackered an' hungry, weren't I?"

Yes, her pitiable ploy had worked wonders on Maisie, but for different reasons. But *they*? "To whom are you referring? Who told you to look tired and hungry?"

"Thems that helped us oot, though ta be honest, didnae help so much as set us up—told us which corners we were ta work an' gave us a scrap o'bread an' a kipper or two if we brought 'em guid money."

"How did you find them?"

"Found us. Trolling the Grassmarket, I reckon they were, like they were netting up herring. This fella asked where we was frae, an' we told him Prestonpans, an' sayed he knew me Da, an' he'd take care o' us as a favor ta our auld man. An' he gave us food an' a place ta stay. But then, a few days later, 'e sayed how we owed him frae the fare, an' how we needed ta beg ta make money ta pay him back. So, he put us oot ta our corners. But no matter how much we take, it's ne'er enough, is it, ye ken? An' if we don' give it all—like when I tried ta hold back the money ye gave me—he lamped me hard an' guid, an' left me black and blue." The child twitched within her bruised skin.

Maisie was horrified, as much by the casual violence of this unknown man as by Agnes's casual acceptance of it. "I'll give you work so you don't have to go back to him," she swore.

There had to be a position in the house for the girl—something that would keep her close and safe. Perhaps she could even train the girl up as an assistant—teach her to keep the studio tidy and organized and mix colors and block canvases, all the harder, physical labor that often tired Maisie out.

"Work here?" Agnes looked up at the tall stone edifice with open skepticism. "Inside? Is it warm?"

"Yes," Maisie averred. "I'm sure something can be arranged."

"Truth? I don't fancy leaving Fergus on his own, missus."

"I will take you both," Maisie said before she had thought seriously about how she was to achieve such a feat. But she meant it. "I'm sure there's a place in the stable, or with the gardener, or maybe even in the house."

And perhaps this Fergus could also pose for her. Perhaps she might consider painting other biblical figures—the shepherd boy David, quaking in front of the giant, but facing the fight in spite of his fear. A young St. George, similarly facing down the dragon. Or even a young Jesus, working his hands raw in his father's carpentry shop.

The possibilities were delightfully staggering.

"I swear to you, Agnes, I will see it done." But before she put paint to canvas, she needed to get the girl clothed and fed. "You leave it to me."

Maisie led the child around to the stableyard entrance and said a silent prayer that the servants would be too busy in the public part of the house, fetching hot water for baths or laying the evening fires, to see her sneaking the girl up the stairs into her attic.

Her prayers were answered—she had just gotten them safely behind the door and divested herself of her cloak, when Flora called up the stairs behind her. "Maisie, are you up there? Do you need anything before we head out for the evening?"

Maisie signaled quiet to Agnes and shut the studio door behind her as she came out onto the cramped landing. "I'm quite fine, Flora. You needn't take on so."

"My dear sister, you must take better care of yourself," Flora chided as she came up the stair. "You look done in. I fear you'll need all your strength for your Lord Carrington."

Flora's smile was enigmatic, but not so mysterious that Maisie could not divine its meaning—Flora was well and truly enchanted by Carrington's rogue charm. "He is not *my* Lord Carrington and he is not to come today. But I will say," she added in an effort to divert Flora from the studio, "he was far better housebroken than I had expected."

"Do tell!" Flora laughed. "I've just enough time for a comfortable little coze before we're to leave."

Maisie quickly blocked her. "Not this evening!" She held up a hand in mock surrender. "You are quite right, as usual, my dear— I fear I have overdrawn my strength." She gave way to the fib—let her infirmity be useful instead of damning. "Would you be a dear and send someone up with a good supper of egg and ham for me?"

"Have you not eaten? Are you ill?" Flora made a show of laying the back of her hand against Maisie's temple. "You must have a fever—or perhaps I do, because I could have sworn I just heard you say, I was right."

Maisie swatted her sister's hand away good-naturedly. "Don't make me regret my honesty. But be a dear and have some supper —some soup perhaps, a big bowl of soup—sent up for me, will you please? I'm too tired to tramp all the way down to the kitchen myself."

There was a slight hesitation that acknowledged the strangeness of Maisie's request, but Flora was too kind to cavil. "All right. But only if you promise to take a nap after you eat."

"I hate naps." Resting felt like a relic of the long purgatory of her teen-aged infirmity and recovery. "But I will promise to do so, if you'll leave me be."

"Done."

"And done," Maisie echoed. "Have them leave it outside the door, but just knock to let me know it's there, if you please."

"Maisie, you really need to let the servants into your room sometime to clean."

"I don't like my work or my supplies disturbed," she protested out of habit before she saw her opening. "But again, you may be right. Perhaps, if I trained someone of my own choosing to work to my specifications and not to Mrs. Smyth's, both the housekeeper and you would be satisfied?"

Flora bestowed her smile as if it were a gift. "You've hit upon just the thing, Maisie. What a wonderful idea. I'll speak to Mrs. Smyth directly and put out a notice—"

"No! Thank you, but I would prefer to take care of this particular assignment on my own. You can leave it to me, Flora." Maisie smiled back at her sister. "You leave it all to me."

CHAPTER 6

*A*rchie promptly answered his summons to the Aiken Townhouse, which sat facing St. Andrew's Square like a squat, vigilant bulldog guarding the greensward in the twilight.

The equally vigilant, bulldog-like Marquess of Aiken wanted his report. "Well?" His father was characteristically abrupt. "What have you found out about this Conway?"

"Good evening to you, too, sir." Archie straightened his cuffs to make sure no trace of grubby, tradesman's ink marred his appearance. The marquess was not an easy man at the best of times and was infinitely worse when he couldn't get what he wanted—especially before he'd taken his supper. "Is there no whisky to be had in exchange for my reportage?"

His father waved a hand at the drinks tray before reiterating his demand. "Well? What have you learned about Conway?"

"I reckon the new Lord Advocate hasn't been in Edinburgh long enough for word of his history to come to light. But I am also pursuing some leads in London, where information about the man may be more widely known."

"See that you do," Aiken growled. "It's been nigh on five weeks since Conway's arrival. Don't let the grass grow under your feet, lad. You've been in his house, I hear—for some bloody 'salon'? What goes on there?"

"Nothing out of the norm." Archie stuck with solid ground. "It was a lively mix of peers, politicians, intellectuals and the wealthier tradesmen. Best behavior from everyone, including the convivial host, who, I will note, had a very liberal hand with the libations."

"He would, wouldn't he," his father groused. "Coming back here out of nowhere, a 'successful merchant' nobody has heard of! He was a bloody gardener, grubbing in the dirt back in the day. Likely made himself rich enough with some dirty dealing— I'm sure of it. My guess is he was neck deep in slaving for years, but covered it all up to curry favor with Pitt, when he was Prime Minister."

"As have many men, over the years," Archie added mildly, without naming his own esteemed grandfather—but he didn't have to.

"Don't take that tone with me, lad," the marquess snapped. "I know full well what my father did. And I have done everything in my power to atone for that moral failure."

Everything except give the money back.

But his father's conscience must be his own, just as Archie's was his. He had, in fact, given the money back—paid back his father for both the cost of his education and the original cost of buying the Review. But if Archie had not inherited his charm, or his money, from his father, he had certainly inherited his determination—and he was determined to make his success on his own.

"I will continue to pursue Conway as I see fit. If his hands are dirty in any way, I will find out and I will expose him."

"Yes, by God," his father swore. "He has no business being Lord Advocate here. The Prime Minister should never have shunted such an unknown, untried man off on us, as if we've no better men to represent us to the crown."

Men like the Marquess of Aiken, presumably.

Archie had heard his father's complaints before, but after having met Sir Richard Conway, he wondered if there might not be something more between the two men—one so amiable and seemingly open handed, and the other so irascible and demanding. However much Archie might agree there was something fishy about Sir Richard Conway, there was something equally off with his father.

"I'll be honest father—I liked him." Archie worded his statements carefully—the way he always did with his father. "I found him convivial and welcoming and seemingly wanting to do his best for Edinburgh. I find it hard to reconcile that man with the personal animus you seem to feel for him."

"Aye, I've bloody personal animus," the marquess roared. "He's a rot at the root of Edinburgh, this man with no experience, no reliable reputation. He's an Englishman now, not a Scot. He holds no land here, but for the Kirk Brae Head parcel he somehow connived out of the Widow Fraser. He married an Englishwomen and from what I hear, his pretty, simpering daughter is English, through and through."

"As to the two daughters, sir, I see an interesting opportunity—"

"Two daughters? No, no! You've got it all wrong, as usual. The wife died, soon after birthing the girl—whom I hear is a pretty enough young thing—who has come north to act as her father's hostess, though she is more than old enough to have been married off by now—she must be twenty."

"Miss Flora Conway is, I believe, the lass you mean and at nineteen years of age, she is a very pretty young lass, indeed."

"As old as that? Don't be so stupid as to take any real interest in the girl, lad," his father interrupted in his preemptory way. "Nothing could be so ruinous. You'll get nothing but spleen from me there."

Archie felt his spine stiffen, the way it always did when his father chose to be so belligerently insulting. "Thank you, sir, but I need nothing from you." As grateful as Archie had been for his upbringing and education, he owed his father nothing now. He was his own man—an influential man in his own right. He would disabuse his father of this tendency to think of him as a lapdog. "Save your spleen for other, more deserving men—men who haven't made careful, well-considered plans."

This gave his father pause. "You have a plan?" And then, in typical fashion, the marquess answered his own question. "You plan to seduce this pretty daughter for more information about Conway."

"Something like that," Archie admitted, because the idea now sounded crass and crude the way his father said it. "Conway has two daughters, as it happens." His correction, as always with his father, was careful. "The elder Miss Conway is an accomplished portraitist, whom I've engaged to paint my portrait. So, I'll be sitting in her studio in the house at Kirk Brae Head at irregular hours."

Although he had already used up one of the three sittings Maisie Conway had said would be required—he would have to think of some way to extend the visits. "But the important thing is that I will therefore have access to the house and its inhabitants."

"An entrée into Conway's past? Aha, I see." His father finally smiled. "I suppose it doesn't matter which daughter you fuck out of her family's secrets—though from what I hear, you've always had a weakness for the pretty ones. Pray don't let your predispositions get in the way of the business. I didn't raise you hard for you to go bloody soft on me. Do you understand?"

Archie was not surprised by his father's descent into profanity and as near blackmail as the old man could get—he was inured to his father's underhanded ways. "I have always understood you, sir."

"Good. Well, what are you waiting for?" His father waved him away. "Make it so."

Archie would make it so—for himself and the Review, if not his irascible, un-pleaseable father.

And so, he made his chilly pre-dawn way to the Conway house the next morn through the darkened stable gate, taking a groomsman in the stableyard by surprise.

"I beg your pardon, sir!" the lad jogged over to take his mount. "Wasn't told to expect anyone."

"Pay me no mind," Archie assured the lad as he tossed him the reins. "Miss Conway is painting my picture and I am instructed to arrive in her attic before the first rays of sun hit the window-panes. I thought the stable gate and kitchen stair would be best, so I didn't wake the rest of the house."

"Aye, right, sir," he agreed. "Straight up to the top landing, sir. And good luck."

Archie waved his thanks. He didn't need luck—he had charm. In another few days he would become as invisible as a servant himself, coming and going with impunity. But failing that, he would have better access to the servants and be better placed to judge which of them might be most useful to him.

But the most useful—and surprising—person in the stable-yard turned out to be Maisie Conway herself, creeping through the stable gate behind him in her quiet, uneven way, like a wraith from the mist. "Miss Conway?"

How marvelously curious.

She started, much as she had the first night he had surprised her in the dusky dark, nearly dropping the bound sketchbook she clutched. "Lord Carrington!" She immediately put him on the defensive. "What are you doing in my father's stables? Again."

"Seeing to my horse." He pointed to the dark hunter the groom was leading away as a way to turn her attention—and assuage his own guilt at trying to butter up the staff. "I've come for our appointment," he reminded her, for it certainly looked like she had forgotten. "You bid me be early, so here I am. But I'm also a sportsman," he averred with what he hoped was a bit of diverting dash. "Always eager to take a look at good horseflesh."

She looked skeptical. "My father is not known for sporting pursuits and does not keep particularly fine horseflesh."

"Does he not?" Archie decided in this instance, some portion of honesty was the better part of valor. "But I do fancy you can tell a lot about a man, or a woman, from the state of their stable."

She looked even more skeptical—one brow rose over those narrowed eyes. "I fancy you can tell more about the sort of man who actually does the work of keeping the stable and the horses in good tick, than you can about the man who simply employs him."

He could not tell if she was knowingly trying to keep him from prying into her father's character, or if it was her own contrary nature that made her rebuff his inquiries.

"You are right, of course. But bad employers can seldom keep good stablemen, so we'll split the difference, shall we, and put it down to the character of both." He made her an elegant little bow of contrition. "Shall we go up?"

"Certainly. Please, precede me." She looked away and firmed her posture, as if she were determined not to be embarrassed by her infirmity. "I prefer to go at my own pace without anyone behind me, waiting as I make my way."

"As you like." He turned her suggestion to his own purpose, rising rapidly upward to get a head start, while also wondering idly how she had so easily kept him from asking about her whereabouts—though it certainly was little of his business—when a sleepy young tweeny went pelting by, barely sparing him a glance as she flew downward, jamming her mobcap on her tousled head. "Easy there, lass," he counseled.

"Sorry, sir! I didnae see ye," she exclaimed in a broadly Scots accent as she keeked up at him—and revealed a floridly bruised face.

Rage rose within him like a tide.

He controlled it to say, "Nae bother." He gave her an easy, we're-all-in-this-together smile, even as he seethed at the injury done to the young lass. "But tell me true—who skelped ye so? Yer mistress?"

"Ach, naw. Nae her—she's pure lamb, my missus."

The roar of outrage receded from his ears. "Good to hear, lass. I'm after heading up ta see Miss Conway, now—told I've tae be there sharpish for her painting."

"It's ye, then?" she asked with delighted wonder. "I'm ta get the coffee fer ye the day."

"Excellent." He slipped a penny into her palm. "That's for your trouble."

"Tapadh leat, sir!" The coin disappeared into her pocket in the blink of an eye. "Have it up ta ye in a jiffy, sir." And away she went.

He climbed the rest of the way to Maisie Conway's aerie and took the opportunity to make a quick poke around—while most of the contents of the attic looked to be part of Maisie Conway's studio furnishing, perhaps there were other relics of the Conway family's past life stored and hiding along the attic walls.

While he kept an ear cocked to the sound of footfalls, Archie began by peeking beneath the Holland cloth over the small easel, where he found the rudimentary outlines of a vaguely religious, Madonna-esque figure.

He shuffled through the loose papers stacked at one end of the work table and found a bound notebook—much like the one she had tucked under her arm in the stableyard—filled not with any telling details about her father's life, but with page after page of vibrant, watercolor pictures of the city.

Those people she said she was interested in, brought to vivid, colorful life. Archie recognized a number of the characters depicted on the pages—the baker's boy running up Prince Street and the dairymaid with her wooden yoke and pails making her way down Kirk Brae Head. There was the thin, bald apothecary, polishing the multi-paned window of his shop on the corner of Hope Street. Here were the farmers leaning over the temporary fences at the Cattle Market Place, and the barefooted children chasing chickens up the sweep of the Queensferry Road.

Page after page of perfectly observed, perfectly rendered street life—Edinburgh at its most colorful and lively. All this she saw from her window? Or perhaps, that was what she had been doing outside the stable gate in the early dawn—making pictures.

"Remarkable." He said it out loud, because it had to be said. Because it was the bloody truth. Maisie Conway, a plain, unremarkable spinster was actually a genius hidden in plain sight. "Well, I'll be damned."

CHAPTER 7

"You needn't sound so surprised." She came into the room with her uneven pace, although, he noted, she did so silently—her infirmity did not render her any less stealthy. "Although, I thank you for the compliment, the next time you are tempted to rifle through my personal things, don't. That is not for public view."

"Why not?" Archie asked with the bravado that usually saw him out of sticky situations where he had his intrusive fingers in other people's goods. "The paintings are charming."

"That would be your measure of worth," she muttered before she said. "They are not for view, because I do not want people to see them," she said as if that were reason enough, before she added, "They are private."

"You needn't be ashamed of them—they're very good," he protested with a smile.

She raised one eyebrow at him in tart humor. "How kind of you to say so, Lord Carrington."

"Archie," he protested with what had always been a thoroughly winning smile.

But Maisie Conway remained resolutely uncharmed. "Lord

Carrington, let me be very clear—I am in no way ashamed of my art. But I will choose both what is shared with other persons and when. You may do with your portrait what you like—hang it out your window in Cowgate, for all I care. But my private work is to remain private."

"What is the point of art if it is not to be shared?" he countered. "Hidden beauty does no one any good."

"That is not the point of art—to merely be good. Or horror of all horrors, be good *enough*."

Her surety, combined with her ardor, intrigued him. "Then what is the point of your work?"

"To please the eye as well as the mind," she answered immediately. "To embody the finest balance between thought and execution, between conceptual *ideas* and the making of physical objects *by hand*," she explained. "That is what the finest and best painters do."

He had never, in all his years of looking at and talking about art—even with his friend Rory Cathcart, who was a *bona fide* connoisseur—heard such a succinct and ardent definition.

Archie had to admit it—he was more than intrigued. He was impressed.

"And who are the finest and best artists, in your opinion?"

Her answer was immediate. "The Renaissance masters— DaVinci, Michelangelo and Raphaello, for light and color. Oh, and Sirani, for the use of color. For drama, especially the storytelling of the Baroque, Caravaggio and Gentileschi. And any number of the Dutch—I do so like their restraint."

Several women, but no portraitists, he noted. Curious. Did she have ambitions beyond making peoples' likenesses?

"What sort of restraint do you mean?" For his part, Archie's head was full of his last encounter with a certain countess who had been enamored of being tied up. But such was clearly not Maisie Conway's thinking.

Her serious expression grew animated as she warmed to her

subject. "I like thinking of what they chose *not* to paint—especially the Dutch. Of the balance in their compositions. There is nothing extraneous—take out one single element of any of Vermeer's works and the whole composition begins to fall apart —like a house with bad lintels."

"Why, Miss Conway, you're a philosopher as well as a painter."

"I am not." Her denial was firm. "I will admit to being only a keen observer. I've told you, you needn't try to flatter me, Lord Carrington—"

"Archie, please." He would accustom her to banter and harmless flirtation.

Her sigh was nearly biblical in its patience. "Let us get on with the business of trying to flatter *you* while the light is good."

"So, you admit flattery is your aim?" he teased.

"Flattery, according to that windbag Dr. Johnson,"—and here she flashed him the most delightfully arch smile—"is both excessive and insincere regard, undertaken especially to further one's own interests. My interest in you," she clarified, "is entirely sincere—to capture what exists in nature in both the flesh and the spirit."

Archie felt several of the more unruly parts of his flesh fill with the spirit of the conversation. "I stand corrected—you are not just a philosopher, but also a poet, Miss Conway. A poet with a romantic's heart."

"I am a realist, Lord Carrington and—"

"Archie, please." He kept his voice low and easy, unperturbed in the face of her determination not to use his given name. "I like it far better than Archibald—but perhaps it's the 'bald' bit that gives me the jim-jams. Shouldn't like to end up like my un-dear pater, as bald and shining as an empty pot." He gave her one of his best, most endearing smiles, all warm eyes and harmless intent.

"As you seem blessed with at least as much hair as wit," she returned, "I'm sure you'll do fine. Now, if you'll stand quietly there?" She pointed to his spot in the light between the window bays. "Please."

He went, but did not want their diverting banter to end. For reasons other than the ones he had originally planned—he was the one charmed.

How curious.

He needed to reapply himself. "I thank you for the compliment, Miss Conway. Although I must say, I like 'Maisie,' much better than Miss Conway." He gave her the sort of lazy smile that had worked to weaken the countess's knees. "It suits you, Maisie." He liked the way it buzzed like a drowsy bee on his tongue.

She sighed. "If you're done?"

"Actually, no. In consequence of your compliment to me, I'd like to offer one of my own—you look very lovely this morning, Miss Conway." He would not call her Maisie again until she gave him leave. And he would not relent until she did so. "I like the lovely soft effect you've achieved with your hair."

Her hand went up to her rather messy, undone chignon involuntarily—the moment she realized she had done so, she retracted it immediately. And sighed. "Is it possible, Lord Carrington, for you to have an unexpressed thought for five minutes running?"

He kept her waiting for a very long moment for his answer. "No."

Her smile breached the corners of her mouth against her will. "Exert yourself, Lord Carrington, I have confidence in you. Pray see if you can be quiet now for a moment or two."

"Why?" he asked just to be contrary.

"So I can sketch your mouth. Look at me."

The sudden command did something uncomfortably gripping to his insides. And some other, rather more outside, places.

She was looking at him in a way that made him aware of himself—in a not entirely comfortable way. Which was ridiculous—he was a man normally deeply comfortable with himself, body and soul. He was a generous and confident lover. Why should this plain, lame, red-headed spinster make him feel so... strangely inadequate?

Archie swallowed his misgivings and gave her the gift of his silence. Not that it really was a burden—despite what he had just said, there was ample fuel to keep his mind occupied. He could plan her seduction standing on his feet, couldn't he? She was already warming to his charm—a few more smiles, a few more compliments to her discernment and she would eventually succumb.

He wondered idly what her legs would look like under all those skirts while she succumbed, the rosy, fresh color of her skin heightened by—

No—that was entirely too idle.

He wrested his mind back to more productive, professional thoughts about her father, Sir Richard Conway. Archie had already worked up a draft review of the new Lord Advocate's decisions through Hilary Term, but wanted fresh information.

A grubby gardener, his father had said. How did a gardener with no formal education become a knight for services rendered to the crown? What could those services have been?

Archie cast his eyes back at the enigmatic Miss Conway. Did she have the answers he sought? She was certainly hiding something behind that plain facade—including what she liked to do wandering beyond her father's stable gate. But were they her secrets, or her father's?

He would have to exert himself a great deal more if he hoped to win her over. His inquisitive eyes alit on her hands—articulate, but strong and capable in an interesting, artistic way. Perhaps strong enough to—

No.

Archie forcefully navigated his inquisitive, impertinent thoughts to the Review's upcoming coverage of the imminent opening of the Edinburgh office of the Embassy of the United

States of America—he had capable Red Fletcher on that—as well as his own essay on the proposed union between England and Ireland, but more importantly the effects the rebellion fomented by the United Irishmen would have upon the fair and just distribution of powers between the two countries—

"Lord Carrington, I hate to burden you, but is it possible for you to be still as well as silent?"

"Apologies." But the words were gathering in his brain—he needed to write them down immediately. "Would you mind terribly if—" But he had already risen and taken a blank sheet from her table and brought out the pencil he habitually kept in his pockets.

As soon as the implements of his trade were in his hands, the words began to march through his brain like sentries, neat and organized and more brilliantly incisive than he had a right to expect.

Whenever the question of an Incorporated Union between England and Ireland comes to be discussed in the Legislature of this country, it may justly be presumed that the following principal points will be particularly attended to: an equality of right and privileges....

He had no idea if he took two minutes or ten, or even twenty—he forgot himself so completely he didn't know where he was, or for what purpose he had come. He knew only the immediacy of the task before him.

"There." He came back to himself to find Maisie Conway had calmly kept drawing him, even as she left him to his own devices. "Forgive the interruption, Miss Conway."

"Not at all," she replied far more easily than he might have expected. "I recognize the impulse." She came toward him in her uneven way. "If you don't mind?" She put her hands to his upper arms this time, firmly backing him into the shaft of light from the window, but he felt the surprisingly assertive press of her hands through the fabric of his coat in such a way that he had to suppress the strange urge to flex his arm muscles in response.

Because her adamance was astonishingly attractive.

"Just stand thus, holding that paper out, perhaps as if you were reading from it, or mean to show it to me?" She thrust out her own hand to show him the pose. "Yes!"

Her eyes pored over him and for no reason that he could rationally fathom, his skin went hot and tight.

"Just so," she said with a sort of wonder and her eyes were bright with her own, different excitement as she took up her charcoal, outlining his new posture with quick, bold strokes. Her eyes held his, as if she were trying to see through him, or into him, deeper than the covering of mere flesh and blood.

He felt his own flesh and blood prickle—under the cover of his clothing, his body was alive with awareness. And attraction. For nondescript, sharp-witted, plain Maisie Conway, who stared at him with such blazing intensity, it brought a rush of blood pumping through his veins.

She was all animated purpose and intent and that blazing intensity, pulling a tray of pastel pencils near without her eyes leaving her paper, to hastily find the colors she wanted.

Archie forced air in and out of his lungs, willing his unruly body back to normal.

But she was back, approaching him again, coming nearer to stare at him intently. "Yes, I think better, with your eyes blazing like that. More dynamic—athletic but intellectual at the same time. What do you think?" She reversed the board to show him.

And there he was—in living, livid color. Just as she said, somehow athletic and intellectual all at the same time. This she had seen—had found—in him.

He did not know when he had ever felt so…exposed to his better self.

The realization was daunting—*he* was daunted. By quiet, nondescript, lame Maisie Conway who had powers of perception beyond his ken.

In the face of such a revelation, Archie did what came natu-rally—he flirted. "And you said you wouldn't flatter me."

"I don't think I have," she said in all seriousness, as if she truly did think flattery an insult. "Not at all."

Her earnestness made it easier to tease. And to admire. "But you have flattered me. You see me better than I see myself."

"Good." She nodded in satisfaction. "Aristotle said the aim of art is not to show the outward appearance of things, but their inner significance."

Archie was surprised to find he had any inner significance. His philosophy was much more temporal: life was short—his friend Ewan's recent nearly lethal woes stood as a vivid example. So Archie went at his life and work with energy and passion, pursuing pleasure as if it were a virtue.

Maisie Conway's virtue was genius. He saw it in both the way the pose created import and action in an otherwise static painting—making him seem as if he were about to walk straight off the canvas while talking directly to the viewer—and in the color, confidence and skill with which she had so quickly achieved the composition.

God's bawbag, she was talented. "Remarkable."

"Yes, much better," she agreed.

There was no pride, no boasting or preening in her voice, only satisfaction. She was all about the business, adding in a final highlight of smudged white chalk. "There."

Watching her work had been illuminating. He could see the fresh color of excitement in her face. The flush of creation. The warm glow of—dare he say it—genius. She fairly glowed with a vitality he hadn't noticed before.

But then again, perhaps he had not been really looking.

Because Maisie Conway was beautiful. Not particularly elegant like the polished women of society. Not pretty like her charming, stylish, younger sister. But simply like herself—entirely, freely herself, alive and enchanting.

God's bawbag. He was seriously attracted.

"Here ye are, missus." As if on cue, the voluble young tweeny from the stairwell clambered through the door with a tray laden with two steaming pots of coffee. "I got sir's and missus's coffee."

"Thank you, Agnes," her mistress said. "All my Lord Carrington's talking has undoubtedly parched him dry."

"A lord, is he?" The scrawny child keeked at him from behind her mistress. "Looks pure young ta be a nob, though his claes and breeks is fancy enough."

"Nobs come in all shapes and sizes and ages, Agnes," Maisie explained with that ever so slight smile. "But nobs pay well to have their portrait painted. Especially the handsome ones."

"So you think I'm handsome?" he teased the way he always did.

But Maisie Conway was not the sort of woman he usually teased. She looked him square in the eye and smiled. "No. But you knew that. What I find you, Lord Carrington, is useful indeed."

Useful? *She* was using him?

That pleasant hum in his ear rose until it was like the roar of the tide.

It was worse than he had feared—he wasn't just curious. Or even charmed.

He was damn well smitten.

CHAPTER 8

"What I also think, my lord,"—Maisie felt the spirit of their easy conversation called for truthfulness, if not some well-deserved flattery to help him recover himself—"is that you have a strong, interesting face, with clear, solid features that look carved out of dark Scots granite rather than the doughy, pink and under-baked consistency of a great many Scottish men."

"Oh, aye," Agnes, bless her, agreed artlessly. "He's pure braw."

"Thank you, Agnes." Maisie gave the girl a smile to make sure she knew how much Maisie enjoyed her forthright opinions. "That will be all for now, until after Lord Carrington leaves—then we'll work on learning to mix colors." All the madders swirling deep.

"Aye, missus."

Maisie brought her attention back to her subject, only to find him recovered enough to saunter dangerously close to the almost-finished portrait of Agnes as the Madonna, along with the other oil sketches that she thought of as her waifs and saints canvases hidden against the far wall. "I'm glad you wore your 'pure fancy' breeks," she said to turn his attention. "But that waistcoat is still wrong." She recognized the ensemble from their first encounter in the stableyard—the crimson waistcoat still all but smoldered with sulfur.

"It is a rather too-obvious choice for a portrait, although this black evening coat works very well, indeed. I prefer my subjects to be clad in fabrics that catch and hold the light," she explained, "and textures that appear to best effect upon the canvas, like velvet and satin."

"I can see that." He had wandered in front of her well-organized shelves and pointed to a small oil sketch she had propped up there. "Is that Frances Percy?"

"That is the Duchess of Northumberland, yes," Maisie said, though it was everything she could do not to thump across the floor and snatch the painting from his hand. She settled for defending the work, lest he think it crude or unfinished. "That painting is merely a study, done to work out the details of color and pose and size." It was also the first portrait Maisie had undertaken of someone who was not a member of her immediate family. Despite its defects—or perhaps because of them—she was deeply proud of that study.

"The *primi pensieri?* I believe that is what you call these preliminary drawings? And *invenzione e disegno*—working out the design through investigation. What you just did—with astonishing speed, I might add."

While she was gratified by his praise, she was also astonished to realize that however handsome he was, Archie Carrington was more than a just pretty, animated face. His education had been extensive and his learning was vast—far more extensive than her own, mostly self-directed learning.

How interesting. And potentially useful.

"I thought I recognized her," he said with a thoughtful nod. "You've captured her air of kind enthusiasm."

Maisie was again flattered, but more impressed by his acuity. "Yes! That is the hallmark of Her Grace's character, I think, that kind enthusiasm." It had certainly been a kindness to invite Maisie to paint her portrait. "Do you know her well?"

"She is a patron of my very auld friend Rory Cathcart," he enthused with a return of his roguish brogue, "who is a great connoisseur of art and painting. Anything I know of art is thanks to him." He replaced the study on the shelf and moved back toward the stacks of canvases with their backs turned against the far wall. "Are these more of the same? Who else have you got hiding back here?"

All her ease fled. "No one!" Maisie heard the stridency in her own voice and hoped it was mistaken for irascibility, instead of what it really was—fear. "Please don't touch them. Those, like the sketchbook, are not for public view." She lurched across the floor to impose herself between him and the paintings. "Some of them are not yet dry and they must not be disturbed—the paint is too wet," she lied.

Something of her urgency must have finally communicated itself to him—he raised his hands in a gesture of surrender. "Calm yourself, Miss Conway, your precious wet canvases are safe from me."

"Thank you."

His apparently rampant curiosity swung back to her shelves. He leaned close enough to read the labels of the glass jars. "Lamp black, coal black, ivory black—now, that last one makes no sense," he observed wryly. "Ultramarine blue, cobalt blue, cerulean blue? They all look the same to me—are they really such different colors?"

"They are," she assured him, "very different."

"All those colors, every time?"

Carrington's curiosity about the work was a novel experience —none of her previous sitters had had so much to say. Papa never said a word, preferring to read from his papers. The Duchess of Northumberland had dictated letters to her secretary. Other ladies had gazed out their windows or upon their houses with perfect silent equanimity. None of them had expressed such particular interest.

"No, not every color, every time—just the ones I'm working with on the day. For the duchess, there, I did use all those different shades of blue. But for you, I feel certain I'll use every shade of black."

"To depict my soul?" he joked.

"To capture the eight or nine different tones in your hair," she said honestly. "I keep them in the order I like to lay them out on my palette—always in the same order, so I am always oriented and therefore efficient." She showed him the thin, oval wooden disk she had used for her painting of Agnes last night. "From the darkest black to the lightest, to give depth and texture, along one side. White is up in the corner where I can get to it easily, because I tend to use much more white than any other color, for blending." She warmed to her topic. "So you see my white"—she indicated one out of the line of jars—"is dangerously low."

"If you need a new color maker," he advised, "you'll want Alexander Hill, Publisher and Colorman, just a short walk down the way on Princes Street—Number 67 to be exact. He'll be your man. Tell him I sent you. He'll treat you right."

Maisie strove not to look astonished—this was information she could actually use. "Will he treat me wrongly if I don't tell him so?" She made her own try at teasing.

Carrington laughed good-naturedly. "Nay—Hill's a stand-up man, who has a subscription for his advertisements in the Review. As does Raeburn, by the way. We carry a lively mix of arts, poetry and literature along with the politics. You might like to take a subscription."

"Do you let unknown English spinsters take advertising subscriptions?"

Now it was his turn to be surprised—as if he saw absolutely no reason why she might not do as she pleased. "My dear Miss Conway, I would be delighted and honored if Edinburgh's newest and most promising portraitist—not to mention keen observer and painter of the city's daily life—would subscribe. I'll bring you a copy of the latest issue—out just a month or I would not have so much time to meet with you. You ought to take a gander at Mr. Raeburn's advertisement—no doubt you can do better."

Again she was flattered. And very near charmed. "I'll see if I can talk the city's most promising portraitist into it." She couldn't help her smile. "And I thank you for the recommendation to the colorman."

"You are most welcome." What she had thought was already an easy smile relaxed a measure or two. "And thank you for the conversation. It makes me less nervous."

"Nervous? You?" And now she was astonished as well as charmed. She had pegged young Lord Archibald Carrington as an unrepentant rogue. This uncomfortable truth—if it was the truth—was decidedly un-roguish.

"I assure you, Miss Conway," he appealed. "Despite any appearance to the contrary—which is only the result of a lifetime of habitually imposing myself into uncomfortable situations—I am not at all at ease. Under your gimlet eye, I am most decidedly uneasy."

Gimlet? How unflattering. "Do you now find me 'indelicate' as well?" she asked dryly. "You said you had been painted before by a woman."

"True." His acknowledgment was rueful. "But I was young and unaware of everything but my own handsomeness. And unlike you, Madame LeBrun was too used to flattering her subjects to make me question myself."

"Madame LeBrun?" she all but gasped. "Madame Vigée LeBrun? Queen Marie Antoinette's court painter?"

"The same."

"Then you were there—in the French Court?" So much more than just a handsome face—his education, understanding and experience were more than extensive. And unconventional. "How astonishing."

"It didn't seem so astonishing at the time. I had not yet learned to be so quizzical, or question either our surroundings or our privileges. Now I do—and I know when I am being judged lacking."

Did she really have such a piercing, unforgiving, *indelicate* gaze? "Nonsense. I am here to paint, not judge."

"Can you do one without the other?" he asked. "I don't reckon I could."

"Do you not write or carry articles of explanation of fact in your newspaper? Does that not require you to set aside personal judgment?"

"On the contrary!" He immediately began to defend himself. "I must use my professional judgement to ascertain the correct facts. There is an old adage amongst newspapermen—if one man tells you it is raining and another tells you it is not, your job is neither to believe one and report that it is raining, nor to believe the other and report that it is not. Your job is to stick your head out the ruddy window and ascertain the true fact if you are wet or not. No other way to make a splash."

And there was the passion that lay well-hidden underneath the roguish facade.

She had instinctively known how she wanted to depict the members of her own family, and she had also understood what was required by the aristocratic women who had commissioned her portraits—Lady Ivers had remarked upon Raeburn's tendency to show all his women in the same pose, but she, too, had almost always chosen a pose that showed the wearer's clothing to best advantage while also giving her scope to show their personality. But their status also had to be personified—she was to show them as society wanted to see them—sophisticated, urbane, delicate and beautiful. And still.

Young Lord Carrington was none of those things.

But what was he—besides a rogue?

"Lord Carrington—"

"Archie, please."

"Tell me how you came to be the youngest-ever editor of the Edinburgh Review." Clearly, he had deeper merit—however he might try to hide it. "How old are you anyway?"

"I am the ripe old age of six and thirty."

"As old as that?" How was it that she had thought herself older than him? "That 'youngest-ever' epithet makes it seem like you're fresh out of leading strings."

"Hardly," he laughed good naturedly. "I'm afraid I am decidedly middle aged. Starting to worry about going bald."

"Nonsense. A man is not middle aged until he has a head full of gray hair. A woman," she noted with some asperity, "is middle aged the very moment she passes beyond six and twenty." Having perhaps revealed too much of her own feelings, she added, "The editorship?"

He laughed and looked uncomfortable and reverted to his ready charm. "I'm sure they only picked me because I'm the only educated, liberal young Scotsman with a working vocabulary and the inclination toward satire they could find. Who is also the son of a marquess."

Ah. Was this the source of his 'nervousness'?

He briefly winced up one eye before he smiled. "It is true that that my father originally bought up the Review, but I have since bought it back. Although the marquess still sits on the board, there are other investors who together own three quarters of the shares of the business. I do own the last quarter free and clear and entirely on my own," he emphasized as if it were important for her to know. "I manage the day-to-day operations and exercise final editorial say, though I control only a quarter of the voting shares. But they leave me well enough alone if I'm making them money."

"And are you making them money?"

"Certainly." He was all casual, surface assurance again. "But that's not what's really important."

"And what is important?"

"Why, changing the world." He tried to make it appear as if he were joking, but there was something earnest beneath his bluster. "And having a great deal of fun while you do it! My job is generally to plumb the depths of human depravity, but I love the rawness of it all. I like calling people out for their hypocrisy and false outrage. If politics is a fisticuffs brawl—and I assure you, it is—then journalism is the knife you want to protect yourself in that fight."

"Is it always a fight?"

"Only if you want to win."

"And what is winning?" she asked.

"Rousting out the frauds, exposing the cronies, roasting the hypocrites." He said it quickly, a litany he might have repeated many times before, but there was something about that speed that said he meant it—his eyes lit with that righteous light that had animated him while he was writing. "Making an unholy splash."

There was assuredly the man she wanted to paint.

"Why, Lord Carrington, you are on the side of the angels."

"Archie. And perhaps," he admitted, "but I am certainly not one of them. I'm a cynic—an opportunist. In my business it helps to be a bit morally flexible in pursuit of the truth." He shook his head and smiled out of the side of his mouth all at the same time, and something lazy and curious and strange painted her feelings a fresh, new color—vermilion with a touch of turmeric yellow lightened by lead white. Warm and rosy.

But she wasn't painting herself. She needed to capture the blazing verdigris of his eyes on the page. She took up her colored chalks. "Tell me more about your education—how came you by these morally-flexible ideas of yours?"

"I was originally educated at home with my older brothers, by tutors, before I was packed off to France and Italy for a Grand Tour—three years we were on the Continent, mostly in France. After that, St. Andrews University. A very thorough but old-fashioned Scots education."

She envied him the experience and the sights, but she did not begrudge him the subtle loneliness she fancied she heard in his voice—she knew too well what it had been like to be separated from her family.

"And which part of your education was most influential in forming your views of the world—your tastes, your preferences and your morals?"

"My friends," he chose instead. "My three best mates—we were all educated together, you see, on the Continent and at St. Andrews. Far better men than I. Rory Cathcart, Alasdair Colquhoun, Marquess of Cairn and Ewan Cameron, Duke of Crief—the Four C's we called ourselves. Fate brought us together but nothing will break us apart—not even differences in taste, preferences or especially politics. They are the men I admire most in the world. I would do anything for them—and have!"

Maisie was so struck by the ardor of his sentiment—and his openness in all but declaring his love for his friends—that she did not think to ask *what* he had done for them. She could only think of capturing that gesture of generosity—the open reach of his palm.

And she, who had no one besides herself and her sister on whom she might depend, could only wonder what she might do to have such a friend for herself.

CHAPTER 9

"May I come and see your printing press?"

The impulse—and the fact that she had spoken it out loud—astonished Maisie. Normally, she was usually not in the least bit impulsive. Rashness had gone with the fullness of movement in her leg. Since then everything had been thoughtful deliberation.

"That is, may I make an appointment to come and see your press?" It might be a fitting emblem for him, as part of the background of the portrait.

"Aye." He cocked his head to one side, like an inquisitive, attentive fox, but smiled easily. "Our hour is up, I suppose," he noted. "Come with me now."

"Now?" Excuses piled into her brain. She was not suitably attired to go out in public—and Raines might not be available to put her to rights. And going out meant…going out *publicly*. With him. Which would surely be noted—such a man must be noticed everywhere he went. "Tomorrow would suit my schedule better." She could order a sedan chair in advance.

"Tomorrow, the presses won't be running like they are today," he explained. "The Review is a quarterly, meaning we only put out four editions a year—we have to make them count. But when the need arises, we also print special issues. Today, I've engaged the presses to print an extra edition for an essay on the water problem."

"What water problem?"

"In the old town, for the most part." That blazing sense of purpose came back into his voice and posture. "A great deal of the clean, potable water for the city was diverted up here, to the New Town, where the gentry can afford the latest sanitary practice of having clean water piped in. In the old town, access remains only from a limited number of public and private wells. Most people have to buy water a pail at a time from dealers on the High Street."

"I had no idea," she admitted.

His smile turned grim. "Most of the wealthy people who live in the New Town don't realize—they don't have to. They only think of the convenience to themselves, not the inconvenience to others. But the outcome is that the old city seems to have been abandoned to the poor, with predictable results."

"And what is that result?"

"You'll have to read the special edition to find out." He was already gathering up his coat and reached for her hand—as if he saw nothing wrong with so personally escorting her. As if he saw absolutely nothing wrong with her attire. Or her person.

"We'll not find the presses running at this time of day anytime soon. It's now or next quarter, Miss Conway. Come," he urged. "You don't want to miss out on all the fun."

Fun was not a concept she allowed herself to think about much anymore. Fun had been summer afternoons in balmy England, rowing on the river, the glassy liquid as bright blue as the sky. It had been riding ponies across the green and yellow fields, the breeze bright on her face. It was all the things she couldn't do anymore. All the things she had missed out on for years and years.

"I'll give you fifteen minutes to get ready and change into your habit while I see to the horses," he offered.

"Horses?" She sounded stupid to her own ears. "I don't ride."

"What? Never?" He frowned at her. "Flora said you used to."

Flora, it seemed, had been excessively chatty, for no particular reason that Maisie could conjure. "I did used to." Before. Before she had learned the lessons of discomfort and peril.

And after, riding had been deemed too strenuous and too risky.

"Shall we not give it a try?" he asked as if it were the easiest thing in the world. "Your stable houses a very sweet pony that I'm sure your sister wouldn't mind lending to you."

Flora was not the only one who had been chatty—clearly the stablemen had fallen under Carrington's spell as well.

"Forgive me if I presume too much," he went on. "But I have a friend who has what we call a hitch in his walk—the result of a childhood fever. While he is a…determined walker, he says he experiences greater freedom of movement while riding. And I think, perhaps, you might like that…freedom."

It was as if he could see straight into her lonely, thwarted heart.

"I would," she whispered, almost afraid to say the words out loud. "I do think I would."

"There," he said as if he had every confidence in her, but understood her hesitation as well. "We'll take it at a sedate walk up to the Grassmarket, but I vow, it will be fun anyway."

His smile warmed her through. "Fifteen minutes," she pledged.

"And not a minute longer," he called as he headed down the stair.

"I'll meet you in the yard." Maisie followed him down to the next floor with alacrity. She might not be as fashionable as Flora, but she wanted to at least be equal to the occasion, if not equal to the handsome man.

Raines was thankfully a wonder, improvising with one of Flora's longer walking skirts—long enough to look well upon a saddle but not so long as to trip Maisie up after she dismounted at the printing office—along with the bodice of Flora's habit. "You'll do, miss," she said as she set a jaunty plumed tricorn atop Maisie's head.

"Thank you. Wish me luck."

"You don't need luck, miss," Cora Raines stated plainly. "You've pluck and plenty of it. Go on now."

Maisie met Lord Carrington at the stable gate thirteen minutes later, armed with her courage—as well as her stout, steel-shanked walking parasol, which she would need for support once she dismounted—only to find Carrington waiting by the mounting block to leg her up.

"Such favors, Lord Carrington," she observed coolly to cover the rose madder color she could feel staining in her cheeks as he came to stand behind her. He was so very near, she could smell the starch rising from his shirtfront.

"I have told you, Miss Conway," he answered with that ready laugh of his, "I stand ready to serve in any way I might."

She tried not to sound ungrateful, but ungrateful was better than afraid. "You needn't go to such trouble. I'm not in need of cosseting."

"And you shall certainly not be cosseted in a working press warehouse. But for your first time back on in the saddle, I think some gentle help won't go amiss. May I?"

Before she could neither agree nor object, he placed his hands around her waist and lifted her into the saddle. She all but gasped, but it was over nearly as soon as it began.

He had stepped away and she was sitting atop the pony. "Behave," she beseeched the animal in a low murmur while she gathered up the reins and situated herself more securely in the saddle, hooking her lame leg over the lower pommel before arranging her skirts.

But she could do nothing about the hammering of her heart beyond taking a quieting breath, lest her nervousness communicate itself to the animal.

But Flora's gray pony proved more stalwart than her rider, doing nothing more than giving Maisie a long side eye, as if to say, behave *yourself.*

And they were well away, Carrington walking his glossy black mount easily at her side, chatting in that unaffected way he had. "As you come to know the sights of Edinburgh, you may come to understand that they are accompanied by smells."

"Yes! That I do know." Maisie felt secure enough to turn slightly into the prevailing easterly wind. "The smells are mitigated somewhat in my aerie, but on the ground, your city has an underlying dank I cannot place."

"And where have you found it especially dank?" His gaze was newly assessing.

"I walk a bit from time to time," she hedged to account for her appearance at the stable gate that morning. "I generally live retired from Society—that is, I do not care to socialize, which is not at all the same thing as being a recluse. The benefit of being thought shy of people is that they underestimate me—they never expect me to be out and about."

"So noted. Good for you."

As they made their sedate way down Kirk Brae Head to the Lothain Road and beyond the West Kirk to the Queensferry Road, she grew comfortable enough to carry her part of the conversation. "We lived on the river west of London," she explained, "so I thought I was used to urban smells, but your Edinburgh—I understand fully now how it came to be called Auld Reeky."

"On a river west of London?" he queried "Though I lived in London in the early years of my career, I've only traveled along the Thames to visit the old Palace."

"Hampton Court? Then you have been near to my home in

the countryside outside of Richmond."

"The countryside. Sounds lovely. Must have been a wrench to leave to come to the city."

It might have been a bit hard, but not for any reason he might suppose. But Edinburgh was growing on her—the variety of people alone gave her such vast scope for interest. Richmond had never provided such a seemingly infinite variety of characters for her study.

Or maybe she really was making a new start—a fresh view on the world that came with a new place. Because there she saw a prostitute leaning wearily against a doorframe—the sinuous s-curve of her body and casually crossed ankles calling out for Maisie's pencil to immortalize as the Samaritan woman at Jacob's Well. Over here was a butcher's wife, leaning over the sill, arms crossed like a veritable wise woman of Abel Beth-Maacah. And another three or four doorsteps up the road was a young woman greeting an older one—Mary calling to her Aunt Elizabeth, with the baby stirring in her womb.

So many characters she would paint, had she the time.

She tried to fix the scenes in her mind's eye, but the needs of the present moment kept her firmly in the here and now—the pony tossed her head and snorted, as if exhorting her to pay attention. Once she calmed her momentary start, Maisie could only agree with the mare. "What is that peculiar dank, briny smell?"

He took a hearty sniff. "That, I would reckon, is the sticky, sickly smell of urine and liquor mixed with malt from the distilleries and the putrid smell of overflowing gutters and sewers." He flashed her a mischievous grin. "I'll warrant it makes for an overwhelming brew. Still, Auld Reeky is a grand old town," he opined. "The best town. I wouldn't trade it for Glasgow or even London."

"No?" Maisie queried. "I thought Mr. Johnson said, 'When a man is tired of London, he is tired of life; for there is in London all that life can afford.'"

"He did," Carrington agreed. "But the poet Mr. Tobias Smollett, a Scots, said, 'Edinburgh is a hotbed of genius,' and that is the just sort of bed I like to lie in," he told her on a wink.

Maisie felt the distance between them grow exponentially closer. Or perhaps it was just the dank miasma of the streets infecting her. After a decade of daily exposure to the dense smells of linseed oils, paints and turpentines, Maisie had thought herself quite used to noxious smells, but the further they went into the narrow heart of the old city, the more putrid it became.

Yet people trudged along the pavement, seemingly inured to the stench. "I don't know how they endure it."

"Nowhere else to live—nowhere else they can afford," he observed. "Poverty is a great prison keeper."

Maisie decided she liked the grim but determined light in his eyes. "I think I like your politics."

"My politics are meant to be invisible—even though the Review is known as a more liberal publication, the editor needs to keep an even hand. Politics matter far less than the truth."

Yes—this was the side of him she wanted to see. "And the truth is that it is an awful thing to be poor?"

"Always has been." He shook his head in grim confirmation. "The poor will be with us always, as the vicars say. Especially beneath, in the closes."

Maisie had heard the word "close" bandied about, but had never thought it was anything more than a quaint Scot's word for an alleyway. "What do you mean, beneath? Do you mean the sewer drains?" Though she might live retired from society, she was not ignorant of its more pressing needs—water closets had to drain somewhere. "But I thought you said the newer water and effluent pipes were only available in the New Town?"

"So I did. The closes are not drains, per se, although they do drain, since most of them run downhill," he digressed. "But the closes are more like layers of streets one atop the other, starting at the narrow alleyways that run downhill from the High Street."

"You mean those long, narrow staircases with all the interesting and disgusting names?"

The roguish eye winked at her again. "You've been past Fleshmonger's Close."

She could only smile at his acuity. "Indeed."

"Think beneath, as in the basements of the buildings going down to the rock beneath, and so the passages beneath the top pavement of the close are down there too, sometimes two and three stories deep, connecting on to other passages that run across them. There are mazes down there that run for miles, in layers, going down into the very rock upon which the city was built."

"What are they for?"

"Whatever they're needed for—storage, manufacturing, rooms. Homes, too, some of them, like the vaults under the South Bridge." He pointed up the lane where a stone bridge cut across Cowgate's path.

"You mean, people live inside that?"

"Poor people do. People who can't afford sunlight and air, nor certainly clean water."

She had never before felt so affluent. "They live there?"

He was patient with her disbelief. "Hundreds of them. And throughout the old city, nigh unto the thousands. There are even closes under the Exchequer and the Parliament House up on the High Street, filled with dispossessed crofters and such. It suits the government, I reckon—if they can't see the deserving poor, then they don't have to think about them or see to their needs. They can pretend they're the undeserving poor and consign them to their fate."

Maisie was shocked into silence. She had thought herself so well-informed, so aware of the challenges and improvements of the day. But she hadn't seen the poverty as well as the water-closets. And this—this knowledge that such conditions existed quite literally under the government's feet—nearly defeated her.

"At least you're not worried about the pony anymore," he teased. "Come, we're here."

They drew rein alongside a narrow close, where Lord Carrington whistled up a lad to hold the horses while he came to hand her down.

Maisie had to steel herself against the press of his hands about her waist and school herself to keep her composure. But there was no time to dwell on the tumult of her feelings when he took her hand to help her make her slow way up the damp, slick cobbles of Liberton's Close, where a brightly painted hanging sign announced the offices of the Edinburgh Review.

The bell over the door clanged cheerfully at their arrival.

"This way." Lord Archie Carrington strode into his office where he promptly divested himself of his coat, leaving him attired only in his shirtsleeves, which he immediately rolled back to reveal arms muscled more like a stableman than a scrivener. "What do you want to see?"

"I merely wish to see you in your more natural state."

The moment she saw the answering expression of wicked amusement on his face she wished her words back. "I meant, I should like to observe you at your work," she attempted to clarify. "That rousting out of the frauds."

"We're short a fraud or two today." His laugh was her reward. "But turnabout is fair play, I always say—I've watched you work, so why should you not watch me, if you've a mind to?" He gestured toward two stout, workaday chairs that were arrayed in front of a huge oaken desk strewn about with pens and foolscap paper. "Catch your breath—I don't have any want to return you to your sister worse for wear."

The stark reminder of his attraction to her sister helped Maisie quiet her pulse and harden her purpose. The youngest-ever editor of the Edinburgh Review was revealed to be of an entirely utilitarian bent—there wasn't even the thinnest veneer of aristocratic favor about the place—everything was hotchpotch and ad hoc. A number of smaller, mismatched desks and tables were strewn about the primary room behind the railing, manned by a veritable wolf pack of idly curious-looking, pipe-chewing characters of various ages.

Lord Carrington's smaller office sat to one side of the larger room, behind an interior wall of dirty windows that provided an obscure view of his rag-tag collection of likely looking fellows—his apostate apostles, for they looked as heretical as all get out with their long clay pipes and short, battered hats. She would paint them as a rogues' Last Supper.

But behind Carrington's head, his shelves were filled with a marvelous variety of titles, with everything from the poetry of the Scots bard Robert Burns to large folios of botanical drawings laid on their side. There were even a few sentimental novels, dog-eared enough to prove they'd been read.

How interesting. And fair minded.

Archie Carrington, the man she had pegged as an unrepentant, sly rogue, had many other facets of his personality, it seemed.

"You're a reading man."

He looked up, not exactly surprised, but curious. "Food for the mind, books and reading—I'm in the business, you see."

"And the poetry of Burns for the youngest-ever editor of the vaulted Review?"

"The vaulted, most especially, need the food for the soul that poetry—and Scots poetry in particular—gives us."

"Proof, one must suppose, that you do indeed have a soul under all those vaults."

And under all that cynical charm. But, if she had to pick the trait that best summed up the youngest-ever editor of the Edinburgh Review's appeal, she would have to say it was his ready and steady acknowledgment of people. Of their differences.

That was what made him so damn charming.

Not to mention, so devastatingly, dangerously attractive.

"I am sorry not to be able to offer you any refreshment," Carrington said between pen scratches, "but we don't get many visitors to the pressroom. I can send one of these motley fellows out for tea and cakes if you need to revive yourself?"

"Though I will admit to being a bit challenged by your cobbles, I am not in the least overset." The exercise had actually done her good. What a cheering thought. "I confess, I thought there would be a printing press or some sort of machinery hulking up the place."

"They're around the back, our presses." He gestured over his shoulder and Maisie was taken by the curious and interesting play of muscles along his forearm. "The pressworks is a separate business actually, available to other printing businesses besides the Review, since we only run issues four times a year. The rest of the time, the lads are printing pamphlets, tracts, waybills, advertisements and the like, along with my friend, the publisher Hamish Cathcart's books."

She had heard of Cathcart Publishing—according to Flora,

they were the publisher of Lady Ivers' niece, Elspeth Otis Cath-cart. "How economically mercenary," Maisie teased.

She was rewarded by his laugh. "Are you ready to see them? I've a proof to take through for the typesetter."

"Certainly." She was there to see whatever she could.

He led the way through the gauntlet of heretic pipe-chewers and on through to a set of hanging doors, which slid sideways to reveal a barn-like stone building.

"My pressworks," he said with the same sort of pleasure a new father might evince on announcing a newborn son.

"Yours?"

"While I am the editor of the Review, with final say over what we publish, I have to answer to a board of directors, who together make up the controlling shares—at the moment. I am always working to buy the shares back. But the presses them-selves, they're all mine. And if the pamphlets and tracts we print aren't to the board's political taste, it's none of their damn concern."

As they drew closer, his voice was drowned out by the rhythmic din of the presses. Along with the sound, the dense, pungent scents of industrial oils, wet paper pulp and something thoroughly acidic filled her senses.

Carrington raised his voice to be heard over the clack of the tympans and the heavy whirring groans of the presses, but she could still hear his pride. "We've three wooden, 'common' presses," he explained. "Two pressmen per machine, Smitty and Big Davy, here"—he introduced the pairs of broad-shouldered, thick-armed pressmen by clapping them on the back—"Duncan and Craig, and Braw Jim and Wee Wally, turn that large screw on the top with one heavy swing of the levered arm. You, with your experience might have guessed that the ink which is assailing your nostrils, is a thick black paint of boiled linseed oil and lampblack—applied by the ink boys, Jonesy here, Tad there, and Double D, Dumfries

Davy, on the far side." His affection for the men was evident. "The paper's dampened for printing, so that's the other stink, along with the lye used to clean off the type after the page run."

He pointed her toward the large slanted desks where nimble-fingered fellows picked up tiny letter blocks and slatted them into place on a deep board. "This fellow, here, is Craig, our chief typesetter, and those young printer's devils are Andrew, Keith and Stewart who help where they're needed, keep order, clean the place up and are meant to be learning the processes so they can become pressmen themselves one day. They practice on small waybills we print both to keep the presses from sitting idle and to earn a few extra pounds on the side."

His obvious enthusiasm was enchanting.

"We print the Review four times a year," he explained. "For every issue, we run no less than twenty pages, front and back. Craig keeps the sets of columns that don't change—subscription advertisements for trades and services at the back, so we can press those in advance, or at least begin the run with those pages before the others are set."

"Or even written," the typesetter joked.

"Always on our feet, we are," Carrington agreed with a laugh. "Getting express dispatches up from Westminster on the regular, so we're never more than two days behind the news from the government and Crown." That fire of purpose lit his eyes. "Making sure the Review's readers have the best, latest information is vitally important to the political health of the city—and the country, at that."

Definitely on the side of the angels. And definitely far more interesting when he wasn't trying to charm, so much as convince.

Oh, yes. This was the man—the rabble-rousing editor, the urbane, educated man of allegedly flexible morals and implacable ideals, not just charm.

The stretch of his arm, palm up, in appeal. The length of his legs seeming to stride off the paper. The light in his eyes and the set of his jaw. The power of his mind and body.

At the scale she was envisioning, she might have to buy canvas already stretched on a frame. Did she have enough treatment medium and rectified spirit of turpentine to underpaint such a large canvas? And then she would need a new, larger easel to hold such a piece…

She began a list in her head. "What was the name of that fellow on Princes Street?"

Somehow, he followed her obscure train of thought to its rightful destination. "Alexander Hill, the colorman? Number Sixty-Seven Princes Street."

"I must go there straight away. I shall require an excessively large canvas."

"Excessively large?" His laugh filled the vaulted space. "How big is excessive?"

"How tall are you?" From her vantage place, he loomed larger than life.

She fetched out her pencil to begin an actual list. "I need poppy oil clarified with charcoal—do you know if your Mr. Hill carries that?"

"I have no idea, but I am all agog to find out. Let me call for the horses—" At that he strode to the open window and let loose a piercing whistle. "—and I shall accompany you there."

She was about to wave him off, thinking she had already taken up too much of his valuable time. But the truth was, she might so much more easily visit the establishment as well as transport her purchases home without the nannyish interference of either Flora, or God forbid, her father, who would quaver and lecture about her being on her feet too long—or worse, desporting herself dangerously upon the pony, when nothing of the sort had occurred. "That would be lovely. Thank you."

Carrington did not quaver—he easily put her back upon her

mount in so matter-of-fact a manner that she had no time to ponder his surprising effect upon her pulse.

It was well done of him. And charming in an entirely different way.

As was the way his hair ruffled in the brisk breeze as he swept off his hat to hold the door to the shop and let her make her slow, uneven way under the sign that read: Alexander Hill, Publisher and Colorman to the Scottish Academy of Painting, Sculpture and Architecture: Artist's Materials of the Best Quality, Constantly Fresh, Picture Frames Made to Order, Drawings Lent to Copy.

It was as comprehensive an offering as she might need.

A brass bell jingled them inside, where the warm, welcoming scents of linseed oils and turpentines bid her make herself comfortable. Maisie let the blessed sense of familiarity wash over her. Back in Richmond, her forays into the village had been few and far between—she had been fourteen the summer the fever had left her so weak she could not walk, and when she had recovered, she had hated to be seen dragging her lame leg behind her, having the townspeople pull their skirts aside as if she might be catching.

But the colorman's shop had been different—the first place her burgeoning talent for painting mattered more than her infirmity.

"My Lord Carrington," came an enthusiastic greeting from behind the tidy counter. "So very good to see you, my lord. What brings you to visit us today?"

"Mr. Hill, I bring you a new and important customer whom I predict will shortly become one of your favorites. Miss Conway, may I present Mr. Alexander Hill, Colorman. Miss Conway is a portraitist new to the city, already receiving commissions."

"Is she?" Mr. Hill was all enthusiastic delight. Trim of body, dark of face and wearing a meticulously clean workroom smock, he reached across to offer his hand. "You are most welcome, Miss

Conway." His greeting held the mellifluous accent of the West Indies. "How may we be of assistance to you?"

Maisie was instantly taken by the warmth of the colorman's character. She could easily see him as one of her saints—Saint Peter guarding the gates of heaven like a welcoming shopkeeper, ushering his ecstatic believers in.

Maisie met his enthusiasm with her own, as well as her list. "If you please, Mr. Hill, I shall need a large canvas of your best Belgian linen, stretched on an ash frame of at least four inches by one and a half inches thick, for a canvas approximately ninety-five inches by sixty inches."

"A 'Bishop's Whole Length,'" Hill nodded along, copying out the specifications. "Splendid, splendid. At that size, you'll no doubt want a prepared canvas?"

Maisie hesitated. "I generally prefer to undercoat my own canvases with Bell's medium. That way, I am assured of the quality—"

"Just so, just so," Hill nodded in sympathetic agreement. "Bell's medium is an excellent preparation. But if I may, we have newly developed our own treatment that I would submit is an improvement upon Bell's. Our preparation contains no resin, but consists of thickened linseed oil dissolved in oil of spike. To prepare it, we oxidize pure linseed oil until it has acquired the consistency of fresh honey. Now, this change occurs when a layer of oil is exposed to the air in a large flask, the mouth of which is lightly plugged with carded cotton—"

"Thank you, Mr. Hill. That does sound quite thoroughly prepared and exactly what I require." Clearly the man knew his business. "My next problem is the stretching—my studio is accessible only by narrow corridors and steep stairs, so the framing would need to be done there, *in situ* as the academics might say. And later, once the portrait is finished and cured, it will need to be taken off, and re-stretched and framed wherever Lord Carrington might choose to display it."

Maisie included Carrington in her explanation, as it was only fair that she delineate the logistical problems that came with the size of portrait she was proposing.

"Lord Carrington?" Mr. Hill was all enthusiastic delight. "His lordship is finally sitting for a portrait?

Carrington stepped in to explain. "Don't let that get out, will you, Mr. Hill, until I have acquired an abode suitable to the dignity of the canvas?" he added with easy humor. "At present, I haven't got any space fit to purpose."

"Ah! Splendid, splendid. A canvas assembled at Miss Conway's studio in Kirk Brae Head?—if I may be so presumptuous, Miss Conway, but your family's arrival in Edinburgh has been well reported," he added as an aside. "Then disassembled there, at a date to be determined, and then reassembled and mounted at Aiken House, if you are still lacking a suitable abode at that time, my lord." Hill poked his spectacles up the bridge of his nose. "I do have stretchers of the required dimensions, but of the finest West Indies mahogany, well-cured and cut to a finished length of eight feet, ten inches by five feet, ten inches."

"Thank you kindly, Mr. Hill, that will do admirably."

The tradesman beamed. "I assure you, you will not be disappointed, Miss Conway." Mr. Hill handed off the specifications to an assistant. "I have it in mind that you shall become one of, if not *the* favorite of my customers."

"I look forward to finding out, Mr. Hill." No doubt the dapper little man heaped such blandishments upon all of his customers, but it still felt nice to be so complimented. "I would also like a number of superfine oil cake colors, please, starting with lamp black and vine, and massicot lead oxide as well as orpiment."

"Splendid, splendid." Hill flourished his hand before the well-dusted shelves of color-filled glassware. "We prepare all our colors here, on the premises. You may be assured that if I sell you lapis blue, lapis you shall get." He brought a compacted cake of that hue out for her inspection. "We shall have everything packaged up presently and will deliver it to Kirk Brae Head directly," Mr. Hill was saying, "where I hope I may I request the honor of a tour of your *atelier?*"

"I should very much like that," Maisie laughed, since there was no other way that the hardwood stretchers for the painting would be assembled if he did not see her aerie, but she was sensible of the courtly manners that bid him ask.

She was, in a word, charmed. Perhaps Edinburgh was growing on her.

Or perhaps she was finally, after so many years of being angry and embarrassed and afraid, perfectly ready to be charmed.

CHAPTER 11

"*L*et me see you home." Archie could see that she was far more knackered than she would admit—two high spots of color tinged her otherwise pale cheeks.

"Oh, no," Maisie protested when he would have helped her mount. "I had much rather not. It is such a fine day. Do you mind if we walk?"

Archie was glad of any excuse to prolong their time together. She was proving to be someone very different than he had assumed her to be based on their first few meetings—and someone very different from how her family described her.

"I don't mind, if you don't," he said. "You must know your own strengths better than I." He took up the reins to walk the horses.

Her smile was small, but as bright as a new penny. "Thank you. I do know my own strength. And I have had enough of being coddled to death by my family. Or censured, which I will undoubtedly be for riding again—although, I do thank you for suggesting the ride. I thoroughly enjoyed myself. I had forgotten how much I loved to ride."

"Perhaps we can do so again," he found himself suggesting.

"I'd like that." Her simple delight made her smile anything but plain.

"I would, too," he said, even as he wondered why it was true. He ought to be sticking with his original plan of probing her father's affairs instead of trying to make an assignation with his eldest daughter. But there he was. "I hope after so many years away from the saddle, the ride was not too…" He found heat rising up the back of his neck—since when had he become so delicate in his manners? "Too uncomfortable?"

She laughed, but her cheeks were stained an enchanting pink as well. "I am not too saddle sore, if that is what you mean, though I wanted this walk to prevent just that. But I don't need to be wrapped in cotton wool. And I have a stick to assist me should I become fatigued." Maisie gestured to her heavy-shanked walking stick masquerading as a parasol, even as she used it to detour across the pavement to hand a penny to an old beggar woman.

"You have my arm as well."

Her cheeks turned even rosier with her pleasure and he could not imagine how he had ever thought her plain. "Thank you."

"Think nothing of it," he replied to keep any corresponding ruddiness from his own face.

"But I do think a great deal of it," she insisted. "To my way of thinking I cannot improve my strength if I do not take exercise, but I cannot take exercise with my family dissolving into puddles of apprehension every time I put a foot wrong."

"Your sister doesn't seem the type to dissolve into puddles of anything, let alone apprehension."

At the mention of her sister, Maisie Conway's expression instantly became more guarded. "Don't let that dainty facade of Flora's fool you, my lord—"

It wasn't Flora's dainty facade that had first caught his eye—it was Maisie's supple form he had caught in his arms.

"Archie," he cajoled out of habit. And to bring his wayward thoughts back to some semblance of respectability.

She was all seriousness. "Just because Flora seems to have formidable control over her apprehensions and emotions, does not mean she does not feel them."

The Conway sisters were clearly very protective of each other. "This formidable control runs in the family then?"

Her brows rose over those sharp hazel eyes. "Such control would more likely be a reaction *to* our family circumstances." Then, perhaps thinking she had said too much, she added, "Not that I'm ungrateful for my family's comfortable circumstances when so many others are not so fortunate, or have less—I just don't subscribe to the same philosophies as my father."

Archie saw his opening to encourage her confidence. "You must have been very proud of his knighthood?"

"Must I?" she asked with the same wry humor she had evinced that first night in her father's drawing room.

"Are you not? I didn't read the particular court circular announcing the New Year's honors—may I ask what was his service to the crown?"

"I have no idea," she said as if she were mildly surprised by the realization. "I did not ask. My father is only lately returned to our lives," she explained. "He was away, traveling abroad for many years."

"Ah, travel!" he pretended to enthuse. "For business or pleasure?"

"With him, I can only assume they were one and the same." She ducked her pinked cheeks down, as if the admission embarrassed her. "As I said, he is only lately returned to our lives, much to the interference of our prior philosophies of living."

Archie decided sharing his own confidences might help her along. "I know that feeling well enough. Despite my father's best efforts, I see the world very differently than he does. Which infuriates him, of course. 'I didn't pay for your damn expensive education just to have you disagree with me,' he fumes on a regular basis."

"Yes," she laughed. "How inconvenient for us to be our own persons. But here is another inconvenient person—who is also my friend." She waved to the crossing sweep at the intersection of Hope and Princes streets, where the well-regulated lines of the New City gave way to the older, more irregular lanes like Kirk Brae Head. "Good morning, Fergus. How's business?"

"Nae too bad, missus, but it'll be a sight better if yer man'll gie us a few pennies!" he said without shame. "How's our Aggie?"

Maisie supplied the pennies before Archie could do so. "Agnes is doing quite well, Fergus, looking more herself every day. There's a place for you in the stable as well, if you like? Better work than sweeping the street for pennies."

"Nae," the lad refused the offer of employment. "I like my chances oot here. But ye'll tell 'er I was asking after 'er, will ye? Yer not workin' 'er too hard, are ye?"

"Yes, Fergus, I certainly will tell her you asked after her," she promised. "And no, I am doing my utmost not to work her too hard." She slipped him another penny. "And neither should you work too hard—why don't you get yourself a meat pie?"

"Aye, missus." The lad tugged his dirty cap and disappeared back across the busy street.

"Well, well, well," Archie chuckled. "Under all those terse, forthright opinions, Miss Margaret Conway is a soft touch. You'll put yourself in the poor house paying all the beggars like that. The august gentlemen of the government—amongst them, the Lord Advocate—advise strongly against encouraging their idleness in that way."

"Because it keeps them from being useful in the workhouses? I have a decidedly different philosophy than your august gentlemen," she explained. "I think God puts the beggars in our path not to test their discernment about what is right or wrong, or useful and sinful, but to give the people who claim to believe in charity the opportunity to show that charity, which, people seem to forget, is a virtue not a sin. *He who shuts his ear to the cry of the poor, will also cry himself and not be answered*—the vicars ought to say that more often, instead of *the poor shall be with us always*."

"Now, who is on the side of the angels?" he teased.

"Oh, I most assuredly hope I would be—they have tested my faith enough." Her expression was so animated, there was nothing of the older sister who was shy of people.

How had he—how had her family—got her so wrong?

"And how many beggars are in your regular pay?" She seemed to know this Fergus by name and the old woman a few streets back had been liberal with her blessing of the Hirplin Miss. As for the aforementioned Agnes, Archie had a very good idea of how she had benefitted from Maisie Conway's largesse.

Her smile was delightfully wry. "A fair few," she stated before she turned more serious. "There is someone on every corner it seems. I see them from my aerie, you see." She pointed upward to the windows of her attic across the street.

"And on forays out with your notebook, I'll wager?"

She did not exactly answer. "I have long made it my practice to do what little good I can, whenever I can." She shrugged. "It is a simple enough thing to offer pennies, or even employment to a beggar boy and girl, though it does little to stem the tide of poverty I can see at every turn, abroad in the city."

They passed another bewildered-looking woman sitting on the curb of the pavement of Kirk Brae Head with her hand out, which Maisie filled. "These poor people, especially these children, seem exploited at every turn. I've discovered that more often than not, they are caught in a vicious cycle of addiction to blue ruin—amongst other things—at the direct behest of … let's call them kidmen or gang men who give them a taste of the gin to start, or then opium to get them addicted, and then force them to beg or worse, to pay off their debt for the drug. They get used up like cord wood, spent and smoldering before they're even fifteen years of age sometimes—especially the girls."

It was an extraordinarily clear-eyed view for a newcomer. Clearly, she was an astute observer of mankind. "Why, Maisie Conway, you do see a great deal from those windows of yours."

"I see enough," she acknowledged with an astute glance at him. "As clearly, do you."

Archie was not surprised that her views of the convenient hypocrisy of the powerful aligned with his, but he was delighted. "Would you care to write an essay on the topic for the Review, Miss Conway?"

She shook her head. "That would be too much for even Flora to explain away to my father—he'd have my head and my studio aerie, and then where would I be?" She smiled, but at the same time stumbled on the curb. "Damn and bother."

Archie caught her up, delighted by her mild oath and glad for the chance to put his hands around her supple, lithe waist. But she was also exhausted—he could hear it in her voice. "I've over-tired you—"

"Don't you dare!" She laughed. "I am not tired—I am heartsore and weary which has nothing to do with you and everything to do with the injustice of the world we live in." She poked her hand playfully into his chest. "Don't you dare try and coddle me out of my opinions."

"I would not dare," he swore, laying his hand over hers for the pleasure of its small weight, if not to keep her from poking him again. "I had much rather you were aggravated with the world and not me."

"I am quite capable of being aggrieved with you both," she declared quietly.

She was so close, her face was turned up to his, full of animated, artistic appeal, and it was suddenly everything he could do not to kiss her.

The impulse staggered him.

Not the kissing—he was always up for a bit of amorous play. But that he wanted to kiss *her*, the lame spinster sister, the plain, prickly recluse.

The object of his sudden fantasy seemed not to notice his fascination. "I must save my breath to cool my porridge as you Scots say, or I shall arrive home out of breath and then there will be no end of Papa's doom and gloom and Flora's flutterings."

"Your sister seems to take great care of you." Yes, better to focus his thoughts on the beautiful and far less dangerous Miss Flora.

Maisie bristled like a hedgehog, but refrained from poking him with her spines, though her chin came up. "I am perfectly capable of taking more than adequate care of myself."

This, he no longer doubted. But still, he teased, "Then why are you avoiding your own front door?"

"I had rather go round to the stable gate," she admitted under her breath, "where the servants' stairs lead straight up to my aerie." She steered them up Kirk Brae Head and around the side of the house. "It usually keeps me out of my father's way, which suits us all better."

Archie handed off the horses to the groom, lest he miss the opportunity to see the prickly object of his unhinged attraction to her door, which was opened from within by the same small servant child he had met on the stairs. "There ye are, missus. Come ye on. Miss Flora's left a message fer ye."

"Has she?" Maisie took the proffered piece of paper and promptly ignored it in favor of the child. "Thank you, Agnes. I saw Fergus just now and he asked how you're getting on."

So this Agnes, whom he had thought to befriend on the servant's stairs, was a beggar child Maisie Conway had rescued from the streets? Better and better. Although, it had not come up in their conversation about the hidden economies of kidmen and blue ruin and beggar children, oftentimes such waifs possessed an interesting and larcenous set of skills that might be put to his best use.

"Fine, missus, thank ye," the waif answered, though she looked longingly out the door, as if she was sad of the chance not to see her brother.

"The work isn't too hard?" Maisie pressed.

"No, missus. And Mrs. Cook is a rare hand with treacle tarts and lets me have the kitchen maid's disasters, she called 'em."

"Very good to hear," Maisie patted the girls shoulder. "She's under strict orders to feed you up."

"Thank ye," the girl said again, cheered by the thought.

"I'll see you later, then," Maisie told the girl before she turned and put out her hand to take leave of Archie. "Thank you for an informative and interesting visit, my lord."

"Archie. Please." He found himself holding her hand captive between his own to feel the heat of her presence as long as possible. "I won't take my leave, until you say it."

Under the warm press of what he hoped was charm—but knew was really the inexplicable force of attraction—she softened. "Thank you, Archie. Until next time."

"Thursday morning, at the dawn."

"But if you please—your wardrobe, my lord."

"Archie," he corrected. "I thought we had made progress?"

This she acknowledged with a slow nod, although she lowered her voice, as if she didn't want anyone to hear her take such a liberty. "If you could come again in your evening clothes— the black velvet coat and black satin breeches? With the black silk stockings?"

He had frankly hoped she would prefer his working attire. "I'm really not a silk stocking kind of man."

"Boots, then, if you must, but well-polished, so they shine." She narrowed her eyes. "And a green satin waistcoat, if you can manage it—to match your eyes. And very white linen to contrast with the dark tan of your skin."

The singularity of her regard, combined with the forthrightness of her compliments kindled a pleasurable heat under his skin. "Anything else, my lady?" he teased. "Should you like to inspect the color of my linen drawers as well?"

She stilled—in shock or delight, he could not tell. And for one long, blessed moment, he wondered—and hoped—if she just might say yes.

"That will do, my friend," she said instead. "Agnes," she called over her shoulder, "will you see Lord Carrington out by the front stair? I will leave it up to you, *Archie*"—she gave his name an arch, whispered intonation—"as to what else you should like inspected. And by whom. But I have done enough for one day and will take my leave. Good afternoon."

It wasn't much as far as flirting went, but by God, she *was* flirting. With him.

He didn't even try to hide his pleasure—he smiled over her hand. "I will spend the time until we next meet contemplating nothing but that."

Archie stayed put and watched her go, making her slow but not inelegant way up the narrow servants' stair, before he turned to the tweeny. "Well then, Agnes, is it?"

"Aye, m' lord."

She looked up at him in expectation, and Archie was struck by the sense of something familiar about her. "You worked the Grassmarket, near the Corn Exchange at Cowgate Head, Agnes?" He rarely forgot a face.

"Aye, sir," the child said warily. "Missus was kind enough tae gie me this position."

"That is very good of Miss Conway, so I hope you'll do me a favor and take good care of her as well—see that she doesn't work too hard or tire herself out?" He tossed another penny the lass snatched out of the air like a magician.

"Nae worries there, sir—tires us both oot the way she works, she does." The lass led the way to the kitchen door. "She's the one always looks after me like I were her own, ye ken? But I swear to ye, sir, I'll do the same."

"Good lass. I'm glad I can count on ye." He laced his speech with a heavy lashing of Scots to put her even more at ease. "We're going to be the best o' friends, young Aggie, thee and me. Thick as thieves."

CHAPTER 12

Maisie watched from her window as Archie Carrington ambled across the stableyard to retrieve his mount after waving to Agnes at the kitchen stairs—not the front stairs as she had requested, so he might be seen by Flora.

That was interesting in and of itself, but what was more interesting was that he greeted the stable lad with a handshake, like an equal, before they together admired the dark hunter's withers.

She admired his egalitarianism, which he proved again when he chanced upon Mr. Hill and his assistant arriving at the stable gate with Maisie's order. He shook Mr. Hill's hand as well, and leaned close to speak to him privately, before he tipped his hat and with the barest of glances and a raised hand for her up in the window, was gone.

Maisie had no time to reflect upon his actions, or the nigh perfect pleasure and productivity of her morning with him, before Mr. Hill arrived with an entire loomed roll of prepared canvas.

"Of a suitable size for your grand portrait of young Lord Carrington," he explained, "along with enough for your subsequent portraits of Lady Ivers and others, who will no doubt be lining up at your door. With Lord Carrington's and Lady Ivers' imprimaturs of approval, you're sure to be inundated with ladies who, I don't mind saying, would rather not sit for Mr. Raeburn or any of his studio—some of those fellows have wandering hands, if you know what I mean. But you didn't hear that from me."

"Not a word, Mr. Hill. I'm sure I'm as deaf as an etching."

"Ah! You understand me. Now—" He cast his gaze on her shelves of colors. "Caput Mort violet—splendid, good. Van Dyke brown, burnt umber," he recited as he read her labels. "Most excellent. Alizarin crimson, cadmium red deep, Naples yellow. Now, you'll want Hansa yellow, as well as more vermilion and madder deep, I should think, for Lord Carrington." He made himself a note on a smart little silver-covered pad. "And I'll get in some French ultramarine, Bremen blue, viridian, cerulean and cobalt violet to have on hand, ready for when you paint Lady Ivers."

Maisie was both thankful and frankly a bit overwhelmed by the generosity of spirit in such an offer. "That is very good of you, sir."

"I am entirely at your service, Miss Conway." Mr. Hill made her an elegant little bow. "Because, as you may have guessed, I want something from you—a glimpse at some of your other work!"

These Scots certainly were forthright types—Maisie recalled Archie Carrington's almost identical words to her sister that first night.

"I should so very much like to share your work—which I am told by Lord Carrington is quite good—with others in my clientele, some of my more influential customers." He hesitated delicately over his choice of words. "I have a great many amateur or hobbyist customers—elegant ladies and gentlemen for whom painting is a pastime rather than an avocation. But they come to look at copies of the masters and at some of the other, more masterful works that I might offer them. For instance"—he turned to the study of Frances Percy, Duchess of Northumberland, almost as if he had been told it was there—"This small work of Her Grace might do well to convince them that your brush would be more than suitable for painting their portraits."

"I see." Flora wasn't the only carnival barker in Edinburgh. And Maisie was ambitious enough not to disdain such help. "I hesitate only because, as I told Lord Carrington, that work is but a preliminary study and not the finished portrait."

Mr. Hill turned in a circle. "You seem to have a great many other canvases from which we might choose something more suitable?"

Did she dare? Every instinct she had toward privacy was screaming in her ears that it was too soon, too much of a risk. Yet the rewards might be great—as great as the reward from the risk of taking Archie Carrington's commission in the first place.

She damned her fears and chose the canvas currently upon her easel. "I have a religious painting of the Magdalene." Agnes had been an inspirational muse. "It is nearly finished, you understand, though it is not yet ready to be shown anywhere, but..." She damned the thump of dread at the base of her throat and removed the holland cover.

"Miss Conway." Mr. Hill put his hand to his chest and stood stock still for a long moment. "So arresting! The *chiaroscuro* —almost baroque in its drama, but more restrained."

"More Dutch, I had hoped."

"Just so," he agreed. "The use of layers of green to create the piercing light in the eyes. The detail of the fabric in the headscarf. They're all here—yellow ochre, raw Sienna, Mars red, are they not? Such deep, sententious tones. My dear, Miss Conway." He blinked his eyes rapidly before he turned to her. "I had expected talent—for Lord Carrington is well-known as a man of exceptional taste—but this is exceptional. Your Magdalene is a vision."

Maisie felt her own eyes prickle with a rush of relief and gratitude—it was one thing to believe in one's own abilities, but another thing entirely to have such a knowledgeable and clearly learned person confirm them. "Thank you, Mr. Hill. Your good opinion means the world to me."

"My dear Miss Conway, I am ecstatic to find you so accomplished. I will do my utmost to give my clientele a good report of you until I might be able to show them your finished work. I can do nothing less! It will be my honor."

"Thank you, Mr. Hill. You are very kind."

"I have no need to be kind when I can simply be truthful, Miss Conway." He turned around again. "What other treasures are you hiding?"

Maisie had risked enough for one day. "The Magdalene is all for today, sir. But you will certainly be the first to know when I have canvases suitable for display."

"Splendid, splendid!" Mr. Hill cried. "What an excellent afternoon's work."

His confidence made her bold. "I wonder if you can help me with another request, Mr. Hill. As you may have guessed, I require a far larger and more substantial easel than I currently possess to hold Lord Carrington's canvas."

Mr. Hill brightened. "I think I may be able to help—let me make some discrete inquiries on your behalf, if I may?"

"Certainly. I thank you." In the meantime— "I wonder if we might also postpone the stretching of the canvas on the frame until I can make a preliminary sketch?" She could roll out the canvas on the floor and begin her charcoal outlines immediately while the vision of how she wanted to portray Archie Carrington was hot in her mind.

"Certainly, my dear Miss Conway. I understand you. Certainly! I leave you to it!"

The moment Mr. Hill had taken his effusively polite leave, Maisie set to work, spreading the prepared canvas out on the floor, cutting off the required length and then sketching out the preliminary outline in charcoal.

Carrington's life-sized form was the focus of the scene, standing with arm outstretched in the foreground, while in the background she would depict the pressroom, or certainly at least one press, with its singular long swing arm, to show Carrington as a man of thought and words, as well as action.

But could she do what she envisioned? Did she have the skill to adequately depict him as if he were about to stride out of the painting and convince the viewer of the rightness of his argument? Could she capture his ardor and elan as accurately as she could the mechanism of his printing press?

She had to. Anything less would be failure.

She began with the image she could see most clearly in her mind's eye—his handsome, intelligently foxlike face. The fur-like frame of his hair. The plush, nearly athletic curve of his ready smile. The taper of his strong cheekbones and nose. The straightforward line of his brows. The chiseled arc of his jaw.

And then she was mixing paints, measuring out powders and oils, grinding and stirring until the hues were at just the right viscosity to flow off her brush.

Larger brush first, to lay in the middle flesh tone, then lighter on the left cheek and darker on the right. A subtler tone for the retiring plane of his forehead, temples, chin and nose. Subtler still for the mouth and eyes.

She quickly changed to her finest brush, a smaller red sable tip more suitable for the delicate work of highlighting the full, firm curve of his lip.

Yes, just so. Perfect. As if his mouth were just opening, just ready to press against hers and whisper flattering things. Divine. Delicious. Devastating.

No. No. Certainly not. Ready to speak, then. To tell the truth no one else would say.

Yes. Maisie took another deep breath and refocused her mind

on the task before her, setting away the red sable brush and selecting another flat-tapered brush to work the articulation of his fingers upon his hip.

She dashed a bit of ochre with mummy brown, mixing them for the darkest tones first, working out the shape of the larger knuckles and carefully delineating each individual, capable finger where they sat so casually propped against the turn of his hip.

"You're het up this e'en, missus." Aggie brought in a tray laden with cold slices of beef.

Maisie started before she glanced at the clock on the mantelpiece, surprised to find so much time had elapsed. "Have I missed supper?"

"It's gone nine chimes of the kirk clock, missus— Oh, I beg your pardon. That Mrs. Smyth, says as she's the only one to be called missus, along with Mrs. Cook, and I'm to call you miss. Miss Conway, that is."

"Mrs. Smyth is a fussbudget," Maisie opined. The housekeeper and Maisie had never been on anything more than civil terms. Although the woman had now been with the Conway family for many years, she had come with the house in Richmond, which had originally been leased as a quiet, out of the way place for Maisie to either slowly succumb to the debilitating fever which robbed her of movement, or recover as she could, while the baby —Flora—was spirited safely away.

It had been a terrible time. Mama had died shortly after giving birth to Flora, and with Papa away on one of his long overseas trips, Maisie had never felt so completely and shockingly alone. To Maisie's memory, Mrs. Smyth had run the house more like a prison than a hospital, and had insisted on a forced regimen of idle inactivity—even reading had been deemed too much exertion by the woman. Hours, days, months had passed without anything more interesting than the shadows moving across the ceiling of her room to entertain or sustain her. Or take her mind off the worst fears of her misery.

Since the first moments of Maisie's recovery, they had forever been at odds.

"You may call me whatever you like, Agnes—missus will do just as nicely as Maisie. Have you eaten?" The cook had been doing a wonderful job putting some meat on Agnes's spindly bones, but Mrs. Smyth might be working the girl too hard, despite both Flora and Maisie's stressing that the girl was to work for Maisie in the studio.

"I wouldn't mind a bite o' them tatties, if ye're no mind ta eat them, Miss Maisie."

Maisie was warmed by the girl's use of her name. "This is far too much just for me, Agnes. I'll make you a plate while you light those candles for me and then build up the fire. I have a feeling we're going to be working late this evening." Maisie began dividing the meal onto a second plate.

"We'll want me posing again? I tell you, I won't mind setting down a spell. Fair worked off my feet today while ye were out and about."

"No posing this evening, Agnes—I've other work in mind. You eat your supper and take your ease on the bed there until I need you. You leave it all to me."

She didn't need Lord Carrington to be posing in front of her, either—the image of what she wanted was graven in her brain so clearly, it was as if the painting were already done. Of course, she might have problems correctly executing the perspective, with his hand coming forward, but she especially wanted to capture the elegant vivacity of his fingers and the lovely taper of his wrist into his forearms.

Of course his lovely, sinewy forearms would be covered with black velvet sleeves and white linen cuffs, but it wouldn't hurt to draw them now. Who would see besides her? She would cover the preliminary charcoal sketch with paint as soon as she had the canvas stretched on its frame.

But why should she not indulge in the pleasure of delineating that fascinating stretch of flesh in the meantime? And perhaps his face, which wouldn't be painted over—but the skin tones would be very much in the same color family as the forearms and she had them already laid out on her palette.

Maisie bolted her supper and while Agnes slept, she indulged her imagination, drawing, standing back to judge, redrawing, painting and drawing again all through the night. She was only shaken from her reverie when the footman brought up the coal bucket.

"What time is it?" She squinted first at her clock and then at the early sunlight streaming in through the windows. "Agnes, wake up, love!"

"It is nearly seven in the morn, miss," the footman—ancient Robert—said.

"Oh, heavens!" Archie Carrington was due any moment—and Mr. Hill, to stretch the canvas, too. And she was still attired in her walking ensemble from yesterday afternoon. And her hands were soiled and stained with charcoal and paint.

Stalling was in order.

"Please offer Lord Carrington, or Mr. Hill and his assistant, or whomever might come, some refreshments in the kitchen while I make myself presentable." God help her if Raines wasn't available to work her magic to turn her into appropriately dressed mutton.

Maisie grabbed a turpentine-soaked rag and began scrubbing at her hands as she went. "Agnes, see if you can tidy up a bit—take that dinner tray down, quickly if you please!"

"Aye, missus!" The girl set off immediately with the tray.

Raines was fortunately available and willing to turn Maisie from a charcoal-stained smudge into a reasonable facsimile of a polite person, scouring away all traces of wayward pigments and obliterating the stink of linseed oil with a lemon water wash, before she shoehorned Maisie into one of her better, but still serviceable, round gowns.

But the moment one worry was erased, another replaced it—

Agnes appeared at the door. "I let that Mr. Hill up ta yer room, missus. He sayed as 'e needed ta get back to his shop afore the day begun. Was that no right?"

"Well, it wasn't wrong, Agnes." Maisie began to hear hammering from the floor above—Hill and company banging together the stretcher frame. Which meant that in another moment, they would take up the canvas—her canvas that she had spent all night painting with various evocative and highly recognizable facets of Lord Archie Carrington's person.

"Oh, good Lord. No fichu, Raines, just a sash and a clean smock over the top, immediately!"

Time was of the essence. She was about to be found out.

CHAPTER 13

"No without a cap, miss!" Raines brandished the muffin-style cap made of the same sturdy linen as Maisie's smock and began to stuff her still unruly and no doubt unsightly mop of red hair beneath.

"Yes, but hurry, please!" Maisie had spent far too much time disguising herself, and not enough disguising the portrait of Lord Carrington. "And coffee, please, Agnes—pots and pots of it." The coffee would have to substitute for courage.

Maisie hurried her ungainly way up the back stairs as Agnes went pelting down, but by the time she climbed to her aerie it was too late—Archie Carrington stood in the middle of the attic, gazing at the now-stretched canvas as Mr. Hill adjusted the crank on the large double-rocker easel before him.

Which put Archie Carrington eye level with the image of his sun-lit, unclothed and painstakingly articulated forearm, upper arm and shoulder.

"My dear Miss Conway," he murmured as she lurched to a halt behind him, "why on earth have you insisted I wear these ridiculous evening clothes when you've made me appear to much better advantage without any clothes at all?"

Her cheeks had surely gone as scarlet as if she had powdered her face with Armenian red. She had never felt so exposed. "That is merely…a preliminary study," she began, wishing she could remember his elegant Italian words. "It will be painted over."

"Whatever for?" His smile was all sly, sulfurous amusement at her expense.

"Why, Maisie!" Flora put in an appearance to round out the crowd. "That is most decidedly…large."

"Thank you, Miss Flora." Carrington's smile was pure rogue. "One tries."

It was everything Maisie could do not to grab up the first brush she could find and obliterate the figure upon the canvas under a wash of color—or fling it at someone's head. But she could not bring herself to deface such exceptionally good work.

And why should she?

Why should she be embarrassed at such an excellent representation?

She took a deep breath and stood her ground. "You wanted me to burnish my reputation, Flora, so I decided to paint so large a canvas, it will either make or break my reputation. No reward is without risk."

"And a very interesting way you've chosen to mitigate the risk," Flora said with a mischievous light in her eye.

Maisie could feel her thin veneer of composure crack. "Haven't I just," was her muttered agreement.

"Well." Mr. Hill cleared his throat first. "The canvas is stretched to my satisfaction, Miss Conway, so I will take my leave." Hill bowed himself out. "Do please let me know if the canvas loosens or becomes unacceptably slack and I will hasten to tighten it with as many keys or additional stretchers as you think necessary."

"Thank you, Mr. Hill." Maisie blessed the man for keeping his professional composure. "I will not hesitate to call."

And out they filed—all but Flora, who hung back to quietly

whisper, "Well done, Maisie. To think, I worried about you taking him down a peg, when in reality, you've rather raised him up, haven't you, you clever girl."

"Flora—" Maisie warned.

"I like it—very much," her sister insisted. "Who knew you had all that in you. Besides me, of course. Do carry on!" And with that, Flora was gone, quietly closing the attic door behind her.

Which left Maisie alone with Archie Carrington—both in person and on canvas.

Both were somehow larger than life.

Almost too large—while the lofty piece could be raised and lowered by the large, geared crank on the back of the easel, she was still going to have to rig up a platform, or acquire a step ladder at the very least, to paint the upper portions.

She might have bitten off more than she could paint.

"All teasing aside," Archie began, "whatever alchemy you have performed here, you've done more than flatter me." He stared at the canvas. "You really have painted me as I wish to be, not as I am, Miss Conway. I find myself quite at your service."

Embarrassment surely painted her a hundred different shades of vermilion. "Maisie, please," she tried his own gambit. "I thought we had made progress."

"Oh, clearly, we have."

There was not enough madder deep on the shelf to paint the scorching heat streaking up her cheeks.

She cleared her throat and tried a more professional approach. "Of course, the painting will not remain in this preliminary state. It will be properly finished, in time."

He tipped his head to one side in contemplation, as if it might make him see what she envisioned. "In the meantime, that you see me thus is...." His pause stretched as wide as his slow smile. "...eye opening," he finished.

Maisie decided to refuse to be embarrassed—the painting was

good, even if it was a little bit over-imaginative. "Well, you did say hidden beauty does no one any good."

"Damned if I didn't," he agreed on a laugh. "Philosopher, poet, on the side of the angels," he began, "and perhaps secretly, the pornographers."

Maisie could not help but burst out laughing. "You are the second person this week to suspect me of wanting to make dirty pictures, though nothing could be farther from the truth. I assure you, your..." She could not utter the word "naked," though she seemed to have no trouble painting him naked. "...arm and shoulder"—she could not help but color at least a slight tint of rose madder even as she laughed—"will all be painted over. Although your face should be able to safely remain unclothed."

"Who is hiding beauty now?"

"I am, most assuredly, though I am sorry for it. But it cannot be helped." She had reached the limits of her experience—and very nearly, her imagination. Nearly. "Well, let us take advantage of your correct clothing this morning—thank you for the green waistcoat—and get you into place so I can work out the details of the light on the fabric."

But Archie Carrington was not of the same mind. "I could have just brought the clothing and left it here on a dress form for all you seem to need me to be before you," he teased.

"It might come to that as yet, my lord, but—"

He tipped his head to one side. "Archie, I think, while you're secretly ogling my forearms."

Despite her best intentions not to be embarrassed, Maisie's cheeks advanced in hue from rose madder to madder deep and even Cadmium red deep. "I was not ogling—I was indulging a passion for drawing and painting," she admitted. "It is not often that I get the chance. In fact, I have never before painted a man— with the exception of my father, who is both elderly and a relation."

He tipped his head to the other side, as if it might make him see the painting better. "I begin to see Dr. Johnson's point about the staring into men's faces—but he was wrong. It is not undignified. Not at all."

"No?"

"No. It's downright entertaining. And decidedly invigorating."

Archie Carrington was flirting with her. Granted, it seemed to be his natural state of being, but it was charming all the same to be the current recipient of such *pleasurable* undivided attention.

"Dare I take it this means you've found my forearms please your eye as well as your mind?" he teased. "That they embody the finest balance between thought and execution?"

Clever flirtation, too. "That is my aim no matter if I am painting you or the merest button upon your waistcoat—the work is still the same. Beauty being in the eye of the beholder."

He was all interested curiosity. "Tell me what you mean."

"We all get to decide what is beautiful to us, and I find variety and differences interesting. I really do believe there is an infinite variety amongst people—we all look different from one another, we all think differently from one another and we certainly feel differently from one person to the next. Even people from the same family may feel very differently from one subject to the next."

"Is that true of your family?" he probed.

"Certainly. Even people who share the exact same experience may react and remember particular events or incidents entirely differently. I am constantly astonished and delighted by how individual human beings are. And more than just human beings —all beings." By the warmly amused—and interested—look on his face, her attempt at explanation was only making matters worse. "I find caterpillars fascinating and beautiful, but most people prefer the more conventionally beautiful butterfly. But I would paint them both with the same eye for the telling detail."

"How fascinating." He turned his full regard upon her. "I

suppose I've always been a bit of a butterfly man myself," he said thoughtfully. "What else do you find beautiful?"

"Many things." She shrugged. "Everything—there is beauty in everything, if we know how to look."

"And how do you look? How do you find—what did you call it —the telling detail? I do see what you're talking about in every one of your notebook of drawings—your sketch I saw of the crossing sweep—what was his name, Fergus?"

"You have a good memory for faces."

"As clearly do you."

"It is my job—my avocation as a painter to faithfully render what I see."

"Ah, but first you must see it and not everyone can do that. Very few people, I should wager."

"You see things," she countered. "All the beggars and crossing sweep boys in the streets that most people go out of their way not to see. You know the names of all your pressmen and where they come from as well."

"My avocation as well," Archie agreed. "I try to describe with words what you describe with paint."

"And we both must try to achieve that balance between thought and execution. Between careful consideration and the inspiration and sense of the moment."

"*Sprezzatura*." He said the word like an incantation. "That certain nonchalance, so as to conceal all art and make whatever one does or says appear to be without effort and almost without any thought about it. From Baldassare Castiglione's *The Book of the Courtier* in 1528."

"You definitely need to thank your tutors," she murmured.

"And my friends," he acknowledged. "But I would venture to say the technique is true of both the art and the artist—concealment to appear without effort."

He met her eyes and Maisie fancied she saw something— some shared truth—reflected there. She felt herself poised on the precipice of something she did not understand. Something very new.

"We seem to have come back to flattery," she offered.

"We do." His smile seemed easier, more rueful and truthful, as if he wasn't working so hard to charm. "Are you sure I can't convince you to go on as you've started?"

"Quite sure," she said with a laugh. It was so nice—so fun—to banter with him like this. "There is a limit to my imagination, which normally is as powerful a tool as either the eye or the hand. But we must move on to the next problem."

"Problem?"

"Conundrum," she clarified. "Each different surface requires a different technique."

"Trading *spruzzatura* for *impasto? So quale preferisco.*"

I know...which I prefer? She was not sure exactly what he meant—her attempts to study languages were limited to reading alone—but his eyes met hers and again she felt as if she were on a precipice, paused between one thing and the next.

"I'm sorry, I have read the painting terms, but I don't speak Italian."

"Neither do I," he joked. "I *studied* Italian—whether I learned enough to speak it sufficiently is up for debate. But I had the benefit of a classical education conducted on that long Grand Tour, a great deal of which was spent in Italy so perhaps that experience rubbed off."

"Lucky you."

"Very lucky me," he agreed equitably. "Have you traveled Maisie?"

"My family doesn't like me to travel across Edinburgh by myself, let alone London. They think I'm too delicate." Too damaged. "So imagine, if you will, how they would take to me traveling across Europe? Especially France, with their decade-long revolution."

"Can you not show them you're not too delicate—that your hitch makes no matter?"

"Do you think I have not? Do you think I have dragged my leg around behind me for the past sixteen years because I'm too lazy to pick it up and walk straight?"

"No," he agreed quietly but adamantly.

"I have not," she confirmed. "My education, such as it has been, has been conducted solely from books and in places like Mr. Hill's shop, with his 'Drawings Let to Copy.' I've studied copies of the great masters, made by painters more fortunate—but not always more talented than I—but never seen the original paintings or met the great masters themselves, like Madame Vigée LeBrun."

"I don't see why you might not travel," he offered. "But in the meantime, I wonder how I might best help your education." His expression as he looked at her was somewhere between the easy camaraderie of the past few minutes and the sly, foxy charm of before. "I wonder if you might like it if we conduct ourselves as if we were in the Academy in Rome."

He tipped his head to the side in that considering way he had. "I offer you my services as a model, for the benefit of your education and my entertainment. You can draw or paint me, *Dalla vita* —from true life. *Spogliato.*" He fed her the words like pastries full of tempting sweetness. "Stripped," he translated. "*Nudo.*"

Which needed no further translation.

"In the manner of the renaissance masters," he elaborated as if he were describing a technique and not an intimate state of being. "But privately, behind your locked attic door, without a *studio* or *atelier* full of eager eyes. Just yours. If you dare."

And there was the edge of the precipice, sharp and yawning before her. There was the risk she had so cavalierly thought she wanted to take on.

There was the temptation she had secretly longed to give into.

"I wouldn't dare.

"Wouldn't you?" he coaxed. "I would."

"I thought I made you nervous?"

"I've gotten used to your rather demanding eye. I've grown to like it."

He *liked* it.

Maisie could not seem to make her mouth say the required, sane, prudent words.

"We could start with something easy—innocuous even. An elbow or shoulder?" He spread his arms out, as if on offer. "But you've already imagined those quite correctly. How about something lower—a foot or calf?"

Her gaze shifted precisely to his exceptionally well-turned calves of its own volition, without consulting her head.

"I'll take that as a yes." He peeled himself out of his evening coat before he sat in her lumpy, upholstered chair by the window to shuck off his boots slowly—so slowly she could have stopped him at any point in the proceedings, as he toed off each boot in turn before he peeled off his stockings.

And then he merely stretched out his legs before him, laid his head against the back of the chair and closed his eyes.

She wanted to speak. To say something—anything to ease the tension that coiled through her like a spring, ready to pounce.

So she swallowed. And found her voice.

And said the only thing she could think of.

"I'll get the lock."

CHAPTER 14

*S*ensible woman, to take precautions. How he liked the clever ones.

Archie felt his anticipation and pleasure spread across his smile, but he kept still and said nothing more for what felt like a long while, not even giving into the impulse to keek out at her. But when he felt the fabric of his patience begin to fray at the seams, he stretched a little and then slowly undid the buttons of his waistcoat, and let the satin shift silently open, exposing his shirt linen. And then he went for the folds of the cravat wound around his neck, untying the knot and slowly drawing it off.

Slowly, he cautioned himself. Purposefully. Steadily, without unnecessary flair or folderol. Nothing that might alarm. Or interfere with her work.

Or the fragile balance they seemed to have established between them.

And when he had judged her unalarmed, he went just one small step further—he tugged open the button at the base of his throat, letting the neck of the shirt gape open. And then he spread his hands as if in surrender, over the arms of the chair, tipped his head back and feigned sleep, like a lazy, satiated sable warming itself in the sunbeam blazing through the window.

And listened to the furiously industrious scratch of her charcoal as it flew over the paper. And felt the weight of her gaze just as physically as he felt the warm press of sun on his skin. And let himself be wreathed in the dense, painterly scents of linseed oil and turpentine, so similar to the industrious smell of printing ink that clung to him when he worked.

What would her skin smell like?

Someday soon—very soon—he was going to get close enough to Maisie Conway to find out. He would put his nose to the soft skin at the side of her neck and discern her essence. And then he would taste that skin and—

Archie swallowed, and focused his attention on the rasp of her charcoal against the paper.

By now, her fingers must be dirty and stained black from the work.

He amused himself for a long, satisfactory minute thinking of what else she might do with those stained fingers—tracing them across his body. Tracing them across her own.

Archie shifted uncomfortably. He was a man of action, not idleness, and not even all the naked imaginings in the world could keep him still for much longer.

"Are you quite to rights, Archie?" she asked with quiet concern.

Something deep and satisfying shifted within. "Say it again."

"Are you quite—?"

"No. My name." It was the first time she had said his name unprompted. The first time he had been sure that she was thinking of him and speaking to him as a person as not as a title. "I like the way you say it."

"Archie." Her voice was low, and pleasing, and just warm enough to know she was amused if not pleased.

"Maisie," he answered, putting a bit of Scot's behind it, letting the 's' sound slide off his tongue, soft and slippery like a dozy bee dusted in pollen. "Do you like that?"

"Yes," she admitted, and Archie fancied he could hear that wisp of a smile in her voice, that attempt not to be amused. But she was too honest to not be enjoying herself.

He decided to enjoy himself, too. "If you have not painted a male nude, have you never painted a female?" he queried.

There was a long pause while Maisie seemed to take a long breath. "I do have a mirror."

That was a vision that kept him still for another few minutes before she felt bold enough to go on.

"Though it is a bit messy, trying to hold a palette and paint while also posing. All a bit too smeary. Too hard."

What he would do to such smears. What he would—

He brought his unruly reaction back under control by thinking of other, less *smeary* things. "Why do you not ask your devoted sister to pose for you."

He heard her intake of breath before she answered. "I have drawn and painted Flora many times—as you saw in the salon that first night."

"I meant as a nude. Since the staring in men's faces is indelicate even when clothed, I should think it less so for a woman to draw or paint another woman. Why do the painting schools not have life drawing classes of women by women?"

"You'll have to ask the public drawing schools," she said. Her voice had lost its ease and amusement—she sounded slightly peeved. "None of which admit women."

He took the moment to keek out at her, half hiding behind the enormous easel—at her unfashionably ginger hair, half-fallen out of the soft artist's cap, loose strands wreathing her face. She pushed a tress behind her ear, smearing her temple and cheekbone with the red stick of color she was using to draw and he was instantly beside himself with attraction.

She never noticed, didn't so much as pause in her intense

staring as her hands danced across the paper he could not see. She blinked and frowned at the work before her, nodding and pursing her lips.

Her intensity, her focus and concentration did marvelous things to him. Her sheer competence made him voluble. "Since I don't suffer from any indelicacy—or delicacy for that matter—why should we not go on as we've started."

"Yes?" She made a rather delicate sound of consideration. "I had noticed your cravat seems to have fallen by the wayside. As for your shirt…"

Archie opened his eyes to find her staring at him—at him and not through him. At him as a man and nothing more. "How do you find the view?"

"Extraordinarily educational." Her tone was even, if her voice was a little breathy. "One might even say downright entertaining. And decidedly invigorating."

How he liked the clever ones. How he was becoming more and more attracted to this particular clever, honest one.

"I would not have offered if I did not mean it, Maisie. I am at your disposal—all you have to say is yes."

"Yes, then," she whispered. "Yes, please."

Archie felt the rhythm of his breathing change. He sat up. "Then why don't I—"

"Maisie?" The door rattled against the lock. "Are you there?"

The sudden sound made Maisie jump out of her skin—her box of charcoals clattered to the floor. "Damn and blast."

As oaths went, it was mild enough, but it seemed to alarm her sister. "Maisie?" Flora called again. "Are you all to rights?"

"Yes, yes," Maisie called, abandoning the mess on the floor to pick up his cravat and toss it to him. She made a shooing motion at him to put his clothes back on while she quickly stashed away her drawings and attempted to cover the canvas with her Holland cloth. "Just a moment, Flora."

Archie stamped his foot into a boot and jumped up to help

her drape the unwieldy Holland cloth over the high top of the easel.

"What was that— Maisie? What goes on there?" Flora rattled at the door.

"Art!" Maisie all but yelled as she climbed onto her worktable to pull the cover over the high top of the easel. "I am attempting to make art, which is best done in solitude and silence."

"Is Lord Carrington not still there with you?"

"That is generally how portraiture works, Flora."

"Is Lord Carrington all to rights?"

"Fair enough," he answered as he wound his cravat back around his unbuttoned neck, hurriedly did up his waistcoat and was shrugging his way into his coat when Maisie motioned him near.

He grasped her about the waist and lowered her swiftly to the ground before she nodded in thanks and moved to the door. She spared him one last glance before she nodded in agreement and unlocked the portal.

"What do you want?" she demanded of her sister.

"Civility, for a start," her sister said tartly. "You missed breakfast—not to mention supper last night—so I brought you up a tray." Flora pointed to the food balanced on the chair outside the door. "I meant no harm."

"I am sorry, if I was rude—"

"You were."

"—but we were having a very productive session."

"Were you? I am glad to hear that." Flora's smiles were meted out evenly between Maisie and Archie. "I have also come to rescue Lord Carrington."

"Miss Flora!" Archie fell back on charm to disguise his wildly uneven pulse. "I thought you agreed to call me Archie."

"I did." Flora returned his smile easily. "How do you progress?"

"Quite nicely, thank you," was Maisie's answer.

"Your sister is very talented," was Archie's.

"I told you," Flora asserted.

"You did," Archie agreed.

Flora moved toward the easel. "May I see?"

"No," they said together.

"I must be on my way," Archie said at the same time Maisie assayed, "You know I prefer my work to remain private until I am satisfied with the particulars."

"Yes, Maisie, you're very particular." Flora all but rolled her eyes, before she turned her attention back to Archie. "Will I see you this evening at the Queensburys, Archie? I'm counting on you to introduce me to some new acquaintance."

"Yes, of course," he began before some look in Maisie's eye—a flatness, an erasure of happiness—bid him prevaricate. "Provided I can make up some time on the production of this quarter's edition. We're very busy, what with the binding of the printed pages. I was just telling your sister the same."

"Yes, I can see how busy you are." Flora gifted him with a smile, before she stopped and raised a hand to her face. "You've got a smudge of something on your cheek"—she nodded at him and pointed—"on your cravat, just there, and on your coat. Is that ink or—"

"Oh?" Archie feigned nonchalance. "I've always got a bit of printer's ink somewhere. Occupational hazard."

"I'm surprised Maisie didn't mention it—nothing escapes her notice. And on the shoulders, there." Flora gestured. "As if—"

And then she glanced at Maisie. At the dark charcoal stains on her fingertips. And the vibrant heat staining her face. "Maisie?"

"My apologies, but I must go," Archie said before either of them became any redder. "Miss Flora. Miss Conway"—he made Maisie a small bow—"as always, it has been…an education. I look forward to the morrow." He would leave her with that. It would have to do until something, anything, better should arise.

CHAPTER 15

$\mathcal{M}$aisie hid herself away. This time, she kept track of the time, though she had painted long into the evening, trying not to dwell on the knowledge that at that very moment, Lord Carrington and her sister were out at the Queensbury mansion forming new acquaintance. And cementing old ones. And most likely flirting.

Because Archie Carrington was a flirt and rogue even if he was also a crusader on the side of the angels. And a man who had seemed to be on her side, even if only for a while.

But that while had been wonderful.

Too wonderful—it had tempted her beyond reason. And reason told her that if she wanted Edinburgh to be a new beginning, it had to be the right beginning. If she wanted to have a career, a future, she needed to choose more wisely than she had that morning.

Reason told her that she needed to paint over that elegant slide of calf and that tawny slice of chest—she picked up her palette and brush to do just that, to clothe the painting in velvet and propriety.

But instead of sweeping her wide brush in madder black, she

found herself choosing the tapered sable to add a subtle luster to the warm pulse at the base of his neck. And more definition to the curve of his shoulder. More structure to the strong slide of his nose.

It might damn her, but the painting was too good, too engrossing.

He was too beautiful to cover up just yet.

She would paint over his figure when she was ready—in a few swift strokes with no one the wiser. In the meantime, it would be her gift to herself, this secret, this knowledge that she alone would have—that under his finery, from whatever lofty hall his framed figure would look down, Lord Archibald Carrington had once bared his gloriously, athletically nude limbs. For her.

Maisie left the canvas and returned to the drawing she had made that afternoon—Archie in his shirtsleeves, reclined in his elegant sprawl, feet and arms bare, the strong cords of his neck arched back and slackened in his ease.

And even in his ease, everything about him had seemed alert and waiting, like a dog fox lazing in the sun, seemingly unconcerned with where his next meal was coming from, when all the while, his teeth were still sharp and white.

She would do well to remember that and not get bitten.

When the bells on the nearby kirk tolled midnight, Maisie stretched the cramp out of the small of her back before she built up the small fire and began setting her worktable to rights, putting brushes into jars of turpentine to soak, saving useful pieces of charcoal and pencil.

Putting off thinking. And feeling. And deciding.

Outside the windows, moonlight frosted the rooftops in silver light, illuminating the pavement below. Across the road, she could see Fergus curled up on his corner, waiting to sweep for the last of the fashionable *beau monde* who were still out and about.

They push the needy aside from the road; The poor of the land are made to hide themselves altogether. The Bible verse, taught by Mrs. Smyth as an antidote to Maisie's in-acceptance of her state, in the long hours of her convalescence, came back to her clearly, prompting her to act.

Maisie thought for the merest moment of waking Agnes to fetch the boy. But what was a small amount of ache and strain in her hip compared to the life these poor children had lived—were still living.

She wrapped herself in an extra shawl and made her slow, silent way down to the kitchens, where all was still and quiet. It was easy to slip out the kitchen door and begin the short climb up to the yard, where the stable gate was securely and heavily latched. But Maisie had learned the trick of the heavy bolts and soon had the gate propped open for her safe and easy return. All that was left was securing the lad's cooperation.

"Fergus?" She approached cautiously. "It's Maisie from the house."

The boy came awake in an instant. "Aggie all right?"

"Yes, she's fine. Quite fine. She's asleep—I came myself since I didn't want to wake her."

"Must be nice," he muttered.

"It is nice. Why don't you come with me and we'll make it nice for you, too. We'll get you warm and out of this terrible mist and chill."

"Yer off yer heid. Don't want to work wit' no horses." In his cold and hunger, the boy was vulnerable. Maisie thought she could see his lower lip quiver. "I'm afraid of 'em."

"You don't have to work with the horses," she promised. "You don't have to work for me or my family at all, if you don't want to. You can come back out here in the day and sweep, if you like. Only do come with me now, so I can get you some food and get you warm."

She might also see about getting the poor boy a bath, but first things first.

"Come on, lad." She helped him to his feet, and then needed his help to straighten up from her crouch. "The blind leading the blind," she muttered.

"I'm no blind," he groused. "But I am 'ungry."

"Bread and cheese, at this time of the night, but we've plenty of it." They slipped back through the gate and into the house, where she directed Fergus to raid the larder for a small wheel of cheese, bread and butter. "Now, quietly, straight up the stair, right at the top, stay out of sight until I get there."

Maisie took her time, hauling herself slowly up step after step, pausing frequently to ease the knot of cramp in her hip.

Fergus was waiting patiently, carefully out of sight behind the door. "Ye all ta rights then, missus?" he whispered.

"Yes, Fergus," she answered in her own hushed tones. "Thank you." Maisie glanced at Agnes to make sure she still slept and then made her way to her stool where she happily rested her wearying bones. "Now, we'll have that cheese, shall we, but while you eat, I wondered if you might do me the favor of letting me draw you. There's a sitting fee of two shillings." She used the excuse to give him the money she had in her pockets. "To make up for the time away from your work on the corner."

"Two shillings makes up for it, aye." Fergus's smile was sheepish. "No many folk to sweep fer this time the night."

Maisie set about cutting the cheese and slicing bread—making him feel more at ease. "Would you like to see some other drawings that I've made—of Agnes?" She made her sore way over to the canvases she had carefully stacked with their faces to the wall. "What do you think of this?" She chose her depiction of Agnes as the Magdalene, grieving Jesus's death.

"Jings! She looks like a duchess, or them of old."

"Yes, doesn't she." Maisie liked that description. "She is supposed to be a saint, but I like your description better. I'd like to paint you similarly, like the apostles who were friends of

Jesus." Fergus would make an excellent Doubting Thomas, all leery disbelief.

"Ye kin do that? With yer paints and all?"

"Yes," she answered simply. "If you'll sit for me."

"Fer two shilling I'll stand on me head fer ye."

"Just sitting, or perhaps a sort of kneeling, will do." She didn't want to keep him on his knees for long—he was a boy not a medieval monk. "But let's poke up the fire first, shall we?"

"Aye. Gie it laldy," he encouraged in the local dialect.

Together they coaxed a small flame—enough to illuminate the boy's face perfectly.

"Why don't you sit right here?" She plumped up the small pile of cushions left over from Agnes's pallet. "And just eat and watch the fire."

Fergus took another piece of bread and closed his eyes in something that was more relief than satisfaction.

Maisie quickly took up her red charcoal stick and set to work. In no time at all she had the outlines of the beleaguered saint, gazing longingly at his lord, hoping against hope, wanting more than anything to believe.

And didn't they all? Wasn't that what all of them wanted from this life—to believe that goodness and true, perfect, unconditional love existed in the world? And that even the lowliest amongst them were still worthy of that love?

By the time Maisie's eyes grew dry and scratchy, dawn was poking its blue-tipped nose over the hilly horizon to the east. She glanced at the clock on the now-cold mantlepiece.

"Damn and bother," she swore. "Agnes, dearling, I've done it again. Fergus, wake up. Time to go."

He came to with a feral sort of alertness that must have come from living rough and feeling sharp, snatching up his hat and the last few crusts of bread to stuff into his pockets. "We done then?"

"For now. If you'd like to come again to pose—"

"For two more shillings?"

"For two more shillings," she confirmed. "Come to the stable gate anytime of an evening and knock and send a message up with Agnes."

"Aye, I can so."

"Agnes, dear, coffee after you say goodbye to your brother. Now quietly," she advised. "I'll walk you out. Stick behind me on the stairs and we'll make a go of it."

With Agnes as a lookout, they got down the stairs and out of the house without being seen. Maisie pulled the bolts of the stable gate and let him out.

"Grand to be working with ye, missus."

"You too, Fergus. You too." She felt the strange, elated exhaustion of a job well done. The satisfaction of doing what she was meant to do. The thrill of purpose in knowing the rightness of what she was doing.

"Maisie?" The low voice startled her out of her reverie.

Archie Carrington stepped through the unlocked stable gate. "Dare I hope this means you're as eager to see me as I am to see you?" He smiled in his bright fox way. "Here I am, precisely three minutes earlier than yesterday, just as you so presciently specified." He presumed upon their prior...intimacy—there was no other word to be used, though they had not actually touched—in saying her name. "Been out carousing the night away, have you?"

He seemed like he was joking, but he reached for her suddenly cold hand and came close. So close she had to look up at his face as he looked down at her, searching. "But you have been up all night, haven't you?"

"Yes," she answered because there was no hiding her fatigue. Or her vulnerability. Because the way he was looking at her made her feel glad she hadn't painted him over. "But I'm glad."

"I'm glad you're glad. But you look done in." He swept her up in his arms, off her feet, and carried her across the yard and down the kitchen stair. "Pure scunnered, as your young friend Fergus might say."

The sensation of being picked up was extraordinary. Unsettling, but not unappealing. She felt a bit dizzy—giddy perhaps. Upended and uprooted, as if the distance to the ground were a few miles instead of a few feet.

"Thank you." She sounded out of breath, as if she were the one carrying him. "But best put me down now."

"I think not," he answered, shouldering open the door, and whisking her past the astonished early kitchen staff. "Don't mind us."

And up he went, tailed by a gaping Agnes and a few of the housemaids, though Maisie tried to shoo them away over his shoulder.

But Agnes was not about to be shooed. "I've the coffee, pots and pots, missus. Just as ye said ye'd be needin'."

"Yes, thank you, Agnes," she said as he set her onto her feet next to the daybed, though it felt like he perhaps let his fingers trail from her waist as if he were loath to let her go. No, clearly she was so tired she was hallucinating. "And thank you, Lord Carrington."

"Archie, please. I thought we were well past this. And you are most welcome, Maisie."

She nodded and swallowed and took a breath but could think of nothing to say that was not idiotic or revealing, though she knew by the heat under her skin, her face must be flaming. She was going to need another cake of vermilion.

Especially when he stepped close. So close she had to turn her head up to look into his dark honeyed eyes. So close she could smell the crisp, homey scent of starch and the more earthy scent of freshly washed man.

It was nearly overwhelming. "Lord Car—" She who was rarely at a loss for words or poise had nothing of it now.

"Archie," he teased softly, "while I've come to bare my body for you."

"Archie." It was nearly unbearable to say it. Because she had been longing to. Longing from the very first moment he had offered his name to her like a sweet she was forbidden to taste.

But why should she not have what he so freely—so temptingly offered? Why should she not have the pleasure of painting him as he was made, even if she would never be the one standing next to him at a soiree?

"Thank you, Agnes," she said in what she hoped was a firm, normal voice. "You may leave the coffee and get your own breakfast."

"Thank you, missus."

The girl shut the door on the gaping housemaids. And Maisie was finally alone.

With Archie.

She took off her cloak and hung it on a peg, and ran her hands down her skirts and had nothing more she might do. Which made it the time to speak, to finally say what she really wanted.

"I *am* as happy to see you as you are to see me," she told him in a voice that went quiet with her earnestness. "And I should very much like to see more."

"**I** am very glad to hear that." The slyly teasing note was back in his voice and he gazed at her through narrowed, lazy eyes. "Let us take up our lesson in the anatomy of the human body." He stripped off his gloves. "How shall we decide what next to bare?" he teased. "Shall I take a look? Have you added more?"

A shiver worked its wicked way under her skin. "Only a little," she admitted as together they took down the Holland cover. "More detail to your feet and hands."

But after a glance at the painting, his eyes were all for her. "For a woman who claims ignorance of the male body, you're a delightfully quick study."

The thrill of his attention made her bold and even proud. "Though I have not had the privilege of a life class—I have had some education in human anatomy." Self-educated, she might be —but she had studied earnestly. "I have my own drawings—a copy, of a copy if you will—of Vesalius, one of the great anatomists of the Renaissance."

"Do you mean done in your own hand?" He turned those hands over within his, as if searching.

"I do." Her confidence rose with his admiration. "I was given a chance to look at a copy of Vesalius's *Epitome*, by my physician, who was an Oxford educated fellow, residing in Richmond. It was he who encouraged me to study art and paint." And move and walk as much as possible. To struggle until it was no longer such a struggle.

"When did— Forgive my curiosity, but as I am about to bare my all for your benefit, perhaps I might ask you to bare your past for mine?" The tension in her hands must have communicated her discomfort to him. "I'm sorry, have I hit upon a sore topic?"

"Exceedingly sore," she admitted. "My hip aches to this day. Mostly only when it rains, but this is Edinburgh—the only place wetter must be some godforsaken Highland heath."

"Had you rather stayed in Richmond?" he asked carefully.

Had she? In Richmond, she would be slowly gaining 'some renown' as a ladies' portraitist. But in Edinburgh, she really had —just as Flora had promised—a new beginning. She had met Agnes and Fergus and was more than pleased with the paintings she was secretly making with them. And she was just as pleased to be secretly painting Lord Archie Carrington's manifest charms.

"No." The understanding gave her some relief. "I'm glad I came." Not that she had a real choice—a spinster, even one with her own occupation, lived at the behest of her father. She supposed she ought to be glad he had allowed her with them— this time.

"But it always aches? When was your illness?"

"In the summer of 1786." She laced her fingers together to stop her hands from shaking, but it was hard to recount such an experience with perfect equanimity—the paralysis had left her, but the fear had not. Likely never would.

"It was a summer fever that came on like a humid wind. One afternoon I was swimming and sailing on the river and by the evening I felt as if I couldn't breathe." She drew a deep breath just to prove to herself that she could—that the crushing pain had long ago been banished, unlike the fear. "And it hurt—a deep aching pain in my bones, while my skin felt like I was being stuck by pins. In my delirium, I thought that's what the first physician was doing to me—for some strange reason I felt it was all his doing that my legs wouldn't work." She wiped her suddenly damp hands on one of her rags. "And his doing that my family went away. Papa left, you see, taking Flora to safety so she wouldn't get the fever. She was only four."

"How old were you?"

"Nearly fourteen."

"God's bawbag." He wrapped his arm around her. "I thought you had been a wee child who couldn't remember anything different. I told you about my acquaintance, the writer, Walter Scott, who suffered what he called a 'teething fever' as a bairn, but it, too, left him with a hitch in his gait. He was taken to the seaside several times for a cure. How did you recover?"

She had never talked to anyone besides Flora—and then only fleetingly—about her illness. No one else had ever asked. "Stubbornness, I suppose. And luckily, about a year after, that physician moved in next door—the one who gave me his Vesalius to copy. And as I was fifteen by then, his encouragement and my own restlessness and spite eventually drove me to teach myself to walk again. And to paint. In the end, I was one of the lucky ones, even if it didn't feel like it at the time."

"I'm very glad you recovered." His smile felt like a gift.

"I am glad, too, I suppose. I'll admit I have bad days, when half of me aches and I want to do nothing more than curl up and hide in bed. But there are other days, when I feel like I never want to sleep again—when I feel as if I should paint forever."

"Like last night?"

"Yes," she confessed. "I know it might seem strange, because I'm exhausted now, but I like being in the throes of…I don't know what to call it—inspiration, I suppose." She drew in a deep breath. "There was a time when there was so little that I could do, that to lose myself in painting was both reward and escape."

"My acquaintance, Walter Scott, has spoken of how he believes his infirmity of body, as he put it, enabled him to achieve a greater genius of mind."

"I don't feel infirm," she insisted, even though the exhaustion she had kept at bay with anticipation crept into her bones like a chill. "I just don't walk evenly or picturesquely—which is what society seems to want from a woman, the picturesque."

He smiled at her then in such a way that told her what Archie Carrington might want from a woman had little to do with the picturesque. "Do you feel like a genius?"

She could only laugh. "I suppose only time will tell."

"Let us hope it does. But thank you." He closed his eyes briefly, and quietly said, "Thank you for telling me what happened to your leg."

"It happened to all of me," she amended. "My leg is the just the only part that didn't get over it."

"Fair enough." He smiled at her again. "Then I thank you for enlightening me."

"You're welcome." She felt entirely exhausted—or exposed, she wasn't sure which. "As much as I would like to take you up on your very gracious and very appreciated offer, the truth is, I'm too tired to do you justice. And I should hate not to do you justice."

"Do you know what?" He clasped her hand again. "I like you." He said it as if he had just discovered the fact himself. "You're an entirely unique person, Miss Maisie Conway. I like you very much."

She could hardly think of what to say to such an extraordinary speech. She felt all the remarkable power of that special, steady regard for people he seemed to have. "Thank you. But do stop complimenting me before someone thinks you're flirting with me."

His smile was slow, spreading across his face like a sunrise. "I am flirting with you."

"Are you also flirting with my sister?" Maisie felt her own breath bottle up in her chest at the rash boldness of her question. But she had to know.

His smile dissipated, but he was honest enough to answer, "I thought I was, too. At first."

A sliver of air found its way past her dry lips. "But you're not, now?"

"No," he shook his head, his eyes never leaving hers. "I am not."

Something within her shifted—like a canvas that had been under pressure for too long giving way at the edge. "Archie." It was such a pleasurable pain to say his name. She could feel the landscape of her wariness shift, as if the tight fabric she had woven like a cloak of armor to keep herself safe, was loosening.

He took a careful step nearer. "What would you do if I kissed you?

She would die.

She had never been kissed—never kissed anyone. She was nearly thirty years old and had been considered an invalid for more than half of her life.

And she wanted it more than she could say.

But so might her sister. Even if something had changed for Archie Carrington, it might not have for Flora—she might still be in expectation of his attention—and his kisses. And while there were many things Maisie felt she might do to experience her first kiss—and with such a man—she would not disappoint Flora. "I... don't know.

He slowly, carefully reached out to brush a stray lock of hair from her face. "Dear, sweet, hesitant Maisie. I think it's time we found out."

∼

THE ONLY THING ARCHIE WAS SURE OF AT THAT MOMENT WAS THAT he could not go another day—another minute—without tasting her particular brand of tart Englishness from her lips.

But despite her avowal of interest, she still had reservations. "Why?" she asked in her straightforward way.

"Because I *like* you," he repeated, as if the answer was self-evident and not a riddle he wasn't sure he could solve. "And I want to kiss you. More than ever."

"What about my sister?" she asked quietly. "Do you want to kiss her?"

Trust Maisie to be so straightforward. But Archie had already come to his own decision. "Not anymore."

She was too clever not to understand all of what he had said. "Did you want to, before?" But she, with her acute gaze, could read the truth upon his face, because she drew back. "Did you kiss her?"

"I might have done," he admitted. "Once, briefly. On the cheek," he hedged. "It felt like I was kissing a sister." That at least was the truth.

She wanted to believe him—she worried at her lip with her teeth. But she was still her wry self, even in her wariness. "Do you even have a sister?"

"Two." He was happy to tell her. "Both of whom I love. Neither of whom I should like to kiss." He reached for her hand— for anything that would connect him to her. "Same for your sister."

"And you think kissing me would be different?"

"Maisie." He reached out to stroke a single finger along the sweet, soft line of her jaw and gave her the only truth he had left. "There really is only one way to find out."

He waited, standing there with his hand warmed by the febrile heat of her skin while he tried to let her decide his fate.

But he could not be still. He would convince her. He would persuade her. "Have you never kissed anyone before?" he asked.

It was important to know—to get it right. Not to overwhelm or underestimate her.

Her answer was weary and a little sad. "You do realize that I am quite on the shelf? And the years when I might have been expected to be sneaking kisses behind potted palms in ballroom antechambers were spent learning how to walk again instead of learning to dance."

"Fair enough," he murmured, his voice low and easy. "Time better spent, I assure you."

He would kiss the sadness away. He would make her glad.

"But you've kissed …" She was looking at him in that way that saw all. "Many?"

He shook his head in disagreement. "Enough."

"Enough for what?"

"Enough to know what I like." He would convince her. He would kiss her into trusting him. "And how to do it properly."

She stared at him—at him, not through him.

And then, after it seemed she had taken her fill of looking at him, she looked into him—into his eyes as if she saw more than just the happy accident of his face. "And will you show me how to do it properly?"

"Yes. I swear it," he vowed. "I will give you my all."

To you and no other.

She bit her lip, hard, as if she were afraid to believe him.

"If it helps," he gave her the God's honest truth, "I'm just as startled by the fact as you."

And even with all her wariness, she said, "I'm not startled."

"Good." He smiled to show her this strange tension between them was not too heavy a burden for him to bear. That he liked carrying the weight of her expectation.

So he lowered his face to hers slowly, so she could change her mind. So she could turn away. So slowly, he thought he would lose his mind before her lips finally, infinitesimally, raised up to meet his.

He met the cool firmness of her mouth and moved his lips against hers gently, taking his time, pressing into her so sweetly, she opened to him. And just that easily, he fell into a softness so profound and so deep, it was as if the attic floor gave way beneath his feet.

He grasped at her to keep from falling, wrapping his hands around her arms until he found his feet. Then he thumbed the high line of her cheekbones, his blunt, printer's hands rasping along her jawline, urging her to part her lips in astonishment and pleasure.

"*Archie.*" Her gasp was a sound of wonder and delight. And encouragement.

Archie drew her closer, holding her face, fanning his thumbs along her cheeks as he slowly slid into the soft, open warmth of her mouth. His tongue caressed as his lips had, lulling her with gentleness, drugging her with sweet sensation, drawing her out to join him, until she began to make instinctive sounds of pleasure. And hunger.

Every fiber of his being was heated, rushing toward the intoxication of her mouth. She tasted new and fresh, like clear, cold water that left him gasping for breath. His hands slid into her brilliant, soft hair as he kissed the side of her mouth, trailing kisses along the sensitive underside of her jaw while she made astonished sounds of pleasure. His nose probed there, along the side of her neck, where her soft skin held the heady, lingering smell of paint and solvents.

When had linseed oil become an aphrodisiac?

Maisie raised her arms and looped them around his neck, pulling herself even closer, pressing herself against his chest and arms. She ran her fingers over his collar and up around the nape of his neck, caressing and exploring, driving his self-control to the brink.

Archie sought her mouth with a new urgency, a more insistent pressure against her lips, until she was pressing back, greedily taking all he would give, unselfishly giving back all that she could.

Their tongues tangled and tasted, and he let go of his self-restraint and gave in to the overwhelming need to touch and excite her. She was surprisingly responsive, as if, once she had decided to enjoy herself, she would give in to their mutual pleasure as thoroughly as possible.

God's bawbag, he wanted her badly. His hands slid around to mold themselves against the contours of her arching back and a deeply possessive sound—a very Scots combination of curse and growl—rose from within him. He could only pull her more tightly against him, urging her surprisingly pliant frame closer, until he could feel every swell and indentation of her compact, lithe form.

There was that same thought again—surprising. Why was he so surprised? Had he expected that just because she was lame and sometimes moved awkwardly that she would kiss awkwardly, too?

He had never been so happy to be proved so wrong.

Especially when her hands tightened in his hair, pulling his mouth down to hers so she could suck delicately on his tongue.

It probably lasted only moments in reality, the give-and-take, the sharing and wanting, but it felt like time stood still—or better yet, stretched on and on, until Archie somehow began to remember where he was—with a young woman he had commissioned, within her family home.

With only an unlocked door separating them from the rest of that house.

In the middle of the morning.

God's bawbag, indeed. But he wouldn't apologize. He had never been less sorry for doing something in his entire life. "Sweet Maisie." He had to work to draw a steady breath. "For all your inexperience, you catch on fast."

Her gasp was a laugh. "I'm exceedingly glad to cultivate any new talent."

He laughed, too, because the thought made him unaccountably happy. Happy to have shared her first taste of delight and desire. Happy that he had been the one to show her that delight. "As sorry as I am to have to stop kissing you, Maisie, I think it best if we end our day before we get ourselves into trouble."

She exhaled on a sigh. "Why is this trouble? I am nearly thirty years of age and not some green girl."

"No, lass." He clasped her shoulders to gently push her away. "But for all your years—"

His attentive ears caught the sound of footfalls advancing up the stairs.

"Maisie?"

She sprang away from him, hastily clambering onto her table. "Help me!" She gestured frantically to the holland cover heaped upon the floor by the base of the easel. "Hurry!"

He hurried, finding the edge of the thing and lofting it up toward the top of the canvas where she caught quick hold of it, pulling it over the painting and obscuring it from view.

She breathed out her relief. "You sit," she whispered. "No—stand! No—you open the door. I'll stay here. Well apart."

Archie nodded and took a deep breath. And went to the door.

"Good morning," Flora came through the portal wreathed in a smile. "I was coming up to see…and I thought I heard your voice, Lord Carrington—Archie." She turned to her sister, poised like a sneak thief atop her own table. "What in heaven's hour are you doing up there, Maisie?"

CHAPTER 17

*A*rchie.

Maisie felt her breath bottle up in her throat. She had not adequately prepared herself for the idea that whatever designs on her sister Archie may have given up, Flora had not given up hers.

Despite what he had told her, despite what they had just shared, Flora clearly had expectations of him.

"You know I don't like to show the work to anyone while it's in process," Maisie stammered, while keeping tight hold of the Holland cloth as if it were a lifeline. "Not even the subject."

"So particular," Flora teased. "Though I'm sure you have your reasons, they don't particularly make sense to the rest of us." She included Archie in her 'us.' "Do you need help getting down?"

"No, thank you." Maisie took a more composed moment to turn away and secure the cover over the canvas. "What do you want?"

Besides the obvious.

But Flora was focused on Maisie, not Archie Carrington. "I wanted to see if I could talk you into attending the Cathcart Salon this evening, with me."

"Me?" Maisie squawked. It was guilt, no doubt, making that sour feeling in her stomach—guilt that she had been kissing a man Flora might still quite rightly consider her own suitor.

"You." Flora enunciated as if Maisie were hard of hearing and not hard of understanding. "Although I'm sure Archie has already been invited—Mr. Cathcart is one of his oldest friends, is he not?" She looked to Archie for confirmation. "Which is why I was asking you, Maisie."

"You know I don't attend evening parties."

"And why not?" Flora broadened her appeal to Archie. "Have you told her about Mr. Cathcart?"

"Only in passing," he replied.

"Mr. Cathcart," Flora began, "is a very well-known connoisseur from Mr. Christie's Auction House in St. James's, in London. He's an expert in the tracing, detecting and exposing of art forgeries—isn't that the most interesting thing you've ever heard? But more importantly, he serves as a sort of consultant to art collectors—like the Earl of Aberdeen and Lady Augusta Ivers—telling them what art they ought to buy."

"Good thing I'm not a forger," Maisie said with some relief. "And can therefore be of no interest to the man."

"Maisie!" Flora scolded. "Don't you see, he's exactly the sort of person who could be recommending you to his aristocratic clientele as a portraitist. Once it's known that you're painting Lord Carrington and Lady Ivers, others will want the honor."

It was no more than Mr. Hill had said—but Mr. Hill had not required her attendance at a soirée. "Absolutely not." Maisie put her foot down—well actually she put her bottom down, sitting upon her worktable. "Firstly, I do not want to discuss or reveal the portrait until I am pleased with the result—which will likely not be for some time." A very long time, if she kept interrupting her progress by spending the mornings kissing her subject instead of painting him. "And secondly, no thank you. I don't like to attend soirées."

"But Archie will be there, too. Surely that—"

Archie, not Lord Carrington.

"No thank you." Maisie firmed her resolve. "You don't need me."

"Maisie," Flora pled, "it isn't right that you always shut yourself away."

"I had much rather spend my evening working—there is much to be done outside the hours of Lord Carrington's sitting, you understand. Much more to be done."

"Flattery takes a great deal of work," Archie put in, in an attempt to lighten the suddenly contentious mood.

Or maybe it was just she who felt contentious. Maybe it was she who was angry with herself and the world because as much as she truly didn't want to go to the party, she resented Flora and Archie going. She hated knowing they would be there together without her.

Guilt and resentment made an acid brew in her belly.

For his part, Archie seemed to understand at least a little of her discomfort. "I do have to say, Miss Flora, I'm not sure my schedule will now allow... The current special edition of the Review is…proving …needs attention."

"Oh, leaving me on my own, are you both? Well then, be it on your head if I get into trouble!" And with that, Flora flounced out the door.

"She's not really going to get into trouble, is she?" Archie asked.

"No," Maisie assured him. "Flora was being dramatic—she never puts a foot wrong." Unlike her older sister, who was expected to put her foot wrong every time she moved. Which was why she didn't like going into society—even the savage society of slushy, smelly Edinburgh.

"May I give you a hand?" Archie asked as he held out his arm to assist her in standing.

At least he asked, instead of assuming like others always did. "Thank you."

He nodded his response, and said nothing more for a long time. But he did not move away. He seemed contented simply by her nearness.

As the moment lengthened, Maisie searched for something to say to break the strange spell. But it was he who finally spoke first.

"You doubt me."

Guilt and resentment were met by some small measure of relief—she didn't like pretending. "I do."

"I'll prove it to you," he swore.

"How?"

But her nonsensical question was ended by his mouth pressing against hers as he caught her about the waist and turned her toward him. His hand was at the side of her face, along the line of her jaw, angling her face up, toward his. The press of his lips against her was both a shock and a delight. Both gentle and fierce. Soft and insistent.

His mouth moved against her, as if he were tasting her in small sips before delving deeper.

And it was nothing like she had experienced before—nothing like she expected. She had thought that somehow she would feel trapped, or taken advantage of, or manipulated. If she had always shied away because she didn't feel comfortable being that close to another person—to a man—she now wanted to get closer. She wanted to wrap herself around him and breathe in the scent of starch and printer's ink. She wanted to taste the sweet tang of his mouth. She wanted to touch his glorious, unruly hair and smooth her palms along the bristled texture of beard below the clean line of his jaw. She wanted to pull him down on top of her and feel the glorious weight and strength of his—

"Maisie."

"Yes," she answered. Yes to any question he might have. Yes to any idea that might cross his mind.

"Maisie." He said her name as if it was the answer to a question. "Maisie, Maisie, Maisie. You certainly are a surprise."

"Yes." She liked surprising him. She liked overturning his opinions and expectations of her. She liked kissing him more. "As are you."

Not that she didn't think he would kiss like an experienced rogue, but that he would be so…sweet and kind and wonderful while he was doing it.

She had thought he would be all piratical and knowing and here he was, almost flabbergasted, holding her face, staring down at her from his great height, with wonder in his voice and touch. "I don't think we're going to get any sitting done today."

"No," she agreed. Even she knew that kissing led to more kissing which led to more intimate exchanges and even more intimate revelations. Which she wasn't ready for. "Your kisses, I will grant you, are very nice indeed—"

"Nice?"

"Very nice."

"Fair enough," he replied. "I'll take that as compliment enough. Though I reserve the right to show you differently."

"How differently?"

"That there is more, my sweet Maisie." He raised her hand to his lips for a lingering kiss. "Much, much more."

He kissed her with force and finesse and the heretofore hidden heat of his pent-up passion, backing her into the door, which shut with a clatter, so he could lean his weight into her.

And she was welcoming the press of his body into hers, the feel of his lips upon hers. His kiss was more insistent, more intense, as if he had used up all his charm and now had nothing but roguish desire to assuage. The whiskers lurking just beneath his clean-shaven skin lightly prickled hers, bringing every other part of her skin into bristling awareness.

This was nothing like the gentle exploration of his first kisses. Nothing like she had imagined. This kiss was hot and tight and close and needy and fierce. This kiss robbed her of breath and thought, and she did not care about either in the moment. She only cared that he keep kissing her. Keep making her feel such delightful, pleasurable, dangerous feelings.

Dangerous because he kissed her as if he wanted her, and her alone. Wanted her lips between his, wanted her tongue dancing with his, wanted to taste her as much as she wanted to taste and lick and suck and explore him.

His hands fanned along her face, tipping her chin, angling her mouth more to his liking, bringing her close and closer still. As if he could not get close enough.

And she was kissing him back, pressing her lips to his. Holding him as close as she could. Giving herself over to each moment of passion as if it were all she had ever wanted. As if she did not need to think or breathe. She needed nothing but him and the sure heat of his touch.

He felt powerful and sure and generous pressed against her. He tasted of coffee and whisky and want that weighed on her tongue like a bittersweet drug. And she could not get enough. She wanted more.

More of the insistently tender way he held her. More of the strength of his body pressed against hers. More of the dangerous want rising within her. So much more.

And as if he heard her unspoken plea, he gave her more, wrapping one arm about her waist while the other began a slow exploration up the side of her cheek to her hair. And then down and around to the sensitive whorl of her ear and down again over the heated skin on the side of her neck.

Maisie felt herself lean into his touch, titling her head to grant him greater access.

And he took it. He turned his hand to let the backs of his fingers trail along the line of her collarbone, over the fine muslin of her chemisette, before brushing slowly—so slowly she all but heard her own aching sigh—across the top of her bodice.

Beneath the layers of shift and stays and dress, her breasts tightened so suddenly, she could not help but cry out.

"Maisie," he answered. "Sweet Maisie, do you want—?"

"Yes," she answered before he could finish. Yes, to any question. Yes, to them all.

His fingers delivered their answer, traveling down around the curved underside of her aching breast, cupping and warming her until he gently closed his thumb over her nipple and squeezed.

"Yes." Her voice was tight with the needy delight that streaked through her.

Thus encouraged, he plucked at the row of buttons lining her chemisette, loosening them turning his attention to the taut drawstring tucked under her bodice. Two long, inquisitive fingers delved into the cleft between her breasts and she could feel her lungs swell with air to try and feel more of the tantalizing pressure. And then he tugged at the bow and the neckline of her dress was loose and opening, leaving her in desperate want of his touch.

"Yes," he said this time, answering what she had not asked, giving her what she wanted—the exquisite feel of his palm rounding her breast before he tweaked the tip of her nipple, rolling it between his thumb and forefinger until she ached with pleasure.

This was what she wanted—to feel alive within her own skin. To escape the prison she had made of her own body. To feel free again.

Her response encouraged him to lower his mouth to join his hand, to take the sensitized tip between his lips, kissing and sucking and nipping just hard enough to send currents of bliss and want streaking deep into her belly. And as if her knew exactly what she was feeling, even as he held and laved her breast, his other hand slid down, pressing into her belly before finding the apex of her thighs and cupping her mons.

Maisie thought her legs would buckle from the needy pleasure.

"Spread your legs for me," he whispered against her ear. "Let me—"

"I can't." She couldn't. Not without risking that her weak leg would give way. But she threw her arms about his shoulder, holding him tight for fear that he would stop.

For fear that he would remove his hand and leave her wanting.

But he did not. Instead, he seemed to take the weight of her with his thigh pressed insistently between her legs, nudging her back against the panel of the door with his chest and strength and clever, clever fingers that somehow seemed to find their way to delving into her cleft even through the intervening layers of fabric and shift and gown, leaving her body arcing towards him, ringing wildly within. Pealing—

No, that was just the bell of West Kirk, tolling the hour, reminding them both that their time was up.

Almost.

Even as the exquisite want spiraled deep into her belly, he was easing back, lessening the pressure and the pleasure.

"For now," Archie promised as if he had heard her thoughts. "Only for now. We must stop, for both our sakes. But the next time we are together, in just this position,"—he pressed the heel of his palm against her aching mons once more—"I predict that we shall both be quite, quite naked. And you, my sweet, curious Maisie, will get the anatomy lesson we both have earned."

CHAPTER 18

$\mathcal{R}$ory Cathcart kept an elegant suite of apartments on Heriots Row, where he and his delightful French wife, Mignon, lived whenever they were in Edinburgh—which was only about four times a year, which was still not enough to suit Archie's fondness for his friends.

Rory was the only other one of the Four C's who worked for a living—not that the other two didn't work, but both Alasdair Colquhoun and Ewan Cameron had inherited titles along with large landed estates.

Which was why Archie made time for his friends' salon despite what he had told Flora Conway—he wanted to talk to his friend Rory alone. But there was no time to be private—the Marquess and Marchioness of Cairn, it seemed, had had the same idea to turn up at the Cathcarts' early.

"Archie, my darling friend," Quince, Marchioness of Cairn greeted him. "Well met!"

"Archie," was her husband Alasdair's more subdued greeting. "I've been hearing things about you."

"What kinds of things?"

"Interesting things," supplied Quince as the door was opened.

"Evening all! Ain't you damn fellows—and pardon me, my lady—got any manners?" Rory greeted them in his typically dry, humorous manner. "Imposing yourselves before time," he tsked, even as he shook his friends' hands and kissed the lady's cheeks. "Damn, but I'm glad to see you. We've been lonely in London without you lazy hoists always dropping by to eat—and drink—us out of house and home."

"With Pitt out of office, I have no role to play, and no reason to be in London when I could be here," Alasdair began.

"No politics," his wife, Quince, warned. "This is an artistic evening, and we can't have you putting off Rory's guests by offending them right out of the gate."

"Which is why we came early," Alasdair objected, "so I could get it out of the way!"

"As if art and politics don't go hand in hand," Rory joked. "As if one weren't constantly informing and inspiring and reacting to the other."

Quince laughed. "Don't I know. But I will leave you political hoists to your whisky while I join Mignon in her dressing room, if I may?"

"She would love it," Rory confirmed. "You know the way. Now." He turned back to Archie and Alasdair. "Let us have that quick drink, for I'm not offering the *hoi polloi* my best Scots whisky while I quiz my favorite scribbling piker on his request for information about one Sir Richard Conway."

Archie put a hand to his ear. "I harken to my name. So, what have you found out?"

"Very little on my part. Start with Alasdair first," Rory instructed.

"As you suspected," Alasdair informed him, "Conway's appointment was definitely made by Pitt in the last days—if not the last moments—of his term as Prime Minister."

"Why?" Archie echoed Maisie's straightforward style. "Was it a reward?"

"Of sorts, because handing out plum positions always is," Alasdair said. "But why did Sir Richard Conway, a former merchant from what I can find out, and sometime backbench Member of Parliament for Richmond Park, qualify for this particularly plum legal position of the Lord Advocacy, when he might be thought to have earned a far more prestigious or lucrative reward for a successful merchant, like being offered a directorship of the Bank of England?"

"What kind of merchant?"

"East India Company, which may explain the influence, although his tenure there was some time ago—and not in the official record."

"My first instinct," Archie said, "was that the appointment was a convenient way to remove him from the new government's line of sight, as it were, while still rewarding him."

"Sound thinking," Alasdair reasoned.

"Yet from what I can tell," Rory interjected, "he left London, and the house in Richmond in particular, in something of a fire sale state—a great many things were offered for auction that one would have thought would have been brought to Edinburgh when he moved house."

"What sort of things? Like things that could be sold for cash?"

"Anything that's not entailed to an estate can be sold for cash," Rory reminded him. "And although Chinese porcelain and other imported goods are a little out of fashion at the moment, there is always a market with collectors."

"Chinoiserie?" Archie asked. The fashion for expensive items of decor originating in China had been wildly popular some forty years ago. "Perhaps his tastes have lately changed and he didn't wish to burden himself with such unfashionable stuff?"

"Perhaps," Rory agreed. "Either way, he made a tidy bundle in the sale. Christie was lucky enough to find a particularly acquisitive buyer in Sussex, who took the whole of Conway's collection."

"I hope the commission made you your own tidy bundle?" Alasdair asked.

"Naturally," Rory confirmed. "I am a working man and not a landed gentleman—I never turn up my nose at a commission. And speaking of which—"

"No, don't distract me—I haven't got time," Archie interrupted to bring them back to their purpose. "Was Sir Richard's elevation to knighthood also given as a reward for services or loyalty to Pitt's government, do you think?"

"It's termed as services to the Crown, but that's usually how it works." Alasdair sighed. "It's an ugly business, the granting of the King's favors, rife with cronyism and open to corruption, but such is our world."

He would get no argument from Archie. "So, he was a merchant with the East India Company? That's a big enough umbrella to cast a great deal of shade. What was his profession with them?"

"My sources, which, funnily enough, include my botanist papa-in-law," Alasdair said, "have told me he started out as a gardener's lad at the Royal Botanical Gardens here in Edinburgh before he eventually earned a spot at Chiswick."

Then Archie's father, damn him, had been correct. "A gardener, who then becomes a successful merchant? Successful enough to curry such favor?" Archie could not fathom such a leap.

"It is Lord Winthrop's recollection that Conway originally became employed by the company when he was sent to India as a plant collector—something to do with tea plants specifically, but Winthrop's memory is hazy."

"But India didn't have tea plants—they were embargoed by the Chinese." Archie began to see the beginnings of a pattern. "Was he sent as a plant thief?"

"If he were," Alasdair agreed, "that might explain why he was secretly rewarded with the favor to run for a seat in Parliament upon his return."

"But that was years ago, yes? It doesn't quite explain his recent elevation to the knighthood, and the Lord Advocacy post, does it?

"Does favor really need explanation?" Alasdair asked dryly.

Archie answered with a rude sound. "So generally," he began his list of known facts, "he sold everything in Richmond, where his family were happy, by all accounts. He disposed of a collection of Chinese porcelain and furniture, perhaps to erase that earlier, illegal connection to plant theft in China? Which was technically not illegal under British law? He's no sportsman, though he keeps a single, modest carriage and a good-enough stable. He employs two footmen, and two only, to be seen riding on that carriage. He is not ostentatious or extravagant in dress or his style of living. He does not subscribe to the Review."

"Now that is a sin to you," Rory put in.

"So, the question focuses itself down to why does Pitt—or one of his ministers—" Here Archie looked directly at Alasdair. "—reward him now? Why is he shunted up to Scotland where he has not lived since his youth?"

"And my answer is, I don't know," Alasdair said. "It was not something that was ever under my purview or notice."

"My father is sure it was something unsavory—he thought it was something to do with slaving," Archie suggested.

"And how is the irascible old bastard?" Alasdair asked in reply.

"The Marquess sends his best—nothing less will do for him," Archie joked.

"But as to slaving, I can't see it," Alasdair opined. "If Conway was involved in slaving Pitt would never have had him in his government, let alone reward him."

"Fair enough." Archie had to agree.

"But let us turn for the moment from matters of politics to matters more personal," Rory said.

"Politics are personal," Archie and Alasdair said together.

Rory smiled at them. "I *personally* heard a delightful rumor about the youngest-ever editor of the exalted Edinburgh Review." Rory turned the sharp blade of his smile on Archie.

"Do tell. I wonder if it is the same one I heard?" asked Alasdair.

"That our resident rabble-rouser has commissioned a portrait of himself," Rory told him.

"From the pompous popinjay Raeburn?" Alasdair asked.

"Give him marks for having better taste!" Rory exhorted. "And better opportunities. He has very cleverly commissioned a lady portraitist. I had it from the colorman, Mr. Hill, on Princes' Street."

"Color me astonished," Alasdair looked at Archie with amusement. "Archie, what have you to say for yourself?"

Archie said only what he must. "It is all in the name of my investigation into Sir Richard—the portraitist is his daughter." Even as he said it, he felt the sharp prick of his conscience, paining him for his disloyalty. And his lies.

"You don't say?" Rory was nonplussed. "So, it's all a ruse in the name of advantage?"

Archie knew he looked uncomfortable, but he could not yet divulge his true feelings to his friends. He settled for something just less than the truth. "To be fair, I did attempt a far more straightforward inquiry, a series of unobtrusive but serious questions submitted by the Edinburgh Review, seeking the answers to all these questions from Sir Richard himself, first."

"But you did not get honest answers?" Alasdair guessed.

"I got no answers at all."

Rory was nonplussed. "But the man made no objections to your commissioning your portrait from his daughter?"

"He did object, but Miss Conway overrode him," Archie answered.

"Well, the pretty young Miss Conway is on my clever wife's

invitation list," Rory confirmed. "So, we will not have long to wait until we see if the other rumors I have heard about Archie spending a great deal of time with Miss Conway are true. Finish your drinks, my friends, for the appointed hour draws nigh—here are the ladies now."

Archie did as Maisie has once advised and hushed his whisht until the lady in question—or rather the sister of the lady in question—arrived.

"My Lord Carrington," Flora Conway greeted him in the drawing room. "How nice to see you. I hope this means your business at the Review was concluded favorably?"

"Indeed, Miss Flora, it was," he gave way to the polite, expedient lie.

"Maisie tells me that you are nearly done with your sittings for her. I daresay you will be glad to reclaim your time."

"Has she?" Archie was not prepared for the strange pang that came with the thought of ending his sessions with Maisie—he felt as if he had taken a blow to the sternum. But surely he had known that his time with the delightfully enigmatic artist would sometime come to an end?

Not unless he found some way to prolong the acquaintance.

Flora was clearly thinking along the same lines. "But it will take her some time after the sittings to finish the painting, during which time our door surely lies open to you, Archie, however much you should like to visit."

Was she asking for her own part? Was Flora Conway flirting with him?

It was hard to tell. She lacked her sister's straightforward manner. Though Flora smiled as she spoke, her motives were altogether more opaque.

Which was why he needed to concentrate more upon his original assignment than on his current obsession with her sister. And surely, once he had the information about her father, the reason for seeing either of the Conway girls would be at a natural end. And when the Edinburgh Review published its exposé, neither sister would want bloody anything to do with him.

God's bawbag.

"Archie? Mr. Carrington?" Flora was looking at him. "Are you all to rights?"

"Oh, yes, of course," he lied. But the thought of never seeing Maisie Conway, of never talking to her or joking with her, or kissing her ever again, was an idea so abhorrent that it was physically painful.

"Of course?" Flora looked at him expectantly.

"No, I'm sorry," he confessed. "I was thinking of a story we're gathering information about…"

"Of course, you were." Her smile was full of warm indulgence, almost as if—was she humoring him? Her sister would have given him a gimlet eye and told him to either listen or leave. He was never bored when he was with Maisie Conway.

But their conversation was about to be interrupted by Quince, who was leading her husband their way. "May I have the honor and pleasure of introducing you to my friends, the Marquess and Marchioness of Cairn, Miss Flora?"

"Yes, please!"

"Good evening, Archie!" Quince was all purposeful delight. "And you must be the famous Miss Conway we've heard so much about. I'm Quince. So very pleased to meet you."

"As am I, my Lady Cairn." Flora dropped a perfectly charming curtsy.

"Quince, please," the lady demurred, "for I am sure we are to be friends. But you must tell me what it is like to work with our Archie. Is he a tolerable subject for your study?"

"I think you must have me confused with my far more talented sister, Miss Margaret Conway," Flora clarified. "It is Maisie who is painting Lord Carrington's portrait."

"By jimble!" Quince turned her own gimlet eye on him. "Two

sisters?" she asked him with wide, questioning eyes, in a way that asked without speaking, *How will you choose?*

Her teasing could not ruffle him—he had already chosen.

But Flora could have no idea, though she was all easy charm. "I am flattered to be thought my sister, for she is truly the most talented person I know. I would be honored and very happy to introduce her to you, my lady."

"You are very kind—I would like that, very much," Quince answered. "But perhaps it is I who needs must make amends for my error. We must have you and your sister—and your father, the Lord Advocate, of course—to dine with us, soon. I'm already excited by the stimulating conversations we will surely have. Now, tell me everything about your sister's work." She led Flora away in the way only Quince could manage—being peremptory while also being genuinely absorbed. "You've secured Lady Ivers? Of course, but I shall only forgive you for letting her be the first, if you will let me be the next!"

"Two sisters," Alasdair said, calmly, factually, the way a barrister might state a truth in a court of law. "You've been a busy boy, Archie."

"You have no idea." It was something of a relief to have his situation made known to his friends.

"Oh, I do." Alasdair smiled and patted Archie on the back while he asked. "What I want to know is which one is leading you a merry chase?"

"The painter," Archie said without thinking. "When I am with her, I can scarce think of anything—anyone—else."

"Quite," Alasdair agreed. "That will be the one then. Let me be the first to wish you happy."

While Archie was happy to admit his attraction to Maisie, Alasdair's leap of logic took him by surprise. "Don't be an ass, Alasdair."

There would be no marriage. First of all, he wasn't like his friends—he wasn't the marrying kind. And secondly, once he had published his exposé on Sir Richard Conway, Maisie Conway would have nothing to do with him.

"And don't be a stubborn, unthinking or unfeeling mule, Archibald. Society is linking you with *that* girl." Alasdair gazed across the room at Flora Conway. "While not knowing the other young woman exists."

"Hardly young," Archie said. "She's of an age with us—she's nearly thirty."

"And what does her age have to do with attraction, Archie? Or, more importantly, reputation?" Alasdair shook his head as if Archie were a particularly dim pupil. "My point is that you play a dangerous game, being linked to each of the sisters differently —but potentially amorously—whilst you are investigating their father. While I agree there are irregularities in Sir Richard Conway's history that warrant investigation, I would bid you not do the two things at the same time. Pray do not play with two young women's hearts. Especially sisters—there is more at stake here than an exposé in your Review. If you create a rift between two sisters, then not even hell would be hot enough to take you."

"Come on now," Archie protested. "No need to do it that brown."

"I'm not joking, Archie. Be careful with their hearts. Be careful with your own." Alasdair gave his pronouncement with all the gravitas of a judge. "I am never wrong about these things."

"And which things are these, my dear?" Quince was back to bedevil her husband.

"Matters of the heart. You may tell Archie that I was a slow study, but that I learned my lessons thoroughly. He is falling in love, but he won't admit it to himself yet."

"The painter?" Quince guessed.

"Indeed." Alasdair rewarded his wife with a kiss. "But how did you guess?"

"Because Miss Flora's conversation is full of 'Maisie and

Archie'—together like that. I don't think she has a thought for Archie that is not in relation to her sister."

"Really?" Archie didn't know whether to be relieved or outraged that his charm seemed not to have worked in the slightest on Miss Flora. "Do you really think so?"

No, it was not relief, but unadulterated excitement—and lust, damn him, pure unadulterated lust for Maisie Conway—that had him instantly glad that particular hurdle might be cleared from his way. He was already planning his next seduction. It would be just as he told her—they would both be left naked, but certainly not wanting.

Not if he had his way.

"Absolutely," Quince's smile dazzled. "We must have this mysterious Maisie over for dinner. Gird your loins, Archie. Your kettle is about to be put on the boil."

CHAPTER 19

Flora knocked before she let herself into the studio. "Hello, my dear," she greeted Maisie. "I've come to warn you that your recluse days are nearing an end."

"Have you?" Maisie had enough time to put down her palette and cover the canvas of Agnes as the Magdalene before Flora reached her. "What have you done?"

"Nothing specific or out of the ordinary, I assure you." Flora's smile was teasing. "Nothing that could be construed as carnival barking."

"That's a relief." Maisie stretched her back. Secrecy was wearying. As was thwarted attraction.

"Only temporary, I assure you."

"Are you going to tease me all night," Maisie asked, "or are you going to tell me what you have in mind?"

Flora mimed trying to make a decision before she held out the letter, addressed to the Misses Conway.

"Who is it from?"

"Read," Flora instructed.

Maisie did so reluctantly. "The Marchioness of Cairn? A small family dinner with a few select friends? You know I don't go to dinners."

"You do now." Flora looked pleased as punch. And as if she was not going to take no for an answer this time.

"Why?" Maisie demanded instead.

"Because she is the Marchioness of Cairn." Flora enunciated each syllable slowly as if that might make Maisie understand. "She, along with her husband, are great friends of your Lord Archie Carrington, and she wants to meet you. Obviously."

"Why? What did you say?" Or worse, what had Archie said? "And he is not my Lord Anything."

"Don't be daft, Maisie. Though I will admit to meeting her at the Cathcart soirée, I said nothing of you beyond your being an excellent portraitist. Obviously, Archie has told her all about you and now she wants to meet you herself."

"Why?" It was as if her brain were stuck in place. "What do you think he told her?" The self-doubt and fears she had lately been able to thrust aside began to creep back. "He knows I don't socialize. You may tell her that. Tell her—"

"I'll do no such thing." Flora crossed her arms over her chest. "It's high time you got out and about. Like Lady Ivers, who is also a friend of Quince—that's Lady Cairn's name, the marchioness— the marchioness could be very influential and help make your reputation as an artist."

"Why would she want to do that?"

"Honestly. Don't be so dense, even if you are afraid." Flora got right to the heart of the matter in an instant. "But you may certainly ask her that question yourself—at dinner, tomorrow evening. I've already answered, so don't think of trying to get out of it." She held up her hand before Maisie could speak. "Papa is engaged to dine at the Thompsons, so we are free of him. Raines will be our chaperone. So that leaves the question of your dress for the occasion."

Flora squinted at her sister, considering. "The dark blue

lutestring, I think, with pearls. He won't be able to resist. Yes, the blue silk, with your coloring—and your affinity for surface textures," she added archly. "I'll inform Raines straight away. This will be fun." Flora was positively giddy with delight.

A new possibility—equal parts horrifying and interesting—occurred.

"Flora? Are you—" The idea was so far-fetched, Maisie hesitated. But faint heart never won fair understanding. "Are you pushing Lord Carrington at me?" It sounded ridiculous even as she said it. "And by that, I mean for something more than his portrait, or my reputation as a portraitist."

Flora was not nearly as surprised as Maisie. "What if I were?"

"If you were, I—" Maisie hardly knew what to think. "I would thank you," she said finally. "With all my heart."

Maisie could have warmed herself on Flora's smile. "Then you're welcome."

"But what of you?" Maisie persisted. "What of your heart?"

"What would make my heart glad is to see you happy," her sister swore. "You've done so much, sacrificed so much for me."

"I sacrificed for you? Nonsense," Maisie denied even as she swept her sister into a fierce hug. "Don't you know I would do anything for you? Don't you know you alone are my solace and joy?"

"Not alone," Flora said. "Not anymore." She set herself away. "So resign yourself, Maisie, to being fêted. Practice your curtsey. And your smile."

Maisie resigned herself. Mostly out of curiosity. Which did not exactly outweigh the fear, but she concentrated on the curiosity to keep herself from dissolving into a puddle of misapprehensions. She didn't want to disappoint Lord Carrington—or live up to whatever horrible things he might have told the marchioness about her—that she was plain, or waspish, or a stupidly soft touch or whatever it was these aristocratic types gossiped about behind other people's backs.

She put up her chin and descended from the carriage—which had been trotted out of the Conway's mews to deliver them the insurmountable distance of an eighth of a mile to the north side of Charlotte Square, where the Marquess of Cairn kept a town house.

"Good evening, Miss Flora." An impish vision in deep viridian green satin and an absolutely stunning set of matching emeralds opened the door—the Marchioness of Cairn was her own butler.

Maisie was impressed.

"And you must be Miss Conway." The Marchioness of Cairn reached for Maisie's hand. "So wonderful to meet you. Do come in, you are very welcome. I'm Quince."

"My Lady Cairn." Flora bobbed a curtsey before kissing their hostess the marchioness on both cheeks in the continental style. "Quince, thank you for your kind invitation."

"My dear Flora, you are most welcome. Do come in for it's a raw night—not that we seem to have any other kind in Edinburgh. But come right through—there's a roaring fire in the drawing room to keep us all toasty. Miss Conway, let me conduct you in."

Maisie found herself being taken on the marchioness's arm and walked at a measured pace towards the drawing room. "You must let me know if I rush you, Miss Conway. I'm a terrible rusher, Alasdair tells me. Don't you, my love?"

"I do indeed." A tall, stately man with a mane of ginger hair bowed to Maisie. "Good evening, I am your blithe hostess's husband, Alasdair, and I am very happy to welcome you here this evening."

"My Lord Cairn." Maisie made the serviceable curtsey she had practiced, but had had no time to give to the marchioness.

"Alasdair, please. We are all friends here." He looked to where Archie and another man stood nearer to the mantlepiece. "You already know Archie."

The Archie in question made a charming bow—to her first,

she noted, and then to her sister. But his eyes came back to her. "My dear Miss Conway. Miss Flora."

Something inside clenched and unclenched simultaneously. Maisie could not decide if the feeling was pleasant or not. She didn't have time—there were more introductions to be made.

"And this elegant fellow is Mr. Rory Cathcart."

"Miss Conway, Miss Flora." The man made an elegantly brief bow. "My wife, Mignon."

"*Enchanté.*" The petite dark-haired beauty at Cathcart's side made them both an elegant little curtsey. "But I am so very pleased to meet you both. Miss Flora and I did not have time to speak at the salon the other evening, much to my regret, so I am so very happy to have another chance—and to meet you as well, Miss Conway. I am always pleased to meet an *artiste.*"

"And these darling people are Ewan Cameron, Duke of Crieff and his lady wife and duchess, Greer."

"Your Graces." Maisie sank as low as she thought she could without being unable to get up.

"Such a pleasure to meet you." The duchess offered a surreptitiously supportive hand to help Maisie rise. "We've heard so much about you, Miss Conway."

"Call me Maisie, please," she heard herself saying. Clearly she had been infected by the bonhomie.

Archie's smile spit into a wide grin. "Was that so hard?"

"Yes," she said, even as she smiled. "Terribly."

"You're doing fine," he assured her. "I'm so glad you came."

And suddenly, so was Maisie. Because he was speaking to her. He *liked* her. He had kissed her.

And she had kissed him back. Passionately.

But such thoughts were not for now—the marchioness was leading Maisie to a comfortable divan. "Now, you must tell us all about your sessions with Archie. We are all agog to hear how he conducts himself out in the world."

"Are you?" Maisie felt her face must be painted in every shade of cinnabar. She hardly knew where or how to begin. "Surely you must know this better than I? Have you all not been friends for years?"

"Yes, by jimble," the marchioness said with a laugh. "But we are as used to his eccentricities and deficiencies as he is to ours. Yours is a fresh impression, not guided by misplaced affection." Her smile was full of the affection she claimed was misplaced.

"I will say," Maisie began carefully, "Lord Carrington has been an interesting, though difficult subject."

"Difficult?" Archie said in mock protest. "How, when your every wish has been my command?"

"Every wish?" Lady Cairn's eyes grew wide with delight. "By jimble."

Maisie drew a deep breath to cool the crimson in her cheeks before she attempted her explanation. "Difficult because he is a man of action, and I must torture him into standing still for at least an hour a day."

"But the results speak for themselves," Flora put in. "Maisie has captured the essence of Lord Carrington, not just his likeness. The results thus far are magnificent."

Flora looked—knowing, somehow. "When did you see?" Maisie could hear the tart rebuke in her voice, but know it for what it really was—fear.

But the others were looking at her—and at Archie who looked just as astonished as she at Flora's revelation. "To depict the sitter's character is the goal of all portraiture," she exclaimed in defense. "To depict their life and livelihood, not just their looks."

"How very well put. I should very much like to see that!" the marchioness said.

"No," Maisie objected. "You must pardon me, Lady Cairn. No one is meant to see the work before it is ready, especially not the sitter. For a variety of reasons," she hedged. "I prefer to keep my works in progress private—not even Flora is allowed to see them." Maisie fixed her sister with a reproving look.

"I refuse to be cowed. Or sorry." Flora gave her as good as she got. "Maisie is far too apt to keep her work from public view even when it is finished. There must be a hundred canvases that she has painted over the years that no one has ever seen."

Rory Cathcart made a sound of distress. "My dear Miss Conway, as a gallerist and agent of artists, I beg you would let someone see them. Preferably someone who is in a position to help you make the most of them."

"And are you that someone, Mr. Cathcart?" Flora asked, despite Maisie trying to hush her.

"I hope I might be," Cathcart answered cheerfully. "I'd like to be. I'm with Mr. Christie's Auction House in London, but we represent a number of important Scottish artists."

"I told you about the lovely watercolor paintings of the city she's made from her window," Archie began. "Miss Conway has both an excellent eye and a kind, magnanimous heart. It is an irresistible combination."

Maisie felt assailed from all sides. "I specifically asked you not to—" She looked from Archie to Flora. "Both of you! They are unfinished."

"The paintings I saw are too good to let molder hidden away in your attic," Archie said.

"Not moldering," Maisie protested. "And it is not as if I keep the portraits—they are always finished and presented to the sitter."

"Speaking of which," Lady Cairn put in quickly, "I am all agog to get on your list—I hear Augusta Ivers has the honor of the next spot—but we are all anxiously awaiting our turns, Greer, Mignon and I.

First a lady, then a marchioness, and now a duchess and an important gallerist's wife. Maisie could see by the way Flora's eyes lit up that she was delighted by the prospect. "I'm sure Maisie will be happy to accommodate you," her sister pledged.

"Yes, my ladies, I should be honored," Maisie agreed. "But in the meantime, I have other work that must be finished first."

"And exhibited," Rory added sternly.

"I'm afraid I have nothing ready," Maisie began to give him the same excuse she had Mr. Hill.

"I protest that those charming watercolor scenes of the city are more than ready. You should see them," Archie explained to the others in the party. "They are brimming full of life. You'd recognize both the places and, I don't doubt, some of the characters. She's captured Jeanie's seamstresses coming out of Rose Street, their arms linked together with their sewing baskets swinging from the crooks of their elbows."

"Oh, by jimble!" Lady Cairn clapped her hands. "I must have that for Jeanie's shop! Jeanie Smith is a great favorite of mine—she was my lady's maid in my wildly misspent youth before she set up her own shop. And by the by, if you haven't found someone you like to make your dresses, I would be happy to offer you an introduction."

"How kind," Flora answered. "Is her shop the one with the embroidery samples on the south side of Rose Street?"

"Aye! South side to keep the sun off the fabrics in the window," the marchioness responded. "But I'm assuming your frocks are both London made, judging from their fineness. Your blue silk, especially, suits you perfectly, Maisie."

"Thank you, but the credit for both the choice of material and my appearance in it is all due to my sister—it's she who has the eye for fashion."

Flora, bless her, was just as generous with her praise. "While my sister has an eye for character and a talent to depict it. I think we all know which is the greater talent."

"Well put, Miss Flora," Lady Cairn approved before she turned back to Maisie. "We will certainly give each sister what they are due, but I cannot wholly believe that a woman who sees and recreates so much beauty in her art—Augusta Ivers has raved about your technique for depicting fabrics and eye for what she called insight into character—does not have an eye for color and fabric in her own dress."

It was a novel sensation to find she had been talked about—that her art had been discussed favorably. "Lady Ivers is too kind."

"Nonsense. We are none of us too kind, we Scots," Lady Cairn insisted. "We're a hard-headed and probably heard-hearted lot up here in Scotia. If she said it, it must be true. Now!" She clapped her hands together again. "We have heard fair praise of Archie—just as we should. And Archie has praised your work—just as he should. But now Archie, you must tell us what it is like to sit for our new friend Maisie and put yourself, quite literally, in her hands."

aisie felt her face flame so hot she feared the neckline of the silk might darken and char from the heat—cerulean and vermilion combusting to dark puce brown.

"Sitting for Miss Conway is…mostly quiet, but for the sounds of the city below coming up from the street and into her window, and the near-silent sound of her working," Archie said. "But perhaps I only fancy I can hear her charcoal making sketches, or her brush lapping into the paint and then brushing purposefully against the canvas, because I can't really see anything of her, hidden behind her easel. So, my imagination runs a bit wild."

Maisie felt as if everyone could hear her own breath, slewing wildly in and out of her chest.

"But *you* are silent the whole time?" The marchioness laughed in disbelief. "My dear Maisie, you appear to be working more than one miracle if you are making our garrulous friend be quiet, along with lending him an air of *gravitas* suitable for a portrait."

Maisie was moved to defend her subject. "We are not always quiet, for Lord Carrington has a great deal of interesting and intelligent conversation about the events of the day, but I did not have to give him any air—the *gravitas* is all his own. I only hope I will be able to do justice in capturing the force of his personality."

"Oh, brava!" Lady Cairn applauded quietly. "It would take a decidedly discerning eye to understand the force of our Archie's personality."

Maisie felt as if Lady Cairn could see right through her. The heat in her face and neck became nearly scalding—so scalding she judged it better not to make any response.

As the conversation went on around them, Lady Cairn lowered her voice to speak to Maisie alone. "If I may be so bold as to speak more privately, I sense an air of...caution about you, Maisie. As if... Forgive me, if I overstep, but that is what I do— overstep. But it is as if you have a secret you perhaps don't want any of us"—she cast a glance at Maisie's sister, Flora—"to know about."

Maisie hardly knew where to look or what to say. "I beg your pardon, my lady, I do not seek to conceal," she lied.

"No, do not think I criticize," Lady Cairn explained. "Quite the contrary. I might even say, I approve." This time, her ladyship cast a meaningful glance at Archie.

Maisie was definitely going to run out of red pigments. It was everything she could do to keep her gaze on her own hands and not risk her own glance at him, across the room as casual and easy-going as you please. As if he had not been teaching her the wonders of kissing—and more—less than twenty-four hours ago.

But the object of her illicit thoughts seemed to have the hearing of a fox, for he joined them. "I had a very good feeling that you two would enjoy each other's company. Maisie and I were just talking about the beggars the other day—"

"Beggars, you call them, as if that is all they are—parasites," the marchioness began with some spirit. "They—the wretched poor you see on every corner—are not lazy or stupid—"

"That fact is debatable." Lord Cairn joined their circle.

"It is not." His lady wife was adamant. "They are people.

People who would in most circumstances much rather be doing work, on their crofts and crafts and trades had not—"

Archie held up his hands in surrender. "I agree with Quince. As I also agreed with Maisie, who gave me a great deal of insight I did not have before. The economics of Edinburgh's poverty are complicated."

"Then un-complicate it for us, Archibald," Lord Cairn bade archly.

"What most of the beggars are is in debt. Especially the young. In debt to kidmen—for want of a better term for the villains who prey upon them when they first come to the city. The kidman—for most of his victims are younger—finds them and befriends them, or his minions do. And they'll give these young people a place to stay and food to eat out of the goodness of their heart. And they'll slip them a little something to keep the chills or blues at bay—a little gin to start and then it's just a taste of opium, and the next thing you know the lad's addicted and then begging on the corner he's assigned by the kidman as a way to work off the debt he's accrued in housing and food and above all liquor or narcotics. It's a predatory, vicious cycle that turns a huge profit that then goes into other things that drive the economy."

"I had no idea about the opium. That is worse than even I imagined," Lady Cairn put in. "And I already imagined it was awful.

"It is indeed, but it's a business. That's what no one, especially the esteemed town fathers and lawmakers, seems to grasp with any kind of proper understanding."

"Then you should write an essay," Lady Cairn declared. "No, a whole series, in that newspaper of yours exposing the practice."

Archie smiled. "Actually, I asked Maisie to do just that."

All eyes that had conveniently forgotten her during the course of the conversation, turned back to Maisie. "I declined," she demurred. "Lord Carrington is much better placed."

"I suppose, I am," he admitted. "But I don't know who the

kidmen are, and have had the devil of a time trying to find out. I have no real connections or informants in the world of crime—nor have I ever cultivated any, for it's a damn dicey business, with lives on the line."

"You must instigate an investigation," the marchioness urged. "Surely there are some suitably stout-hearted fellows amongst those rough and tumble rogues your call your scribes, who wouldn't object to rubbing shoulders with the criminal element?"

Archie's frown deepened before he returned his regard to Maisie, "Agnes, your tweeny, was one of those children? And Fergus, her brother? Perhaps I should talk to them?"

"I don't suppose that could hurt." And it certainly might help. Anything to help the children ought to be encouraged.

"What else have you got planned in your latest issue, Archie?" Lord Cairn asked. "I like to anticipate any trouble you're going to stir up before the pot goes on the boil, as my wife would say."

The gentlemen moved back toward the liquor cabinet and Maisie was once again left alone with the marchioness.

"I am glad to find a fellow rebellious spirit in you, Maisie," Lady Cairn confided. "A spirit I share."

"Do you, my lady?" Maisie hardly knew what to say. She had often thought herself defiant and stubborn—and had been told she was those things often enough to believe it—but never rebellious.

"Oh, yes. Perhaps when we know each other a little better I will convince you of my *bona fides*, but for now—" Lady Cairn sat back on the divan and looked at Maisie with a serious, but very kind eye. "—leave it to say, I would like to be your friend, whenever you might need one."

Gratitude made a lump of Maisie's throat. "Thank you." This was all clearly for Archie's sake, but as Maisie had never before been offered friendship under the aegis of another, she was grateful.

"You are most welcome," Lady Quince was all sincere

graciousness. "And not to be too interfering, but if you find yourself in need of a…shall we say, a married woman's frank advice, *vis a vis* our mutual friend, Archie, please know that I am neither judgmental, nor a prude. I am instead, happy to be your friend."

Gratitude gave way to absolute astonishment. "Thank you," Maisie said, because she had to say something.

But she had never felt so exposed.

Or so hopeful.

Flora had been right—Edinburgh had been a new start. Maisie had met new people and had begun new and wonderful work. Work that she was proud of—work she would be proud to show others. Because it was work that satisfied—work that pleased her eye as well as her mind. That embodied the finest balance between thought and execution, between her conceptual idea and the painting before her.

And she needed to keep right on doing. Despite what she had told Archie, her vantage point over the busy corner was no longer sufficient to satisfy her curiosity.

Agnes, with her wildly sad eyes and her faraway gaze, was a perfect Mary the Madonna, or Mary Magdelene, but she could not be every saint Maisie needed. But there were so many others: the New Testament heroines of Martha, Tabitha and Lydia. Old testament matriarchs, Sarah and Ruth. The clever and queenly Esther.

So many saints, so little opportunity.

No, not opportunities, for the city was open to her each and every day.

All she needed was nerve.

CHAPTER 21

"Agnes!" Maisie called the next morning. "How well do you know the city?"

Agnes looked up from cleaning brushes. "Aye, missus? What d'ye need?"

"Direction. And accompaniment. And companionship. As well as your two strong arms and legs." She had a small portable painting box she had last used some years ago in Richmond. Where had she stored it? "There! Take that box off the shelf. No —the light-colored wooden box, not the dark one—that one is medicine we don't need. The light-colored box is a traveling paint kit. And that folded up easel behind—yes, that thing that looks like a parcel of folded sticks."

"Here y'are, missus." Agnes glanced at Maisie's face as she handed over the kit. "Ye sure are het up 'aboot a clarty old chest."

"I am, indeed, for that little chest is our means to a day out. We're going to put that chest in a pony cart—which I hope you can lead." If the wicker governess cart had made it with them to Scotland and hadn't been sold along with the piles of other household goods that had been deemed too much trouble to bring north.

Her father had originally purchased the small governess's cart as an aid to Maisie's convalescence, all those years ago. Fresh air had been deemed beneficial, even if riding had been forbidden. But with Papa subsequently gone off on his work travels, the cart had somehow been deemed the purview of Mrs. Smyth, who had used it to get around Richmond—after she had decreed it too fast and too dangerous for Maisie or Flora's use.

But no matter if the cart were still there—they would find another way if need be. "We're going out!"

"Are we?" Agnes didn't know what to make of this idea. "Where to, missus?"

"The Grassmarket," Maisie enthused. "Where I found you—I want to paint the most interesting people we can find. I want to paint them, much as I've painted you."

"Nae the Grassmarket, surely?" the girl protested.

"And why not?" Maisie heard the hesitation in Agnes' voice—and too late, she remembered Agnes's bruised, blackened eyes.

Agnes hung her head. "I want tae keep well clear o' there, missus. Don't want tae give them lot any chance o' finding me."

"Then we shan't go there," Maisie decided. "We'll find somewhere else."

"Happen we could wander o'er Cannon Mills way?" Agnes readily pointed out the window toward the tip of green countryside peeking over the rooftops to the north. "There's a distillery there, just a ways down frae the village. But it looks so nice and green. Reminds me o' Prestonpans and home. Happen ye'd find sommat worth lookin' fer there?"

"Happen we will try, Agnes." Maisie rewarded her suggestion with a smile. "It certainly can't hurt to try."

And off they went at a snail's pace, with Agnes leading the docile pony and Maisie riding comfortably in the neat wicker basket. But productive snails they were—that prostitute Maisie had seen dozing against the doorway on Vennel Street had a comrade in arms, if not legs, sitting on the stoop of a cottage at

Stockbridge Crossing, who made an exceptional foolish virgin lamenting letting her lamp go out before the bridegroom had arrived, and was easily bribed by the pennies Maisie sent over by Agnes to stand still at least long enough for Maisie to complete her sketch.

The marketplace at Cannon Mills Loch proved her best ground—the wide-open space gave excellent light reflected off the water of the small loch, while the denizens of the modest village provided her with no shortage of shopkeepers' wives willing to spend a quarter hour in their doorways, while Maisie turned them into biblical matriarchs and prophetesses.

So busy was she that she didn't note the passage of time until the afternoon light began to wane and the excitement and energy that had pushed her out of her aerie ran flat, leaving her depleted. Thank goodness for Agnes's wiry pluck—she made no objection to loading up the equipment by herself, before leading the pony and cart back up the hill to Kirk Brae Head.

"Will we do it again, missus?" she asked. "Them ostler lads at the inn all wanted a go at posing for ye. Ye'll have no shortage of takers the next time we go out, I've no doubt. Word'll get round."

"That sounds like a very good plan indeed, Agnes. You are a commendable artist's agent. But I fear we shall have to put off our next exhibition for at least a few days, while I see about transferring these ideas from the watercolor sketches to canvas and oil."

"Like the paintings yer after making o' Fergus an' me?"

"Very much like. Oh, and look at the sky," she exclaimed as she cast a glance back toward the northwest. "What an excellent day." Which would turn into an excellent evening, if they could slip in by the stable gate in the gathering dusk without a fuss.

But such a thing was not to be, as the housekeeper, Mrs. Smyth, seemed to have stationed herself at the top of the kitchen stairs in wait like an unlit beacon, unseen until they were nearly upon her. "Pardon me, Miss Conway, but your father bid me ask you to attend him in his book room."

Maisie started, but kept her composure. "Certainly, Mrs. Smyth. Agnes, please take the equipment up to my studio and put it away. You know what to do. And thank you for your excellent help today, Agnes. Well done."

"Aye, thank ye, Miss Conway," Agnes said very correctly, before she curtseyed and went up.

Mrs. Smyth pressed her lips together in a seam, but couldn't hold her tongue. "These stairs are certainly the best place for these backward girls, but surely the front door and stairs would be far more suitable for a member of the household, Miss Conway?"

And there was that ungenerous nature. Maisie had been surprised—and frankly annoyed—when Smyth had insisted on accompanying them north to Scotland when the house in Richmond had been sold, even though she complained bitterly under her breath about everything from the weather to the unmannerly inhabitants of their new city.

"Am I interfering with the flow of servants?" Maisie asked instead of answering.

"No, Miss Conway," the housekeeper admitted.

"These narrower stairs are easier for me, Mrs. Smyth, since I can pull myself up by the handrail whilst bracing my other arm against the wall. You see—" Maisie gave a demonstration of her technique. "And here, I'm not as…conspicuous." That should appeal to the woman's barely disguised opinion that Maisie was best kept from public view. "The front stairs are a better stage for Miss Flora, not me."

Smyth pursed her mouth again but couldn't think of any way to object to such a logical explanation. "I will inform his lordship of your preference, Miss Conway."

"Thank you, Mrs. Smyth." Maisie was unfailingly civil—antagonism did no good with a character like Smyth. "Just let my father concentrate on Miss Flora and leave me to fend happily for myself up and down the back stair. We'll all be happier that way."

"If you say so, Miss Conway."

"I do." Maisie smiled politely. "That will be all, Mrs. Smyth, thank you."

"Yes, Miss Conway."

Maisie took a deep breath to let the tense, wary feeling Smyth always managed to engender in her fade away. She would not let the woman's disapproval ruin what had been a lovely productive day.

So many new faces. So many new ideas for apostles, prophets and saints—she really ought to see if she could sketch Mr. Hill. Perhaps a quick visit to his shop would suffice to render him as St. Peter. Or the Angel Gabriel acting as God's messenger—

Yes!

As if she had conjured the apparition from her imagination, he appeared above, entering onto the narrow landing above from the first floor.

No, Maisie chided herself. It was more likely only a servant coming down from her father's book room on some errand.

But the figure wasn't going down—he was heading up, climbing swiftly upward past the second-floor apartments, upward toward her attic, where no servants but Agnes were welcome. Her father, then, deigning to come up to her aerie to chide her about something when he had never done so before?

She had hoped to change into cleaner, more presentable clothes before facing him, but perhaps if he saw her studio and some of her paintings, he might be less inclined to think so little of her work.

"Papa!" she called up. "If you'll but give me a minute or two—" But the tail of the coat she had seen disappearing around the turn of the stairs wasn't the plain broadcloth of her father's everyday coats—it was velvet black. "Archie?"

But what would Archie be doing sneaking up the stairs to her aerie from her father's book room. Had he come to speak to Papa? Was that why Papa wanted to see her?

Misgivings—and something far more alarming and rewarding —gripped her like a fist, stealing her breath and drowning out all other thought. Why else would he—

"Maisie?" Footsteps pattered rapidly downward. And then Archie appeared, smiling as if nothing were wrong. "There you are!"

Here she was. With him. So why didn't she feel any relief? "What were you doing?"

"Looking for you," he said as if it were the most obvious thing in the world.

"On your own?" She could not shake the uneasy feeling. "Just wandering around the house?"

"I was looking for you," he repeated, easily. "Why, what is wrong?"

"Nothing," she lied, because she could find nothing to say in support of her unease. "Why are you here? We had no appointment today."

"I know," he admitted, reaching for her hand to lead her upward to her aerie. "But I wanted to see you anyway."

"Did you?" The idea seemed newly astonishing—despite what he had last said to her, she hardly knew what to think or feel.

"Have you not wanted to see me?"

"Perhaps," she hedged, knowing she ought to be wary, but giving in to the warmth of his regard anyway.

"Just, perhaps?" His smile was somehow both roguish and sincere. "I couldn't get you off my mind. Or more specifically, what you wanted off my mind." He smiled, that sly clever, amused fox smile. "To pose *nudo*." He pronounced the Italian word with relish, as if it filled his mouth with flavor.

"Ah." Her mouth was suddenly dry, but all traces of her

previous exhaustion vanished—unless she counted her ability to make a well-considered decision.

No. The daring that had prompted her to accept his earlier proposition had been replaced by clearer, more rational thinking. "As tempted as I am by your manifest charms, my lord—"

"Archie, while I am offering to make my charms manifest," he teased. "I left off my waistcoat and cravat in the hopes they wouldn't be needed."

"Archie." It was pain and pleasure once again—but mostly pleasure. "I cannot keep wasting time and pigment on an illicit portrait that will need to be painted over." And she certainly ought not even entertain such an idea with her father seeking to speak to her.

"Why not paint two portraits?" he countered. "One for public view—although who is to say if I want a clothed version of myself? Perhaps I prefer to be painted nude?"

"Archie, be serious."

"I won't tell if you won't," he came closer to whisper. "It can be our secret."

As tempting as that sounded, Maisie was old enough—and even though she did not have much experience of the world—wise enough to know that secrets had an insidious way of not being kept.

"Archie, it is already known that I am meant to be painting your portrait—your illustrious friends, not to mention my family, all expect me to furnish a portrait of Lord Carrington, youngest-ever editor of the Edinburgh Review, appropriately dressed, not indulge myself with a nude painting of my friend Archie."

His smile was slow and spreading and entirely sulfurous. "Then why not just make a nude *study* of your very good friend, Archie." He smiled. "A drawing in the style of the *invenzione?*"

That offer was too tempting to refuse. She had kept all her other drawings private—why should she not keep any life studies she made private as well? And her father had never yet ventured to her aerie—the changes of him doing so were so slim as to be non-existent.

And any chance to see Archie Carrington as she had first envisioned him would be worth the risk.

"Just so." She took a deep breath. "I accept your proposal." Maisie felt breathless with the hazard of her decision, but light and thrilled and full of anticipatory delight. She made her careful way to the door to the attic and flipped closed the latch. "You may safely strip. *Spagliato.*"

"Brava, Maisie." That he was astonished by her showed only for a moment in the lofting of his eyebrows, for in another moment he began the slow growing smile that looked calculated to melt hearts. Or moral fortitude.

But she was made of sterner stuff. "I would have thought you pleased."

"Oh, I am." His puckish smile spread across his face in a slash of gleaming teeth. "And so will you be."

"Will I?" She moved to drag the small chaise she had been using in posing both Agnes and Fergus into the bay of light.

Archie quickly came to her aid, picking up the upholstered sofa as if it weighed nothing.

"Just there," she instructed with what she hoped was a normal voice, but knew must be tight with nervy excitement. "Where the light can warm you."

There was a very long moment when he did nothing, but was entirely still—the way she fancied a bomb was in the last moment before it blew off. And then he moved with a swiftness that would have left her breathless had she any concept of how to breathe.

His coat he shucked first, shaking it off his shoulders impatiently, the way a fox shakes rainwater from his fur. Then the linen shirtsleeves, dispatched over the top of his head, baring the rangy expanse of his chest, before his nimble, beautifully articulated fingers went to the buttons of his breeches, loosed one by one, until the breeks were sagging from the now-exposed ridge of his hips.

He sat before anything more pressing might be revealed, tugging off his boots and sliding down his stockings, which he tossed on the growing pile of discarded clothing. And then he stood.

And locked his eyes upon hers. And smiled.

And then, as she stood there holding what little was left of her shredded breath, he shucked off the rest.

CHAPTER 22

*M*aisie hardly knew where to look—except that she knew exactly where her curiosity bid her look. So she did.

She kept her own mouth studiously straight while she took in the sight of him, from the tip of his toes, up those impressively shaped calves to even more impressively shaped thighs.

Maisie was astonished into speech. "My Lord."

"Call me Archie whilst you're ogling me, if you please."

"I was complimenting your divine maker, Archie." She would not be embarrassed out of this opportunity—she certainly might never have another. "I promise not to ogle, only to observe."

"Can you not do both?"

Heaven help her, she could. She was.

"Yes," was all she could manage as she reached for her charcoal. "If I may be so bold, *Archie*"—she took pleasure in teasing out his name just as he had so often teased her—"Could you just perhaps bend one knee, slightly? And put one hand on your hip, if you will, to draw your shoulder back and your—" Her vocabulary nearly failed her. "—other hip, forward?"

The asymmetry of the positions of his legs and shoulders

would give the composition balance, and she hoped, make it easier for him to stand for her longer. A very long time.

He smiled at her suggestion, all knowing, vulpine delight. "*Contrapposto?*"

Trust Archie to know the formal term. "Your tutors would be impressed." Her hands flew across the paper, capturing the astonishing beautiful, arcing juxtaposition of muscles around the curve of his hip bone.

"I only care about impressing you," he told her.

"Oh, I am," she confessed even as she knew her cheeks were colored deep madder pink. "Deeply, gloriously impressed." She recorded that impression with a thick sweep of charcoal, capturing him in all his glory.

And when she looked back, the strangest thing happened—his eyes shuttered closed, as if he were unwell, or overcome. His cheeks colored the deep shade of cinnabar, and his member grew ruddy and stiff before her gaze. And his hand, which had been hanging loosely by his side seemed to rise of its own volition to brush up the underside of his now proud phallus.

And then his eyes were open, looking straight into hers. "As a gentleman, I'm sure I ought to apologize, but I find I cannot apologize for nature. I want you, Maisie."

Maisie found it difficult to breathe, much less speak, with such heat coursing through her body. "Is that what happens, naturally?"

"When I am aroused," he answered in a low voice. "Usually by the sight, but more often lately, by the mere thought of a pretty, talented, curious lass. By you."

"But I—" She would have protested her involvement in this arousal of his, but she knew very well she had asked to ogle him —this must be the natural result.

"You," he confirmed. "And only you." But then he cocked his head to one side and asked, "And you?"

She hardly knew—the sensations arising from the moment

were so new. "I could not say aroused, exactly." Certainly, she found herself in some state of excitement, not the least from the forbidden circumstance of drawing him naked. Yet she found herself looking at his body more dispassionately than he suggested. "I doubt if I were allowed to walk up the steps of the academy in Rome, or Paris or London, and gaze upon a similarly fine specimen of a man—"

"So you think I'm a fine specimen of a man?"

"Assuredly," she explained. "But I doubt I would find myself attracted, or aroused, by the mere sight of a man I didn't know."

"Mere?"

"There is little mere about you, Archie," she assured him.

"Are you humoring me?"

"I am trying to explain that while the sight of you is very interesting"—she chose her words carefully—"it is not especially *arousing*."

His head tipped to the other side, considering. "Were you aroused when I was kissing and touching you?"

She could name it then, that sensation that once again coiled deep in her belly—this glorious tension that came from within and spread its touch under her skin from her fingers to her toes —at the memory of the moment his hand had covered her mons. "Yes."

His smile grew kinder, but no less intent. "Would you like me to kiss and touch you now?"

"Not just yet." Because it seemed she didn't actually need him to touch her to feel the same erotic effect—all he had to do was remind her.

And she wasn't willing to stop drawing him yet. She wasn't willing to give up the spectacular sight of him as God made him for a feeling she might create on her own again if she thought of the moment his fingers had touched her through the intervening layers of her clothes.

The mere thought brought a flush to her skin.

And excitement to her fingers. "Not when I might draw your buttocks." Their shape, nearly round, but somehow also angular along the line of his flank, took some concentration to render correctly.

"Coward," he teased.

"Exhibitionist," she countered.

He laughed. Which was a spectacular thing—he threw his head back to loose the laugh and his stomach muscles jumped and capered from his chest down to his loins. "Oh, certainly." He touched himself again, unselfconsciously. "You see how it is."

"I do see," she confirmed.

"And what, my sweet, highly observant Maisie, are you going to do about that?"

"Observe." For now. "I am going to ask you to turn around, so I might turn my *exacting gaze* upon the intriguing shape of your shockingly fine behind."

"Be my guest." He turned to give her what she had asked for— a view of his rather spectacular backside. And then, as if he already understood the power of memory and words, he bade, "Tell me what you see?"

"You," she said simply, her hands too busy to let her mind alone. "If you will let me look."

"I will let you look to your heart's content if you talk to me— so I can think about you when I can't see you."

Maisie's hand stilled. "Does that mean that you are not...as aroused when you can't see me?"

"Perhaps," he admitted. "But not really."

"How intriguing." Her hands took up their profession again, shaping the long slide of taut muscle tapering down the back of his legs on the paper. "You get a physical feeling of arousal when you see things—"

"Not things—you," he corrected simply.

"How interesting," she commented, and set her fingers skimming down the page, delineating the teardrop shape of his calves dissolving into the singular line of his tendon.

"Whereas I see things without getting a feeling—only when you make me feel, do I get aroused."

"Say that again."

"You seem to get a physical—"

"No," he interrupted. "Tell me what arouses you?"

Maisie thought about it for a moment. "When you look at me in that way you have."

"What way?" He looked at her over his shoulder.

"As if you like what you see. No," she amended. "As if you see *me*. Really see me, for who I want to be. Not just some…lame spinster painter."

"Maisie. I do see you," he swore. "The same way you see me as the man I want to be."

She started to answer that she didn't want to be anybody but herself, but the moment she thought the words, she knew they were not true—that she had wanted to be any number of people over the past fourteen years. Anybody but her own lame, damaged self. But in the last few days with Archie, she hadn't felt that way at all.

"What else?" he asked. "How else can I make you feel…?"

"When you say things to me," she said immediately. "Things you'd like to do." Her voice strangled itself into a whisper. "Or see."

"Ah," he said as if that made all the sense in the world. "Like how I'd like to see and touch every inch of you beneath that gloriously shapeless smock?" He closed his eyes and tipped his face up to the heavens. "How I'd like to undo every single button, one after the other, all the way down from your neck, until they were all gloriously open? And then how I'd like to peel it away from your body and discover you like a land I've only dreamed of visiting?"

She had to force herself to breathe before she could answer, "Yes."

There was another, longer moment of silence before she heard his intake of breath. "And what makes you want to be touched?"

Maisie thought about that more a long moment, her hand poised over her paper. "When I'm done drawing, may I..." She swallowed, not out of any sort of embarrassment, for her gaze was clear and focused. She knew what she wanted. "May I touch you?"

ARCHIE FELT AS IF HE HAD BEEN WAITING HIS WHOLE LIFE TO HEAR her question. "I wish to God you would."

His skin felt tight and fresh in the chill of the attic as he drew in a great lungful of air and let his chest expand in his first full breath in minutes.

He had been aroused simply by watching her draw. Watching as she pushed a strand of her her gingery hair, half-fallen out of the proper knot at the back of her head, behind her ear, smearing her temple and cheekbone with the red stick of color she was using to make her drawing. She hadn't paused to notice—her hands danced across the pad he could not see.

He had watched as her eyes darted down slightly. "Yes," she had half muttered. Or at least he thought she did, as she rubbed at the paper, making shushing sounds. He had watched as she pressed her lips together and chewed to the side of her cheeks, looking by turns displeased and anxious and eager all at the same time.

Finally, she blinked and saw him, as if she were again awaking from slumber.

"Please, do. Touch me everywhere." His answer didn't so much catch him unaware—he knew he was attracted to her—as surprise him by its intensity. He felt the need like a hot coal in his own chest.

Maisie set down her charcoal, carefully putting it away in her box, replacing the lid, and wiping her hands on both a clean rag, and then, on the skirts of her smock as she approached him.

His body was practically vibrating in anticipation.

She touched her hand to his elbow first, nearly drawing back at his reactive twitch, but when he moved his arm into the weight of her hand, she smoothed her fingers against the back of his arm, moving higher around the curve of his muscles and over the top of his shoulder.

A world of sensation grew from beneath the surface of his skin. It was everything he could do to stand still beneath her exploration, to hold his need—to touch her skin, to hold her tight, to taste her essence—in abeyance.

But hold himself still he did. Because he had pledged her this opportunity and he owed her at least these few moments. So he swallowed his pride and his aching need and put himself, quite literally, into her hands.

She trailed the soft pads of her fingers from his shoulder down the seam of his spine slowly—the muscles in his back contracted and released one by one in turn. But when her inquisitive hand turned to trace the curve of his waist, along the belt of muscle that divided his hip from his leg, he felt his resolve begin to crack.

But it did not crumble. Not yet. Not until she came around in front of him and her cool, curious, articulate fingers curled into the dark springy hair at his groin at the same time that she glanced up to meet his eye.

His eyes crashed shut—it was too much. Too much to see her and feel her and want her all at the same time. He had to limit his losses, ration his endurance, parse out his patience.

"Yes," was the only articulate word he could push from his suddenly sluggish brain.

And she did as he had somehow bid and rounded her palm under the base of his cock.

"Yes," he said again to ease some of the hunger growling its way out of his chest. "Take hold. By all means," he encouraged.

And when she did and her hand closed around his cock, he was sure he had never felt such perfect, unadulterated bliss. He clenched his hands into fists at his side to keep from putting them on her. To keep from gripping her hands to teach her how to fist his cock up tight.

"So soft," she whispered against his chest.

And it was all he could do not to laugh at his own bemusement. "That, my clever, curious woman, is most assuredly not soft." He let out a breath. "That, under your excellent tutelage, has gone decidedly hard." And harder still when she closed her grasp and squeezed ever so sweetly. "God, yes."

"You like that."

"Yes," he admitted without hesitation. "The only thing I should like more—" The effort to think and speak and still feel left him short of breath. "—is to bury my cock inside you." He dragged in an unsteady breath. "And that will only happen if you want me to. And only when you ask me to." And another deep breath. "And that can only happen when I make you feel the same way you are currently making me feel—like heaven."

"I feel that way when you kiss me," she offered.

He kissed her. He took her face in his hands and held her lips to his and kissed her with every ounce of his thwarted desire. Every inch of feeling in his body. Every hope of passion between them.

And she was kissing him back, opening her sweet little mouth, wrapping her arms about his neck, and pressing those luscious little breasts of hers against his bare chest.

They kissed and kissed, tangling tongues, tasting, biting and sucking at each other with hedonistic abandon until all he could think of was putting his hands to her stays, and lowering her bodice so he might put his mouth, if not his hands, to what he was sure would prove to be the delicate pink whorl of her nipple.

"I want to see you," he confessed against her ear. "Just as you have seen me. I want to feel you, just as you have touched me. I want to touch you and taste you and—"

He stopped before he could actually say the words clanging like a struck gong in the back of his head. Before he said exactly how long and how well and in how many varied positions he wanted to fuck her.

He settled for, "I want you very much."

"I—" She had to catch her breath. "I think—" She calmed her breath. "I think I want to think about that."

"I understand," he said. Because he did. Because he had to. He had to go slowly and carefully and think and know what he was doing before he plowed ahead and did it.

He had to choose as carefully as she.

Because the key to her father's desk was burning a hole in the pocket of the pants he was no longer wearing. And he no longer knew what he was going to do about that.

CHAPTER 23

The key was actually burning a hole in his conscience.

The flexible morals he had joked about had come back to haunt him—just like the key, which he had snatched up from her father's desk when he had heard someone coming. Even though he had no idea just what it was the key to.

Maisie set herself away from him, taking a moment to recover her composure, while he attempted to do the same—which was damned difficult without clothes on.

And so he gathered up his scattered clothing from the floor and began to get dressed. He focused on the small, unimportant details—the tie on the waist of his small clothes, the button at the throat of his linen shirt, the pulls on the cuff of his boots—until he was clothed and composed enough to speak to her.

"I hope you got what you needed," he said, gesturing to the loose sheaf of drawings now scattered on her work table, though he could have been talking of any number of things between them.

"Yes," she said, though her cheeks pinked up in rueful embarrassment. "Very much so. More, even."

"Happy to be of help," he tried. And he was, genuinely happy

—thrilled to be with her. Which made him all the more miserable.

"Happy to have been instructed," she teased.

"Maisie, I—" None of the words he kept at the ready in his brain seemed adequate to the moment. None of his feelings were articulate enough to be spoken. "Thank you for the gift of this time. For the gift of your trust. Until next time."

"Until next time," she echoed, and there was just enough warmth and pleasure in her voice to give him hope.

Hope that he had not endangered everything he felt for this singular young woman by taking the key that now dug into his flesh like a thorn, reminding him he had a job to do.

Archie kissed her on the cheek, straightened his clothes, and stole back out onto the landing. There, he took a long minute there to take stock and listen.

Below, the house was slipping into an afternoon lull—the maids' to-ing and fro-ing subsided. The footmen put out cutlery with civilized, subdued clinks of silver and clanks of glass. From the kitchen at the bottom of the stair came a low hum of activity that signaled that luncheon would soon be served.

Sir Richard would shortly vacate his book room. And return Archie to the activity he had been engaging in before he had stripped off his kit for Maisie Conway as a way to distract her from her all-too-pressing questions about what he had been doing abroad in the house.

Going over her father's study would have been the honest answer, pocketing the key to the desk drawers when he had heard approaching footsteps and exiting out the nearest door, which turned out to be the servants' stair.

He had thought to take advantage of her absence to have a poke about the aerie, as she called it, to see if there was anything there that might give him any clues into her father's past.

Until he heard her call from below.

But what he had glimpsed in the study before he had been forced to abandon his search, made him anxious to return.

"All done then the day, sir?" It was the garrulous young tweeny, making her way up.

"Ah, Agnes, lass!" Archie greeted her. "Ye're just the one I hoped to see. Your mistress informed me of her intention to take a nap," he lied.

"A nap, sir?" the lass asked. "Aye, then, she'll have worked all the night."

"And a good part of the morning," he added for good measure, though his conscience pricked him like a thorn for his part of her morning's labors. But needs must when the devil drove.

"Agnes, lass, do you think you could do me a bit of a favor? I've a little something that fell into my hands that needs to get put back." He held up both the key and tuppence, which she took in one hand, as if she dared not refuse. "And after that, I've a question or two for ye and yer brother out there, Fergus." He held up another coin. "Do ye think ye could answer them for me?"

"Aye, sir. Why not?"

MAISIE WAS SO ENTIRELY TAKEN UP WITH HER PRIVATE DRAWINGS OF Archie, she worked on nothing else, filling her sketchbooks with one rendition after another of his sculptural form.

She neglected his portrait, not wanting to add anything that would later have to be painted over. But the sketches she drew from her mind's eye gave her ample scope for study—both of the anatomy of the human body and the workings of the mortal heart.

Because she was well and truly smitten—she was falling in love with Archie Carrington.

The acceleration of her heartbeat when his boots were heard on the stair was only the latest proof.

He burst through the door like a fresh breeze, clearing all before it. "Maisie!"

"Archie," was her more subdued greeting. "Do come in." She hastened to shut the door behind him before she headed to her easel. "Let's see if we can manage to get any real work done today."

"Real work?" He laughed before he paused, frowning. "Are you all to rights? You're …different today."

"Am I?" she asked, reflexively. "I'm just a little tired—all these late nights drawing and painting."

"Late nights?" His slow spreading smile returned. "Dare I ask if you've been having trouble sleeping? Is it all the thinking about kissing, sweet Maisie?"

"Does that mean you've been thinking about kissing, too"—her own voice fell to an intimate whisper—"Archie?"

"Aye. All about kissing, Maisie. And more."

"More?"

"Yes, more." His smile was all contented, soft, sly fox as he prowled closer. "But kissing first. How would you like to be kissed, do you think, Maisie?" He queried close to her ear. "Hard and fast, or soft and slow?"

"Must it be one or the other? Can it not be hard and slow?"

"Oh, such a good question and a very good choice indeed. And yes, yes it can be hard and slow." He reached out, with his palm up, waiting for her to bestow her hand. And when she did so, he brought her palm to his lips, pressing a kiss to the sensitive spot at the soft bend of her wrist. "Never thought the faint scent of linseed oil and turpentine would be such an aphrodisiac. But then again, I never bargained on falling for a painter."

Maisie felt as if the world faded away into nothingness around her. Even her very breath felt suspended, as if she were falling and floating all at the same time even though he was the one who had 'fallen for' her. "What do you mean?"

"I mean I want to kiss and taste and smell every inch of your body. I want to delve into every soft, sweet, scented part of you, from the crook of your elbow to that delicate spot behind your ear, to other less accessible, more arcane spots."

"Arcane?" She wanted to laugh but her breath was already coming in shorter pants as his words sent arousal sliding under her skin and swirling deep into her belly.

"Unknown. Mysterious. Secret," he whispered to that spot on the side of her neck he had just mentioned. "All your secret places."

Her heart was going to collapse in her chest from the suspense. "Such as?"

"Ah." He drew out the sound like a sigh. As he came to stand behind where she was perched—rather precariously, she now thought—on her stool. His hands encircled her. "Like these well-hidden beauties." He swept his palm across her bodice, and beneath the layers of chemise and stays and dress and smock, her skin went taut with awareness. A need that was barely assuaged by the passage of his thumbs across the slight swell of her breasts above the edge of her bodice.

She felt her body moving of its own accord, arching into the curve of his hand, wanting some greater contact.

And then he gave it to her—but it an entirely surprising way.

He swept the flat of his palm down, across the scoop of her tummy, pressing inward until she felt the rounded point of her stays press into the flesh of her belly. And then lower still, until his hand was cupping her at the juncture of her thighs, heating her with the warmth of his palm through the intervening layers of fabric and clothing. "Where we left off—here," he whispered. "Arcane, sacred and profane. And if I had to guess, never yet explored. Such a crime." His voice insinuated its way under her skin and into her bones and sinews until they all melded together deep within her. "A sin to stay so unknown. So unloved."

And while one hand cupped and pressed, impressing her own needs upon herself, the other rounded her breast, teasing her with pressure and pleasure until her nipples peaked inside her clothes.

A sibilant sound of pleasure escaped her lips, and he bent his head to press a sweet kiss to the corner of her mouth, even as she mustered her response. "I don't think—"

"Don't think. Feel."

"I am feeling," she assured him on a gasp. "I am feeling there is a very great difference between kissing and your arcana."

"That is where you are wrong, my sweet Maisie. Because kissing is a deeply arcane art." His mouth found hers, confident and brash and wily and sure. So sure, she felt as if his strength was the only thing holding her up. Because she couldn't feel her knees. She could only feel the smooth, rough texture of his lips and taste the tang of whisky-laced coffee on his tongue. She could only hear the rush of her breathing and feel the delight of her body warming to his.

He broke the kiss by whispering, "Let me show you more."

Her body said yes, while her mind tried for sanity. But the truth was, she was never going to be courted the way Flora was. Archie was never going to get married—at least not to her. What did it matter if she salvaged an hour or two of passion and pleasure with this clearly passionate, clearly pleasurable man?

No one could stop her. No one but herself.

Archie felt her hesitation and guessed at her misgivings. "Do you trust me?" he finally asked.

"No. Not really," she answered honestly. "But I trust myself. And I trust my choices. And what I want is for you to show me exactly how you can kiss me—"

He stopped her speech by picking her up and carrying her to the door where he set her back against the portal. "It ought to be locked," he said without taking his eyes from hers. "So we're not interrupted this time."

She reached over her shoulder and shot the bolt through the hasp. "No interruptions."

"Agreed," He kissed her hard, pressing her back into the oaken panel, leaning his weight into her. "It's a good stout door, is it?"

"Yes," she managed.

"Then I think—" He stepped back and as he trailed his large strong hand down the length of her torso, he knelt before her, "we put that to the test."

There was something wicked and wild about his kneeling before her. Something decidedly carnal about the way he laid his hands on her thighs. Something that both delighted and scared her all at the same time.

She swallowed. "Will it hurt?"

"No, lass. Only please. I give you my word." And there was that smile of his—sly and nearly cunning in its focused intent.

The low words sent her already hectic pulse pounding in her veins. "And what exactly is it you are about to do?"

"What I'm about to do is make you come." The twinkling laughter left his face as he looked at her solemnly. "But if you don't want to, if you should like me to stop, even for a moment, or call a halt, you have only to say so." His smile softened the wicked corners of his dark eyes. "But I am confident, my sweet Maisie, that you will find everything—and I mean every thing— to your liking."

Everything within her stopped and started and tensed and eased all at the same time. She didn't know when she had ever felt so uneasy and excited all at the same time.

Because, she realized, she trusted him. His words alone seemed to enflame her in a way that was different than the sight of his body. Even if she wasn't quite sure what he meant.

"Then by all means, make me come."

CHAPTER 24

*B*ut he seemed to be done talking, because he slowly—so slowly that she felt herself taking a deep inhalation, as if she might draw courage in like a breath—hauled up the hem of her skirts.

For a quick moment she wished she was wearing something nicer, or more feminine, or at least less workaday than her felt slippers and short, warm woolen stockings, but all thought fled when his clever fingers found the sensitive skin at the back of her knees.

The effect of that first touch was instantaneous—she had to be kissing him. She had to be pressing her lips to his and opening her mouth to him. She had to be taking his lapels and pulling him closer. But she could not. "Archie."

"Easy—we've just barely begun." He pressed a kiss to the inside of her knee. "Steady on, lass."

"Archie," she said, because she had kept herself from saying it for so long, until it had echoed around and around her head, day after each more interesting day.

"Maisie," he murmured against her thigh and everything within her, every ounce of her blood and every inch of her skin went hot and tingly with anticipation. As if her body knew what her mind did not—that she had been longing to hear her name whispered so softly and intimately.

"Yes," she said, as if that would hurry things along. And because she was still herself even if she was desperately aroused, she asked, "Why is it taking so long?"

He was unperturbed by her urgency. "Oh, no, lass. I'm going to be taking my sweet time with you. Hard and slow, you wanted. You'll see." But he took her plea for the permission it was, delving his tongue into the crease of her thigh as he exposed another inch or so of her body to the chilly morning air.

Her breath left her lungs in a whoosh and came back to land there, where his hands and his mouth came together to touch her intimately.

Maisie tried to lean back into the solid surety of the door at the same time she leaned into him, into the warmth and ease the tension his tongue began to build within. She closed her eyes to thought, tipping her head back, giving up all semblance of control, hoping the exquisitely slippery feelings were leading to someplace...more. "Yes."

His lips curved against her bare skin. "I'm glad you approve." And then he raked his hands through her curls as a prelude to his intentions.

Wondrous, wicked, clever, clever man. Her mouth felt as dry as her nether region felt wet. "I want—"

"Steady on, lass," he counseled one last time before his hands cupped her bottom to press her nearer so he could blow softly against the sensitive skin of her mons. "Shouldn't like to overwhelm ye."

She could all but hear the smile in his voice, though she shivered at his words. She felt breathless and light, buoyed up by his wicked sense of humor. "I'm not overwhelmed."

"You will be—if I get this right." He let the delicious weight of the words settle upon her. "How do you feel now?"

"Ridiculously giddy," she admitted, feeling the excitement and anticipation rise up against her uneasiness. "And a little achy."

"Tell me what aches." His mouth brushed against her, sending heat pooling within. "Tell me what I need to soothe."

Beneath the layers of her clothing her skin seemed to be alive with sensation. Her breasts felt heavy and tight. Deep within, her belly constricted. Her thighs clenched together in unconscious spasm.

"Everything."

"Then everything it will be. But I need your help." Another long, shiver-inducing lick. "Take down your bodice—or don't, however you choose—and ease your own ache by touching your lovely breasts."

Her hands immediately fluttered up as if she might cover herself. But she didn't. She wanted this—she had asked him specifically for this. Pretending otherwise was disingenuous.

But he understood her even if she didn't understand herself. "Do as much or as little as you like—I will. I will give you my all."

"Archie." His name was answer and entreaty all at the same time.

"Yes." His answer was encouragement. "So lovely," he murmured, his lips stirring against her sensitive skin. "So sweet."

She felt herself arching into the warmth and weight of his hands and mouth.

"Steady on, my lass, steady." His murmur echoed in her ear. "Because there's more. A vast deal more."

"I want more," she insisted.

"So determined. So curious," he teased as he slowly slid one strong finger within and Maisie felt her body clench and release and clench again in an agony of pleasure and anticipation that was so strong, she found herself needing to cross her arms over her breasts, pressing against them within the confines of her stays to allay the feel of his clever, clever fingers teasing needy pleasure from deep within her belly.

A low hum of something more, something deeper began to thrum within as his clever fingers plucked and played her body. And he knew just what chord to play.

"Spread your legs for me, sweet Maisie," he urged. His big hands covered her knees, pressing them lightly, showing her the way. Leading her to expose more of herself to his touch.

"I'll fall." She didn't know what to do, pinned to the wall by her pleasure, but wanting more.

"Then fall," he said, pressing his hand to hold her against the wall. "Let me help you," he urged, before he traced his beautifully articulate fingers along the length of her thighs until she thought she would burst from the anticipation.

And then he cupped her mound, and it was…*everything*.

"Just so," his low voice crooned. "Exactly so."

He set his fingers in a gentle rhythm upon her until it was almost too much—all pleasure and need and achy, incandescent joy. Until it wasn't enough, and she began to move her hips, chasing her rising passion, riding his hand as it played against her.

"That's the way of it."

He rose to stand with his hands still on her and in her, pressing into her with the surety of his weight. She turned her head toward him in mute appeal and he kissed her deeply, his tongue tangling with hers in rhythm with his hands.

He backed away from the door, and picked her up. She was weightless and dizzy and giddy all at once. She tried to tether herself to him, pressing hot, ardent kisses along his jaw. Kissing her way up his temple. Tangling her hands in his riotously curling hair, tugging it back until his neck arched and his mouth fell open to her exploration.

She fell into his kiss and warmth and surety, stroking his tongue and stoking the slowly building fire within. A fire that seemed to be spreading like a flame through dry tinder. She tried to tamp it down, tried to hold back the heat. She wanted to kindle it slowly, but her desire rose rapidly with his.

Her skin heated, her breath shortened, and her hands fisted tight on his lapels. She took everything he gave as he lay her down on the creaking old daybed, the springs and coils protesting under their weight.

But she didn't care. She loved the feel of him on top of her, the weight of his body, pressing into hers. He held her still with his hands as he ravaged her mouth and gave in to the mounting fire of need. His hands were strong, not gentle, as he held her, pulling her into him, letting her feel the hard length of his arousal between them, willing her to give him more. More of the sweet taste of her mouth, more of the flushed silk of her skin, more of her very essence, her very self.

When he insinuated his tongue into her mouth, Maisie gasped with gratifying astonishment and she opened herself to him whole-heartedly, with no hesitation or affectation.

He cradled her jaw, to angle her head, and kiss her more deeply, and she answered him stroke for stroke, kiss after kiss, until they were both breathless and gasping for air.

He slid his hands down to her shoulders, and pushed himself gently away from her so that they lay side to side, mouth to mouth, eye to eye.

In the next moment, he eased another long finger alongside the first—a rush of heat and desire blossomed from her belly and spread to the edges of her being.

Maisie closed her eyes to stop thinking and only feel, as he touched and played and murmured. Her body wound itself higher and higher. Closer and closer to some unseen place—some not-so-distant meeting of mind and body and soul and pleasure so beautiful she wanted to laugh and cry all at the same time.

She wanted this. She wanted more. She wanted nothing less than absolute bliss.

Maisie could not stop the sound of want and desire that flew from her lips when he touched her *there*, at the center of her pleasure and need, grazing ever so lightly against the sensitive nub his fingers exposed.

She arched wildly one last time and he swallowed her cry as her climax shuddered through her, hot and delirious and imperfectly perfect.

Archie wrapped his arms around her and held her, safe and secure, as she collapsed against his chest, sated and numb and more alive than she had ever felt before.

She put lips against the hollow of his throat and feel the strong pulsing of his blood and hear the hard pounding of his heart. "Heavens."

She could feel his smile as it all be vibrated through her. "You're welcome."

"Yes. Thank you." She suddenly felt ridiculous all splayed and awkward beside him.

Maisie sat up, rearranging her clothes as she carefully put her weight upon her rather unreliable legs. But funny, how she hadn't thought about her leg the whole time they had been—

Doing that. And doing that rather well.

She checked her clothing and hair more attentively. She knew she must look a fright, but she was too happy and sated to care or blush. She was too happy to do anything but smile. "For everything."

His smile was quietly reciprocal. "You are most welcome."

What else did one say? What else could one possibly feel? What also was there?

It was as if he could read her thoughts. "There is even more. Next time," he promised.

Maisie was simultaneously amazed and delighted that there would be a next time. "And when will that be?"

He laughed, a lazy satisfied, animal sort of sound. "Soon," he promised again. "That's why I like you."

Like you.

Not love. Not lust. But something infinitely more valuable to her.

He liked her. Just as she was—by turns inexperienced and afraid, confident and curious to find out more about the world. More about life. He never questioned her choices or told her what to think. He never once corrected her.

Archie Carrington was that rarest of rare creatures—a rogue who could become her friend. Perhaps he already was.

The only question that remained as she kissed him goodbye— what was she going to do about it?

CHAPTER 25

The painting of her Magdalene was nearly finished, so full of inspiration had Maisie been, with the small, but important caveat, that she was running out of mixed lead white paint. She would send a note down to Mr. Hill.

"Agnes?" Maisie called through the door. "Are you there?"

She returned to her work, alternately standing back from the work and then moving in close to add necessary corrections and additions before stepping away again. "Agnes?"

And yet, no matter how many times she called, no Agnes came. Which was odd.

Maisie descended to the second-floor bedchambers, where she found Flora in consultation with Raines, discussing this week's plan for Flora's clothing.

"Yes, the pink lutestring for the Marchioness of Huntley's soirée, but I must go tell Maisie, now."

"Tell me what?" Maisie asked. "Do either of you know where I can find Agnes? I thought she might be here with you, holding bandboxes, but I can't find her anywhere."

Raines looked to Flora, and then Flora said, "Why don't you come in and sit down?"

"Because I want to find Agnes. Surely someone knows where she is?"

Flora stood. "I'm afraid she's been let go."

"Let go where? When will she be back?" It wasn't like the girl to hare off without telling Maisie.

"She's not coming back, Maisie," Flora said quietly. "Mrs. Smyth let her go."

"Turned her off," Cora Raines added with some asperity. "Said she didn't care where the poor lass went."

"Mrs. Smyth turned her off?" Maisie was aghast. "Why didn't you tell me immediately." And enraged. "Where is she?"

"I don't have any idea where she's gone," Flora answered. "Raines only just told me."

"I meant Mrs. Smyth." Maisie plowed down the central staircase, headed for the kitchen level. "Smyth!" She bawled at the top of her lungs, bringing maids peeping around covers and over the baluster. "How could she do this?" she asked no one in particular and everyone at the same time.

Raines was right behind her, muttering. "Has a particular set of prejudices against we Scots, she does."

"Bloody cheek," Maisie agreed. "Smyth!"

"She said she consulted with Sir Richard, miss," Raines tattled. "I only just found out, but I told Miss Flora straightaway when I did so."

"When did she talk to Papa?" Maisie demanded as she pushed down the last set of stairs. "When did this happen?"

"Turfed her out before breakfast, miss," Raines answered.

Before the poor child had had any breakfast? At least Maisie was sure that she had a decent bit of tea late last night. "That monster."

"Maisie," Flora cautioned in her wake, "Mrs. Smyth has every right—"

"She does not," Maisie contradicted with heat. "And I intend to tell her so, immediately." She dragged herself through the kitchens to the service corridor, where she did Mrs. Smyth the discourtesy of entering into her parlor and office without knocking.

"Miss Margaret!" The woman stood in clear affront.

"Did you turn Agnes MacDonald off?" Maisie demanded.

Mrs. Smyth's alarm eased. "Ah, yes, indeed, I did. I don't mind saying that I did not care for her from the start and she did everything she could to live up to that low expectation. These Scottish girls... Well." She let her particular set of prejudices against the maids go unsaid but not unmeant. "But the absolute last straw with MacDonald was that I found she did not sleep in her room last night, but was out—"

"Did she not explain—"

"I am not interested in these girls' excuses." Mrs. Smyth put up her chin and reprised her pinched expression. "Standards of conduct are to be maintained at all—"

"Did you not let her explain," Maisie raised her voice, "that she was not in her small, unheated, crowded chamber she shared with three other girls"—who, Maisie noted with some satisfaction, were crowding the entrance to the corridor—"because she was working for me in my studio, assisting me in all the various and sundry things with which I need assistance and for which she was hired in the first place?"

Mrs. Smyth was surprised, but not apologetic. "I was not made aware of this."

Maisie threw her hands up in the air. "Perhaps you would have been aware if you had let the poor girl explain. Or if you had listened to me in the first place when I hired Agnes."

"Be that as it may." Mrs. Smyth drew in air through her nose as if she had smelled something rank. "Those were not MacDonald's official duties as tweeny, for which she was engaged—"

"Those were the *only* duties for which she was engaged!" Maisie heard her voice becoming strident, but she was done with the sort of politesse that Mrs. Smyth was always shielding behind. "I was the one who engaged her!"

Because she had been as scared for Agnes then as she was now. Because Maisie knew what awaited her on Edinburgh's cold, icy streets.

"Indeed, if you had consulted with me, Miss Conway—"

"I saw no need to consult with you, Mrs. Smyth, because Agnes's work for me had nothing to do with the rest of the bloody household!"

"Maisie." Flora's quiet but firm tone was a warning.

A warning she might have heeded, had Mrs. Smyth not said. "If you require a girl to assist in your studio"—she said the word the same way one might say serpent or scorpion, full of aggravated suspicion—"then we will hire you another girl."

"Another girl won't do," Maisie fumed, thinking not only of the nearly-finished Magdalene upstairs, but of poor Agnes herself, who was afraid to walk back through the Grassmarket. Where was she now?

"What won't do, Miss Margaret, is having these girls get above their station, talking to guests out of turn, haring off to shops—"

"Doing errands for me," Maisie insisted. "Doing the walking I cannot."

"Taking money from guests," Smyth went on as if she hadn't even listened to Maisie. "Conducting guests through the servant's stair instead of—"

"Are you speaking of Lord Carrington?" Since he was her only guest, Maisie felt on sure ground. "He chooses to come up the servant's stair because he comes so early and it is most convenient for us both—"

"It is highly irregular," Smyth was just as insistent. "Not to mention entirely out of line for the MacDonald girl to solicit monies from the man, chatting him up like one of these young Scottish doxies."

"Scots," came a muttered correction from the corridor.

Smyth glared at the cluster of girls before she returned to her subject. "And if, as you say, the MacDonald girl had no business within the household but the things she did for you, then there was no reason I should have found her in your father's book room, pilfering items."

"Pilfering? There must be some mistake." Of this, Maisie was sure. "Agnes would have no reason or need to pilfer—she was paid well, both for her duties as my studio assistant and for the extra work of posing for me."

"Posing?" Mrs. Smyth pruned up her mouth and nose as if she'd encountered a particularly awful smell. "Probably how the beggar girl got ideas above her station, singling her out like that."

"Yes, how dare she try to improve her lot and keep herself out of the filth and mire?" Maisie gave vent to her fear and frustration with sarcasm. "Is she only allowed to get so high as a servant, and no higher? Have you never accepted vails from my father's guests, Mrs. Smyth?"

"That is entirely different."

"It is not," Maisie insisted, again. "It is no business of ours if Lord Carrington is liberal with his money."

Mrs. Smyth remained unmoved. "When you have lived as long as I have and worked as long as I have with these girls—and these Scots girls especially—you will know that some of them can't be taught and can't be saved, miss."

Maisie gasped along with the girls in the corridor. "Then I hope to God I don't live as long as you," she told Smyth, "to become so jaded and cold to the suffering of my fellow human beings."

Silence rang for a long minute, while Mrs. Smyth made a show of shaking out her handkerchief and dabbing at her eyes even as she said icily, "I don't know when I've ever been spoken to in such—"

"I don't know when I have ever witnessed such unfeeling, unthinking behavior in this household," Maisie returned.

"You always were a fractious, willful, ungrateful child," Mrs. Smyth accused. "And you are an ungrateful, unnatural woman."

The words struck Maisie like a slap. It was as if she were fourteen years old again, abandoned to the "care" of Mrs. Smyth, whose regimen of cold water baths and forced inactivity did nothing to ease the intolerable ache of her infirmity.

But she was no longer fourteen. And she was no longer under Mrs. Smyth's oppressive thumb. She was her own person—a spinster must have some occupation, Smyth had warned—well, she had an occupation now!

"And you, ma'am," she returned, "are the sort of person who derives pleasure and purpose from the unkind subjugation of others. I daresay you felt a sort of holy glee at the prospect of teaching Agnes what you thought was a deserved lesson."

"Rude, ungrateful child," the woman repeated.

"Mrs. Smyth, that will do!" Flora was aghast.

Smyth paled, but kept her icy composure. "As you wish, miss. But, I'll be speaking to Sir Richard—"

"By all means," Maisie agreed. "Let us speak to him now."

Smyth defended herself. "I undertook this action under your esteemed father's direction."

"And I'm sure he believed your mis-truths. But you've had it in for that girl since the first moment I brought her—"

"Foisted her upon us with no training, no skills, no moral character—" Smyth insisted.

"That is not true." Maisie had had enough of the woman's spleen. "Agnes MacDonald has moral character to spare."

"Then why wasn't she in her room? Gone all night doing who knows what with who knows who!"

"She was with me, Mrs. Smyth!"

"Was she in your father's book room with you? Or merely

under your direction? In which case, you have only yourself to blame for introducing low moral character—"

Now it was Maisie's turn to defend herself. "Why, you nasty old biddy!

"Margaret!" Papa stepped into the corridor. "What in heaven's name is going on here?"

Sir Richard's appearance in the servant hall had the predictable effect—those in the room pressed away, toward the doors, while those out of the room pressed forward to get a better look. But the silence into which Maisie spoke, was deafening.

"I am taking Mrs. Smyth to task for dismissing our tweeny, Agnes."

"A tweeny?"

"The girl I told you about, sir," Mrs. Smyth put in.

"Yes?" Papa looked from between her daughter and her housekeeper, dumbfounded. "Troublesome, untrainable and absent from her duties?"

"Just so, sir," Mrs. Smyth confirmed with obvious satisfaction.

"Not so," insisted Maisie. "Agnes MacDonald was not in the least bit troublesome to me, nor was she untrained by me. She worked very hard for me, often forgoing her dinner in the servants hall to stay with me and learn how to mix my colors and paints, and cleaning the studio, too."

"Cleaning!" Mrs. Smyth huffed. "One can hardly call it cleaning when nothing in the *studio*"—she pronounced the word with disdain—"is ever changed or improved or—"

"You have never understood my requirements," Maisie countered. "I need things done precisely—vignettes repositioned exactly as they were, poses recreated exactly. The window panes dusted and cleaned daily so the quality of light remains the same. I need to know exactly where everything I need is and Agnes understood that, and was learning—" Maisie felt the heat of tears blister her eyes. It wasn't so much the work Agnes had done, so much as the plain fact that the girl had become a sort of kindred spirit, both a muse and a companion. "She had become indispensable to me and now she's gone, through no fault of her own."

"But Mrs. Smyth said the girl had absconded after she found her in my book room, going through my manuscript pages?"

"Your manuscript?" This was the first Maisie had heard of such a thing. "Smyth must be mistaken, for Agnes could have no need of any manuscript pages—the girl could barely read."

"Most irregular." Sir Richard was non-plussed, but still somehow sure of his point. "Can you tell me why the girl wasn't in her bed when Smyth performed a bed check?"

"That's right, sir." Mrs. Smyth was happy to confirm. "I can't have girls under my roof—"

"She wasn't under *your* roof." Maisie didn't care that she raised her voice. "She was under mine! She was quite literally, in my attic studio with me, doing the work I assigned her, not going through pages of a manuscript that she could not have read!"

"But Mrs. Smyth said the desk drawer where I keep my papers was unlocked," Papa charged.

"And?" Maisie was non-plussed. "Have you not got the key?"

"Yes," her father hedged. "But I can't have my papers getting into the wrong hands."

"Well, they weren't in Agnes' hands, I'll swear to that," Maisie averred. "And now Agnes is gone and has nowhere to go. No one to look after her."

"Didn't have so much as a cloak," another of the maids whispered before Smyth shot her a vicious look.

"Find her," Maisie charged the housekeeper. "Find her, or so help me, I will make sure this is the last job you ever have."

"Sir Richard," Smyth appealed to her employer. "This is an outrage. I have only done—"

"As *you* wanted," Maisie broke in, "without giving Agnes either the benefit of the doubt or a chance to explain herself."

"I did as I saw fit."

"Will you now do as is truly fit and bring her back?" Flora asked with a calmer diplomacy.

"I don't know how she can be found," the woman sniffed.

"That is no excuse." Maisie would move heaven and earth—she would only ask that Smythe join her. "Find her, Mrs. Smyth," Maisie charged. "Right the wrong. Bring her back. Find her and bring her back safe."

CHAPTER 26

She was not to be found, Maisie was told—Mrs. Smyth left a tidy little note under the door to the aerie the next morning stating that she now considered the matter closed.

"Not bloody likely." Maisie let out an unladylike curse. "There hasn't even been time to look properly."

Maisie began immediately at her window, scanning the streets below her aerie for Fergus, but the lad seemed to have disappeared as well, likely gone to ground with his sister. Another sweep was already stationed on the corner of Hope Street.

"Yeah, I ken Fergus," the lad, who identified himself only as Jock, admitted narrowly when Maisie made her laborious way down to the corner to speak to him. "Who's askin'?"

"A friend." Maisie bolstered the lad's cooperation by handing him a coin. "Who might be persuaded to become your friend as well."

"Friend, is it?" He narrowed an appraising glance at her. "You the one making the pictures?"

"So you've heard about that?"

"Easy money's what I've heard."

"And easier still if you can tell me anything about Fergus or Agnes MacDonald's whereabouts."

"Nae chance, missus. I'm no clipe. No worth meh hide," the boy advised. "You give 'em up, missus. Be best if ye did."

But Maisie could not—would not—give them up. The guilt would eat her alive.

Her next mission was to send a note over to the offices of the Review, begging both that Lord Carrington excuse her from their appointment and also, soliciting his help in the search. Surely a man as connected in the city as he—"Ask anyone over Cowgate way and they'll tell ye where Archie lives"—might have better ways of finding the children than she?

Maisie was gratified when a note was immediately returned, pledging his assistance—he would do anything he could for her relief. The cold feeling of dread was temporarily replaced by the warm flame of reliance and, dare she say it, charm.

But the appeal of charm faded with the reality of no success. While Maisie tried to immerse herself in the work of finishing the Magdalene, staring into Agnes's wildly sad eyes brought little relief and more guilt. She moved on to painting her weeping Madonna and her Doubting Thomas from memory, while she worried and fretted and cursed and spent her pennies on every vendor and beggar and crossing sweep she could find in the vain hope that one of them might be able to either pass on information or bring word back.

Neither happened.

Maisie was left with the unsettling understanding that everything that had happened to Agnes was entirely Maisie's fault. Perhaps Smyth was right—she should never have brought Agnes into the house. She should have left well enough alone.

But Agnes hadn't been well enough alone—she had been all but starving. Was Maisie to have turned her back and simply walked away, knowing she might have helped?

No. She had to try.

And she would try again in the morning today in some other way—perhaps she might ride over to Cannon Mills village to see if she might have taken refuge with one of the shopkeepers there. Perhaps there were other jobs a poor, illiterate girl who had been let go without a reference might find there.

But it struck Maisie again, the wrongness of the charge that Agnes had been in her father's book room, pilfering pages from this manuscript that Maisie had never heard him speak of before. But her father had lived abroad, away from his family, for long expanses of time, a life that they knew nothing about.

But 'can't have them getting into the wrong hands,' her father had said. What wrong hands? What could possibly be in this manuscript that made it so special, or volatile?

Maisie decided to find out.

The rest of the house remained safely abed as she crept down the back stairs and through the unlocked door that led directly from the second-floor landing into her father's book room at the back of the house.

The chamber was paneled in bookshelves. On the wall opposite the servant's door hung another portrait of Sir Richard—this one less flattering than the hanging in the drawing room. While this likeness did not depict the proverbial 'warts and all,' Maisie had tried to create a portrait of her father that was both realistic, showing a man well past his prime in life, and sympathetic, giving him warmth and personality.

Here was the face of a man who had told them he meant well. That he wanted a fresh start with his daughters—though there was evidence that might prove otherwise.

The books lining the shelves behind the central desk revealed his past interest in horticulture, with titles ranging from *The Profitably Arte of Gardening*, to *The Practice of Gardening* and *The Gardeners Labyrinth*. There were also notebooks covered with a great many planting schemes—some for the house in Richmond —and some for other unidentified places. And on the wall between the shelves was a framed print, a hand-tinted engraving of the plan of Chiswick House gardens, surrounded by various scenes of the gardens, none of which she had seen before, as none had adorned the walls of the house in Richmond.

She turned to the desk, where a set of ledgers as well as several notebooks, similar to the ones containing planting schemes on the shelf, were stacked to one side. A glance through the ledgers showed her father was both meticulous and economical in the recording of his household expenses—nothing extravagant or out of the ordinary.

But there, to the other side of the desk—stacked neatly in two piles, one face up and one face down, as if he had been paging through them, making a count—were hand-written pages of what appeared to be his manuscript.

Maisie set down her candle, marked her father's place, and turned over the title page,

A Residence Among the Chinese, being a Journey in Disguise. And she began to read her father's account of how he had been set up as British Cantonment merchant—all of whom had been forbidden by the Chinese government from venturing into the interior of the country past the limits of the established trading cantonments—specifically to find his way into the country. Not once, not twice, but repeatedly. Because what were Chinese laws to British subjects? Traders like the British East India Company made their own laws to suit wherever they wanted to go.

And so she read on and learned and was astonished long into the night.

IT WAS THE CLOMP AND RATTLE OF THE FOOTMEN CARRYING COAT scuttles up the stairs that roused Maisie from the account. She marked her own progress before she returned the pages to their previous state as she had found them. But she had a

number of questions to ask her father—not the least of which was the real reason for their removal from Richmond to Edinburgh.

Maisie returned to her aerie just as the faintest streak of dawn purpled the hills to the south. Archie she hoped, would either arrive with the dawn or send some word of Agnes and Fergus's whereabouts. But until then she would search—

Below her window, on the corner below, Maisie's eyes were instantly arrested by the sight of Fergus, who darted forward on the pavement, looking and waving up at her, as if he had been writing for her to appear.

"Missus!" His voice was thin and raw when it reached her ears. "Please, missus," he called. "Please."

Maisie all but tumbled down the narrow back stairs in her haste to get to him. "Fergus," she called as she threw open the stable gate. "Where have you been? I've been worried sick about you and Agnes."

"Ye cannae be more than me," the boy objected. "She's sick, our Agnes, missus. Terrible sick."

"Where is she?"

"She were at Mrs. Bigelow's," he gulped.

"Yes?" Maisie prompted. "Is this Mrs. Bigelow the house-keeper at Agnes's new place?"

"Nah, missus. She's naught but a rotten old bawd, Mrs. Bigelow."

"Do you mean, a…" Maisie forced herself not to gasp in shock. "…prostitute?"

"A bawd," he explained as if it made a difference. "Runs the house. For hired fucks, if ye'll pardon my French."

It wasn't his French that she would have to pardon. But that didn't matter—Agnes did. "Agnes is only twelve."

"What's that got to do wi' it?" The boy protested miserably. "I'm eleven and I've done ma share o' the hochmagandy."

Maisie decided the word would remain untranslated—it's

meaning was clear enough. "And I am sorry for you, but where is Agnes now?"

"Tossed her out like a worn bauchle when she took bad, but I found a room for us. Only she's no gotten no better. She's gotten worse."

"How exactly? What's wrong with her?"

"Shiverin' an' shakin' the day and night through. She's off her heid, she is, talkin' mince. Pure naff, ye ken? I'm afeartie for her."

"Of course you are." Maisie did not ken, precisely, but she got the undeniable fact that Agnes was desperately ill and in need or nursing. "But you've done the right thing in coming to me. What has been done for her so far?" She would stock her traveling medicine kit accordingly.

"Told ye—got her a room, like?"

"Like? Where is the room?" she asked, though the moment she did so, apprehension gripped her chest.

It was as if she knew before he said the words. "Down the vaults."

Fear shot through her like a lead-cold arrow. She had learned much since Archie had first told her about the closes, the long narrow passages from the top of the old town leading down the sides of the ancient escarpment Edinburgh had been built upon. Sometimes enclosed with buildings on top of them, the underground closes were dark and dank and close and often fetid.

But the vaults were worse, narrow, reeking brick rooms built under the arches of the South Street Bridge. Cut off from fresh air and light, the vaults were a sort of home of last resort.

"We must get her out immediately and bring her home." She began making a list in her head of the necessary supplies. "But we'll take the medicine chest, blankets from the daybed, clean rags from the basket with us to get her."

"Aye, then." Fergus drew a deeper breath seeing her resolve. "Aye, she needs medicine and she's cold. So cold she's blue."

"Is there no heat?"

"Had a brazier, but what coal we could buy from the money we had left gave out."

"Has she eaten anything?"

He shook his head.

"Come with me." Maisie led the way down into the kitchen, where the cook was just poking up the fire under the hob.

"Feed him," she bade the woman tersely. "Pack up a nourishing pot of soup or stew or whatever you've got that I can carry. And bread. Warm, if possible, wrapped up well. It's very important. I'll be back for it as soon as—" She was wasting time explaining. "Feed the boy first, if you would. I'll be back for him presently."

Maisie clambered back up the stairs to her aerie to pull down her dusty medicine chest. As disused as it was, she had been afraid to leave it behind when they left Richmond. Though she had not needed to dose herself in years, the chest had been a fixture of her young adulthood, when any sneeze might fill her with apprehension. She had hated the thing, but was glad to put it to some good use now.

She rolled up the blankets as compactly as she could manage, before she found her stout country boots and her old woolen country cloak to put on over her wool pelisse—she could only imagine that it would be cold and dank inside the vaults.

The cook, bless her tender heart, had a stout basket hurriedly packed by the time she returned. "Take a footman to carry the load, Miss," was the only advice Mrs. Rattle offered. "I've put in fortified wine and bone broth, and a few other things—brandy and a jug of warm willow bark tea. Packed tight and heavy. Have you turpentine?"

"I have," Maisie gestured to the medicine chest. Though she hoped against hope she wouldn't need to dose the poor child with it—her own memories of the vile, burning brews that had been forced down her throat when she'd been gripped with the fever were so deeply unpleasant as to be fearsome. "Blankets as well."

"He's told me. It's not right what happened to Agnes," the woman whispered. "She was a good girl, hardworking and honest."

"Yes," Maisie agreed. "I'll bring her back, I promise."

"Let me wake Robert to accompany you." Mrs. Rattle set to ringing bells. "He'll be down in a minute."

Young Fergus shook his head and shouldered the basket. "There's no time for palaver."

"No," Maisie agreed—ancient Robert would never make it down in a minute, let alone ten. "Robert can meet us in the stables," she said as a concession as she ushered the boy out. "We'll ready the pony cart." If Robert were ready by then, she would certainly take him.

Maisie put her hand on Fergus's shoulder to steady herself across the slick cobbles of the yard, setting him to fetch out the cart while she dealt with the placid old pony in deference to his fears. But the boy's fear for his sister was greater than his fear of the animal, and he worked alongside her to fasten the harness to the shafts.

It took them more than a few minutes of trial and error before a sleepy groom came shuffling his bare feet down the ladder. "Miss? It's only gone four-thirty?" Davie stuffed in his shirttail. "You can't be thinking of going out in all this wet?"

"I can and I will," she assured him—and Fergus, whose terror seemed to compound with each potential obstacle. "If you will only check the harness to make sure we won't come a cropper down the Lothian Road. Here, Fergus, pack in the basket and light the lamps."

"I'll get that, miss." Davie sprang to help light the carriage lanterns with his flint, then checked and adjusted some straps before he rearranged the reins. "I'll drive ye, myself, miss, if ye'll give me a moment."

"Yes," she agreed only because it was faster than arguing, but the moment the groom ran for his ladder, she clambered into the basket and took up the reins. "Get the gate," she called to Fergus.

He sprang across the yard, and she was right behind him, slowing only to let the lad clamber aboard before she set the pony to a trot out the wide-open gate, and they were away.

"Just point me the way," she directed Fergus.

"There." He gestured right, across the front of the house and down the Lothian Road, down the path that had become so familiar since she had ridden with Archie that day that now seemed so long ago.

The cart rattled down the empty street, though with every second feeling as if it were an hour long, it took both forever and no time before they were hurtling across the gray, cavernous expanse of the Grassmarket. The pony's hooves echoed off the buildings lining the empty square as they passed onto Cowgate Head and down the narrow length of the coal black street.

The weak light from the carriage lantern shivered in the foggy half-light before the dawn. Ahead, the Cowgate Arch of the South Bridge loomed out of the mist, hulking over them like some hellish portal to the netherworld.

"There." Fergus pointed, and she turned the pony up the chasm of Niddery Street. "Here."

They stopped before an unlit door that gave way to an inky ribbon of a corridor. "Come on," the boy said before he grabbed up the medicine chest and plunged into the darkness.

And Maisie was on her own.

"Fergus!" she called. "Don't leave— We can't just leave the pony unattended—" But of course they could, for there was no other alternative.

Maisie put out the lamps—for she would need them on the way back—and took up the basket and bedding as best she could, for she did not want to leave anything on the rough street. Not even the sweet old pony, but that couldn't be helped.

She stepped into the unlit interior. "Fergus?" She felt her way along with the heavy basket while calling softly for the boy as she went—God forbid someone else should hear her and come for her.

It seemed an age before his footsteps pattered on stone and then echoed a bit more on wood before he appeared. "Come on," he urged.

"Take the basket," she pled, needing all the strength that was left to her to keep up with the boy's desperate pace.

The place was a warren of stone and scaffolding and dank sheets—or dingy laundry—hanging to block drafts of the rainy damp that seemed to seep in everywhere, and rough, stained hessian sacking tacked to cover doorways to keep some semblance of privacy.

Fergus finally darted beneath one such tattered hessian scrim and entered an alcove of a room with a low, curved ceiling.

"There." He pointed to a pile of rags that had been fashioned into a pallet, whereupon poor Agnes lay, before he busied himself opening the folding cabinets and myriad drawers of the medicine chest. "Which do we give her?"

"I don't know yet," Maisie said as she went down on her knees to see the girl in the wavering light of a single candle. "Hold the light closer."

"Left it burning where she couldn't get to it," Fergus explained of the stub. "She don't like the dark but she kept coming over all funny like to try and touch it. Burnt her fingers, she did."

And it was no wonder she wouldn't like the dark in such a dank, fetid, close space—neither did Maisie. The room the poor boy had procured for them was no more than the size of a closet —she doubted another person could be admitted.

"Agnes?" The poor child's brow was hot to Maisie's touch and her face was purpled with bruises running sallow. "Agnes, who did this to you?"

"Mam?" Agnes blinked and tried to focus.

The poor child was calling for her mother. "Yes," Maisie said instantly, laying the back of her hand against the girl's cheek. "I'm here, Agnes, darling."

"I'm sick, mam."

"But you'll be better soon, now that I've come," Maisie soothed even as she boiled with rage. She would find out who did this to Agnes and she would run them through. She would kick them to the cobbles like the curs they were. She would hurt them as much as they had hurt her girl.

"The willow-bark tea from the jug in the hamper," she whispered to Fergus. "I've brought you medicine and food," she told

Agnes as she slipped her hand behind the child's head to try and raise her up enough to take a sip of the tea.

"Hurts," Agnes whimpered, though Maisie cradled her as carefully as possible.

"I know, love," she soothed. "Try to get some of this down."

Maisie held a tiny cup from the medicine chest up to her cracked lips—a few sips were all the poor child could get down.

"Do you know who did this to her," she asked Fergus.

"Himself," was the boy's terse answer. "King of the Beggars they call him. She tried gettin' work again, but in a different place, like, farther away but not so far—"

"Cannon Mills?"

"Aye. How'd ye know?"

"Intuition, I suppose." A young ostler at the inn there had had a bright eye for Agnes. It would make sense that she would go where there was the chance of a friendly face.

"But word got back. I tried to warn her—tried to get there myself," Fergus fretted. "But Himself'd got 'er first, like, and lamped her good an' hard an' put her to auld Bigelow's as a skivvy for punishment for having' left in the first place."

"What is the man's name?" Maisie demanded tersely.

Fergus dropped his voice to the barest whisper, as if he were afraid of being overheard. "Big Nickerson." The boy shook his head. "But ye din't hear it frae me—I don't clipe. Not worth my heid. I'd end up as black an' blue as Aggie an' then where'd we be? Scunnered," he declared. "That's where."

"The man must be exposed," she insisted. "Exposed and punished."

"That's no his real, proper name, ye ken?" the boy countered. "They reckon Himself is about the third Big Nickerson to run Edinburgh. Younger than t'others. And meaner, too."

"Nevertheless," Maisie said, "he must be stopped. One can't go about beating twelve-year-old girls with impunity."

"An' yer mon did come back an' give 'er a bit o' soma for the pain—a black drop."

"What is that?" Maisie asked.

"For pain, in a little gum, like licorice candy," the boy explained. "Tho, she took it and went all jakey, like she were doolally. Laid down and ne'er did get back up. The fever come on when she were scunnered."

"Opium?" Maisie guessed. "He beat her and then gave her opium? Odious, awful man."

"Don' go gettin' that look in yer eye, missus. Aggie said t'same ta him, bold as ye please. Said as she'd give his name to that nob yer painting—Lord Archie frae down the Cowgate."

Then Archie already knew, which saved Maisie the trouble of 'cliping.' Lord, knew she had enough trouble as present without adding any more.

Maisie swallowed her rage like a bitter pill and concentrated on changing the bedding for clean linen and warmer blankets, and propping Agnes up so that she might continue to offer the girl sips. But the work of changing the linens so taxed the poor child that blood began to seep out under her nose and she was so weak, she couldn't even hold a rag up to stop it.

Maisie held the rag instead, tending her as carefully as possible, while trying desperately to keep her own rising panic at bay. Clearly, the girl was so fragile she couldn't be moved—or at least Maisie realized, too late, she couldn't be moved by a boy and a lame spinster. Should have waited for the ancient footman after all. Or far better, the stout young groom, Davie.

Damn her unthinking rush.

Fergus hovered behind her, shifting restlessly—and hopelessly —from foot to foot.

"Go to the nearest decent apothecary—not a quack," she advised. "And get him to attend us as soon as possible." She dug into her pocket to find enough coin.

"Don't ye think I've tried?" Fergus cried. "They'll none of

them come 'ere, missus. That's why I come to ye." His frustration had him near tears.

But they had to have help.

"Archie Carrington." He had already pledged to help her. "In Liberton's Close—the office of the Edinburgh Review. Or the presswork behind. Get him. Tell him I sent you. And if he's not there, tell the men in the press works to send for him to bring him here. Tell them I sent for him. Do you understand? Don't come back without him." It would be dawn soon, and Archie had proved himself to be a dependably early riser. "Find Archie."

"I ken ye, miss. I fuckin' ken." And away he went.

Which left Maisie with a weak, helpless girl, who was probably dying.

But she was going to do everything in her power—everything to prevent that. She set cool compresses to the child's brow and chest to break the fever. She spooned down alternating sips of willow bark tea and bone broth—the tea for the pain and the broth for strength. She cooed and hushed and sang sweet little songs about nothing to ease her agitation when the shivering fits shook Agnes like a leaf in the wind.

And when the cloths warmed, she changed them. And when Agnes swallowed or licked her lips, Maisie spooned liquid in. And when she cried out, Maisie held and calmed her. Over and over and over again. Until the candle guttered and she had to grope her way in the dark, hoping and praying that Mrs. Rattle was as clever and prepared as Maisie needed her to be, and had packed extra tapers in the bottom of the basket. And when her prayers were answered, and the candles found, it was agonizing moments before she could strike a light and chase back the gloom.

And then her prayers were answered again when Fergus reappeared. And dashed when she realized he was alone. And sopping wet. "Could you not find him?"

"Nay, missus. Gone tae Prestonpans, they told me. Nae telling' when he'd be back."

"Looking for you there, I'd wager," she reasoned. "Good man, though he can do us little good here."

They were on their own.

Together, Maisie and Fergus took up the litany of prayers and potions, rotating the various liquids they spooned down Agnes's throat, taking turns changing the cool cloths and soothing the girl.

"D'ye remember the last time we went out on Pa's boat, Aggie. Clear day it were, flat and pretty as a mirror. And Pa sang and laughed and told tales while 'e fished? I think that's the last time I was happy. 'Spect it was for ye, too." The boy swiped his eyes with his sleeve. "Wish we'd ne'er left Prestonpans. Would'a been better off taking Pa's boat an' tryin' our best on our own for all the good Auld Reeky's done us."

"We'll get you back there again," Maisie promised him—and his sister, for all she didn't seem to be able to hear them in her insensate state. But the poor boy had been up through the night, too, and looked it—the circles under his eyes were so dark he looked as if he'd been lamped across the face as Agnes had. "Why don't you see if you can eat a bit of food,"—for he'd touched not a thing in the basket—"and take a bit of rest."

Again and again Maisie tried to cool the fever, and again, somehow, Agnes seemed to grow hotter. The fever did not break. Time stretched in every direction but nothing changed. And Maisie began to give in to despair.

And then he was there, his hand on her shoulder in the cramped space. "Maisie."

"Archie." His name was both prayer and plea. "You came." She had help now. She could do more with his help.

"Of course, I came as soon as I could." He cast off his dripping greatcoat so he wouldn't get them wet and crouched at her side, his lantern illuminating the small space like day. "How is she?"

Fergus was awakened by Archie's arrival. "Is she better now?" the boy asked.

"No," Maisie had to admit. In fact, now that Archie had brought the lantern, she could see that the poor girls neck and chest were covered in rose madder-colored spots. "I fear not."

Over Agnes's head, Maisie's eyes met Archie's—he saw the spots, too. "I've seen that before in these stews—the closes. That's an inflammatory, malignant fever. You shouldn't be here," he began. "You'll get it, too."

"I've had the fever," Maisie argued. "It's already done its worst."

Archie shook his head grimly. "You can't know that."

"Will Aggie be lame?" Fergus asked.

If it was the sort of fever that only attacked her muscles. If she were lucky. If she recovered.

Maisie had little hope and no prevarication left in her. "I don't know. I just want her not to die."

"She cannae die." Fergus began to cry. "Ye cannae let her die, missus. Ye cannae."

"I'm trying, Fergus," she promised. "I'm doing my best."

But her best was clearly not good enough. When the girl wasn't insensate from the fever she was agitated to the point of confusion.

"Where's Mam? Mam!" she called as she picked at her bedclothes restlessly. "I want Mam."

"I'm here," Maisie said over and over to calm her. Every time she slipped a spoonful of broth down past her lips, and put a cool cloth to the child's fever brow. "I'm here with you, Agnes." But she wasn't enough.

She turned to Archie. "Can you not get an apothecary or surgeon here? Do you not know someone who will come?"

"I sent word with one of the press devils to an old friend—a former Navy surgeon. He'll come if he can. But the vaults…"

The vaults were living up to their reputation as dangerous,

feral places that one entered only at their peril. Maisie did not know where she had ever felt so trapped.

No. She knew—when she had been the one sick with a fever in the bed, too ill to even pick at her covers.

"Thank you." The hope helped hold back the tears that burned behind her eyes. As did the work of spooning in medicine and broth, and wiping Agnes's arms and chest with the cool cloths, as well as making sure Fergus ate enough from the well-packed basket to stay strong and healthy himself and urging the boy to sleep. Doing whatever she could.

But it never seemed enough.

The fever continued to burn, though the willow-bark tea seemed to have done some good—Agnes stilled and was silent some time. Maisie sat quietly with her on the cold brick floor, silently saying the same litany of prayers that had kept her company and relatively sane throughout her own illness.

Archie saw her weariness. "Why don't you try to rest. Or take some nourishment or food yourself," Archie urged.

"I will later, nearer tea time or supper."

"Maisie." He looked at her with growing concern. "It's gone eight o'clock."

"In the morning?"

"In the evening—you've been here for whole day. I've no doubt your family must be worried sick."

"Mrs. Rattle, the cook, knows I've gone out to help Agnes. She'll have told Flora." Maisie would not put her own safety or well-being ahead of Agnes's. "This is all Smyth—the housekeeper's—fault. She made up an excuse to turn the girl off behind my back. Made up some spurious story about the girl pilfering from my father's book room— Bloody woman." Maisie gave vent to her feelings. "Do you think we might move her? Would the surgeon come see her more readily if she were at Kirk Brae Head and not here?"

"We could try, Maisie, but I think—"

"Mam?" Agnes's cry was nothing more than a whisper, but Maisie heard it, and took her hand.

"Yes, Agnes. I'm here. I'm here with you."

But the only sound in the room was the painful rasp of the poor child trying desperately to draw breath. And then the sound came no more.

Maisie at first was thankful that her breathing seemed to have eased, but when the moment of silence stretched out, she finally understood that Agnes, bless her, was no longer there with them.

And the tears and fears that Maisie had held at bay through the long terrifying hours began to pour out of her—hot, scalding tears streaking down her cheeks. "No. Agnes. Please."

"Is—" Fergus came closer, then stepped back. "Is she dead?"

"I'm so very sorry, Fergus." Maisie tried to compose herself. Tried to draw her own breath over the aching tightness in her throat and chest. "But—"

The boy let out a desperate sob and would have bolted out had Archie not caught him up in a fierce hug and held him tight, letting the poor child bury his face in Archie's coat and howl out his misery and grief.

But Maisie could not give in to her grief, not yet.

There was still work to be done.

She settled Agnes into an easier pose, folding her hands composedly, smoothing her hair back away from her face. Making her presentable so she could be taken home. Even if it were now too late.

"I'll see to arrangements," Archie said quietly. "See that she's decently buried."

"Yes," Maisie agreed. "It's the least we can do. The very goddamn least."

And it would never be enough.

CHAPTER 28

There was nothing more that could be done. He had to get her out of there. "Come, Maisie. Let me take you home."

"Home?" She said with a sort of belligerent confusion. "No."

She turned back to the lad, Fergus, who had emerged from Archie's embrace wiping his face on his sleeve, as if he would wipe the whole of the memory from his mind. "What am I supposed to do now?" the lad asked, his voice choked with fear and impotent anger.

"I'll take care of you," Maisie promised.

"The way you did Agnes?" he countered.

"Better," she swore through the tears that salted her cheeks. "Far better. I swear it. I'll make it up to you. And the first way is to see that Agnes is decently buried. Who is the nearest undertaker?" She turned to Archie in mute appeal.

"Angus Marin, down St. Mary's Wynd is the best of the closest."

"There," Maisie confronted the lad. "Go to Mr. Marin in St. Mary's Wynd and tell him that Lord Carrington will be in to see them first thing in the morning, but could they please collect Agnes's…body—" She had trouble saying the word.

"Yer no going to just leave her?"

"I'll stay with her until you come back," Maisie promised. Seeing the boy's hesitation, she added. "Archie, perhaps you had best go with him."

"I had rather not leave you," he said. "You know the way, lad—it's only a few streets over."

Fergus scrubbed his face one more time with the coarse wool of his sleeve. "I'll go," he finally said and left without further ado.

"Be as quick as you can," Archie called after him. He didn't like having Maisie down in these damp, crypt-like corridors any longer than absolutely necessary. The place felt rank with death and disease. But Maisie gave no indication that any of that bothered her—with her head bowed as if in prayer, she held fast to Agnes's cold white hand until the lad reappeared some thirty minutes later.

"It's done then."

"Thank you, Fergus. You're a good boy." Maisie reached for his hand as well, but he shied off, moving back toward the crude doorway where other faces—the wretched inhabitants of other "rooms" of the vaults, all peering in to get a look.

"She dead then?" asked one of them.

"Pish off, Doris," Fergus said as another person said, "Hush," and pulled the offending Doris away. "Everyone can pish off. All of you. And you, too," he said to Maisie. "Nothin' you can do for her now. Nothin' anyone can do for her now."

The lad's mood was turning surly in his grief. "Easy, Fergus," Archie advised. "There's no call for that kind of talk. We'll stick together." He helped Maisie to her feet, but felt for the first time how cold her fingers were. "But you'll thank Miss Conway for all she did, first."

"Didn't do nothin' that worked, did she?" Fergus spat. "Made Aggie's life a misery."

"What'd she do?" came the murmured questions from the edge of the small crowd. "Did she kill her?"

"No," Archie's voice echoed in the stone close. No matter how much the lad was hurting, Archie was not about to stand idly by while he badmouthed Maisie. His own guilt would not allow him to stay silent. "No one could have done more. No one did more—or did anything. You know that, Fergus."

"All I ken is Aggie's gone."

"Fergus, I know you are grievously sad," Maisie appealed. "But please—"

The child's lip quivered. "I want to go home."

"And we'll take you home. Our home to start," Maisie promised. "And then to Prestonpans or wherever you want. We'll find a boat for you to work on if you want to fish like your father. Or you can stay and learn painting. Or printing." She turned to Archie for approval after the fact, but he agreed with a nod—nothing less would do for the poor lad. "It's up to you."

A shuffle at the door interrupted. "The baneshanks has come, but they'll not come along insides, they say. You're after having to carry 'er out to their cart."

And so he would. Archie nodded grimly to Maisie, who tucked the linen sheet respectfully over Agnes's head and smoothed the covers before he knelt down and carefully picked the whole bundle of bedlinen and lass up in one go, to carry out.

"Give way," he ordered as she shouldered his way out of the coffin-like room. "Get back."

Maisie picked up her things, took Fergus by the hand and together, they led the long, winding way down and out of the fetid vault and into the pouring rain, where the undertaker's hand-drawn bier waited for him to gently lay Agnes's body into the cart.

They stood there, the three of them, in the pouring rain, getting soaked to the skin, watching the bier be trundled away until the lad could stand it no more. He tore himself away from

Maisie's protective embrace and went pelting off down the street to God knew where.

"Fergus!" Maisie called after him. "Please come back!" And then she raised her hand to her mouth to yell, "You can come home anytime!" as his footsteps faded from the cobbles.

"He'll come back," Archie consoled her. "He knows where to find you."

And then there was nothing for Archie to do but take up the heavy medicine chest and lead Maisie under the spine of the South Bridge and back down Liberton's Wynd to the Statesman's offices a few yards up from Cowgate. But this time, he led her through the empty office to a narrow stair at the back, which led upward to a small but comfortable apartment of rooms.

His private rooms. With his private bed.

"It's not much. But it's clean and warm—my landlady always keeps the fire laid." In another moment he had coaxed forth a flame and the fire slowly caught, chasing the damp chill from the room.

"Let's get these wet things off." He began by peeling his own sodden, multi-caped greatcoat off before he helped her with her own heavy countrywoman's red cloak, spreading them over the back of a chair to dry before the fire.

"And a hot drink, I should think, to warm us through. Hot whisky should do the trick." He banged a kettle on the hob before searching a cabinet for a whisky bottle. "Here." He passed her the bottle. "Get a dram of that into you, while the water heats."

She was past the niceties and took a swig straight from the bottle. "Lord!" she muttered on a gasp. "I've had wine, but that's—"

"Strong Scots whisky. Good for what ails ye."

"I don't think anything could fix what ails me. Not tonight."

"Well," he said, "were still going to try. Keep working on those wet clothes." He shucked his waistcoat and toed off his boots before he drew his wet linen shirt over his head, leaving it where it landed with a splat next to the fireplace. "I'll get some blankets."

By the time he padded back barefooted, but carrying an armful of blankets from the other room, Maisie had not even managed to loosen the tie at the neck of her plain woolen chemise dress, let alone peel off her sodden stockings.

"Here, let me help," he offered. "My hands are warmer."

"I left in such a rush, I didn't think to take gloves."

"You took the important things." He nodded toward the portable medicine chest he had deposited next to the door when they came in. "And you went, which is more than most people in your position would have done." He loosened the neckline until it gaped wide.

"Don't make me out to be a heroine for merely trying to be a decent human being," she scoffed. "I'm no saint."

"No? You've said yourself you're on the side of the saints. I think I can see the halo, though it is a bit dim at the moment." He kissed her forehead and undid the wet knot of the tie at her waist.

"You're being willfully kind." She pulled her arms out of the sodden dress and let it fall to the floor. "I thought newspapermen were supposed to be hard and cynical, having plumbed the depths of human depravity?"

"Perhaps, but along with the view of what I will admit is some pretty shocking depravity, I've also seen some wondrous acts of kindness, generosity and gratitude. I try to think of those first when contemplating my view of mankind. Or womankind. Not hard to do when you give me such a sterling example of kindness." Archie took her hand to lead her closer to the fire.

"For all the good it did."

Archie could hear the tight heat and hurt in her voice. She seemed to cave in upon herself a little, as if the purpose that had stiffened her spine suddenly gave way—she looked deflated.

He steered her into the only armchair that wasn't covered in wet clothes. "Maisie, you did everything you could."

"I did everything too late."

"Not too late," he tried to assure her. "You gave her ease. You showed her care. You made sure she didn't die alone. You held her hand." He took her own cold hand within his own to warm them. "I don't know another woman of my acquaintance who would have done that. And I doubt even the most skilled apothecary could have done more."

"And still it was not enough."

"We need to get these wet things off of you." His hands went to the laces on the front of her stays, but the sodden knot resisted all his attempted to untie it.

"This was all my fault. I should have done more. I never should have let Smyth think she had any dominion over Agnes in the first place. I should *never* have let Smyth stay with us all these stupid, long years. I should have made her go years ago. I should have done more."

That was her guilt talking. "You did all you could." Archie's own guilt—for being the one who had in fact sent Agnes to return the key he had swiped from Sir Richard Conway's office—was so great that he could not even begin to articulate it in the present circumstances.

Maisie sighed out her weary frustration. "Do you have a scissors?" she asked.

"Here." He fetched the letter opener on his desk and levered the sharp edge to sever the taut lace with a snap that seemed to rouse her from her chilly stupor. "I'll hold the blanket while you peel that off."

He held the blanket up like a wall around her as she stood before the fire, shielding her modesty from his gaze. But it was impossible to shield her from his thoughts—on the other side of this rough woolen blanket, Maisie Conway was slowly taking her clothes off. And there was every chance that he was finally going to get to see every beautiful inch of her.

It was slow, nearly laborious work because she was cold and tired and exhausted, but she kept on doggedly peeling the clammy garments away from her chilled skin.

Finally she took the blanket from his hands and pulled it tight around her as she stepped out of the puddle of her chemise, and, for no reason and every reason all at once, began to cry. The composure she had kept through the ordeal gave way to grief and she began to weep—deep, heart-wrenching sobs wringing their way out of her chest.

Archie wrapped another warm woolen blanket around her before wrapping another around himself, whereupon he sat, gathering her on his lap and into his arms. "I'm sorry," he said when her sobs finally began to subside. "I'm so very sorry." He kissed the salty corners of her eyes.

"I am, too," she agreed as she swiped at her wet cheeks with the edge of the blanket.

He thumbed his hands across her cheeks to wipe away the rest of her tears and found himself following his hands with his mouth, kissing away her hopelessness, pressing his warmth and reassurance into her as if it were a living, breathing thing.

"Please," she said.

Because what she needed in the face of miserable death was the delight of life in all its frailty. And because she was still cold— far too cold.

"Yes." He kissed her with all the force of his pity and understanding. With every ounce of kindness and decency in him. He kissed her with longing to heal the broken, frightened part of her. He kissed her to warm her from the inside out.

"Archie." His name was a sigh upon her lips. "Please. I don't want to be alone. And I don't want to be sad. Make me glad, Archie. Kiss me and make me glad."

"Maisie, I—"

She cut off his words with her mouth upon his.

Maisie gripped the bound hem of the blanket and levered herself against him, angling her mouth to his, offering him her body, her self, her very soul. She would not just passively wait for him to accept her offer. She would not let this opportunity slip from her grasp.

She moved her mouth softly at first, feeling her way toward pleasure. And passion. Anything to obliterate the empty feeling inside. Anything to feel something better.

She pressed her lips against his lightly, shifting to place little busses along the rough line of his jaw, until her mouth seemed to want to move of its own volition, until she was opening her mouth and delving in to taste him.

And then her hands were no longer on his blanket, but around his neck and in his hair, holding him still and near, so she could kiss him as she pleased, as she had always wanted to do.

"I don't want to be alone tonight, Archie," she whispered again, as if she had to convince him of all the painful longing she had bottled up inside. "I don't want to sleep alone. Please. Please don't turn me away. Please let me be with you. Please."

If she could have tonight, if she could have just one chance to be with him, then she felt she could bear the awful burden of the grief that was like a wound inside.

"Now." She pressed kisses to the lovely slide of skin beneath his ear. "Please," she said again, because she did not know what else to say to his silence. "I want to be with you, Archie Carrington. I need to be with you. Please, if you care for me, if you love me even a little, then you'll do this for me."

"Maisie..." He shook his head as if he would gainsay her.

"Please, Archie."

He looked at her for a long time, it seemed, his eyes dark and unfathomable, roaming over her face. And then his hand came up to follow the path of his gaze and he caressed her, carefully outlining each and every curve and plane, brushing his fingers lightly over her lashes, skimming along the outline of her lips. "Why on Earth do you think you need to convince me. Don't you already know?"

She wasn't sure what she knew and what she didn't anymore. The only thing she was sure of was that she could rely upon him. She could trust him.

She pressed her mouth into the hollow of his throat where his pulse beat strong and steady beneath her lips and in answer, he cupped her face with his hands, drew her toward him and kissed her. A sweet, gentle kiss that filled her with bittersweet ease.

She felt the moment when his caution and care gave way, and he began to kiss her in earnest—his arms tightened, his hands gripped her arms and drew her hard against his chest. Archie delved into her mouth and let his hands roam over her blanket-covered back, until they came up to rake through her hair, cradling her jaw and holding her still for a blistering kiss.

"Yes," she gasped. Heat began to pulse through her veins,

warming her enough to drive out the cold dread that was knotted in her chest.

She abandoned herself to the warmth of his care, losing herself in the blessedly forgetful force of each new sensation. When his hand came back up to stroke her cheek and cradle her jaw, Maisie placed her hands over his and tipped her head, leaning her cheeks into his hand.

She rested there, safe in his arms for a blissful moment, until he lifted her to her feet and stood.

"Come," he said simply, holding out his hand.

He led her the six awkward steps to his bed chamber—they were both gripping the blankets—but the distance was as great a divide as any she had ever crossed.

His golden face was solemn in the glow from the fireplace embers. "Maisie, we cannot do this lightly. I couldn't do this—I mean, I could—I can," he said a little sheepishly, giving her a bit of his lopsided smile. "But what I mean—"

"Shh. Archie" she whispered. "You are the best, truest friend I have ever had and I want this more than I can say."

He took her into his arms carefully, reverently, as if she were fragile and would break. He cupped her face with his hands, tenderly caressing her cheeks with his thumbs.

"Sweet Maisie." He touched feather-light kisses upon her salt-stained cheeks, pressed infinitely light busses upon her lips. His mouth came down and gently covered hers. "You will tell me if I hurt you. If your—"

She did not want infirmity between them. Her answer was to press her lips to his. He tasted of whisky and warmth and strength. She gave herself up to the kiss, using her lips and tongue, and the force of her desire. She felt mad with it, consumed by the need to become one with him, body and soul. She needed to be near him, be with him now.

She stepped back to let the outer blanket fall and although her fingers shook, she loosened the second blanket enough to let it slide off her shoulders. She wanted to be naked, with nothing between them, bare of all traces of cloth and restraint.

With nothing left to hide.

Archie simply tossed his blanket on the bed as he came to her. "My sweet Maisie."

"Why do you call me that. I'm not sweet."

"I beg to differ." He kissed her gently before he scooped her up and laid her carefully upon the soft mattress. He came down next to her, and his hands immediately began roaming over her torso, lightly skimming over the length of her body, up and down her arms, around her face and into her hair.

Each touch, each whisper of his breath along her skin wound down through her belly until the sweet tension coiled throughout her body.

He speared his fingers through her hair, pulling out pins, unraveling her braid and spreading the long strands out around her head. He buried his face in it, inhaling deeply.

"Maisie," Archie whispered into her ear. "How I have wanted you. How I have thought and thought of this moment." His fingers traced the contour of her lips.

He was so tender under all that brash, careless charm. The glorious tension pulsed upward through her veins, leaping and tumbling up her heart.

She thought he might say something else, but after a long moment he simply closed his eyes and, breathing deeply, lowered his head to hers.

He kissed her again, with slow, careful kisses, taking his time and relaxing into her embrace. Maisie's eyes fluttered closed as she let the soft, slippery sensations wash over the surface of her skin. Archie's hands heated her wherever they touched, gliding over the curve of her hip and smoothing down around her bottom.

His lips were at her ear, even as his hands cupped her, the

words the same evocative murmur. "My sweet Maisie. So fiercely kind. So determinedly sweet."

She needed little else to inflame her. The heat of his hands, the touch of his tongue at her ear, were all she needed to set the inexorable tide of longing rising within her.

She opened her eyes and inched closer, wanting and needing to see more of him. She reached up to touch his dear, dear face, holding his rough cheeks in her hands, guiding her thumbs across the strong planes of his cheekbones as she set herself to memorizing each and every facet of his handsome face.

This was Archie, with the sharp foxlike chin and the dark luminously warm eyes. This was the man she had chosen—was choosing now. Her hands delved into his long locks, and she could feel the strong cords of muscles in his neck as she pulled herself back up to his mouth.

She wanted to be closer. She wanted to consume and be consumed by him. She slanted her mouth across his, deepening the kiss, needing all of his comfort. Needed to feel the heat of his skin next to hers, to feel the comforting weight of his body wrap around her and banish the last vestiges of the cold inside.

When their tongues met and tangled in her mouth, she gasped aloud with relief from the bittersweet joy of the sensations streaking across her skin like lightning. She was fair jangling with feelings—her palms felt hot and tingly as she ran them over his body and her breath felt intoxicating within her chest.

The strong, corded muscles in his neck and shoulders flexed as she kneaded her fingers into his taut flesh, so she ran her hands down his neck and onto the sleek sculpted curves of his chest, marveling in the difference of texture and feel from her own skin. His chest was sprinkled with dark curling hair that lightly abraded the sensitive tips of her fingers and palms.

Her breath began to come faster, that might have been embarrassing had they not been matched, pant for shallow pant, by the bellows-like push of Archie's breathing sawing in and out of his chest. Somehow, Maisie could only laugh at the dire comedy of the two of them—at herself, the dreadful, lame spinster who was somehow naked with the only man she had ever fancied who had somehow, thankfully, fancied her back.

Archie's answering laugh vibrated through her as she trailed her hands down his long torso, to the glorious member at the apex of his thighs.

"Easy, sweet," he whispered on a low laugh, covering her hands with his own, guiding her to clasp him firmly. "Slowly, love. We have all night."

"Then let us make the most of it quickly," she heard herself say. It felt as if it had been night for too long. But it was the darkness within that needed to be kept at bay. "Please." She slid her hands along the intriguing ridge of muscle that ran along his hips before she took him in hand again.

"God's bawbag—you are exceedingly good at cultivating new talents." He closed his eyes in momentary surrender to the ecstasy of having his cock stroked, before she shook his head. "But let us not get ahead of ourselves. Let us not rush, my love. Let us savor each moment as it comes."

"I'm sorry but—"

He kissed her again. "I want every moment to last as long as possible. I want every kiss to last a day. I want every time I touch you to feel like as if it will last all night."

He illustrated his delightful point by tracing the sensitive underside of her breasts, before his hand brushed lightly across her tight nipples. First one breast and then the other, until she felt the pink flesh contract into an almost painful burst of bliss.

She gasped, a sound of need and desperation, and arched her back, pressing herself forward into his hands.

"Yes, please," she begged again, unsure of exactly what she pleaded for. "Please, Archie."

❧

For the first time in his life, Archie Carrington was afraid he would be unable to keep up. Maisie's ardor was a desperate thing—heedless in her desire to throw off the shadow of death.

In his waking dreams, her seduction had been all slow, gentle caution—he had reasoned that she was a virgin who should have needed easing into the intimacy of sex. But he had not counted on the determined woman who knew both her mind and her own capabilities.

Damn his eyes, but he kept getting her wrong—he kept making assumptions that clearly could not be true. She was neither infirm of purpose nor of body.

What she wanted for her body was respect—the respect of treating her with all the passion he felt. And so he drove his hands into her hair, and put his mouth to her breast, running the edge of his tongue lightly across the sweet peak of her nipple, wetting the lovely tight bud before he abruptly nipped, abrading the sensitive flesh against the sharp edge of his teeth.

Maisie cried out with pleasure and threw her head back, her eyes clenched shut tight to absorb the intense sensation. Clever, clever, responsive lass. Oh, how he liked the responsive ones. As he watched her, some of her intense abandon began to creep under his skin.

Archie rasped the other peak while his hand dove down across the sleek scoop of her belly and into the nest of titian curls between her soft thighs. She was almost keening now, urgent little panting cries that rose with each shallow, rapid breath. "Please."

"Please, Archie," he whispered before he kissed her one last time, before he rose over her, and ran his free hand all the way down her legs, kneading the tired muscles rhythmically until she began to move her hips in time, riding his hand as it covered her mound.

"Please, Archie."

"So polite. So very English." He slowly slid one long finger inside and felt her inner muscles close around him, hot and slick and encouraging. God's bawbag.

The sight of her, long and lithe and pale and pulsing and so very, very responsive sent his own need roaring through his body. Archie sent up another blasphemous prayer as he covered over her body to still her with his weight and ease his own arousal. But he could not forget what she had said about arousal—how the sight of his body didn't inflame her nearly as much as his words.

"Look at you," he whispered. "You're bloody beautiful."

She clasped her arms about him, holding him tight, and tighter still when he moved his finger within her. He kissed her deeply, his tongue tangling with hers in rhythm with his hands.

When he felt her body ease a fraction, he eased another long finger alongside the first. A rush of heat and desire ripped into his gut at the scalding heat of her passage as it closed tightly around his fingers.

"Sweet Maisie."

She sighed and moved with the gentle pulse of his fingers. She was so bloody close, he resisted the urge to find his own release within her and instead concentrated on grazing his thumb ever so lightly against the sensitive nub shielded by her petal-soft flesh.

She opened her eyes wide in astonishment before she clenched them tight as her back arched off the bed. And he was wrapping his arm to support her and kiss her and swallow her cry as her climax broke through her.

Archie kissed her again and again letting her breath level and her ardor cool before he slowly withdrew his hands from her body. But he could still feel the strong pulse of her blood where their bodies touched. Still glory in the soft slide of her skin against his. Still tangle his hands in her glorious red hair.

Her skin was beautifully flushed and a light sheen of perspiration bedewed her even in the chill of the cool room.

"Now ye look like a proper Scotswoman," he teased. "Who knew ye were hiding all this ginger glory under those paint smeared smocks of yours."

"I knew," she said. "I always knew."

How foolish of him not to see. To try to slow her down. Why had he not realized she would make love with the same fierce determination that she lived, with the same controlled genius she displayed in all facets of her life?

Her ragged breathing began to slow and ease, gradually returning toward normal, but he wasn't done with her yet. Not by a long, long shot. Fate had been both persistent and kind in delivering her to him, and he was damn well going to make the most of the opportunity.

He ran his hand down the long, sinuous line of her side, relishing the way her body was splayed in contented abandon across the bed. One leg was bent and falling inward, shielding his greedy view from the bright whorl of red curls atop her mound, and the other was kicked out to the side. Her arms, which only moments ago had been clutching him, now lay still and relaxed against the sheet.

He dipped his head and breathed in her familiar, evocative scent, the acetic blend of linseed oil and turpentine—the scent that somehow moved him so.

He closed his eyes and indulged his other senses, letting his hands flow lightly over her sinuous, responsive body. Her skin felt so soft and inviting.

His cock twitched insistently, as if to remind him of his own need.

He nosed her damp hair aside to kiss the sensitive hollow of her neck, and her eyes fluttered open on a beguiling, inviting sigh. She turned into his embrace, coming fully against his chest.

Archie wanted her so badly he ached. For her, this supposedly fragile, determined lass in his arms, and he wanted to keep her there as long as possible. She was here and they were together, and she was naked. And she was his and no one else's.

He kissed her again, and again his hands delved into the silky glory of her hair, sliding the long, fine tresses across his palms. He meant to kiss her lightly, to give her time to recover, but she stirred and nuzzled delightfully at his throat, and his lust and his cock rose with each supple stir of her body, every subtle rustle of the soft sheets. The fire flared, and light glanced over the dewy slide of her skin, illuminating the beautiful contours of her long, sleek body.

Merciful God, but he couldn't wait another moment to have her.

CHAPTER 30

*M*aisie came back to herself slowly, not wanting to let the sweet, wondrous sensations go, wanting to linger in the satiated twilight as long as she could. She felt physically depleted in the best way, empty of worry for the first time in what felt like forever. Because Archie was warm and safely by her side, his arm wrapped around her loosely, as if he held her because he wanted to, not because he thought she was too fragile or delicate to be left alone.

She reached for his hands, clasping their palms together. "Thank you, Archie."

"You're more than welcome, my sweet Maisie." He kissed her fingers where they were enmeshed. "But we are not done yet."

"No?" She certainly felt done—complete and whole in mind and body.

"Ah, lass." The rough Scots brogue warmed his voice. "I've only just begun to demonstrate what I can offer ye. Let us resume our lesson in the anatomy of the human body, for the benefit of your education and amusement."

He was teasing. And she was warm and satiated and more than ready to be charmed. "Yes, let's. Impress me then, Archie."

"Oh, lass. There's naught I'd like more." He rolled over her, straddling her hips with his tawny thighs, pressing her legs together with the inherent strength of his legs, while he rose above her.

Maisie reveled in the absolute classical perfection of him. His arms and torso were sculpted, as if from warm golden marble—her own Apollo of the Belvedere or Borghese David.

His skin was tanned all the way from his arms, down his chest to his waist, where the skin turned paler again. His chest was very sprinkled with dark hair, as Mars black as his head. It glinted in the firelight, leading her eyes down to where the hair trailed lower past his waist.

She could feel heat flush up her neck and across her face. And lower, where the hot pulse of her desire stirred restively.

He didn't seem to mind her stare. When she tore her heated gaze back up to his face in embarrassment, he just looked back steadily, not laughing, certainly not expressing shock or censure. "Tell me what you see?"

"A very fine specimen of a man." She sighed with all the happy pleasure of teasing him. "But what I find arousing—what has aroused me, Archie—is that this specific specimen is you." She stretched her hands, still clasping his, over her head to bring him poised over her. "Nobody else but you."

Archie smiled and reached to move the candle on the small table next to the bed closer. "I want to see you."

"I want to see you, too," she agreed quietly. She smiled up at him, sure in her wants and secure in his love. "My exhibitionist."

Archie went momentarily still, looking down at her. "For you and no other, *mi amore*. Only for you." Then he kissed her again, lightly tracing the indentations of her dimples with his tongue, before he followed the angled line of her jaw up to her ear. "*Dalla vita*—from true life. *Spogliato*," he whispered against her ear. "Stripped. You as well as I."

Maisie's heart expanded and filled with something deeper and more profound, something more exalted than mere physical bliss, and she kissed him back with all the love and heart-wrenching, bittersweet happiness she felt. But kisses alone, no matter how glorious, were not enough.

She ran her hands down his finely muscled chest, thrilled to touch what she had only drawn. To feel what she had only imagined. She let her palms smooth over elegant taper of his wrist into his forearms. Of course his lovely, sinewy forearms

But there were other limbs, just as lovely. She swept her hands across his belly and then lower, curiously seeking his sex.

"Oh, God, yes," he bit off, the words deep and guttural with gratification.

"Archie." Her own voice was high and needy. "I want you in—"

He kissed her more deeply as her hand settled firmly about him, hungrily delving into her mouth with his tongue, until she felt the urgent press of his pelvis against hers, and he pushed her legs wide with his knees.

Then, he replaced her hand with his own, and she felt the blunt push of his manhood as he guided himself into her quivering flesh.

Maisie felt an uncomfortable, burning sensation. She tensed and gritted her teeth as he pushed more deeply into her, stretching her past where she wanted to go.

"Adesso fai silenzio ... girati," he whispered, his voice easy and smooth. *"Fammi concentrare che—"*

She had no real idea what he was saying but it sounded so lovely and soothing.

"Si, amore mio," he encouraged and Maisie relaxed into the warmth of his regard.

Her hands rose to his face, seeking the reassurance of his lopsided smile. "Archie. Tell me more."

"Certamente amore mio." She could feel his warm laugh reverberate through her from the place where their bodies joined.

"*Dulce Maisie,*" he soothed. "*Sei nel mio cuore! La tua bocce, il tuo seno.*"

He lowered his head to her breast, and took her nipple into his mouth in a way that made her forget the discomfort, and transported her back into the realm of pleasure.

A little frisson of something slippery and spontaneous crept through her. Something warm and terrible and wonderful. Something that made her gasp and smile all at the same time.

His hands rounded her bottom. "*Il tuo sedere.*

His hand replaced his mouth at her breast, and Maisie pulled his mouth back to hers, kissing him back, sliding her tongue with his, wondering at the taste, the smell, the feel of him around her. Her body began to move in response, her hips shifting restively beneath his lovely weight.

He pressed up higher on his arms, taking his weight off her, and flexed his hip muscles against her.

Oh, sweet heavens, yes.

"Adonis."

"Archie, while I'm in your sweet *piricocu.*"

She breathed his name as if it were a prayer. "Archie."

"Yes, that's it. *Daverro. Ti adoro.*"

That she thought she understood. Maisie wiggled closer in response, arching her pelvis toward him. "Bless your Italian tutors," she gasped. "Each and every one of them."

"I'll write them with your praise, *tesoro mio.*" He nudged his hips against her again, and lowered his head to her breast, suckling her in time with the pulse of his body into her center.

Maisie felt the erotic cadence catch hold inside her, urging her hips to move in time to meet his. She closed her eyes and concentrated on the rhythm, and the wonderful, powerful sensations skating under her sensitized skin. Her palms tingled with the need to touch him, to worship his body and his love.

She ran her hands up the living sculpture of his sleek, powerful arms, kneading the sinuous muscles there, before riding upward around his neck, over his wide shoulders, and down onto the sculpted plain of his chest. Her own god beneath her hands, to worship and glorify like a heedless pagan, drunk on the addictive bliss.

She danced her inquisitive fingers across his curiously flat nipples, and he made an inarticulate sound nearer to pleasure than pain.

Maisie opened her eyes to see him rising above her, his teeth gritted and bared in something too much like anguish. "Archie?" She whispered her question.

"*Ancora.*" He smiled down at her. "Do that again."

"This?" She ran her hands across his chest again, slower this time, her fingers tracing over his nipples in imitation of the way he had touched hers. "Do you like that?"

"Yes. Like that." He rose higher upon his knees, pulling her tight against him before he let go of her hips, and molded his hands to cup her breasts. "*Proprio così.*" He flicked the tight rosy peaks with his callused thumbs.

A carnal sound of encouragement and need broke from her mouth on a cry. Her eyes crashed shut as the first wave of pleasure pushed deep into her belly. And then they flew open as she felt him capture her hands again, but she relaxed as he brought them to her breasts.

"*Toccati.* Touch yourself," he urged. "Just with your fingertips. So you can do this for yourself when I'm not here to do it for you. So you can think of me and give yourself pleasure with just your imaginings."

His hands guided hers, teaching her how to best evoke the pleasurable feelings curling low within herself. And by watching him as she did so, she learned that he liked watching her pleasure herself as well, that his breath became even more shallow, and his eyes glazed with that strange haze of intensity as he watched her.

In response he ran his hands down over her hips and around

to her bottom. He traced the curve of the taut globes with his palms, kneading her flesh as he rose up upon his knees.

She watched his hands round to her hips and pull her up high against him, and felt a jolt of such intense, joyous pleasure streak through her, and something inside, some last vestige of restraint came untethered and ran riot—a heady, insistent, intoxicating mixture of pain and pleasure that rose higher with each escalating thrust.

His body surged into her, stronger and stronger, feeding the need, stoking the fiery heat that built where their bodies touched.

Maisie felt herself slipping away, losing herself to the inexorable whirl of sensations. She clutched at the sheets, fisting up the smooth, fine linen, trying to anchor herself against the relentless onslaught of pressure and pleasure.

Oh, she wanted. She wanted, she wanted.

She had to get it.

She tried to plant her feet flat against the sheet to angle her body to appease the all-encompassing need. But her leg wasn't strong enough to hold her—she slipped and the pleasure skidded away, out of reach.

Archie immediately grabbed a pillow and stuffed it under her bottom, leveraging her up.

But it wasn't enough—he was too tall and the feeling was slipping away.

She made a sound of frustrated anguish, clutching at him in desperation.

Archie made an echoing sound of frustration very near to a curse, and shoved the pillow away. Then he drove the breath from her lungs with the simple efficacy of lifting her legs flat against his chest.

The sharp, aching pleasure bolted back through her. She heard a high keening moan and knew it came from her, that it was a sound of approval as much as distress, because it felt so good, too good—a pleasure so intense it was almost pain.

But Archie was relentless. He held her legs and she watched him, rising above her with such strength and beauty that her heart constricted.

She felt him, apart from her and yet in her all at the same time, and she knew in that instant what it meant to be undone— to let go of every last tie to reality, and give way to the glorious physical wash of upending emotion that shot through her.

She closed her eyes and felt him stroke his hand down her belly, into the thatch of curls shielding the place where they were joined. He teased his fingers through the hair, then slipped his fingers lower, ever so slightly lower, to the sensitive engorged flesh below.

Maisie cried out and bucked up hard. It was too much and not enough all at the same time. She felt her head begin to thrash against the sheets, from side to side.

But Archie wouldn't let up. He pulled her back hard against him, holding her hips still against him as he surged inside her.

He held her just so, so that something changed and sharpened, and it felt good, so good. She felt like she was going to break into a hundred pieces of bliss.

And then she did. And he grabbed her neck and pulled her to his mouth just as she cried out in bliss. Heat and joy and peace and relief cascaded through her body in rushing, tumbling waves, leaving the glorious serene warmth behind.

And then, in the next second, it was he who tensed, and with a sound that was both joy and anguish, pushed himself into the heat, into her, one last time.

Maisie felt strange and weightless, as if she couldn't feel the sheets or mattress beneath her, as if all the feeling had drained from her body, leaving her pleasantly, gloriously numb.

She watched with a sort of detached amusement as Archie let go of her and sat back on his heels, slipping away from her body.

He looked dazed and disoriented as he tried to catch his breath.

The two of them were huffing and puffing like a bellows.

Maisie felt her lips curve into a wide smile, heard the puff of laughter that blew across her lips.

"Laughing? Are you laughing at me, Maisie?"

She heard the wicked amusement in his voice. "No, goodness no. That was… 'glorious' doesn't seem adequate."

"It's not." He reached out to stroke her thigh as he collapsed down alongside her. "But you're quite glorious, as well."

He hooked his hand around her belly and turned her to her back, pulling her snugly against his chest. "Maisie. My sweet, surprising Maisie," he whispered against her hair.

Maisie smiled in wonder at the strange scratchy feeling of his chest against her back and closed her eyes in contentment.

She felt happy, so safe in his arms that she wanted to stay and savor the moment for just a while longer. She took a deep breath and felt his breathing slip into the shallow regularity that signaled he was already asleep.

She curled herself tight against him, and stayed awake for a long time, listening and feeling and thinking of the wonderful strangeness of the heat and scent and texture of the man surrounding her.

It was overwhelming and yet not enough, knowing that this night, these last minutes would have to last her the rest of forever.

CHAPTER 31

*A*rchie woke to the sound of rain and of Maisie, beside him, making distressed noises in her sleep. "Maisie, my love, wake up." He wrapped his arms around her to awaken her. "Your heart is pounding."

"Oh," she exhaled sharply and put her hand to her chest. "I suppose it is."

"Bad dream?"

"Bad reality," she contradicted wearily. "Poor, dear Agnes. And —" She exhaled again. "It just comes back now and again—the fear."

He brushed her hair away from her face. "What are you afraid of?"

She took a long moment before answering. "There's this moment every now and again." She turned within his embrace with her back—and her bottom—spooned against his chest and belly. "When I wake up thinking I can't move again. And… it's just awful until I wake up enough to prove to myself that I can move." Another gusty sigh. "I'm sorry. I need coffee."

"I'll make some in a minute." Right after he reassured her that she could indeed move—and move him.

"Thank you." She kissed his hand, laced with hers. "What time —? Oh, good lord." She spied the clock on his mantelpiece. "I hope to God my clothing is dry." She took the linen with her as she rose hastily, wrapping herself but leaving him chilly and alone on the bed. "So sorry, Archie."

"Think nothing of it. I'll fetch up coffee." And arrange for a carriage.

Archie threw on his clothes and padded down to the offices of the Review to send messengers for both, while Maisie hurriedly dressed.

The carriage came before the coffee—within a half hour, the Marquess of Aiken's lacquered equipage took up half of the roadway at the end of Liberton's Close.

"Such favor," murmured Maisie. But she held tight to the hand he gave her to help her into the carriage. "May I ask you to see me home?"

"I would do no less," he said instead of insisting because she didn't look as if she could take even gentle teasing at this point. She was pale and tense, her fingers clenched tight around his.

She only let go when they reached her father's stableyard and Flora came running out of the house to greet them. "Maisie! Where have you been? We've been worried sick."

Maisie clasped the hand her sister held out. "She's dead."

"What? Who—"

"Agnes!" She said a little too forcefully before she lowered her tone. "Agnes is dead. She died. We were with her." When Flora only stared at her, Maisie asked. "Did Mrs. Rattle not tell you I'd gone to her?"

"Yes." Flora tried to recover herself. "Yes, she did. I'm only shocked at such news. I did not imagine— Maisie, I'm so very sorry."

"Thank you. And I hope you never do imagine it. It was awful, Flora, the way those people live. And die. She died in the vaults of the famed South Bridge," Maisie told her sister. "It's a rat's warren inside—a maze of rooms and bolt holes, none of them fit to store so much as a turnip."

"Maisie, heavens. Dearest, you sound—and look—done in. Your clothes look as though you've slept in them."

"There wasn't much sleeping." She managed not to look at him. "Lord Carrington and I were at Agnes' side when she died."

She nodded at him in some sort of warning before she assumed a pose of formality, putting out her hand to shake to take her leave of him. "Thank you, Lord Carrington, for all your assistance. And for your escort home. I am very much obliged."

"Miss Conway." He bowed over her hand to do his part. "An honor to escort you, although I am sorry for the circumstances. My condolences upon your loss."

She nodded. "Most appreciated. I, too, regret the circumstances."

"We should get you in," Flora advised.

Archie found himself loath to part from Maisie, and so offered his hand, to lead her down the steps, when her father's voice bid them stop. "Margaret? There you are. Come inside. All of you."

Maisie and Flora exchanged a speaking glance before Maisie said quietly, "It looks like we will not be getting out of this gracefully. If I might prevail upon your escort for a moment longer, Lord Carrington?"

"Of course, Maisie." He gave up the pretense of calling her Miss Conway. If they were to be called upon the carpet, he was more than ready—but Maisie looked as if a stiff wind might blow her down.

He offered her his arm, and kept a steady grip of her hand as they made their way up the steeper steps to the stone terrace outside the drawing room, where Sir Richard awaited them.

Curious that the man had not come to assist his own daughter. Curious.

"Margaret," he began even as they made their way into the

room, "I should like an account of where you have been these past twenty-nine hours, if you please. I have had nothing but an account from the cook that you left with a hamper and a boy in the pony trap and had not been heard of since. I should like—no, I demand an explanation."

Maisie trembled a little as she put up her chin to speak. "I went to the aide and succor of our former tweeny, Agnes. I hope you'll remember her—the young girl wrongly turned off by Mrs. Smyth?"

"What of it?" Sir Richard was nonplussed. "What's done is done."

"Indeed," Maisie agreed, though her gaze hardened. "Quite done. She's dead."

"Ah." Her father nodded. "That is too bad. I shall speak to Mrs. Smyth about hiring another girl."

"No." Maisie's voice was chilly but firm. "I have already made private arrangements in which Mrs. Smyth will play absolutely no part. Not now, not ever. And if she interferes with my work or my workers again, I shall personally see *her* put on the street to see how she likes being abandoned."

"Margaret! That is uncalled for."

But Maisie was too spent for such unnecessary, prim outrage. "Why on Earth did you name me Maisie, Papa, if you never call me that?"

The question seemed innocuous—rhetorical, even—but Archie could hear the tension in her tone, like a rope turned so tight it begins to fray.

"You're no longer a child, to be called by childish names. And I've a position, now, to think of," Sir Richard stated with some heat.

It was nothing more than many men in his, or similar, positions—Archie's own prestige-conscious father amongst them— might say. But Archie was watching Maisie's stoically expressive face, and her father's attitude struck him anew as callous and calculating.

Maisie was more philosophical. "Mama used to say, 'That's your Scots Papa for you.'" She quoted. "Do you remember?"

"I don't remember Mama at all," Flora answered quietly. "More's the pity."

Sir Richard looked as if his collar were suddenly growing too tight for his comfort. "Be that as it may," he blustered. "You have been gone from this house for over a day. And have come home unchaperoned, in the company of a man? What in heavens name were you doing, though I hardly want to ask? You might have injured yourself, or worse, sullied your good name."

Maisie made an exhausted little exhalation of dismissal. "I hope my name is good enough to withstand one mission of mercy before succumbing to being sullied."

"Indeed," Flora agreed.

But Sir Richard was not having it. "Your wit is not appreciated, Margaret. Can you not see how immoral your actions look for a man in my position?"

"It looked far worse in the vaults of the South Bridge. Do you know these vaults, father? They were vile. A vile place for a poor child to live, let alone die."

"Of course I know them." Sir Richard drew himself up. "It is my business to know." But his expression of satisfaction faded as understanding dawned. "You cannot mean that you— You went in there?" Sir Richard asked with dawning horror.

"Of course I did." Maisie had no care for his concerns. "The child was ill and needed tending. I did what I could, which in the end was only to see that she did not die alone."

"You were inside—" He drew back suddenly, his hand to his chest as if he was afraid to leave it in any closer proximity to her. "You might have brought the contagion back with you! Did you think of that? Did you think of your sister? Flora come away."

Flora did not move. "Papa—" Her voice was tense with warning.

"No!" Their father was adamant. "What might have happened if she had caught this malignant, putrid fever? Why she might end up—" Too late, Sir Richard stopped himself.

But Maisie's pale, stony face showed she knew what he had been about to say. "Like what, Papa? End up like me?"

"Exactly," their father countered, convinced of his rightness. "One would think that having experienced such a devaluation of your own health and wellbeing, you would be more careful with your sister's."

"Papa!" Flora was aghast.

But Maisie trod onward. "As careful as you've always been with us? But you were rarely here? Did you mean when you were away on your travels, that you were careful never to contract a malignant fever? But I suppose one can catch such a fever anywhere, not just in foreign climes."

"I caught a malignant fever from Lady Doughty, that time," Flora added. "Do you remember, Maisie."

"I do," Maisie answered.

"Maisie nursed me through it," Flora informed her father. "She thought nothing of herself. Only of me and my comfort. She didn't want me to be left alone, like she had been when you took me apart from her when her fever left her lame."

Sir Richard was taken aback, but stood his ground. "A sensible precaution that needed to be taken."

"And then, when I broke my arm falling from my pony, Maisie nursed me through that ordeal, too," Flora added, "and made sure I was not made afraid of horses, though she herself was forbidden to ride. Do you remember?" she asked her father.

"I wasn't aware," he said stiffly.

"You were away," Maisie agreed quietly, "traveling. As you were for Mama's funeral."

"My travels, as you call them, were my work."

"Was that your work in India, securing the monopoly for your company's opium trade?" Maisie asked. "Or before that, when you were stealing tea plants for your company from China? Or after, when you went back to China securing smuggling routes for all that monopolized opium, finding ways to circumvent the Chinese Emperor's ban on the drug?"

Archie could feel his skin grown cold while his blood went hot. Maisie had clearly discovered what he could not. This then was the source of Sir Richard's wealth and privilege—a privilege he clearly meant to keep at all costs.

"How did you learn—" The man stared at his daughter as if he had never truly seen her before. "It was you then, getting in my papers, reading my manuscript?" he accused before he turned hostile. "Well, what of it? We are not speaking of my past. Your behavior of last night has nothing to do with either of those things."

"But we are talking of good names and immorality, Papa, are we not? I wonder how you found nothing immoral about smuggling an illegal narcotic—"

"It is not illegal under our laws," her father challenged.

"No, but you weren't setting up smuggling routes *here*, were you? You can simply import it here, where it more often than not ends up as a vicious tool to numb the minds of the poor to the true foulness of their situation. But there's no law to prevent that from happening is there, like there is to stop the poor from drinking gin, because there's no profitable English monopoly to be upheld for the gin."

"You are talking about something you know nothing about," Sir Richard decreed. "You are getting yourself overwrought. This is what comes—"

"This is what comes from watching children die," she declared fiercely. "This is what comes of being sick of the avoidable death and senseless waste. This is what comes from having your stomach turned at the hypocrisy of turned backs and conveniently blind eyes. This is what comes of being exhausted by anger."

"There, you admit it—you are exhausted. And I hold you responsible, Lord Carrington." The search lamp of Sir Richard Conway's blame swept over Archie. "A man of your station ought to know better than to take my daughter—"

"I took myself into the vaults, Papa," Maisie cut in before Archie could answer. "I went to find and help Agnes of my own accord. I sent for Archie, who was kind enough to come to my aid."

"Archie?" Sir Richard drew himself up again. "He is 'Archie,' now, is he? What does that mean? What goes on here?" The man fixed Archie with a baleful stare.

But before he could give his answer that he was both happy and ready to discuss their imminent marriage, Maisie spoke again, as if she were determined to keep the topic from being broached. "Don't be ridiculous, Papa. I am painting Lord Carrington's portrait—as well you know. Such a circumstance has naturally brought us much together. We are professional and friendly acquaintances, no more."

Archie was disappointed in the lie—assuming it was only a convenient lie. He certainly felt that they were far more to each other than mere professional acquaintances. They were lovers. They were intimate friends.

But Sir Richard seemed to have accepted her word. "And how much longer is that exercise going to take?" he demanded.

"As long as is necessary," Maisie answered.

But her sharp tone seriously displeased her father. "Then go!" Her father waved his hands in the air in agitated frustration, dismissing her. "Go paint. I wash my hands of you. Paint and be damned."

Maisie was not content to let him have the last word. "Certainly, Papa. You may be damned certain I will."

CHAPTER 32

*I*t only seemed appropriate for Maisie to hold Agnes' funeral in the comforting confines of the West Kirk, where she had met Agnes to bring her home that first day. Thankfully, she was not alone—Agnes was mourned by Archie, Flora and Maisie, as well as the cook Mrs. Rattle, Flora's dresser Cora Raines and all of the maids who were bold enough to brave the housekeeper's chilly disapproval.

Mrs. Smyth did not join the mourners, though Maisie would not have wanted her to anyway—her presence would have been an affront.

They made a dolorous sight, the lot of them growing cold and wet in the kirkyard beneath their black umbrellas barely sheltering them from the dripping skies. But Maisie was glad of their solidarity, especially from Flora, who stood staunchly at her side throughout the services.

After their argument with their father, Maisie had been reminded of the terrible confusion of the days surrounding her mother's funeral, when she had been too young to know what she ought to do, but old enough to know that she had to do something.

Still, no matter how properly observed, the funeral was a sorrowful affair. Her best solace came during the burial, when she caught sight of Fergus hanging back behind a tombstone on the far side of the kirkyard. Maisie had to hope the rector would understand, and left him droning the burial service, while she made her slow way across the uneven ground to stand by the young lad and cover him with her umbrella.

"It's no good," the boy mumbled into her skirts when she put her arm around his shoulders.

"No," Maisie agreed. "It's no good at all."

"Ye've given her a decent burial, tho," the boy sniffed, "in a proper kirk."

"Yes," Maisie answered. "It is the least we could do."

"Sorry I said what I did, then, missus."

"Nae bother," she gave him her answer in Scots. "I forgave you then, but I'll forgive you again now," Maisie told him. "I know how hard it must be, missing your sister."

"Aye," he agreed. "Miss 'er summat fierce."

"Oh, aye." She hugged him close to her skirts again. "Do you think you'd like to go closer?"

"In a bit."

The bit proved to be quite a bit later, after the small coffin had been lowered to the ground and the dirt filled in. Only then did Fergus venture closer.

"Fergus, lad." Archie shook his hand and nodded respectfully. "You have my condolences on your loss."

"Not my loss, is it?" The boy wiped his nose with his sleeve. "It's Aggie's. Tho I did lose my hat—left it behind in tae vaults, 'an couldn't go back after they turnt the place oot."

"They turned you out of your room?" Maisie questioned. Not that such a foul place could rightly be called a room. "Please know you have a place with me, warm and safe."

"Nuthin's safe, missus." Fergus shrugged far too fatalistically for such a young boy. "But it weren't just me, they turnt everyone oot—threw it all—pots and pans and claes and clooties oot onto th' pavement."

"They?" Archie stepped close enough to hear. "Who turned the vaults out?"

"Bailiffs, I reckon," Fergus supplied. "Big fellas wi' cudgels."

"They evicted everyone?"

"Ere' they could find," Fergus said grimly.

"And their possessions, such as they were, were thrown out onto the street with them?" Archie asked to clarify.

"Aye. And rubble were carted in tae fill the place up, so there's nae goin' back in."

"Surely that's a good thing?" Maisie asked. "That place was unhealthy and unfit for habitation. Surely you saw—" Her own memories of the awfulness of the place caused a chill to crawl across her skin. "It's to do with the water problem that you were telling me about, surely? The smell of the place—of sewage and filth? That can't have been good for people."

"Quite exactly," Archie said with the sort of weariness she had never seen from him before. Almost as if he were disheartened. "It is most assuredly not good for people. But poverty is a great prison—where else are those people supposed to go? There is still nowhere else—nowhere else safe or clean or affordable. Nowhere with running water."

But the way he was looking at her—as if in some kind of judgment—told her there was likely worse to come. "What else?"

"I'm wondering who could have ordered such an eviction? Who would have such power within the government to close down what is essentially a private property for the public good?"

Maisie's heart sank from her chest deep into the pit of her stomach. "The Lord Advocate?"

"Aye."

Then it was her responsibility to do something about it.

Maisie began by taking Fergus by the hand. "Thank you all for coming." She shook each of the other maid's hands. "But let us all get out of the rain." She squeezed Fergus's hand in reassurance. "Let us all go home."

Archie had arranged for the use of his father's town coach to transport them to the funeral—the second-best, unmarked carriage, of course, for while the Marquess of Aiken was happy to aid in Archie's investigation of the new Lord Advocate, he didn't want his name or his equipage associated with Sir Richard or his family.

Archie waited until the ladies had disembarked in the stable-yard at Kirk Brae Head before he quietly asked Maisie. "May I come see you tomorrow? We have the excuse that we still need sittings for the portrait, but I should simply like to see you. It feels like forever since we've been together."

"Yes, please." She gave him a small smile. "Tomorrow. But if you'll excuse me now, I need to speak with my father."

"Yes, let me see you in," he said because it was the only thing he could say, but he held her arm as long as he could, down the kitchen stairs to the servants' stair where she finally let go of his hand.

For some reason he could not fathom, he needed to watch her for as long as possible as she made her slow, uneven, but somehow stately progress upward to the familiar landing outside her father's bookroom.

Archie was about to turn away and take himself and the carriage back to Aiken House, when he heard his name—and his heretofore unused protective instincts roared into instant readiness.

"Margaret, there you are." Though he was supposedly Scots, Sir

Richard had perfected the English manner of sounding thoroughly bored but somehow peeved, all at the same time. As if he was aggressively at leisure, and had conveniently forgotten his vituperation of the previous day. "Did Lord Carrington accompany you?"

Archie stepped into the bottom of the stairwell to better hear. If he was to be called upon the carpet, he was more than ready— he only hoped Maisie was as well.

"He accompanied us," Maisie answered carefully. "All of us including Flora."

"Ah. Good, good." Sir Richard was all bonhomie, as if he had not cursed his daughter the last time they had spoken. "After our…rather too-candid words yesterday, I am glad to find you finally thinking of your sister."

There was a brief pause in which Archie was sure he could hear Maisie's patience crack, before she asked in a more clipped tone, "And what should I be thinking of her in particular, sir?"

"That she might be better placed to make something of this acquaintance, this familiarity with Lord Carrington, since you will not. Though he is only the third son, he is the third son of a marquess and a lord in his own right. And despite his being something of a rabble rouser with that quarterly of his, Flora could likely make something more amenable of him."

This time Archie felt as if it were he whom Sir Richard had slapped across the face, though the blow was too ineffectual to land. He knew well he was the third son, but had always felt it for the blessing it was—how ghastly to be either the heir or the spare. He much preferred being the freewheeling third wheel.

Which Maisie clearly understood. "Lord Carrington is his own man," Maisie said succinctly, "who doesn't need anyone to make something of him—he has already done so himself. Just as Flora is her own woman who does not need to make something of anyone else, nor be made over by anyone. She has a heart and a will of her own, and can choose for herself."

Just as Maisie had a heart and a will all her own—a heart which Archie rather fervently hoped had chosen him for herself.

"But she will not," Sir Richard complained. "Flora declares she will not set her mind to getting married until she can see *you* happy first—a fool's errand, if you ask me."

There was a mortifying silence before Maisie answered. "I do not ask you. And if I can help it, I never will again."

"Come now, have done with this petulance and rancor. You have had years to accommodate yourself—you know what you are."

"I am an artist," Maisie stated. "A painter and a portraitist. And a damn good one."

"Yes, yes—a spinster must have some occupation." Sir Richard's tone was somehow annoyed. "But you must not stand in your sister's way. You must see the necessity."

"What I see— What I *saw* today and the days proceeding, was that not only are the wages of sin death, but the wages of poverty is also death. Were you the one who ordered the wholesale eviction of the South Bridge vaults?"

"Indeed. What of it?" Sir Richard said in his dismissive way. "Such a den of iniquity and vice, full of brothels and low public houses, if they could even be called that. Do you know, the bailiffs found a damn illegal still operating in the place, much to the injury of the revenue!"

"Because the excise tax is more important than people? People —poor people—also lived there."

"It was unfit for human habitation," the man decreed. "Full of disease, as you so recently became aware."

"As I did so recently become aware," Maisie agreed. "But what I am not aware of, is where are those people to go?"

She had listened. She had understood. And she had taken it upon herself to confront her own father instead of waiting for people like him to do it for her.

Archie did not know when he had loved her more.

"Go?" Sir Richard nearly laughed. "They are supposed to go away. Take their vices and be gone."

"Papa." Maisie's sigh was biblical in its patience. "You are a man of the world, who has traveled widely and seen all manner of people. How do you not understand that these people are too poor to go *anywhere*? Half of them have used what little they had to come here to Edinburgh in the first place—all those crofters dispossessed from highland farmsteads so landowners can run sheep."

"They can find gainful employment," Sir Richard insisted, "as every law-abiding citizen must."

"Where are they supposed to live while they are seeking this gainful employment?" Maisie asked. "What trades are they meant to take up? What training at these new trades may they find?"

Her question was interrupted by the sound of Sir Richard's chair scraping back. "I can see you are determined to be argumentative and difficult."

"I am always called difficult when I ask questions you don't want to answer."

"And you are difficult because you come here bedeviling me instead of being grateful," he railed. "A proper daughter would be grateful to her father for what I have done. But a proper daughter never would have gone into those bedamned vaults in the first place. How do you think it looks?"

The silence that followed was ringing.

Archie very nearly started up the stairs to go to Maisie's aid, when she spoke. "A proper father would care more about his daughters and their cares than the way things might *look*. And a proper Lord Advocate for the people of Edinburgh would include the poor and destitute amongst those people, instead of being so wholly indifferent to their plight."

"What is all this concern, when heretofore, you have largely been indifferent to everything but your bedamned paintings!" Sir Richard advised. "Or perhaps this newfound attitude is the result of too much time with that rabble-rousing editor—that Lord Carrington? His unsound views have rubbed off on you. You had better leave him to your sister."

Maisie's laugh was bleak. "You have no idea! But it shows how little you know me—and Flora—to only think it possible that his ideals and ideas might have rubbed off on me, and not the other way round. Just as Flora's heart and mind are her own, so is mine. Good day, sir. I'll see myself out."

Above, doors opened and stairs creaked, and Archie ducked back into the kitchen corridor, lest he be seen. A long moment went by with the only sound the beating of his own heart hard in his ears, before he realized that he had two clear choices before him.

He could leave and return the carriage to the Aiken stable, and take his awful admixture of guilt and rage away from her until he knew what to do with it.

Or he could scale the stairs and speak to her, and say all the things that he had left unsaid—to admit his own complicity in Agnes' dismissal. To confess the reasons he had begun his campaign of charm in the house of Conway. To announce his intentions of exposing Sir Richard's unseemly past.

And yet, it was as if his boots were nailed to the floor. He was mired in uncharacteristic indecision.

Perhaps he should heed Alasdair's advice and cease his investigation into Sir Richard Conway's conduct. One innocent person had already died as a result of his meddling—albeit, he could not have predicted either Agnes getting sacked or her succumbing to something very like gaol fever.

No, he was letting himself off the hook far too easily—he should have known that any time a servant was caught doing anything even vaguely irregular, they might be turned off. He should have been more careful in his investigation.

Yet, now that he could see more clearly how and why Sir

Richard Conway had risen economically, socially and politically, Archie was loath to abandon his investigation.

And since he could not decide, he did not put his foot upon the stairs to rise upward to speak to Maisie. Not now.

Not now, when so much was at stake.

Not now, when he was so absolutely, completely and hopelessly in love with Maisie Conway that he might not be able to endure it if she did not love him back.

CHAPTER 33

Maisie barely slept. While her immediate exhaustion had passed, it was the grief and guilt and sorrow weighing upon her heart that dragged at her footsteps and made her hip ache more than usual.

And there was something more that remained—the rage.

The rage she had felt when looking down at Agnes' battered face. The thirst for retribution that had not slackened. It was like a cold burning flame within her heart, a flame she wanted to turn into a bonfire of blame—Lord knew there was plenty of that to go around.

She could share the blame evenly between herself, and the damn housekeeper, Mrs. Smyth, and the kidmen, or whatever range of degenerates had taken in the children and preyed upon their vulnerability and need in the first place. And with her father for putting the needs of the empire before ethics. And with all the bloody politicians who had turned blind eyes and profited by simply doing nothing—their complicity ought to weigh upon them like forty pieces of silver.

Her hand twitched and snapped a piece of charcoal she had

idly taken up in her pacing. But now her fingers itched to work, to make some sense out of so senseless a death.

Maisie pulled a sheet of foolscap in front of her and set her grief free upon the paper. A grotesque figure immediately took shape—a governmental sort of official, all red, bloodshot nose and gouty excess, sipping claret while sitting upon a great stone monument to his enterprise. And below the monument, the foundations laid much like the vaults of the bridge, filled with people, entombed below.

And when she was done sketching that, she took up another sheet.

This one had the same sort of government figure, less bilious perhaps, but just as smugly secure, squatting over the parliament building as if it were a privy, dropping his excrement and effluent to rain down into the poor in the closes below.

Better, but not… ugly enough to suit her mood.

She began anew with the structure of the Parliament House, first making it more recognizable as an Edinburgh landmark, then adding the hulking figure—only this time she added features that made the grotesque identifiable as the Lord Advocate, in his robe and collar of office.

Yes.

She drew a lopsided crown hanging off his ear to more visually show him as the representative of the crown. And then she populated the closes with recognizable faces, with Agnes, her Magdalene, and Fergus, her David. And even Doris, the talkative old bawd.

Yes. It was grotesque. And truthful. And not still nearly large enough to hold all her rage.

Maisie went to the corner where the large bolt of canvas—her bishop's whole length—was stored and unrolled it flat across the floor of the studio, much as she had done for her portrait of Archie.

She scissored off a length and set to transferring her drawing from the paper to the canvas, enlarging some aspects while eliminating others.

It felt good to be doing something, even if no one else would ever see it. It felt good to put down on canvas exactly how she felt.

"Maisie?" It was Flora calling up the staircase, which was unusual in and of itself—normally, she simply rapped upon the door—but at least it gave Maisie enough time to stand and straighten her skirts, by the time Flora opened the door. "Maisie, you have a visitor. Lady Cairn has come—"

"To see your aerie for myself. And it's Quince." The marchioness came forward with her hand extended in friendship. "How do you fare, Maisie?"

"Well enough, my Lady Cairn," she lied.

"Quince, please." The marchioness smiled and began stripping off her gloves. "I should very much like for us to be friends. I hope you'll forgive me for all but forcing my way up here. But, by jimble, I should have given more credit to Archie's journalistic prowess, for he did describe your aerie quite perfectly."

"Why don't I see about getting some refreshment," Flora said quietly before she gave Maisie what could only be called a speaking look and bowed herself out.

Though, what it was meant to speak about, Maisie did not exactly know—yet.

"Oh, holy lemon meringue," the Marchioness of Cairn exclaimed.

Maisie turned to find the woman standing before the canvas on the floor.

"I beg you will excuse me," Maisie began, for there was no excusing the canvas itself, or putting it away quietly. "As I believe I explained before, a great deal of my work is private—not for public viewing."

"It ought to be," the marchioness countered.

"Only if I want to be horsewhipped," Maisie said honestly. "And never paint another portrait again."

"Perhaps." Lady Cairn said, even as she made a sound of disagreement. "Do you only want to paint ladies and gentlemen's portraits? Selfishly, I hope you do, or I shall be very disappointed for myself, but what I want is neither here nor there. The question is really, would your time be better spent painting other things? Like that?" She gestured to the canvas upon the floor. "Or like this?" She picked up the portrait of Agnes as the Magdalene off the small easel, holding it at arm's length. "Oh, holy hallowed saints. Very much this."

Lady Cairn put the painting down upon the table and without asking or waiting for Maisie's leave, began turning over the canvases stacked with their faces set against the wall. First Agnes, luminous as saintly Joan of Arc, burning with the brilliant fire of a life quenched out far too easily, stared back at her. And then the others, saints, prophetesses and wise women, one by one, their straightforward gazes fixed upon the viewer.

"Those painting are not for public view." But even as she said the words, Maisie felt they were no longer true—perhaps the time had come.

"No?" the marchioness questioned quietly. "Perhaps they *are* too intimate, too beautiful for the world."

"Yes," Maisie agreed tentatively. "I mean—"

"And too important." Lady Cairn's rather intense gaze switched from the paintings to Maisie. "I recognize her. The girl who used to beg down at the top end of the Grassmarket. I wondered what happened to her."

Maisie could not keep the doubt from her voice. "Did you?" How would a marchioness recognize a penniless beggar? "She's dead."

"Aye. I was very sorry to hear that." The marchioness stood quietly for a moment. "My profound condolences. And the lad?" She gestured to the depiction of Fergus as the boy David. "Her brother, I would guess from their likeness. How does he fare with his sister's death—that was he in your stable? And the others—I've seen them all, here and there about town. This lady is typically stationed near Canongate Kirk, near my parent's house," she said of a depiction of an ancient Sibyl. "I know her of old." Lady Cairn shut her eyes briefly and took a deep breath, as if the sensations the paintings had engendered were not entirely pleasant. "But you've captured something magnificent in them. In all of them. Their humanity. Especially your Magdalene."

The marchioness's generous frankness, aided by her penetrating gaze, prompted the uncomfortable truth out of Maisie. "What I wish I had done was save them—save her."

"Yes." Lady Quince let out another attenuated breath. "I understand. Archie told me about the girl. Agnes? Again, you have my deepest sympathy."

The cynicism Maisie thought she had put away like an old toy, reared up like a wave at the polite, rote words. "Forgive me, your ladyship, but how could you, with your fortune and your safe, warm home, understand any—"

"Ach." Lady Quince made a sound of both distress and anger to stop her. "I do understand, Maisie," she insisted. "I *know*. I wasn't always a marchioness and before I became one, I led a very different, very dangerous life because I did not know how else to help—how else to feed and clothe and warm and house those same children. And no matter how much I gave—and still give—there are always new faces to replace the old. New mouths to feed, new shelter to find, new hearts to mend, new minds to heal, new trust to forge." She came closer, as if she wanted to press her earnestness upon Maisie. "But I remember all their faces, each one. Especially the first one—your Agnes must be that to you. Now." The marchioness clapped her hands together as if breaking—or setting—a spell. "Let us talk."

"About what, my lady?"

"Quince," she corrected again. "Please call me Quince so I may call you Maisie. And I should like to call you Maisie because I should like to be your friend. I had sensed a rebellious spirit in you," Lady Cairn confided, "but never hoped for this!"

"This is just unrequited rage—" Maisie began before the marchioness cut her off.

"Do not denigrate your work or explain it away," Lady Cairn exclaimed. "I won't have it. This is very good, very powerful, and you know it. Or you ought to, so do be clever enough to take my word for it. I may be many things, but I am not a liar. I said I sensed a rebellious spirit in you, because it is a spirit I share. So let me just say, that if you ever find yourself with the need to either unburden yourself, or alternatively, to discuss the problems of your secret rebellion and how you might improve…." The marchioness waved her hand vaguely. "…the circumstances of your rebellion, please, do keep me in mind. I assure you, I am as loyal and silent as the grave in such matters."

Maisie was too astonished to say anything except. "Are you?"

"Oh, by jimble, yes." The very slight beginnings of a sly smile danced at the corners of the marchioness' mouth. "Let me tell you about that wildly mis-spent youth of mine. Do you recall the spate of robberies that were all over the newspapers a few years ago?"

"No, my lady. But I am only lately come to Edinburgh."

"Of course. I should have realized. Well, without gilding a faded lily, let me just say, it was I—I stole things and robbed people, too, but mostly stole to do something to address the deplorable problem of poverty and dispossession that began some ten years ago. And though I am often dispirited to find us still trying to fight the exact same good fight, I am comforted to find someone to fight alongside."

"I am not a fighter, my lady," Maisie confessed. "I could no more fight than walk comfortably down Rose Street."

"Certainly you are," Quince contradicted. "In your own way, with your own talents." The marchioness smiled as if satisfied with this unassailable truth. "I defy anyone to do better, or to see the problems you see so very, very clearly with such pointed critique." She gestured to the beginnings of the painting on the floor. "I wish I had your talent for depiction so I could include him." Lady Cairn closed her eyes, as if she were experiencing a vision.

"The scaffy lad in the street outside my father's house on the backside of Canongate. All those years ago and still I can see him in my mind's eye as if it were yesterday. He was a raggedy child, like yours, a beggar boy who came round with a battered tin cup. Someone from the house or staff ran him off after I gave him some crust of bread or something, but he came back, and I remember his thin hands and the over-wide look of his hopeful, ill-nourished eyes. And I will never forget, as long as I live, what he looked like, the next morning, curled up on the cold pavement like an abandoned kitten, dead from exposure in the gray morning light."

She opened her eyes and looked at Maisie. "Dead because we, who had the power to help him, had not. Dead because I, who had tried to help him, could not. So you see, my dear, I do understand. But what we need to do now, is decide what in blazes are we going to do about it?"

Maisie took a deep breath, inhaling air as if it were courage. "I hardly know." Maisie felt the edges of her rage frayed by her lack of daring.

"Think about it," Lady Cairn instructed. "And know that you have friends on the side of the angels, too. I would be your friend regardless of Archie." She laughed. "And maybe even in spite of him."

The idea that these people who had befriended her on Archie's behalf might shift their allegiance to her—or at least share that loyalty with her—was remarkable.

Lady Cairn left Maisie with a sort of reckless determination that she hadn't felt in years—her determination she had honed, but the recklessness had been leeched away by too many years of being careful, too many years of keeping safe. But some rashness seemed to have come back to her with the arrival of Archie Carrington.

Why should she not find her own way to call people out for their hypocrisy and false outrage like he did in his exposés. What could it hurt?

No.

Maisie felt a sigh boil out of her. Only days ago, she might have—and actually had—said the same words. But she knew better now. Far better.

Everything could hurt.

"Missus?" It was Fergus, at the door with a fresh pot of tea. "Mrs. Cook sent me up with summit for the fancy lady. But I reckon she's gone."

"She is, Fergus. But would you like a spot of something warm to share with me?"

"Aye." But what caught Fergus' attention was not the tea, nor the painting of his sister—it was the cartoon she'd painted on the canvas spread out across the floor. "That's th' way of it, there. The scabby basterts."

"My feelings exactly."

"Ye painted this then, just like them class pictures ye make?"

"Yes," Maisie acknowledged not without pride. "An allegory for our times."

"Don't know Al Gorey," he said. "But that muckle bastert at the top with his pelters noggin' down looks like yer old man."

Maisie might not understand all of his Scots cant, but she understood the last. "My father do you mean?"

"Lord High Advocate, they say," Fergus confirmed. "The one what turfed everyone at t'vaults oot on the pavement."

"Yes, it does resemble him," she agreed. "Though it could do more." And why not? The caricaturists' printshops were liberal with this sort of political and social satire. She was just making a large scale, more painterly version of the same.

"Outta hang it oot th' winda," Fergus declared. "Or paint on th' side o' the building, like the adverts up on the walls." He pointed out the window to the apothecary's on the opposite corner, where an advertisement for Duncan MacLaren, Dispensing Apothecary was lettered upon the wall in gold.

And Maisie could suddenly picture it as clearly as if it were before her—the painting, in all its monstrous glory, hanging from the side of a building as if it had been placed there by a vengeful angel, insistent and watching over the city.

"Fergus, my brilliant lad, I have an idea."

CHAPTER 34

"Gov'nor?" One of Archie's ragtag collection of writers stuck his head into his office, his grin as wide as his intellect. "I've a report for ye that's going to light you up like a Christmas punch." He tossed a much-folded sheet of foolscap on Archie's desk.

Archie picked it up with interest. "What have we here, Red?"

"Happened past it on the wall of West Kirkyard." Red Fletcher was as excited as a spaniel on the scent of a grouse. "Across from the glebe field, just where the kirkyard wall separates the manse?"

"Aye?" Archie knew the spot, at the back foot of Edinburgh Castle Rock, where a long stone wall ran around the perimeter of the St. Cuthbert's West Kirk graveyard.

"Big as the side of a barn, posted up like a pasted placard, big as you please on the back wall of the caretakers cottage."

"Aye?" Archie returned his gaze to the page describing a post bill showing the Lord Advocate, gleaming, golden shovel in hand — "The Lord Advocate burying the poor alive?" He felt the hairs rise on his forearms. "You're havering."

"No lie," the fellow swore. "Saw it with my own eyes, before they started painting it over with lime wash. But I saw it first, big as you please. A fat, cruel bureaucrat holding a golden shovel to pour rubble over the poor, burying them within their vault-like tombs." He shook his head in wonder. "The expression of cruel, unholy glee upon his face—"

"Write it up, just like that," Archie instructed, all his editorial instincts up and clamoring like dogs at a kennel door. "All ten-pound words, Red—anti-government tracts pasted on the walls of the ancient city. Too large to ignore. Pointed critique of local officials."

"Oh, aye, Arch. On it." The fellow snatched back his penciled foolscap and dove for his desk. "How's 'A grotesque figure bearing a remarkable resemblance to a certain be-wigged justice…'"

"'…or *Advocate* of the city mounted upon a wall of indifference.' That's the stuff." He would be able to get his first cracks at the Lord Advocate simply by reporting someone else's incendiary, accusatory opinion of the man.

Red rubbed his hands together. "We going to run a special edition?"

"Yes," Archie said, before he immediately thought better of the idea. "Nae. No, not just yet. Not 'til we've all the information we can glean and we're good and damn ready."

If he was going to try and land a punch against the Lord Advocate—the kind of punch his father and the board of directors wanted to be a knockout—he needed it to be as powerful as possible. He couldn't waste his efforts—or his money—running small special editions. He needed to have all his evidence brought together in one stroke. And he had to make sure. Not only for his own sake, but for Maisie's.

This was the moment for him not to make a splash, but to actually make a difference.

"We'll have another look at the incident at the South Bridge Vaults first," he decided. "You keep working on your report," he told Red, "but we'll hold until we can get all this information put together."

"And see if you can make a rough sketch to show to Arthur Jones." Archie wanted his engraver to take a crack at an illustration before the print shop caricaturists made their own copies—if they'd seen it. "Send for him anyway," he ordered. "Who else do you think saw it?"

"Me and the cows and drovers heading up the Grasssmarket. The sexton and the beadle from the Kirk were pretty fast getting out the lime wash."

"But you're sure of what you saw?"

"Plain as day. Wrote it all straight down." Red gestured to the tattered foolscap.

"Excellent. Then we might get an exclusive." An illustration would put the proverbial honey on the oatcake. If only Maisie were there or had seen it—it was only down the Queensferry Road from her aerie—but she could have tossed off a detailed sketch in less time than it would take to tear it down.

But perhaps not—this particular vulgar depiction was of her father and although she might not 'subscribe to the same philosophies as my father,' the man was still her kith and kin.

Yet, Archie could not help but hope that this opportunity to expose Sir Richard for the very things his daughter had railed against him for, would count in his favor. For his own sake, not only would a comprehensive exposé get his demanding father off his back once and for all, but might also help expiate both his sin for using Agnes to put Sir Richard's manuscript pages back and for having thought to use Maisie to gain access to the house in the first place.

But perhaps it were best not to test that particular boundary just yet.

No sooner had he come to his decision than a note arrived from Maisie, asking if they might resume their previous schedule for the last few sittings for his portrait.

It was on the tip of his mind to refuse, but he could think of no good reason why he should not. And so he went, but not before striding down the Queensferry Road so he might take a long look at the spot along the kirkyard wall where someone on the side of the angels, as Maisie might say, had given form and substance to their criticism about the latest outrage against the poor.

If he didn't know better, he would suspect Alasdair's lady wife, Quince, of being that hand stirring this particular pot—the caper had some of her former bravado and daring. But the Marchioness of Cairn had been everything aboveboard and circumspect in her championing of the poor for years now. Still, Archie would bet good money she would be tickled by the report. And even more tickled by the illustration his engraver was making.

The scene of what Red had described so well for the future readers of the Review, as 'An Outrage against the Powers that Be'—as his headline would blare—was now marked only by the outline of lime wash, as if whatever had been posted on the wall had simply vanished. Or more likely, been scraped off the wall by the verger, who stood, trowel in hand, over a barrow he immediately trundled off.

But the lime wash left an outline as big as a stable door. Archie judged the size to be somewhere about nine feet by six. Big enough to cause quite the stir.

And there, down in the very bottom left-hand corner, a piece of the posted paper remained, as if the paste on the corner had proven too thick for the verger's trowel.

Archie made so bold as to step up for a closer look, because on the corner there seemed to be the very faintest impression of a sort of signature, or initial, beneath the lime wash. The letter C, he thought.

He was immediately taken aback—it was a bit of an open secret in Edinburgh that Archie and his friends had long called themselves the Four C's. Was one of them involved? Or worse, was one of them being set up to take the blame publicly? It wouldn't be the first time one of their fellowship had been set up to take the blame for something they hadn't done. Or had someone found out about Quince's prior profession and decided to implicate her?

Archie was more glad than ever that he had resolved to be cautious. This C was the enemy of Archie's enemy, which might eventually make him a friend. But until that time, he could only be considered a convenient ally.

Archie reached the Lord Advocate's house in good time for his appointment, and was gladdened when he ducked down the kitchen stairs to be met by Fergus, who tugged on a new cap in greeting. "Morning, sir."

"Good morning!" Archie had to stifle the urge to sweep the lad up into a hug. He settled for patting his shoulder. "It is good to see you're settling in, Fergus, my lad. I'm glad you're being looked after. And I'm glad you've come into Miss Conway's service. She'll do right by you. As will I—you have only to call upon me."

"Aye, sir." Fergus nodded his thanks. "Nae bother, sir."

"Good lad. Take care of her, Fergus, will you?" He slipped the boy a coin.

"Tapadh leat, sir." Fergus said quietly, tucking the coin away. "I'm tae show ye up."

"Then lay on my good lad." The feeling of rightness—the prospect of good and calm actually prevailing—buoyed Archie up. "Lay on."

Maisie was waiting for him—she stood in the center of her room, as if she had been waiting—the cracked window told him she had heard his approach from the stableyard below.

She looked tired—dark circles hung under her penetrating eyes—but happy to see him.

He went to her immediately. "Are you well? Have you been

sleeping, or—" He took note that the line of canvases that normally had their backs to the room were now lined up like soldiers, face out. "You've been painting, haven't you?"

"I confess," she said with some relief, "I have. Which is why I wanted to see you."

"You'll exhaust yourself."

"Archie, please. I already have Flora to fuss at me—I don't need you, too. I'm just a little tired because I'm quite heartsore over Agnes. But I'll be fine. I'm not delicate."

"You are," he contradicted. "You are as delicate as a Toledo steel blade, etched and chased with filagree along the central ridge, as elegant and fine as anything." He raised her hands to his lips for a kiss. "But as strong as truth underneath."

"Is that a compliment?"

Archie was glad to see she could still smile through her sorrow. "It is indeed, my dear, sweet Miss Conway. I am entirely enchanted by your charms—and continue to offer you mine."

She let go of his hands. "Please don't tempt me with illicit offers this morning, Archie. I haven't the strength for them."

"No?" he teased. "No glimpses of ankles or forearms?"

"Especially not forearms!" she protested, but she was smiling. "If I am to establish myself as a professional portraitist of any credit, I need to get this portrait finished."

"And I assume, put on display? Hidden beauty does no one any good," he teased.

She sighed. "Yes, I suppose. Your Mr. Hill would no doubt be splendidly happy to hang your likeness in his front window."

But Archie had something else in mind. As wonderful as Mr. Hill was, Maisie's talent ought to be showcased by a more influential hand—Rory's. But before he could tell her his plan, his gaze was arrested by a depiction of the Magdalene propped on the small easel behind her. "Agnes."

Maisie's intake of breath was full of apprehension, but she nodded. "Yes."

He stepped closer to the painting. "This is how you saw her—as this force of truth and life."

"Yes, and others." She gestured toward her canvases stacked against the wall, before she crossed to indicate a Madonna. "I have hidden these for too long. They are all here, Maisie and others—Saint Joan, the Foolish Virgin, the Sybil, the Wise Woman of Abel Beth-Maachah. And I've done Fergus as both the shepherd David and the Doubting Thomas, too."

Archie was both deeply honored that she would finally show them to him and astonished at the profound depth of her artistry. "All this you saw in them?"

"Yes," she said simply, wringing her fingers together in front of her. "I call them my waifs as saints, but not all of them are waifs. Some are simply beggars."

She was nervous.

This unflappable woman who had been able to see through his superficial facade of charm as if her eyes were scythes, was nervous. Because what he thought of her work mattered to her.

"Maisie, if you don't yet feel like a genius, you ought to begin." He took a step or two nearer the array of paintings against the wall. "I see they are still drying, but—"

"I beg your pardon?" Maisie stepped unevenly closer. "What do you mean?"

"Are they not still drying? You said the paint was still wet, when I first asked after these painting, and I can see by this long line of dried paint on the floorboards that you've been moving them about."

"Oh, that. Yes." She waved her hands slightly, in dismissal. "Yes, the paintings are dried now. Would you like to see all of them?"

Archie was beyond elated that she had actually—finally—invited him to look at her paintings. It felt almost like an intimacy—more intimate perhaps than the honor of making love to her. This was the sole product of her imagination, that blazing genius she had for seeing something different and special and clearly holy in people.

He went down the line of paintings he had never seen before —Foolish Virgin, the Matriarch Sarah, Elizabeth, the mother of John the Baptist greeting the Virgin Mother. One after another, saints, prophetesses, kings, queens and heroes, peopled with the faces of Edinburgh.

All this—all these people—she had seen and made hallowed.

"They, like you," he told her, "are magnificent."

She reached for his hand. "Thank you, Archie."

He took it with something akin to wonder—and purpose. "I would very much like to invite Rory Cathcart to see them. His good opinion would mean far more than mine."

"Your good opinion is all that matters to me, but though I thank you, I think this has been enough exposure for one day."

"Hidden beauty does no one any good," he reminded her. "Especially not this sort of profound beauty."

"Yes, so you've said," she agreed. "I'll…think about it."

"You do that." He kissed her cheek and the scent of her—the ludicrously divine mixture of linseed oil and charcoal—did predictable things to his desire. "Are you sure I can't tempt you…?"

"Archie, my dear friend, please." She gestured to his place in between the dormer windows and he went to stand there, before he noted idly that she had a fairly straightforward view across the Lotion Road down to the Queensferry—and she was extraordinarily observant, looking out her window at all hours.

"You can almost see the West Kirk from here," he remarked casually.

"I can hear it," she responded. "Agnes used to tell the time by the bells."

"Were you up last night? Late? Did you happen to notice anything going on down around the kirkyard? Lights, perhaps lanterns or a torch or anything?"

"No." She paused and looked at him before she queried, "Why do you ask?"

Archie pulled himself back from the precipice. He had already decided not to reveal the investigation. "I was just curious."

"Didn't you ride up the Queensferry Road on your way here?"

"I walked, the day being fair."

"Yes, a rare thing indeed." She glanced out the window behind him. "But now that I think on it, there did seem to be some small to do down that way this morning—some boys on the wall shouting, or throwing apples or something, because the verger, or whoever, came out waving their arms…" She made a charming little pantomime of the verger's frantic antics.

Archie laughed. "It must have been the graffito, as they used to call them it Italy for the sort of smutty words boys of a certain age in every country like to scrawl upon walls."

"Oh, is that all?" She smiled before she fell silent, and they both retreated into the comfortable quiet of their own thoughts and actions. Although, only she had action—he was to remain still.

They carried on in this fashion, until she put her brush down in an uncharacteristic show of frustration. "I'm sorry, Archie, but I find I'm suddenly very tired—too much painting into the night, as you said. Would you mind if we put off the sitting…?"

"Certainly not," he agreed. "I am always happy to postpone the moment when I no longer have a ready excuse to visit you alone." He advanced, hoping to steal a kiss from her pale cheeks.

But she eluded him, by ducking around her worktable and picking up her depiction of Fergus as David as if she was distracted by something she saw there. "Thank you, Archie. Much obliged."

He was nonplussed at her sudden aloofness, but as Flora had once warned him, she must have her own reasons. "Then I suppose I'll leave you to it."

"Yes, thank you." She reached impulsively across the table for his hand. "Thank you for being on the side of the angels."

"You're welcome." He bowed and took his leave of her, all the while wondering how many more opportunities to be with her remained.

CHAPTER 35

Quince, Lady Cairn, seemed to have learned the secret of the servants' stair from her last visit, for she appeared the next morning at the door to Maisie's aerie unannounced and on foot—Maisie didn't even hear a carriage in the stableyard.

"Well done, my dear!" she congratulated Maisie. "Though it did not arrive with all the éclat I might have wished, we will do better next time."

"Will we?" Maisie never quite knew what to say to the marchioness, especially when she arrived like a force of nature.

"Yes, by jimble," Quince decreed. "Oh, holy— Why, Archibald, there you are." She came to a momentary standstill in front of the larger portrait canvas. "Would you look at him."

"For hours, every day, my lady," Maisie tried to joke to turn the marchioness's attention. "But thankfully, I am nearly done." Young Lord Archibald Carrington now stood before the world clothed in respectability along with his personality.

"Thankfully?" Quince queried.

Maisie tried to choose her words more carefully. "While it has been both a challenge and a pleasure painting Lord Carrington, as well as an honor, I have other commissions, my lady, that I am anxious to undertake."

Lady Cairn smiled. "Of which, I hope I am one. But your impeccable taste, enormous talent and very politic answer has put me off my plan regarding our current little political stir—little, or too little, being the operative word." She turned a circle to peruse the room. "Have you not got a second placard under way?"

"No," Maisie admitted, for it did not seem productive to prevaricate in front of this extraordinarily penetrating woman. "I mean, not really." Though she had, in fact, made more than one sketch when the idea first came to her. "But I had not thought—"

"That's why I've come!" Quince announced. "To help you along. Now—" She peeled off her gloves. "The report I've received—and yes, as you told Archie, Edinburgh is a very gossipy city. But the—shall we call it a posting? Now the report I've heard of the posting on the West Kirkyard wall is not that it wasn't exactly what it needed to be—and well done to you—but that it was too easily and too quickly removed and therefore, not seen by enough people. Although," she said as an aside, "some of the right people saw it—which is how I came to know about it—but not enough." Lady Cairn carried on until she seemed to finally run out of breath. "So, we must think bigger."

"Bigger?" Maisie's glance shifted toward the large loom of canvas in the corner where she had rolled and hidden that first canvas she had made.

"Oh, by jimble!" Lady Cairn clapped her hands in delight. "Is that the one I saw? You still have it? Good lass. But as I was saying—bigger. Or smaller." The lady's own gaze narrowed, though her eyes fairly danced with mischief. "Or both. I don't know. But what I do know is, in the end, what you need to be, is impossible to ignore."

"How?" was all Maisie could ask.

"I'm not sure yet, but…" Quince tapped her finger against her chin. "I was thinking what a dead shame it was that none of the caricaturists and cartoonists down Jackson's Close got a good look at the first placard to print up copies. One post bill may make a small outrage, but a few thousand handbills can spark something truly incendiary."

Quince, Lady Cairn looked her dead in the eye. "The question then becomes, dear Maisie, if you are ready for incendiary?"

IT WAS AS IF SHE WAS HOLDING AN UNLIT MATCH IN HER HAND, while all around her was tinder.

Maisie paced up and back the length of the studio, the normal discomfort of her hip all but forgotten as she walked from the stairs all the way to the opposite wall and back, calming herself, steeling her nerves until at last she heard the quick tap of boots on the stair. The time had come—in the person of Fergus, who crept silently up the stair, quiet and serious, the dark circles under his eyes eating holes in his face.

"Are you ready?" Maisie asked.

Fergus shook his head. "Don't fancy our chances, together like."

"What do you mean?" Maisie had reconnoitered—if taking a sedan chair like a feeble old lady, in order to slowly take account of the city's available walls in as unobtrusive a manner as possible, could count as a reconnoiter—their chosen location for the deed and seen little impediment.

"I'll gie it tae ye straight, missus, no haver. Ye'll be too slow and too easy for the watch to lift. I'm better off on ma own."

"But the pot of glue is heavy and the canvas vast. And it will take two people and four hands to get it hung properly and quickly."

"I kin use the barrow same on ma own as I would wi' ye. Only

I can ditch it, quick like, and take a runner o'er a wall or so, if I need. Ye can't make a runner, hirplin like ye are."

As little as she had been feeling her lameness as an infirmity lately, the boy had a point. "We could put it off until you find someone to help—someone you trust."

"Don't trust no one but ye, missus," he replied solemnly. "Ye've set it up right enough."

"I don't want you to take all the risk on your own, Fergus. I owe it to Agnes to keep you safe."

"That's fer me tae decide, missus," he stated flatly. "Less risky wi' oot ye, if ye ask me."

"I do ask you, Fergus." She owed the boy at least that respect. "And I will let you go alone, only if you are sure?"

"Sure as day, missus." The boy was as resolute as she might wish.

"All right then." Maisie got straight to the instruction. "It will be harder. The posting is much larger than last time—so large I've cut it into four rolls, here." She showed him the four rolls of canvas, each about two feet wide by ten feet long, with numbers for the order they were to be hung, prominent on top.

"Harder to miss, then, innit?"

"Exactly," Maisie agreed with him. "You're sure of the place in the kirkyard where you can get up on top of the wall?"

"Aye, missus."

"Good lad. Thank you. Now, you'll put them up one next to the other, the rolls. Start by hanging the first one, here, from the top and rolling them down over the paste. Then the next one, here"—she showed him the Roman numeral marked at the top— "next to it on the right, and so on, so in the end, the four rolls make up one big picture. One, two, three, four. Do you understand?"

"Aye," Fergus nodded. "I ken. Greyfriar's Kirkyard—the wall across from Merchant's Street."

"Aye," Maisie agreed. "There'll be a watchman circulating in the kirkyard, maybe, and some bustle down the lane toward the Grassmarket, I'd wager. But it should be quiet and dark along the curve of the roadway, so you stick close to the wall there and you should be well hidden."

"Aye, then." Fergus gathered up the heavy canvas rolls to slide into the basket of the peat creel she had purchased for just this use, and covered them with thick hessian cloth.

Maisie took out the tin pot of glue and brushes. "Here's your wheatpaste. It should look like porridge for your supper if you're stopped or asked." Her heart beat hot spikes of bright turmeric yellow as a warning into her blood steam.

"I'll hide them brushes in the creel," was Fergus's advice, while he hefted the basket onto his back before taking up the pot.

"Ready?"

He looked at Maisie, his wide, solemn eyes too trusting, or too desperate to think of the dangers. Or the consequences.

But she knew them all the same. "If you're stopped, run. If you're taken, say as little as possible. But know that I will work to get you out. And if worse comes to worse, don't hesitate to peach me out. I'm fully ready to take the blame."

To this little piece of bravery, Fergus said, "I'm no clipe."

"Right then." Maisie gathered a far bigger share of courage than she had planned. It was her time to try and make an unholy splash. "Bless you, Fergus. Bless us all. Off you go."

ARCHIE TOOK A FEW MOMENTS TO SCRIBBLE DOWN ALL HE HAD learned from his source—a young botanist at the Physick Gardens on the Leith Walk who had access to the local records of the Royal Horticultural Society—before he ambled out of the public house on College Street into the damp night air. The portrait of Sir Richard Conway as an opportunistic young man—

if his words could be called a portrait—was daily becoming clearer.

He had also consulted with Alasdair the previous night and their conversations had been wide-ranging, covering the former Prime Minister, Mr. Pitt's successful efforts to stimulate trade by cutting import duties on certain commodities such as tea, but also by granting the British East India Company certain monopolies on that trade, as well as on all opium grown from poppies in India—both trades in which Conway had been heavily, if secretly, involved.

Exactly where Sir Richard Conway's appointment as the new Lord Advocate fit into this complicated puzzle, Archie had yet to find. But he would.

It was too early to turn in, but too late to find better company —or was it? He wanted a good long walk—he wanted to think.

Without consulting his head, his more amorous feet had turned northwest, vaguely Kirk Brae Head way. Maisie seemed always to be up working her diligent way through the night— perhaps she'd like some company? He might ask her some discreet questions regarding her father's long absences on trips abroad to India and elsewhere.

He might not.

The plainer truth of the matter was that he missed their daily sittings. He missed their bantering conversations. Missed her slow smiles and quick wit. Missed her kisses.

Though it had only been a day since he had last seen her, he missed *her*.

Archie whistled up his bravado and headed down Candlemakers Row toward the Cowgate end of the Grassmarket, where an urchin, a boy with a basket of peat and a stewpot, skittered by against the shadow of the wall.

"Fergus?" He called before he quite knew why. "Is that you?"

The lad hesitated, then inched forward into the edge of the circle of lamplight. "Aye?" He kept his distance, leery.

"It's Archie, Miss Conway's friend, from the other day. Maisie's," he tried again, when the boy evinced no recognition. "You're out late?"

"I am at that, sir," the lad answered quietly though he frowned ferociously, clearly wishing he was elsewhere.

"Aye," Archie agreed with sympathy. "You should be getting on home for Miss Conway's, shouldn't you?"

"Aye," Fergus agreed again, though he made no move in the direction. "Happen I'm on an errand for the missus, if ye'll pardon me."

Archie belatedly understood the significance of the pot and creel. "Got a hot pot of pease porridge for someone there, have you? And some bread?" It would so be like Maisie to be feeding half the population of the city's beggars. She was not a woman who gave up.

"Aye, sir. That's the right of it. So I'd best be getting on." Fergus knuckled his cap in Archie's direction before he went away up the street at a dead run, his boots ringing against the cobbles.

"Good luck, Fergus," Archie called, though the only answer was the sound of his own voice echoing, overloud off the long wall of the Greyfriars kirkyard behind.

And something about saying Maisie Conway's name out loud in a public square, outside a—frankly low—public house, in the dead of night, brought him something close to shame. Those flexible morals of his were giving way far more often to the dictates of his lately reappearing conscience.

It was the guilt, he knew, that made him question himself. The guilt of his part in Agnes' dismissal. His guilt in trying to use Maisie. His guilt in knowing he was going to be an active agent of her father's downfall.

His conscience had an awful sense of timing.

But for once, Archie heeded its voice and turned his feet for home.

CHAPTER 36

"Master Archie! Master Archie, wake up!"

Archie swam up from a dead sleep to the sight of a small lamp hovering over his head. "What is it?"

It was Andrew, his chief printer's devil from the press house. "There's a lad below, says he's come wi' news for ye."

Archie was up and reaching for a shirt and breeks. "Scaffy newsboy?"

"Aye, sum'mat like," Andrew answered. "He asked fer ye particular like. Sayed ye'd want ta know."

"Aye." He checked his clock—two-thirty in the morning—stomped his feet into boots and tossed on a coat before taking the lantern from Andrew and leading the way to the press house, where one of his ragtag collection of newsboys, Dougal Ferris, sat swinging his feet from a bale of paper as if he were bearing a load of mischief. "What have you got?"

"Bill as big as an elephant on the Greyfriar's wall. Lord Advocate sitting on the top."

Greyfriar's? Where he himself had been walking just a few hours ago?

The image of Fergus, who had not been bearing a load of

mischief but a load of porridge on a mission of mercy, surely, skittered across his brain. "I know the place."

Dougal came to his feet and took up the lantern.

"Anyone else about to see the placard? Constables find it yet?"

"Not that I saw," the boy clarified as he followed Archie out of the press house. "But I jack-rabbited over her, quick-like, the minute I saw it."

"Good lad." Archie passed him a fistful of coins. "Now head over to Cesfords Wynd and wake Arthur Jones, the engraver—there will be a sign over his door with a block cut picture. Tell him to come to Greyfriar's Wall. And tell him to bring his own lanterns." With luck they would steal a march on the other broadsheets and caricaturists. And tease out another piece of evidence in this interesting public campaign against Sir Richard Conway.

Archie took the short distance to Cowgate Head, from whence he turned south along the long wall that ran the length of the Greyfriars kirkyard and burial ground, at a striding pace, letting his mind clear for the business ahead. The streets were empty but for a scattering of idlers in the doorways—people so poor they couldn't afford even the closes or vaults. And true to Edinburgh's form, a light but persistent drizzle began to fall.

The light from his lantern turned the wet pavement into a path of gold leading inevitably toward the painting—for it could be nothing else. Monumental and filled with color, the composition pasted upon the wall was the largest he had ever seen, more like a fresco in its size and scope and position high on the wall, ten feet above the ground.

The image itself was shocking even though he had been prepared by Red Fletcher's early account of the first placard. But this one was a grotesque depiction of an overlarge figure hulking over the Parliament House, squatting almost, as if it were literally shitting on the hapless, tiny occupants of the closes below, who were drowning in what could only be described as the effluent of government filth.

The water 'problem' made manifest.

But it was the colors and the expressions on the faces of those depicted, as well as the sheer monumental size of the thing, that truly managed to awe him. It must have taken a crew of men to hoist it up there.

However it was done, it was radical and revolutionary and incendiary.

"Seditious!"—he was sure the politicians would clamor. "Treasonous," others would hiss and sputter as they rubbed the backs of their necks against the whisper of wind that was their fear of the guillotine—it had only been some six years since the revolution in France had challenged the constitutional monarchists' *status quo* and the memory was still fresh.

Whatever it was, by God, it was powerful and unflinching.

Archie set down the lantern to pull out his notebook and pencil to scratch out some words to capture the grandeur and rage and raw anger that seethed from the painting. And it was a painting of some sort, with brush strokes and blended colors, not printed blocks of color like a regular engraved waybill or posted bill.

He abandoned his pose of rational distance and stepped close enough to see the layer of diluted paint spread thin, and smell the thick odor of linseed oil and turpentine that exuded from the surface.

So, painted quickly and not so long ago that the paint had completely dried.

Archie was irrationally pleased by the new information he had managed to learn in his time with Maisie. He put his hand to test the paint but felt instead a sort of seam. He followed it with his finger until he could discern that the whole of the monstrous thing was not one entity but rolls of canvas—wide rolls at that— pasted together to make a whole.

Clever as all bedamned. Diabolically clever.

Arthur Jones puffed up behind him. "Came as soon as— Holy

fuck, will you look at that?"

"Yes," Archie urged. "For God's sake, do look at that and get a fair likeness down as quick as you bloody can, Jonesy, before the watch arrives to tear it down."

But another idea imposed itself and he was turning out his pockets to find his penknife. It wasn't a trowel but it would do for cutting out a corner—

No, the other corner where a dark "C" was clearly embedded, almost as if it were stamped. Like an artist's mark.

C for…

Archie's mind blanked. He could not guess. He had to print fact. But he could create an identity from the meaning of the work itself. C for Conspirator. C for Crusader. C for Conscience.

Yes—The Conscience of the City.

He took up his pencil and began to write. The 'guilty' conscience would remain unsaid, but implied. Oh, yes.

"How are you coming along, Jonesy? What can I do to help? Let me move the lantern to make sure you can see it all. Get these colors down, especially that blazing red."

Yes, that blazing red of the Advocate's coat. Archie made a note to himself. And took another long moment to gaze at the totality of the scene before him.

Yes, he was going to expose Sir Richard Conway and show exactly how his hands had become so dirty. And he was going to sell a great goddamned many newspapers.

He was going to tell Edinburgh one hell of a story.

But first he needed more information.

"MR. HILL," ARCHIE GREETED THE COLORMAN AT THE COUNTER.

"My Lord!" Hill was all smiles and bonhomie. "How goes your portrait making?"

"Very well indeed, Mr. Hill. But it is not the portrait but the current talk of the town that brings me in today."

"What might we help you with this morning, my lord?"

"Information," Archie returned in a lower voice. "About your wares."

Mr. Hill frowned in consternation at Archie's manner. "My lord?"

"Perhaps you've heard of the placard or post bill that was pasted up on the wall of Greyfriar's Kirkyard?"

"Oh, yes." Hill pulled a long face. "Shocking, sir, I'm sure."

"The sentiment," Archie asked, "or the brazenness of the pasting up on the wall of such hallowed ground?"

Hill drew back a little more. "As you say, sir."

"Aye. They've ripped it down—they had to, of course, in order not to foment riots—but I was able to salvage this remnant." Archie produced a piece of linen about the size of a quarto page.

"Oh." Hill peered over the top of his spectacles and frowned. "From the talk, I had imagined something rather larger."

"Indeed it was. This is but a scrap."

"Ah."

When Hill said nothing more, Archie set himself to draw the man out. "I was hoping you might help me," he began in a confidential tone. "I was wondering, with your extensive knowledge of … preparations, did you call them? If you might recognize how this canvas was treated? I recall you and Miss Conway had a rather interesting discussion about the different ways canvases might be prepared?"

Hill accepted the piece gingerly. He peered at it on each side, turning it over and over in his hands, fingering the frayed edges thoughtfully before he brought it to his nose for a long sniff. Then he placed it flat on the counter. "I couldn't say."

Archie was nonplussed. Hill was—if not lying, then prevaricating. "Could you say if the canvas had been prepared?"

"I could," he admitted, but again, said no more.

Archie lowered his voice to ask more directly, "Do you recognize it as one of your prepared canvases, Mr. Hill? Or perhaps one from a different colorman?"

Mr. Hill's cheek flushed ruddy under his mahogany skin. "My lord, please understand—" he stammered. "I am not a political man. I had nothing to do with this outrage against the government."

Archie belatedly realized his error. "Mr. Hill—" he sought to assure him.

"My lord," Hill countered with low urgency. "You must see how it will be if it becomes known that I prepared this canvas? People will jump to unfounded assumptions and from assumptions they will eagerly make the leap to accusations. I am a black man in this land. Even though I have lived in Edinburgh all my adult life, I will never be Scots—or British—enough to be given any chance to explain. My business will be ruined and—"

Archie spoke over him to stem the tide of very rational fear. "Mr. Hill, I am not accusing you." He reached across the counter to touch the man's arm in reassurance.

But Hill was not assured. "Nevertheless," Hill insisted, "I will be accused if it becomes known that we prepared that canvas." He stared down at the scrap as if it were an adder, ready to strike.

"Mr. Hill, let me assure you." Archie kept his voice gentle and even. "Do not make yourself uneasy. I do not think you are responsible for the placard, for want of a better description. But I think you can help me find who is responsible."

Hill looked only slightly easier. "I don't want to put any of my customers afoul of the law."

And there was Archie's answer—it *was* a client of Hill's.

"I am not the law, Mr. Hill. Far from it. You've been a great help to me, sir. I appreciate your discretion." And in the same manner of discretion, Archie discreetly laid a guinea on the counter, which Mr. Hill just as discreetly covered with his palm. "Just as you can rely upon mine."

Mr. Hill made a very correct bow. "Your servant, my lord."

CHAPTER 37

"Maisie?"

Maisie came awake to the sound of Flora rapping on the door of the studio before she came into the aerie.

"Oh, why do you insist on sleeping on that lumpy old cot?" her sister fussed. "If you can even call it sleeping, for you don't look like you've had any rest at all. You look done in. You had so much better sleep downstairs in your chamber where Raines could see to you properly and where you would at least be warm!"

"You needn't take on, dearest." She said the words by rote, but they gave her time to recover herself after a night that had been spent in anxious, rueful pacing until Fergus had reappeared in the wee small hours, unscathed and triumphant.

"Yes, I most certainly do," Flora argued, "for you refuse to take on for yourself."

"I do about the important things."

"The painting, yes." Flora sighed. "And on that note, the color-man, Mr. Hill, is below, asking to speak to you."

Maisie realigned herself from horizontal to semi-vertical and tried to pull the cotton from her voice. "I'll see him."

"Not looking like that, you won't." Flora was adamant. "Come down and Raines will put you to rights and— Oh, never mind that. I'll send Raines *up* with water and a decent gown that hasn't been slept in."

"And some coffee," Maisie added, before she heard the demanding tone in her own voice. "If you would be so kind."

"I would be so kind," Flora said with another heartfelt sigh. "You worry me, Maisie."

The almost desperate, frustrated sort of love in her sister's voice made Maisie contrite. "I know dearest and I'm sorry." She took a deep breath to try to restore some of her equanimity—and honesty. "I worry myself, too. And I also worry about you."

"I'm sleeping in a real bed."

"No." Maisie reached for her sister's hand. "Is it true what Papa told me, that you've sworn not to marry until you have seen me happy? Have I been so unhappy, to make you take such a desperate pledge?"

"No, not unhappy." Flora frowned and shook her head. "But you were practically buried in the country in England, never seeing anyone. That's why I insisted that you accompany me here instead of staying in Richmond, where you were comfortable, and as you wanted."

"And as Papa wanted," Maisie reminded her.

"Yes," Flora admitted. "Because Papa doesn't understand. And I don't know that he ever will. But I understand more than you give me credit for." Flora came to sit beside her. "I wanted you to have the chance to do all the things you had assured that I got to do—paint and make friends and fall in love. And you have. Haven't you?"

Maisie was too tired for such revelations, but too tired to lie. She settled for asking her own question. "What makes you think I'm in love?"

"I can see the way he looks at you—as he has from the beginning," Flora said. "And I can see the way you look at him. It's right there—in the painting."

Maisie had wanted to make Archie transparent to the viewers of his portrait, but it seemed she had become transparent as well. "I suppose I have," she admitted with some relief.

"And are you happy?" Flora probed gently. "With him?"

"I am…learning to be, perhaps?" Maisie wanted to be helpful for Flora's sake. She wanted everything to be fine and happy and easy. But life wasn't like that. And whatever passions she felt for Archie Carrington were not going to outlast the disgrace she was actively trying to bring down on their father's head.

Because it also meant disgrace would fall on her head. And Flora's.

"What about you? Are you happy you came to Edinburgh? For yourself, Flora," she clarified. "You must have ambitions and wants and a heart of your own?"

"Must I?" Flora echoed in an ironic repeat of Maisie's answer that first night, when she had worked so hard to get Archie Carrington as a commission.

"Yes," Maisie insisted.

"I do," Flora admitted. "But that is a discussion for another day, when your Mr. Hill is not waiting downstairs." Flora enveloped Maisie in a careful, warm hug. "I'll send Raines up. And I'll make sure your Mr. Hill is well-tended-to while he waits."

"Thank you for looking after me so well."

"You are welcome," Flora answered. "And I do know you can take care of yourself, Maisie. But for some reason, at the moment, you're just choosing not to."

"I know," Maisie answered without giving in to the invitation to unburden herself. Because that was also a discussion for when Mr. Hill was not waiting downstairs. And likely, for when she could no longer conceal the reasons why. "You amaze me, you lovely witch."

"Just as you astonish me, my darling termagant."

Maisie had long liked being called a termagant, liked that version of herself as a quarrelsome woman—while it had prevented people from approaching her, it had also prevented people from pitying her. But the past few nights she had become quarrelsome in an entirely new, rather more powerful way. And she had taken care of herself in an entirely different way than ever before—she had finally said exactly what she wanted to say and done exactly what she wanted to do.

She had damned the consequences, which felt good and liberating in a way that was far more satisfying than getting a proper night's sleep. If nothing came of it—and actually, it was probably best if it didn't—she would have the satisfaction of knowing the she *had* done it.

Maisie's satisfaction was strong enough to see her through Raines's attentions so she might ask for Mr. Hill to be sent up. So satisfied that she was entirely unprepared for the news he brought her.

"Miss Conway!" He came through the door in a rush and stopped short. "I came as soon as I might." He seemed to gather himself together before he spoke. "They have found the canvas and are asking questions."

Shock—that what this awful, painful feeling in her chest had to be. As if she had been cracked open from within. As if her heart were leaking hot, spiky blood that would drown her with dread.

"I'm afraid I don't understand." She tried to keep control of both her shaking hands and her shaken confidence. "Who are *they?*"

"Lord Carrington," Mr. Hill clarified on a whisper, gesturing to the large canvas behind them, as if saying the name might conjure the man before them in person instead of in paint. "He came around first thing this morning, asking if I could identify the preparation on the canvas."

"The canvas?"

"Of the placard—the giant waybill plastered on the Greyfriar's Kirkyard wall."

"What does Arch—I mean, Lord Carrington, have to do with this…" She hardly knew what to call her own creation. "This placard?"

"I can only assume he is investigating for his own publication."

"But the Review is a quarterly—"

"—that runs special editions on topics of political importance," Hill agreed. "Whatever his purpose, his lordship is clearly probing the matter—on whose behalf, I cannot say. But he now knows the canvas came from my shop."

"Did it?"

He looked her directly in the eyes. "Yes, Miss Conway. As I so cavalierly told you, ours is a new, special and unique preparation. Lord Carrington was listening that morning. And who knows who else was, as well?"

Maisie felt as if all the air had rushed from her lungs—she could not draw a full breath.

"Do you think he will publish that information?"

"I cannot say." Hill's voice was full of apprehension. "The only thing that gave me comfort, was the fact that he said he did not suspect me, myself. But I fear he will follow this thread of evidence to help him find his conclusion." Across the room, his eyes found the last of the tall roll of prepared canvas.

"Have you told him your…" Maisie didn't think she had ever chosen her words so carefully. "…suspicions?"

"Of who might possess such prepared canvas?" Hill's dark eyebrows lifted. "No. And I will do everything in my power not to tell him, if I am able."

"Thank you…" Maisie swallowed. "…for all this interesting information, Mr. Hill. I am very much in your debt." It struck

Maisie then what an act of selflessness his coming to her was. "Deeply. I will take steps—"

"Excellent. May I suggest, disposing of any remaining canvas you may have as soon as may be possible?"

"Yes," she agreed with alacrity. "There are only a few feet of canvas left, but I shall burn it immediately. Thank you," she said again. "I don't know how I can thank you."

Mr. Hill took a breath that seemed to dissipate some of his tension. "Why, when all this blows over, by letting me display your work—that has nothing to do with the other canvas."

"The watercolors," she offered immediately. Archie had said the drawings were good enough to display.

No. He was Lord Carrington, the youngest-ever editor of the most important political quarterly in Scotland. She must endeavor to think of him as such—especially now, when he might no longer be her friend.

She took up the sketch book and was about to offer it to Mr. Hill when she realized that some of the faces she had painted on the postbill on the Greyfriar's wall were also depicted in the watercolors. And the paintings lined up against the wall.

Everything she had been working on since she came to Edinburgh might implicate her. She needed to be cautious. She needed to be afraid.

Deeply afraid.

She saw Mr. Hill out and immediately she began to build up the fire.

It wasn't much of a chore to feed the last few feet of prepared canvas into the fire, but she had a roaring blaze going—thanks to all that linseed and oil of spike permeating the Belgian linen—by the time her next visitor arrived unannounced. It seemed the quiet, private way Maisie had established for traversing the tall house had become something of a high road, with people coming and going at all hours.

She would need to be far more careful going forward.

"You are to be congratulated." Lady Cairn shut the door behind her and turned with a mischievous smile. "You've certainly put the cats amongst the pigeons."

"Have I?" Maisie tried to steel herself for whatever fresh information Quince might have. "I don't think I like being a pigeon."

"You will if you can learn to fly," the marchioness advised.

Maisie did not share her friend's blithe enthusiasm. "I don't think that's possible, my lady."

"Quince, please, since we're conspirators," she teased.

"Archie is investigating the posting," Maisie said bluntly.

"Of course he is." Quince remained unruffled. "I should have expected nothing less. He'll be preparing a special edition of the Review, no doubt."

Maisie could think of nothing worse. "He had a piece of the canvas from Greyfriar's wall that he took to Mr. Hill—the colorman who sold it to me!—for identification and Mr. Hill thinks he's going to keep on investigating and asking questions —" Maisie stopped. She could hear her voice rising in incipient panic and tried to calm herself. Especially in front of the supremely serene marchioness. "I've burned what little I had left."

"Have you? By jimble, good thinking. But points to Archie for acuity, too. And determination. So—" Lady Cairn hopped up to sit on the worktable and patted the tabletop next to her. "Come sit, before you fall down. All is not lost."

"Not yet," Maisie muttered, but sit she did.

"Not at all," Quince assured her. "There is always another choice to be made. Especially in such sticky situations." She put her arm around Maisie's shoulders. "I can see I'm going to need to convince you." She proceeded to peel off her gloves and settle into her story. "A long time ago—about eight years ago, in fact—a disguised, rather spurious French highwayman named Monsieur Minuit—or as the newspapers like the Review dubbed him,

Captain Midnight—roamed Edinburgh stealing only from the rich."

Maisie nodded. "A Robin Hood of sorts?"

"Aye," Lady Quince agreed with satisfaction. "Just so. Robbing the rich to give to the poor—though the newspapers and broadsheets didn't know about that part. Monsieur Minuit liked to do his bad deeds openly, but his good by stealth."

"And did Archie investigate Monsieur Minuit and expose him?"

"Yes, and no. They tried, but the newspapers and broadsheets never did learn his true identity."

"But Archie knew?

"Eventually." Something about the smile on Lady Quince's face told Maisie that she also knew.

Maisie's mind immediately leap to plausible possibilities. "Was it Archie? Or one of his friends—Alasdair?"

"Oh, holy iced toffee, no." Lady Quince's laugh tumbled out of her like water down a brook. "Certainly not Alasdair—the poor man was tasked with finding and stopping the thefts—though, at one point, he was actually accused of being the Captain himself."

"But he wasn't?" Then it had to be one of the others—Quince wouldn't be telling her the story otherwise.

"No, he was not." Quince patted Maisie's hand. "I was."

"You?" Maisie gaped at her. "But you're a marchioness."

"Don't sound so incredulous—I might not take that as a compliment," Quince laughed. "But I wasn't a marchioness then, just a young woman with itchy fingers and an unholy fascination with theft. To put it bluntly, I stole, both as myself and as Monsieur Minuit because I liked it. Although everything I stole— well, nearly everything—ended up in the poor box at West Kirk."

"That's just down the road—" Maisie gestured out the north-facing window. "Where I pasted the first—"

"Just so," Lady Cairn said with some satisfaction. "I found a sort of poetic justice in that. And the fact that I once jumped a toll gate that used to stand on this very corner, during a midnight foray on my way down to the Kirk."

Maisie did not know what to think. "I am all astonishment." She had never been so daring in all her life—even before. "And admiration."

"Thank you. But the point of this criminal confessional is that I thought I recognized that spark in you when we first met, and I wanted you to be able to see that same spark in me. I am here to help—I offer you both my absolute discretion and my services." Quince narrowed her eyes over her smile. "And the first thing you need to learn from my example, is that the authorities never think to suspect a woman. Your first guesses were men, though I had already told you nearly all. I'd wager that if I were to confess all publicly now, few would believe me."

Maisie felt the first sense of lightness and relief she had felt in quite some time. "Do you really think so?"

"I know so," Lady Cairn confirmed. "You are the last person suspicion will fall upon. You may be certain of that. Now, I think what we need is a printing press. A small one, to run handbill sized versions of your brilliantly insightful and incendiary pictures. So much easier to paste up by the hundreds, and so much harder for the authorities to tear down."

Maisie could immediately see the advantage. "Small paper waybills posted with wheatpaste? I think I've got one last idea that might suit. But the only printing press I know is Archie's—"

"You concentrate on making a cartoon suitable for the engraver and leave the rest to me," Quince declared. "I know exactly what to do. Oh, by jimble, this is going to be such great fun. How I do like putting a pot on the boil."

CHAPTER 38

"Which pot is that, my dear Lady Cairn?"

"Archie!" Quince called, as first Archie and then Rory Cathcart came through Maisie's aerie door. "My dear, we were just talking about you, weren't we, Maisie? And admiring your very handsome, very insightful portrait." Quince hopped off the table to greet each man in turn. "And Rory, darling! What brings you with Archie—longing to get your portrait made as well? Well, you'll have to get in line behind me and Greer and Mignon. And of course behind Augusta Ivers who is in front of us all!"

Maisie didn't know how Lady Cairn could seem to speak without drawing breath, but she was grateful for her rather magnificent diversion. It gave Maisie the chance to pull herself together and arrange her face along more pleasing—and less frightened or conspiratorial lines.

"Hello, Archie. Mr. Cathcart." She nodded at his friend, but she really had eyes only for Archie, who somehow came to her and took her hand as if nothing in the world were wrong.

"Maisie." He said her name quietly, in that warm way he had of making it sound like a pleasure. "I have missed you."

"Oh, yes." She let out the breath she had been holding in a rush. "As I've missed you. But I've been—" She gestured generally to the paintings behind her.

"Busy with other matters—as have I," he told her. "That disturbance I mentioned, down at the bottom of the Queensferry Road? It seems to have spread. There's a sort of political crusader abroad in the city, posting up rather unflattering depictions of some politicians."

He seemed to be regarding her with some expectation.

Maisie's chest began to feel tight. Her blood pounded in her ears. "Has he?"

"Indeed." Archie kept hold of her hands, even in front of his friends. "And this fellow seems to be especially targeting your father as Lord Advocate. I thought you should know."

He thought she would be concerned. He was thinking of her. Warning her.

She tried to think of what she ought to say, if she were not the one creating the unflattering depictions. "I assume my father has made himself a target by his recent missteps in regard to the South Bridge vaults?"

"Yes, very likely," Archie agreed, with a slight smile that told her he was relieved at her taking the news so well. "I know you don't share the same...philosophies as your father," he added. "But I thought you would want to know that the hue and cry is bound to get louder, especially when..."

"When the Review, amongst other publications, starts publishing your story?" She tried to sound resolved. "And when will that be? So we can prepare ourselves."

"We don't have a publication date set, yet," he told her. "We're seeking more information before we go to print."

His hesitation gave her pause. "Are you...asking my permission?"

Nae," he admitted. "I don't have that power as editor to keep this from being published anymore. This fellow's last postbill put paid to any discretion I might have had."

"This fellow?" Quince asked with an almost arch glance at Maisie. "Who is he?"

"I've personally dubbed him The Conscience, for the letter C signed in the corner of the canvases—and they were canvases posted up with wheatpaste like handbills. Very clever, very quick. Ingenious, really."

"The Conscience?" Quince asked. "How dramatic."

"The Review is calling him the Conscience of the City. Whoever it is," Archie asserted, "he seems to have it in for your father. I'm sorry. I just thought you might want to prepare your-selves—you and your sister."

"Yes," Maisie agreed. "Yes, I understand. Thank you."

"I've brought Rory as a way of atonement—of paying my penance in advance."

"Penance?" She looked to the elegant man, who smiled and shrugged.

"Archie has told me of your rather baroque religious paint-ings," Rory explained. "Your waifs and saints—and I am thor-oughly intrigued."

"What does that have to do with penance?" she asked.

"Oh, by jimble," Quince broke in. "Archie thinks that if Rory can exhibit and sell some of your paintings and establish you as a painter of note, then you won't feel the sting of your father's downfall quite so much."

Maisie looked at Archie. "Is that true?"

"Mostly," he admitted, with that wince of a smile. "Actually, exactly."

It was an extraordinarily generous idea—and one he never would have thought of herself.

"And the Review," Quince predicted, "will run a glowing write-up of such a show, by well-known local connoisseur, Rory Cathcart? Am I right?"

"Is it going to be that bad?" Maisie asked. "Do you think my father will face censure?"

"Hard to tell," Archie said. "But you need to be prepared. And if you had your own income…? You might have better choices."

It was a fantastical dream, this idea of choices. The problem was that Maisie had already chosen—she had already put her waifs and saints on the satirical placards. And once Archie found out, he would make different choices himself.

He would not choose her.

But there was no way for her to refuse the request—Mr. Cathcart was already standing in front of the row of canvases, solemnly regarding her painting of the well-known Biblical story of God's command to Abraham in all its filicideal terror. There was Fergus as the young Isaac, both defiant and enraged at being sacrificed.

"Ah." Rory Cathcart made a quiet sound of consideration that both soothed and frightened her. But what did it matter if Cathcart didn't like them—she was likely to be a pariah anyway, a woman who had 'cliped' on her morally bankrupt father.

"Your powers of observation and representation are quite astounding," Cathcart finally said. "You've captured both the character in the story and the actual boy—was that not he in the stableyard?—his hunger and anger and determination."

"More like devastation," she answered, though the heavy hammer of her blood in her ears made it hard to think clearly over her fear. "Or desperation." Any moment now, Archie was going to recognize that the same faces that were arrayed in front of him were also on the painted placards adorning Edinburgh's walls, and her masquerade would come to its inevitable, messy end.

"Is that what you see?" Cathcart asked her. "Desperation?"

"Is that not what you see?" she asked back. "The abandonment and yawning horror and deep, abiding desperation?"

"Yes," Archie acknowledged. "But I also see resolution and a sort of native toughness and resourcefulness in the lad. I saw that in him the other night."

"The other night?" Maisie asked in what she hoped was a normal voice that didn't quaver with fear. "Did you?"

"Away on some errand for you, he said. Off with a pot of porridge and some bread for whatever other children he could find to feed? Finding the hungry and destitute outside of your studio, now, are you? You certainly are on the side of the angels."

Her relief was profound, but only temporary. "Perhaps. I have to try, at least, in some way."

"You are succeeding in your paintings, Miss Conway," Rory Cathcart opined. "Transfiguring these lost souls into saints. And this one—" He lifted one of her depictions of Agnes.

"Saint Joan of Arc before the fire," Maisie supplied uneasily. Agnes with her wildly sad eyes that Maisie had painted so many times—and most recently upon the Greyfriar's wall.

Surely a man with Archie Carrington's regard for individuals and memory for faces, he would put two and two together?

"You've depicted her several times—such an arresting face," Cathcart judged. "I especially like the intriguing way she meets the eye of the beholder as the Magdalene. She is us and we are her. Very effective."

"Thank you." Maisie remained too tense to appreciate the compliment.

"They belong, I think," Cathcart considered, "to the tradition of the *femme forte* paintings of the Italian Renaissance, these ordinary people turned into heroic women."

"Indeed!" Quince smiled serenely and patted Maisie's arm consolingly, as if to embolden her. "These paintings, I think," she added, "are our Maisie's own version of a crusade."

"Aye," Archie agreed. "A crusader as delicate and strong as Damascus steel. And clearly, a secret romantic."

"Am I?" Maisie was astonished at this version of herself. "I must be if I can't be blind or uncaring or indifferent. I am not made of stone."

"No, you are flesh and fiery blood," he agreed quietly for her ears alone as he came near. "Lovely flesh and fiery blood, all housed in the heart of a saint."

He was going to hate her. He was going to revile her the moment he found her out—any moment now. But she had to say something. "Now who is flattering?"

"I am," he admitted unabashedly. "Is it doing me any good? Any good to get you to kiss me?"

"No," she said even as she reached for his hand. She laced her fingers between his and brought his hand to her lips for a kiss, even as she said. "Not in company. Not…" Not when his utter repudiation of her and her family was imminent.

"Then I'll wait," he pledged. "I'll wait however long it takes. And I'll be here, waiting and wanting patiently, for however long it takes, to kiss you."

And he kissed her on the forehead. And set himself away from her. And waited until his friends were ready to finally take their leave, and leave her at last, after such a day, to herself.

And her fate.

Maisie took out a fresh sheet of paper, and took up her pen.

"Fergus," she called to the lad who appeared with her morning coffee. "We're going to need more pots of paste. And a few more friends."

Outside, on the pavement of Hope Street, Archie and Rory accompanied Quince across Charlotte Square toward the Cairn Townhouse chatting amiably.

"Well, you weren't lying," Rory began.

"No," Archie agreed happily. "Does this mean you will represent her?"

"If she'll let me," Rory answered. "I see exactly what she's done —taken the iconography, the accepted visual language, if you will, of religious and history paintings and turned it on its head with her direct, almost challenging gaze. And her technique." He made a whistling sound of admiration. "Quite, quite accomplished. Not as conventional as I would have expected, The Magdalene, but so much more powerful for its unconventionality. And the Madonna—what did she label it? Our Lady of the Grassmarket. Ah." Rory nodded at the realization. "That's where I've seen that arresting face before."

"Seen in the past," Archie put in quietly. "The lass is dead."

Rory made a sound of empathetic distress. "Such a loss. And the lad—her brother I assume? Saint Fergus of Kirk Brae Head she labeled him, even while depicting him as David. She's named them one and all."

"Names them, to shame us," Quince put in, "one and all. Just as we ought to be."

"Never doing enough? I knew you'd take to her so readily," Archie said. "Thick as thieves, you'll be before long."

"Certainly," Quince answered with a laugh. "I'm proud to call her my friend. And proud to be her patron—whatever you don't take to Mr. Christie's to sell in London, Rory, I'll be buying."

"No, no," Rory objected. "They need to be seen as a whole—as a whole collection. In a proper public gallery, where their glory and importance can be shared."

"Is she as good as I think she is?" Archie asked.

"Probably better. Our Lady of the Grassmarket," Rory mused with a smile. "Very evocative, but I liked her first title better."

"Which was?" Quince asked.

"She had painted over something else on the back of the canvas, there. Our Lady of the Gutter, I thought. I think I like it better."

"Very evocative," agreed Quince. "Only our Miss Maisie Conway could have thought of a name like that."

"Or made so much of such an arresting face," Archie began. "I am nothing short of amazed that she could depict poor Agnes in so many different canvases and yet make her so different, and yet so recognizable—"

It was as if a bolt of lightning landed on his head—one moment he could hear and see, and the next moment the world had exploded in his head.

Archie drew the corner of canvas out of his pocket—C for conscience.

And C for Conway.

It had all been there for him to see, had he but looked—the secrecy, the stealing through the stable gate at all hours, the hastily painted placard, the line of wet pigment on the floor of her aerie where the edge of said placard had been laid down to paint, the faces of the waifs and saints painted into the placards.

He should have seen—he *had* seen, but he had not understood.

He had underestimated her.

"Oh, holy ice picks," said Quince. "You didn't know?"

Archie turned on her. "You knew?"

"I guessed," Quince admitted. "I'm still guessing. I just thought…she seemed supremely capable. And you seemed so… intimate and—"

"Why didn't you tell me?" he accused.

"Because I assumed if I could figure it out, so could you," she countered hotly. "You men think you're the only ones capable of taking charge or making a splash. Well, you're not."

"Oh, yes," Rory exclaimed. "Things are always more complicated than anticipated."

"Of course they are," Archie countered. "Especially when dealing with women." He fingered the piece of that canvas from the wall of Greyfriar's Kirkyard. "Of course it's her. It's been her the whole damn time."

Anger, humiliation and disbelief made a sour mash in his stomach. But it was the admiration that gave the strongest kick.

Quince stepped in front of him, blocking the way, as if she expected him to immediately head back to the house on Kirk Brae Head. "What are you doing to do about it?"

"I don't know. Yet." He had to think. He had to piece the whole business together—this was Maisie acting out—striking out against her own father.

"I'll help you decide," Quince declared. "If you meet me at your press house in an hour. And Archie?" She paused on her doorstep. "Wake your engraver, and have your presses ready to run. You said you wanted to make an unholy splash—this is going to be your chance."

CHAPTER 39

*A*rchie paced up and down the length of the cold stone warehouse under the dispassionate gaze of his pressmen, whom he had rousted out of their homes, because if Quince was going to bring him what he thought she was going to bring him, it would be all hands to the press.

If.

If Quince came—if Maisie herself came!

If he accepted.

"Governor?" Big Davy tossed his head toward the door, just as a quick rap sounded on the portal.

"I'll go." He stepped outside and waited for his eyes to adjust to the low light before he saw her, dressed in a long, obscuring cloak and veil, standing just beyond the pool of torchlight.

"Friend," Quince called him.

"I haven't decided if I'm your friend tonight," he said to cover the pang of disappointment that Quince, and not Maisie, had kept her appointment.

"Oh, no," Quince disagreed blithely. "The enemy of your enemy is undoubtedly your friend."

It was nothing more than he had said to himself, but he was

too agitated to admit to the truth of his motives now. "Don't try getting eerie or philosophical with me," he advised irritably. "What have you got?"

She handed him a rolled-up waybill, which he held up to the light to better see. "God's bawbag."

The bill depicted the now-familiar caricature of the bewigged and enrobed Advocate of the Crown, sitting this time upon an arching pyramid of hard-baked opium cakes, which, like rubble in the first placard and the effluent in the second, rained or blew down in an all-engulfing dusty mist, inundating the poor until they choked on the drug, while above, the figure of twisted justice counted his money.

As an indictment of her father's work for the British East India Company, it was specific. As an accusation against the Lord Advocate, it was clear. And it was going to cause an unholy, unbridled stink of a splash.

If he printed it.

"I'm giving you first refusal," Quince offered, as if she could hear his thoughts. "A leg up on the competition—the other journals and newspapers as well as the cartoon print shops." When he said nothing, she continued, "I could run this over to Jackson's Close and be done with it. But this way, you'll make all the profit off the story of the decade. I'm paying a premium," she added, "in cash."

"You would be." Posted all over the city as waybills, the satirical image would be impossible to ignore, giving him the excuse he needed to make his own account of the moral, if not legal, charges against the Lord Advocate, public.

This was the blow that needed to be struck. And he decided to be the man who did it.

He put out his hand for the money.

Quince slipped a heavy purse into his palm. "Leave the waybills, wrapped in bundles of fifty outside the door to be collected. Don't be here. Destroy all the evidence from your presses."

"I know what to do, Quince."

"Good man, Archie. I knew we could count on you." She shook his hand. "But I was never here."

"Of course you weren't. Just keep her safe, will you? Keep her out of the thick of it."

"I can try."

It took Arthur Jones an hour to prepare the engraving and fifty minutes to prepare a second. But the moment the first plate was done, the presses were up and running, adding layers of color in successive print runs, repeating the process until a thousand waybills hung from their drying racks, ready to be bundled.

It took nearly four hours to finish the run and another hour to stack the waybills into the requested bundles. And they were done.

"Not a word, lads. Not a single fucking word."

"Aye, Archie. Aye."

Archie sent Arthur, Davy and the rest of his pressmen home, and cleaned the ink off the presses himself, working until there was no lingering trace of any ink, and burning the rags in a bucket of sand to erase the last traces of his complicity.

Outside, he heard the scrape and creak of a barrow wheel against the cobbles and had to make himself stand in place and not look out the crack of the door to see who collected the job—Fergus, likely, with his pot of glue, hopefully not alone, but then again, hopefully not accompanied by a hirplin lass. Or a damn marchioness disguised in an enveloping domino.

Only when he judged that the danger had passed did he look out to see the waybills had been collected. And only then did he put his hat and greatcoat on and go out into the night.

"Gov'nor." The newsboy, Dougal Ferris, waited in the fog,

silent and practically unseen until Archie was arrived at their meeting spot on the southwest corner of the Tron Kirk porch. "There's all for a scramble tonight."

"Aye?" Archie flipped him a shining coin, which he caught as deftly as a conjurer. "What do ye hear?"

"It's what I seen—a pure swell o'lads heading up the High Street with the rolls of bills, just like ye told me they might."

"Which way?"

"All ways," the lad laughed. "All the fuck over the city."

Archie tossed him another coin and settled his hat more solidly on his head. "Take me to the closest."

"Lay on." The lad led the charge up west, up the High Street, toward the Luckenbooths, whereupon they ducked south into Parliament Close, where the walls had been effectively papered top to bottom—some enterprising waif had even had the brass balls to paper over the august government edifice's door.

"This is the stuff, Dougal. Good work." Archie pulled out his pencil and began his mad scribbling, making a full and florid description of both the posting and the mad method of its posting all over the walls and door and windows of the city.

And when he had finished his descriptive report and put away his notebook and pencil, he turned his collar against the damp. "All right, then, Dougal. I'm away."

Away to find her.

Not for his report. Not for exposure in the Edinburgh Review's exclusive exposé. Not for any newsworthy gain.

But only to assure himself that she was fine and brave and mad and unhurt and safe.

Above all, he needed to know she was safe.

THIS TIME, MAISIE WAS DEAD SURE SHE HAD BITTEN OFF FAR MORE than she could chew. The logistics of the thing alone nearly defeated her. While it had seemed an easy decision to change from posting the placards on walls to posting the much smaller waybills, the very real problem of getting those bills posted on several hundred walls, pillars and posts had been daunting.

Wheatpaste had to be mixed in quantity and distributed in waxed cotton feed bags pinched from their stables. Brushes needed to be found and allotted. A collective of waifs, orphans and beggars, eager to earn a few pennies while poking the eyes of the powers that be, had to be assembled and paid. Locations had to be assigned and sections of the city divvied up. Waybills had to be printed, counted and meted out.

But somehow, between the three of them, Maisie, Fergus and Quince got it done.

The wheatpaste, Maisie had mixed and divided into feed bags with Fergus in her aerie, from whence they had taken the bags under cover of dusk to meet one of Quince's unmarked carriages at the stable gate.

From there, they had ventured near to Liberton's Close, where Fergus had stealthily collected the waybills that Quince had arranged and paid for. In the carriage, they had divided up the bundles of waybills and, while driving seemingly aimlessly about the city, met with several and sundry beggars, crossing sweeps, dairy maids and drovers, and idlers and watchers who had taken delivery of a clutch of goods, and gone away in the night to do their worst.

"Divide and conquer," Quince reflected, "is a very clever strategy. And what a delightful thing it is to have co-conspirators. Spread the complicity out, that's what I say."

That—along with Quince's indomitable attitude of larkiness —finally brought a smile to Maisie's tense face. "Yes," she agreed. "It is a wonderful thing to have friends upon whom one might rely."

They were, for their purposes, done. They could return to

their respective homes, retire to their beds and simply await the dawn, anxious but safe.

But they did not.

Each of them for their own reason, but Maisie, for her own, simply wanted to see it through. Wanted to know that she had done this. And while she had not done it alone, nothing could or would have been done or achieved without her. She had started this crusade of sorts with her own hands and she would finish it out with her own hands.

And this was the finish. Maisie was under no illusions that she could continue.

Perhaps she might in time find some success—or at least an income—in an illicit career as a print shop satirist, especially if her part in this escapade became known, but her career as a public political agitator was over. And if not, if she was somehow clever and lucky enough not to be caught, then she would be clever enough not to press her luck.

Pluck could only take her so far.

But it was also pluck that had her damning her nerves, wiping her hands on her smock under the cover of her enveloping cloak and stepping out of the carriage just beyond Twopenny Custom corner, where Orchard Field and Fountain Bridge met. She would work her way up through the streets of the new Orchard Field Square toward the Lothian Road from whence she would steal home.

It was a good plan. A well-thought-out plan. A plan she ought to have been able to follow.

But time was against her—she was, as Fergus had so sagely predicted, too slow.

The first posting was a disaster—a messy, slap-dash affair made worse by her shaking hands and the use of far too much wheatpaste.

The second, third and fourth—put up at intervals along the road on walls, windows and posts—were better. By the sixth, she finally got into the swing of it, slapping up the first coat of paste, laying on the waybill and then plastering it on with a final brush of paste, up and down.

And then it was smooth, if slow sailing down the street and around the corner, settling into the rhythm of the work and calming her jangling nerves enough to begin to enjoy herself just a little. Just enough to take satisfaction from the doing.

But she had not counted on the constable—young, incorruptible and fleet of foot.

She did not see him cross under the link lights illuminating the doorway of number sixteen View Hill. She did not see him pause and turn her way. She did not hear him raise his whistle to his lips.

"Hoy!" he cried as he started towards her. "Hold there!"

Maisie's pulse throttled her throat. She could barely breathe. She panicked and dropped her bag of paste and brush on the pavement, only to find a blessedly convenient gutter pipe at her feet. She kicked the feed bag down into the hole and stood atop it, and was attempting to conceal the rest of her small bundle of waybills deep within the copious pockets under her skirts just as he reached her.

But the moment he was about to clap hands on her, a hew and cry from her right turned his head.

And she could only watch in fascinated horror as his eyes widened and his mouth drew open as if he were about to shout, but his voice was drowned out by the sound of pounding feet coming hard up the pavement.

Out of the corner of her eye, Maisie recognized wee Fergus and taller, rangier Jock, the crossing sweep who had taken over Fergus' corner, just before they barreled between her and the constable, crashing into her with all the force of youth and violent recklessness.

And she was falling back toward the wrought iron railing on

the square, while the constable had been knocked in the other direction, scattered like nine pins bowls.

Maisie went down hard on her weak hip. So hard it hurt, badly. So hard it made her cry out into the night. And draw attention back to herself instead of the boys.

"Please!" she cried to the constable's back, clutching at the long tail of his coat as if it were a lifeline. "Please, I'm hurt."

The constable wavered, torn between chasing down the lads and helping a woman who now appeared to be in distress. But he finally gave in to the clutch of his coat.

"Here, miss." He put his hand to her elbow to help her to rise.

"Oh, thank you, constable." She tried to speak clearly, to put something ladylike and very English into her accent, though her voice was as shredded as her hems and her leg ached something fierce. She would have a bruise like a beefsteak on her hip by the time she got home.

If she got home.

Because the moment she gained her feet, a second man stepped out of the shadows, looming toward her.

Archie Carrington, his eyes as dark as the devil's waistcoat, looking like God's revenge against murder.

CHAPTER 40

It was as if his boots had been nailed to the cobbles. Archie was riveted with some spiky combination of rage and fear. Because there she was.

Maisie Conway really was his Conscience of the City.

All the evidence had been there before his eyes—the bold, decisive strokes of paint, the rolls of canvas hidden under Holland covers, the withholding, secretive nature. The lethal eye. The deadly genius. The terrible guilt.

He could see all that in her eyes the moment she saw him.

And something else. Something stronger. Pride.

She didn't look away.

His feet felt as if they were encased in lead as he walked towards her, but his mind was clear. He put all his native charm and persuasion into his voice to call out, "My dear? I thought I'd lost you in this cursed mist and fog!" He ran to pick her up off the slick, damp pavement. "I heard you cry out. Are you hurt?"

"There was a commotion," she quavered. "I came to look and then— Oh!" She wilted conveniently and perfectly into his arms.

"You know this…" The constable took a long look a Maisie before he decided upon, "leddy?"

"She is my wife," Archie said without conscious thought. "Lord Carrington of the Review." He gave his own bona fides to help the constable come to his conclusion. "What's gone on here?"

"Dunno fer sure," the young man said. "Looked like she were up to no good, ye ken, but then them lads come howling along, and all—" He gestured eloquently to the half-pasted placard adorning the wall. "Reckon it summit frae that Conscience, they're calling 'im."

Archie settled on, "Did you see him, then, this man?"

"Nae." The constable turned his attention back to Maisie, whose supposedly wilted hands had Archie in a grip that would have done his old nanny proud. "Can ye tell me what ye saw then, meleddy. Did they set upon ye, the wee bastarts?"

"No!" She said quickly, before she corrected herself. "I didn't see them really, to be honest. I heard the commotion and when I came around the corner— I wasn't expecting—" She was all breathless confusion. "And I fell. And they ran off."

"They din't hurt ye, meleddy?"

"Oh, no, I don't think so," she quavered perfectly. "I mean, I am hurt, but I fell you see, in fright."

"Thank you, constable." Archie decided their playacting had gone on long enough. "I'll see to my lady."

Archie picked her up in his arms and carried her around the nearest corner, far enough away from the scene for her to say, "You can put me down now. I'd rather walk the pain off, if you don't mind."

"I mind," he said. But he put her down because, as he had once said to her, she must know her own capabilities better than he could.

"I collect that you are angry with me—"

"How very perceptive of you, Miss Conway. But you always were very perceptive." He took her arm more gently than his anger wanted. But he was a gentleman—he would be damn well gentle as he all but frog-marched her away. "But I am more than angry. I am near livid with rage at your stupidity and your brass and the sheer bloody genius of your deception."

She did not argue with him. "Yes. Thank you. But might we flee the scene of the crime more slowly, please?"

Archie immediately slackened his pace, tucking her arm through his in a more familiar, conciliatory manner. But he still felt the need to give vent to his fear. "Keep your voice down, or there may still be the very real possibility of your being apprehended."

"By whom? No one realizes but you."

"And if I am called to give evidence?"

"Who will call you to give evidence?"

"Any of the Crown Prosecutors who may read the Review's account of the Conscience."

"But I am not 'The Conscience,'" she pointed out reasonably. "*You* made that moniker up out of whole cloth. *He* is a figment of *your* imagination. And with any luck, *he* will remain just that."

Archie was still too afraid for her to admit to any reasonableness. "Or perhaps the Lord Advocate himself—whom you've been poking like a bear in a cage—will ask the Crown Prosecutors to take up the case. Did you think of that before you thought this bloody scheme up?"

"No," she admitted. "I did not think he would do anything. I thought he would be too embarrassed. I thought he was capable of shame."

"And still you did it anyway?"

"There is no reward without risk," she reminded him.

"And what could possibly be your reward?"

"Changing the world." She tried to make it appear as if she were joking as she quoted his words back to him, but there was truth and determination behind her bluster. "And having a great deal of fun—although this particular episode has been particularly painful—while I do it!"

"Fun?" He could not reconcile his fear for her with her blithe response. "Keep your voice down." He cast a wary glance before and after them to make sure the way was clear of eavesdroppers.

"Would you be happier if I denied it?"

"To anyone but me," he answered.

"You have the insight and tenacity of a fox at a henhouse, which no one else seems to have," she complimented. "But who, as Quince reminded me, is going to believe this agitator is a woman, let alone lame, spinster me?"

The look on her face was calmly fierce. "You're secretly thrilled."

She turned to look him in the eye. "Not so secretly anymore," she said. "But yes, I am."

There was nothing he could say. But he said it anyway. "God's bawbag. Bugger all."

"Yes, indeed, I should like someone to bugger them all—all the dirty, thieving, greedy basterts—as Fergus calls them—the landlords and property owners and politicians and functionaries who turn their profit and their blind eyes. Bastards all."

But her eyes were lit with purpose and something else—the barest hint of mirth warmed the corners of her eyes. "Admit it," he charged. "You've enjoyed this."

"Not exactly," she hedged. "It has been far too much work for that. But I've learned to enjoy their discomfort at least."

"You're mad, Maisie Conway." But his arms were already encircling her, pulling her close and safe, snugged up tight against his coat.

"I am," she agreed. "Mad as a march hare to have waited so long to find my way and to speak my mind. To finally find my way back to myself—back to the way I was before."

He wasn't exactly sure what she meant. "Has your hitch disappeared?"

"Oh, no!" Her laugh was low and perhaps a little wistful. "It is probably worse than ever this night. I will never not walk with a limp," she stated. "But I will also never again live with my father's, or anyone else's, opinions crippling my abilities or limiting how I do anything else."

"I hope you will make an exception for me and listen to my opinion until we can get you safe."

"We?" She turned her face up to his in the dim lamplight. "I rather like the sound of 'we.'"

"We," he murmured against her lips because they were there and he couldn't possibly not kiss her. Not take the tart plushness of her bottom lip between his teeth. Not press himself to her clever mouth. Not take all the rage and fear and frustration and turn it into something far sweeter than he could have imagined.

She opened to him readily, kissing him back with an ardor he had not thought possible in such a self-contained woman. God help him, she kissed like an angel, all soft, sighing concession when all the rest of her seemed to be prickly opposition.

His hands found their way to her chin, angling her jaw so he could deepen the kiss. Her arms slid under his sleeves, holding him close. He felt warm and alive and—

"Gie it laldy, lad!"

The raucous call brought him back to the chill cobbles of Hope Street. Maisie hid her face in his coat and he held her there until the boisterous fellow had passed.

"Let me take you home."

"Your home?"

"If you like."

"Aye. Please." Fatigue clouded her features for a moment. "Kirk Brae Head is too…hard. And I'd rather just be alone with you, if I may." She interlaced her fingers with his and he liked the way they walked, slowly, but side by side, as if they had every right to be together, every right to be out strolling and kissing under the lamplight.

"What did he mean, 'gie it laldy'?"

"He meant do it proud, son. Give her yer best." He brought

her wrist to his lips. "And so I tried to give you my all. Did I gie it laldy, do ye think?"

A rosy blush painted her cheeks, but she was smiling. "Aye, you did. You are the man I can rely on—for exceptional kisses, as well as everything else."

Was it his own sense of rightness or did he hear happiness in her voice?

They continued on in silence, walking more slowly than his normal pace so she might not be any more labored over the uneven stone pavement. "Is your leg much hurt?"

"I'll have a bruise like an aubergine by morning, but no lasting damage, I think. Easy enough price to pay to know Fergus and Jock were away. Nothing a hot bath won't cure."

"We'll have a look at it all the same," he said. "I've a tincture or two that work wonders on bruises."

"Do you now? But no bath?"

"I've an old copper hip bath that I usually stand in while I pour cold water over my head."

"I'll pass, thank you."

Her hand tightened in his, leaning more of her weight on him as she became increasingly fatigued. "I'll take care of you," he assured her.

"Archie." She squeezed his hand to show him her strength. "I've said it before and I'll say it again—I can take care of myself."

"I know that," he said, pulling her to a stop. "But I wish to hell you'd let me try. I love you," he began. "I love you, Maisie Conway, you impossible, contrary, beautiful uncompromising, delightful woman. You have brought nothing but havoc and chaos into my life. And I've never been happier." He came to a stop in front of her. "I never want to be without you. I never want to let you go, or let you out of my sight. Ever," he reiterated. "I mean to cleave to you and have you cleave to me all the rest of my godforsaken days."

She stared at him. "Archie, are you proposing? Marriage? Now?"

"I bloody well am," he answered. "Come," he urged as the sound of voices came from ahead. He ducked them into a pitch-black alcove and gathered her close. "Not a word," he whispered.

"But—"

He stopped her protest by kissing her. By wrapping his arms around her and holding her so close he could not tell where she began and he left off. He kissed her so hard, he pushed them both into the future where they would be together, safe and warm and happy and free from—

But life with Maisie Conway was never going to be like that. Life with Maisie was going to be complicated and irrational and contrary and wonderful. "Because I can't live without you."

She looked up at him, her dark eyes shining wide in the refracted moonlight.

"I mean it. I'll not take no for an answer."

She shook her head mutely.

Something within him broke. Something that he had been fighting and holding within. Something he had not admitted, even to himself—he could not imagine his life without her.

"Please, Maisie, don't do this to me." He didn't care if he sounded desperate—he was. "I love you and I'll spend every day for the rest of my life telling you so." He kissed her again as if he could press his urgency and his surety upon her. "Why won't you answer?"

"Because you told me not to make a sound." She whispered against his lips.

"God's bawbag. So I did." He drew in a calmer breath. "I rescind that request."

"I had rather kiss than talk."

"I'll take that as a yes."

"You may take that as a perhaps."

"Perhaps?" He nearly shouted in frustration. "Perhaps?"

"Because it depends. Where are we to live? I must have a studio—with good light. I will need the freedom to paint what I choose without interference."

"When have I ever interfered with your painting?"

"Tonight. Fifteen minutes ago."

"Damn right. I reserve the right to interfere to keep you from gaol. Where you may end up yet, if one of your lads gets caught."

She acknowledged his point with a wry tip of her head. "They're not all lads. And they are all paid handsomely not to clipe."

He acknowledged her strategy with a wry tip of his own head —he paid his sources handsomely as well. And clearly, some of his sources and her lads were one and the same. But he was getting well away from his point. "I will find a house for you with excellent light, a pleasing prospect and as many spacious attics as you may want."

"Something near the university, not in the New Town," she began. "On the north side of George Square, where—"

"Hoy!" A torch was thrust into their alcove. "Who goes there? Show yourself!" A panting watchman glowered in the dancing red light.

Archie held her tight against his chest even as he looked over his shoulder. "It's Archie Carrington—Lord Carrington, from the Review. If you could take that torch out of my face? We're just enjoying a quiet lovers' tryst—no need to blind us or burn us, with your torch."

"Who's that with you?" the belligerent insisted.

"A lady—to whom I was proposing. So if you would be so kind?"

The watchman was not so easy to win over. "Who proposes to a lady in the dark of a close instead of a proper drawing room?"

Maisie spoke up in her crispest, most inconvenienced English accent. "Where's your sense of romance?"

"Yer pardon, milady." The miscreant shuffled back a pace.

"We're after some lads. Rositering and making a bloody nuisance —" He stopped and took another step back. "Yer pardon, mileddy. Have you seen any lads running this way?"

"None," Archie answered for them. "What's gone on? Do you have information for the Review?"

"It's them political placards, going up on the walls in Parliament Close and everywhere else it seems. They say they were up on the Corn Market and the Excise Office as well—all across the bleeding city."

"Then you'd best get after them, hadn't you," Archie suggested, "and leave us alone?"

"Aye," the poor fellow agreed. "They're after us to try an' tear the whole lot down, but there're too damn many."

"Good," Maisie muttered.

"Hush," Archie counseled under his breath. "Thank you, constable." And when the man had trotted off, presumably in further search for the lads, Archie added, "Show some remorse, will you?"

"Not a bit," she countered, "unless it is that they have taken them down too fast before they can be seen."

"We need to get you out of here. Come on." He took her by the hand, and damned if the way her hand fit in his, gripped tight together like cogs in a machine, working silently together, didn't make his heart glad.

It was a dangerous, marvelous, inspiring, wonderful thought.

He led her to his rooms in Cowgate, where he could interrogate her in privacy. But he had also promised to take care of her, so he scooped her up into his arms to stride the last few slippery yards up Liberton's Close and down the narrow passageway at the side of the building that led up to the apartment above. Home. "It's not the Aiken townhouse," he began.

"Thank God, it's not. I doubt I would be comfortable there."

"Can you be comfortable here?"

"Not yet," she laughed. "But I have great hopes to be. If it has an attic."

Archie felt the last of his frustration and fear slip away with her good humor. "I'd be honored."

"Be honored quietly." Maisie interlaced her fingers with his and held tight as she led the way through the narrow door and up the steep stair.

He dropped her hand only to lock the door behind them and to kindle the fire in the grate to take the chill from the night.

She moved across the room where she stood quietly next to a chair, fumbling with the clasp on her cloak, as though she could not make up her mind whether to sit or not.

He would not let her doubt herself. Or him.

He went to her immediately, covering her hands with his and lowering his mouth to her lips. He kissed her slowly, savoring the taut fineness of her lower lip and the soft sounds of assent she made as he took her in his arms.

And just like that, he was aflame for her. The warmth within him was low and banked, but growing slowly into a steady flame. She fanned her hand across the nape of his neck, turning his head down to hers so she didn't have to stand on exhausted tiptoe.

He scooped her up again, cloak, boots and all, and brought her to his bed, where he sat with her on his lap. "Maisie," he said because he liked saying her name. He liked the fresh taste of it, and of her, on his tongue.

"Archie," she answered the way a Scotswoman would, with the rolling "r" and the almost exhalation of pleasure.

And it undid him in the same small way her asking to come to his home had—everything within him eased and came alive all at the same time. He wanted her more than ever, as if the first taste of her could not be enough. As if it might never be enough.

It never would be enough. He would always want more.

More of her kisses. More of her wit. More of her love.

Archie deepened the kiss. His hands cradled her elegant jaw, and he nosed his way toward her ear, letting his incipient whiskers rasp along her cheek in a way that made her part her lips in astonishment and pleasure—a sound of wonder and delight and encouragement.

"Welcome home, sweet Maisie."

CHAPTER 41

*A*rchie answered the summons to the Marquess of Aiken's townhouse far less promptly than his father would like. But the marquess, it seemed, still had a deplorable tendency to treat his son like a lapdog.

So Archie took his time, walking his beloved across the city by the same picturesque route he had taken that first morning, heading to her studio. Auld Reeky was muffled in the gray fog of morning, mostly silent but for the soothing sounds slowly rising around them—the wheels of drays and the low calls of horses and cattle as the markets slowly came to life and the city woke slowly from slumber.

Any moment, they would find the post bills that had been pasted all over the city and talk of the Lord Advocate, of waste and hypocrisy and want of justice would begin.

But they were ready. The Review would release its special edition and the guilty would be damned. They had done their best and would now wait out the storm.

Archie left her at her stable gate with a lingering kiss and made his way down the length of the New Town, determined to settle his last remaining debt with the old man. He would begin as he meant to go on—asserting his independence.

"You may congratulate me, sir," he said as soon as he was announced. "I'm getting married."

His father nearly choked on his breakfast brandy. "The hell you say?"

"Married, sir," Archie repeated helpfully.

The Marquess of Aiken drew himself up. "It's like that, is it?"

"Aye." Archie smiled expansively. "It is."

"Am I allowed to ask her name? Or age? Or situation? What has been done for settlements. What—"

"Certainly, you may ask her name." His smile did not falter.

Which, predictably, nearly enraged his father. "Well?"

Archie was enjoying himself too well to answer immediately. Call it fair play for all the years of aggravation suffered at the old man's hands. "I have the honor of marrying Miss Margaret Conway. The painter," he added to be more specific.

"Conway?" his father sputtered. "Have you gone mad?"

"Of a certainty, sir," Archie answered. "I've been mad from the start. And now I'm madly in love. I'm afraid it can't be helped."

"Of course it can be helped! Madness be damned—you will simply not do it. Not while I live and breathe. And not if you want to see anything from me!"

"Whether you continue to live or breathe is your own affair, sir. As for the money—" Archie place the leather purse of guineas on the desk between them. "Here is a complete payment for your last remaining shares of the Review. You may consider yourself formally bought out."

"Bought out?" his father repeated as if this would make him understand his son better. "I have no intention of selling my shares."

"Your intentions are immaterial, sir. Your shares have been bought per the stipulations and terms of my contract as editor—

the contract you forced me to sign when I signed on. I am exercising those rights."

Stymied on one side, the marquess tried another gambit. "Where did you get the money?"

Archie did not mind telling him. "Both the Review and the pressworks have been turning a lively profit thanks to our coverage of recent events."

"That special edition on Conway—and whose idea was that? Mine!"

"And you have been repaid and rewarded for your idea handsomely, in gold." Archie gestured to the purse. "As well as by the accomplishment of your original intent—the removal of Conway from his position."

"Allowed to resign," the marquess groused. "A disgrace to let him go quietly. Should have bloody turfed him out."

"He is gone one way or another. And been replaced." Archie was happy to be the bearer of the news.

"What? Already? By whom?"

Archie smiled. "Alasdair Colquhoun, Marquess of Cairn. You'll remember him—old school chum of mine."

"Pitt's man." His father was shocked into silence. But only for a moment. "By God," he fumed. "Did *you* do this?"

Archie made his expression purposefully bland. "My dear sir! Of course, I did this—at your behest!"

"Not Cairn, damn it all to hell," he cursed. "By God!"

"Indeed," Archie agreed. "It does almost seem ordained by God. I suppose this is a warning to be careful what we wish for."

The Marquess turned his autocratic eye on his third son with decided displeasure. "Careful boy, or I might wish you'd never been born."

Archie had long become inured to such predictable spleen. "One can't change the past, sir, only the future."

"Well, in the future, if you marry this Conway chit—I'm assuming it's the pretty chit, not the other one?"

"Is is definitely the other one," he was happy to report. "The genius. Brilliant lass. You'll hate her—she's straightforward and blunt like you, although not nearly as predictable."

"The hell you say." His father stared at him in stupefaction. "If you go through with a marriage like that, I will have nothing to do with you."

Archie felt his smile grow even wider. "Fair enough, sir," he acknowledged his father's threat as if it were a polite request. "Consider it done." Such a severance would not prove a hardship —though, he would now have to keep his own carriage. "It will be your loss, sir."

"I'll have nothing to do with her, or any Conway," his father swore.

While his father's vehemence did not surprise Archie, it did intrigue. "I asked you this once before—why this personal animus against Conway? For all his moral failings, he's done no more that many men of your wide acquaintance have always done— take advantage of a situation for personal gain. But you don't cut them and you don't plot their downfalls. You don't ask me to investigate them."

"Maybe I should."

"You definitely should," Archie agreed amiably. "But to what end, sir? One hypocrite has been rousted out—what has all this been in the service of?"

"Truth," his father stated adamantly.

Too adamantly. "There are other truths you seem fine with keeping hidden," he pointed out. "Why this one?"

His father rearranged his face as if he had tasted something sour. "Your mother liked him. Favored him even."

"Mama?" Archie had long ago understood that his parents' marriage had not been a love match, but a suitable, decorous arrangement. Mama preferred the country, while his father preferred town, but they had always seemed to treat each other with mutual respect, if not warmth. There had never been any indication of indiscretion or passions that would elicit such—was it jealousy? "I did not know she knew Sir Richard."

"She knew him," his father accused. "She took up for him. Years ago, when he was a nobody—a bloody gardener, for God's sake, working in her father's garden. She never had any taste."

"Took up for him?" This did not sound like his kind, circumspect Mama—or did it?

"Told her father that she preferred him—a grubby gardener—over the heir to the Marquessate of Aiken. Told me I needed to treat her better, be more considerate."

While Archie had long lamented the polite stalemate of his parents' marriage, he was warmed to know that his mother had so early advocated for herself, in her own calm, unruffled way. "And did you treat her with more consideration?"

"Of course! But I found out, after she had finally agreed to do the right thing—the smart thing—and marry me, that she had arranged for Dick Conway to be given the job with the Royal Botanical Society gardens here, in Edinburgh."

And there it was—the first piece in the puzzle of Conway's career, courtesy of his kind Mama. From the Botanical Society's Physick Garden he had been promoted to the gardens at Chiswick, and from there he had been recruited by the British East India Company as a plant thief—sent in disguise into closed China to steal tea plants suitable to the climate of the company-controlled territories in India.

Once he had proved himself such a useful man with plants, he had presumably been tasked by the company with the efforts to control and monopolize the other great cash crop of the subcontinent, the opium poppy. And then, since he had earlier proved his effectiveness at covert travel in China, he was sent back, to establish smuggling routes into the country to circumvent the emperor's edict against the import of opium.

And in that time and travel and not-quite-legal work for the company, he had made himself modestly rich. And what better man to reward quietly than someone who had done so much to help the former government's successful efforts to stimulate trade by cutting import duties on certain commodities such as tea, as well as on all opium grown from poppies in India.

Dirty dealing all around, condoned by the British government because it benefitted British trade.

But that still didn't explain his father. "You have been after Conway for some—what is it now—forty years since you were married? Because you didn't like it that Mama might have once favored the man? Has she been in contact with him since?" He was almost afraid to ask. "Has she *favored* him in any other way?"

"No," his father admitted, and Archie was sure that the marquess was entirely confident of that answer, or he would not have given it. "But it was…demeaning to be compared to such a nobody."

"You were jealous?" Archie would have laughed at the sheer vanity if it weren't so pathetic. "You continue to be *jealous*. Of a man who did not marry your wife, nor keep in any contact with her, but simply went on with his life?" Archie could feel his ire rise like a tide within, pushing him to his feet. "All this I have done—" All the charm and deception and flexible morals he had employed to such destructive end. To Agnes's untimely end. "—to assuage your *jealousy*?"

Hot color rose in his father's cheek, but he said nothing.

Archie was appalled—at himself as well as his father. "I am done with you, sir. I am done with your demands and your vitriol. Done. You have played with people's lives. You have caused me to play with people's lives." He picked up the purse of money and all but threw it at his father. "Take your forty pieces of silver—"

His father caught it against his chest. "I thought you said it was gold?"

Archie could feel the blood drain from his face. "Take your

blood money and be so good as to never bother me or mine again."

Archie left the way he had come, but with far less equanimity.

He had been a fool—and a tool of his father's, even as he had told himself he knew what he was doing. He had seen the prize—success for the Review and accolades for himself as editor, and damned the costs. He had ended Sir Richard Conway's career. But, which was worst, he had been the reason Agnes had gotten into trouble and caused her dismissal, which led to her death.

His father had his blood money, but Archie was the one with blood on his hands.

And he could not atone for that and could not marry Maisie—not until he admitted that.

To her.

He had to go see Maisie.

CHAPTER 42

Maisie took the remains of her courage in hand and knocked on the door of her father's bookroom, where he had retreated from the indignities of the world.

"Yes?" He looked up from his contemplation of the city beyond the window. "Ah, Margaret. Come to gloat? To tell me I've gotten what I so richly deserved?"

"No," she answered. "I've come to tell you I'm getting married."

"Are you? Well, I suppose that's one good thing." He glanced again out the window. "Lord Carrington, I suppose, is the lucky fellow."

"He is."

"And you don't mind that he's the one who orchestrated my downfall?"

"His publication reported the facts of events. I hardly think that is orchestrating—"

"So you don't mind," he answered his own question for himself.

"No, I suppose not." She was working very hard not to argue. "But you already knew my opinion."

"I suppose I did." He scratched at the incipient beard on his chin. "Where will you get married?"

"I don't know." Funnily, she could only picture being with Archie in the chilly expanse of her aerie, but that would hardly do. Especially as her father was tacitly saying that she ought not to plan on having her wedding at the Kirk Brae Head house. "We'll find someplace."

"Will you invite your sister?"

"Assuredly, Papa. For she is the one who made the match."

This surprised him from his self-pity. "But I thought—"

"You thought incorrectly, Papa. But thankfully, now that my happiness is assured, she is free to seek hers."

"And Lord Carrington does not object to your painting?"

"Why might he object?" she asked pointedly, even as she told herself she had come to make some peace with the man. "Because a spinster must have some occupation, but a married lady need have none?"

"You are talented, I'll grant you—I went up to that aerie of yours as you call it, to see the painting you've made of Carrington. You've shown him as a far better man that he is."

"That was his opinion also."

"Then he is cleverer than I thought. And the other paintings—those are yours as well?"

How strange that she had spent so long hiding them and he had never thought to look. "Yes, they are mine. A series of religious subjects, a sort of lives of the saints."

"Very nice," was his understated opinion. "But not so dramatic as you are seemingly capable."

He knew. Somehow, this man who had never taken an interest in her art, had realized just what she had done.

"No," she admitted. "Not so dramatic, or theatrical, or satirical."

He stared at her for a very long moment. "You were right

when you said I hardly knew you. Have I always been your enemy?"

Maisie had to think before she gave her answer. "No, I don't suppose I thought of you at all for a very long time. Just a stranger who came into our lives to disrupt them irregularly."

"As you have now disrupted mine. All my best laid plans. Funny, how one never knows what is about to happen. If I did, I should have insisted you stay in Richmond, as you wanted."

Two months ago, to be left to her spinster life had been all that she wanted. And now—

Now she stood on the verge of a life she had never imagined —one with art and friends and family and love. "Perhaps you should have, but as you've so often told me, what's done is done. I have not enjoyed every moment of the past two months, but now that I'm here, I'm very glad I came."

She left her father to his contemplation of his sins—or perhaps his contemplation of the unfairness of the world—and climbed back to her aerie to the happy surprise of Archie sitting in her chair by the window, waiting for her.

"Archie. When did you get here? I'm so glad you came—I've just been to see Papa." She went to him and kissed him, and would have kissed him more, but he took her hands to lead her to sit in the chair he had just vacated.

"As have I, been to see my father," he said. "Dare I hope yours was far more pleased for you, than mine was for me?"

She could hear the sorrow in his voice even as he tried to mask it. "Archie, I'm so sorry."

"So am I." He nodded and then took a deep breath, and went down on one knee before her, still holding her hand.

"Archie?" She laughed. "Don't tell me you're going to propose again?"

"I will if you want me to," he began. "If you'll still have me. But I am not going to propose—I'm going to confess."

She had never seen him look so serious—and he had looked truly serious when he had found her last night. "Archie?"

"I came to your house in the beginning already searching for information about your father."

Maisie felt herself on the edge of that precipice again. "Skulking about the stableyard."

"Aye. And I commissioned the painting with the express purpose of having access to the house, which I later took advantage of. I flirted with you in the hopes that I would win your trust and ask you questions about your father. I paid Davie in the stable and Agnes—"

She heard herself gasp even over the pounding of her heart in her ears.

"I paid Agnes to return the key to your father's desk that I had taken," he went on in a rush. "I am the reason she was caught by Mrs. Smyth and dismissed. I'm the reason for all this turmoil and strife. And I'm heartily sorry." He kissed her hands as if in supplication. "I thought that by exposing your father I would put things right, but to my shame, I can see now that I put my ambition before my humanity. Before Agnes. Before you. Even as I was falling in love with you, I didn't trust you with the truth." He drew breath and looked her in the eye. "And I don't know if you can ever forgive me."

Maisie had to force her breath to slow and come more evenly. She had to wait until the roaring in her ears receded. She had to be able to breathe and think and feel at the same time.

And when she finally could, she said, "To forgive you, I'll have to forgive myself. For I am guilty of these same things—of reading my father's manuscript and using Agnes to further my career, and putting my anger at my father and the world before everything else, including you. Of not trusting you with the truth."

"What a pair of fools we have been." Archie pulled her down

onto his lap so he could kiss and kiss her. "What a fool I was not to see that I would fall in love with you."

"Nor I with you."

Relief sagged through him, leaving him momentarily numb. So much loss, so much heartache, and still somehow, all they had ever needed to do was trust each other, and their problems and ambitions and resentments would have been as nothing.

It was far less than he had earned and far more than he deserved. His luck really was extraordinary.

He kissed her then. He kissed her with all the passion and fear and desperation and admiration and charm and luck and love he had within him. He kissed her for the past and for the future. He kissed her because finally, at last, he knew that no one coming up those stairs or through that door—no sister, or friend or waif or saint—was going to stop him.

Finally, she was his.

And he was hers forevermore.

LORD ARCHIBALD CARRINGTON WAS THE SORT OF FELLOW WHO never minded having an armful of lass—and he was especially happy to find his arms full of his exquisite bride on his wedding day.

Because on that day, his darling Maisie became Lady Margaret Carrington, to have and to hold, to paint and to kiss, from that day forward, forsaking all others.

All others, except Fergus, who seemed to have become a permanent part of their household.

They were married in the drawing room of the Marquess of Cairn's townhouse on Charlotte Square, with all their friends and family around them, with Lady Cairn herself, her eyes full of happy tears, acting as a sort of fairy godmother for the bride.

The only person missing was not missed at all—Sir Richard Conway had left Edinburgh. Given up his position as Lord Advocate in favor of a long sea voyage on behalf of the British East India Company.

But Maisie had her sister, Flora, to act as bridesmaid, and cry all the tears of joy that Quince could not make herself.

Maisie did not cry. Her bright eyes were as remarkably clear as always—she looked at him in a way that never failed to make him want to be a better man. For her.

For his wife.

"And now the Four C's have become eight," Alasdair said once they had made their amens. "Welcome to the family, Maisie."

His new wife's smile was as warm and pink as the dawn. "Thank you."

"You might have begun as the Four C's," Quince pointed out, "but we have long since become seven. The Seven Seas are separated slightly by temperature and temperament and location, but keep in touch one with another, flowing freely and sharing the tides."

"Why Quince, you darling reprobate," her husband joked. "You've become a poet as well as a pain in the arse of the powers that be."

"And you, my love," she returned, "are now one of the powers that be, my Lord Advocate, so watch your behind."

Amidst this saucy revelry, Mignon spoke. "As the only other foreigner in this bastion of Scots, let me be the first to bid you, *bienvenu.*"

"That's right!" Archie gave her hand an encouraging squeeze. "Our first Englishwoman."

"Oh, by jimble, but she has the heart of a rebel, so we won't hold her Englishness against her," Quince vowed.

"Englishness, Frenchness—madness!" Maisie laughed. "That is what I see before me!"

"Oh, yes," Quince agreed with a smile. "We are all a little mad around here."

"Aye," Archie whispered as he kissed her ear. "I am mad—completely mad for your love."

*H*e took her to Italy, traveling in such style and comfort that Maisie never once thought of the hideous Bath chair that had once haunted her dreams. Their days were filled with learning—taking in sights, strolling across wide piazzas, floating down canals, visiting ancient ruins and gazing for hours at the masterpieces of DaVinci, Michelangelo and Raphaello, Caravaggio, Gentileschi and Sirani. Churches and castles, villas and viaducts—nothing escaped Archie's extensive itinerary for the benefit of her artistic education.

But their nights, in cool high-ceilinged rooms set on hills overlooking the Tiber, or the Grand Lagoon, or the Tyrrhenian Sea, were filled with pleasure. And passion. With soft sighs and hearty laughs. With whispered plans and hopes and dreams—most of which had already come true for Lady Maisie Carrington.

Because she had found a rogue who was somehow more than that, who looked at her with steady regard for her as an individual—with admiration and respect and love. He had taught her that goodness and true, perfect, unconditional love did indeed exist in the world, and that she was more than worthy of that love.

Together they made a life filled with art and agitation, friendship and felicity, painting and passion. And kisses. Day or night, there were always, always deeply passionate, generous kisses. Because they had learned to adore each other and now, always would.

Maisie's disability is the result of contracting the polio virus —*poliomyelitis*—when she would have been 14 years of age. This virus was known by a variety of names and descriptions, such as "a fever causing a debility of the lower extremities," and another, the "teething fever," as suffered by the great Scottish novelist, Sir Walter Scott, who contracted the virus in 1773, when he was a very young lad.

I have taken the liberty of using some of Scott's real-life experiences— to be sent to the country and to the seashore for various water cures—as a template for Maisie's story, and have tried to use language that was historically used to describe Scott's condition. Both he and Maisie are said to be 'lame,' or walk with a pronounced limp as a result of muscle atrophy due to the virus. Scott and others also called his uneven gait a 'hitch.' Lady Charlotte Bury, recalling her first encounter with Scott, found "something I think graceful in Walter Scott's hitch; it would be a pity he should walk like any body else." [Lady Charlotte Bury, Diary Illustrative of the Times of George the Fourth, Interspersed with Original Letters from the late Queen Caroline, and from Various Other Distinguished Persons, 4 vols., vols. iii and iv ed. John Galt

(London: Henry Colburn, 1838-9), iii. 153-4.] So, I have also taken the liberty of making Walter Scott an acquaintance of Archie's, so that I could use Archie to give voice to both contemporary language and views of Maisie and Walter Scott's difference of abulation.

Maisie's artwork was inspired by several sources, most notably two the artists mentioned in the story—the 17th century Baroque painters Artemisia Gentileschi and Elisabetta Sirani. Gentileschi was a Roman and Florentine painter who gained fame as a painter of female biblical subjects. Sirani, was a Bolognese who painted more history paintings and public works that any other woman painter before her. She was also renowned for her *femme forte* paintings of heroic women, an accomplishment I have passed to Maisie. Both of these painters were known for working from real models and imbuing them with heroic qualities. For more information on these illustrious women, I recommend the monograph accompanying the Metropolitan Museum's Gentileschi show, *Orazio and Artemisia Gentileschi*, W. Keith Christiansen and Judith Mann (ed.), (Metropolitan Museum of Art, 2001): and the new (as of June 2023) biography, *Elisabetta Sirani* by Adelina Modesti (Lund Humphries, June 2023).

The Edinburgh closes and South Bridge Vaults were, and are, real, and remain open for tourists—and some businesses. Historically they were used exactly as described in the book, but were closed and filled in with rubble at a later date than in our story. The vaults remained closed and forgotten until they were rediscovered and partially cleared in the 1980's.

There are several "Easter Eggs" in the story that can lead to further discovery of the Highland Brides series.

Lady Augusta Ivers, who first appears in Chapter 3, features in A FINE MADNESS, which is the story of how her niece, Elspeth Otis become a famous novel writer.

The background to Archie's education, especially his Grand Tour described in Chapter 8, can be found in the letters between the chapters in Ewan's story, MAD, PLAID & DANGEROUS TO MARRY, Book IV of the Highland Brides, which also contains the 'lethal woes' Archie refers to in Chapter 7.

Similarly, the particulars of what Archie has "done for his friends," alluded to in Chapter 8 can be found in the adventures depicted across all of the Highland Brides Books.

The story of Rory Cathcart's detection of forgeries, referred to in Chapter 17, can be found in MAD FOR LOVE, Book I of the Highland Brides.

The "particularly acquisitive buyer in Sussex, who took the whole of Conway's collection," referred to in Chapter 18 can be found in A BREATH OF SCANDAL, in the Reckless Brides Series.

The 'bona fides" of Quince's "rebellious spirit" described in Chapter 20, Chapter 35 and Chapter 37, can be found in MAD ABOUT THE MARQUESS, Book II in this Highland Brides Series.

ABOUT THE AUTHOR

ELIZABETH ESSEX is the *USA Today* bestselling author of over twenty critically acclaimed historical romances, including the Reckless Brides and Highland Brides series.

Her books have been nominated for numerous awards, including the Gayle Wilson Award of Excellence, the Romantic Times Reviewers' Choice and Seal of Excellence Awards, and RWA's prestigious RITA Award. The Reckless Brides Series has also made Top-Ten lists from Romantic Times, The Romance Reviews and Affaire de Coeur Magazine, and every book in the series was awarded Desert Isle Keeper status at All About Romance. Her fifth book, A BREATH OF SCANDAL, was named Best Historical in the Reader's Crown 2013.

When not rereading Jane Austen, mucking about in her garden, walking her beloved dogs, Ghillie and Brogue, or simply messing about with boats, Elizabeth can be always be found with her laptop, making up stories about heroes and heroines who live far more exciting lives than she. It wasn't always so.

Long before she ever set pen to paper, Elizabeth graduated from Hollins College with a BA in Classics and Art History, and then earned her MA in Nautical Archaeology from Texas A&M University. While she loved the academic life of an underwater archaeologist, she has found her true calling writing lush, lyrical historical romance full of mystery, passion, daring and adventure.

Elizabeth lives in Texas with her husband, the Indispensable Mr. Essex, and her active and exuberant family in an old house filled to the brim with books.

Website

ALSO BY ELIZABETH ESSEX

The Highland Brides

Mad for Love (long novella)

Mad About the Marquess

A Fine Madness (novella)

Mad, Plaid and Dangerous to Marry

Mad Rogues and Englishwomen

The Reckless Brides

Almost a Scandal

A Breath of Scandal

After the Scandal

A Scandal to Remember

The Scandal Before Christmas (holiday novella)

A Lady's Gift for Scandal (holiday novella)

The Difference One Duke Makes (novella)

She Walks in Scandal (novella in *A Midsummer Night's Romance* Anthology)

The Dartmouth Brides

The Pursuit of Pleasure

A Sense of Sin

The Danger of Desire

The Dartmouth Brides Boxed Set (with holiday novella *"Up on the Rooftops"*)

The Kent Brothers Chronicles

Between the Devil & the Deep Blue Sea ~ and ~ The Devil's Own Luck

To keep up to date on new releases and events, sign up for Elizabeth's newsletter and get exclusive excerpts, contests and more, visit:

http://www.elizabethessex.com

I also hope you'll take a few minutes out of your day to review this book at your favorite book site – your honest opinion is much appreciated. Reviews help introduce readers to new authors they wouldn't otherwise meet.